CONVERGENT

A Starstruck Novel

BRENDA HIATT

dolphin star
PRESS

CONVERGENT

A Starstruck Novel

Dolphin Star Press

ISBN: 978-1-947205-20-8

.˙.

THE STARSTRUCK SERIES BY BRENDA HIATT

Starstruck
Starcrossed
Starbound
Starfall

Fractured Jewel: A Starstruck Novella

The Girl From Mars
The Handmaid's Secret
Convergent

Contents

M

1

Adaptation

"FINALLY!" The message I've been watching for since I got up this morning shows up on my omni-phone as Rigel parks in the school lot. "I was starting to think the Council changed their minds."

I'm about to read it when I see Molly getting out of Tristan's black Porsche a few spaces away. She and I usually take the bus, but after yesterday's assassination attempt, our boyfriends understandably insisted on driving us today.

With that in mind, I pause a moment to focus on Molly's emotions, to see how she's feeling after such an eventful weekend. I detect a trace of nervousness but no actual fear, which tells me she's more concerned about the impact her new status will have than additional threats to her life. Good.

Scrambling out of the car, I hurry over to them. "Guess what's out?" I say excitedly.

Molly turns, her smile of greeting tinged with alarm. "They sent it, then, did they? Mum checked right before Tristan picked me up."

"Yep." I speak quietly enough that no non-Martian can hear. "The announcement popped up like a second ago. I haven't even read it yet."

Catching up, Rigel throws an arm around my shoulders. "Can you let us all see it, M? The rest of us just have regular phones, not omnis."

"Oh, sorry. Everyone huddle around, then."

My new Martian omni doubles as an ordinary phone—easily my coolest Sovereign perk yet. Among other things, it can produce a holo-screen of any size, but I don't dare activate that in the school parking lot. Instead, I angle the regular smartphone screen so all four of us can read the statement together.

MARSTAR BULLETIN
For immediate distribution

The *Echtran* Council is delighted to announce the existence of a second heir to our Sovereign line. According to recently recovered records, Sovereign Leontine's son Mikal fathered not one, but two daughters before his untimely death. This second daughter was concealed from birth to protect her from Faxon's depredations, raised anonymously by an Agricultural couple until such time as her identity could be safely revealed. Unfortunately that couple was killed in an uprising when the Royal girl was barely a year old. She was then adopted by the O'Gara family when they assumed the Mulgrews' identity in order to continue leading the Nuathan Resistance against Faxon. Prior to the discovery of those long-hidden records, neither the O'Garas nor anyone else had any suspicion of their adopted daughter's true identity.

Last night the traditional *foare rioga* was performed upon the girl known as Molly O'Gara, who for the past year has served as Sovereign Emileia's *Chomseireach*. That test conclusively proved that the O'Garas' adopted daughter, previously believed to be a member of the Agricultural *fine*, is in fact Princess Malena, twin sister to our Sovereign. While the role she will play in our people's future is yet to be determined, we hope you will join us in celebrating this near-miraculous discovery.

As I read, I also do a quick probe of the others' emotions. Molly's nervousness shoots up, no surprise. And though Tristan looks calm, inside he's struggling with a mixture of pride, trepidation and protectiveness.

When I'm sure everyone's done, I click the screen off. "Well, word's officially out now! Wonder how long it'll take everyone to see it?"

"We'll know soon." Tristan links hands with Molly. "Let's go in and see how people act. Our people, I mean. No reason the *Duchas* will treat you any differently."

Molly's still so anxious, I put a reassuring hand on her shoulder. "Don't worry. It'll feel weird at first when strangers come to gawk, but that probably won't happen for at least a few days."

"She's right." Tristan gives her a quick kiss as the warning bell rings. "It'll be fine. M's the only one allowed to have an omni at school. No one else will even see that bulletin before they get home."

Molly gives us both a tentative smile. "Aye, right, then. Let's do this."

Together, we walk through the double doors into Jewel High School. All four of us have Pre-Cal first period and sure enough, Liam—the only other *Echtran* in the class—shows no sign he's heard the big news.

But when Kira shows up in French class next period, it's obvious she has. Athletic, auburn-haired and taller than Molly or me, she exudes excitement as she comes over to us.

"Sean told me everything," she whispers to Molly. "How are you holding up after that attack? And what incredible news! No wonder you couldn't get those rosebuds to open when I was coaching you. Remember how frustrated you were?"

Molly chuckles. "I thought I was the worst Ag ever. At least I won't feel like a loser about *that*, anymore."

"Not about anything," I tell her firmly. "You're way more prepared than I was, when I first found out who I am. Shoot, you helped get *me* get up to speed on everything I needed to know!"

"I guess."

She still looks uncertain—which I totally get. She's experienced almost as big a paradigm shift as I did last year, when I first learned there were Martians on Earth, then that I was heir to the Martian throne. At least Molly already knew all about the secret human colony on Mars, having grown up there. But still.

"Give yourself time," I advise her. "Everybody else, too, including your parents. Things probably *will* be awkward for a while, but they'll all get used to the idea soon."

When we walk into Chemistry class, Mr. Abbot, our *Echtran* teacher, gives Molly a piercing look and sort of half-inclines his head before catching himself. *He's* obviously seen the bulletin. I hope the others can be that restrained when they find out my Handmaid—and best friend— is also my sister.

Sitting at the lab table I share with Rigel, I glance over at Molly, reliving that wondrous moment two days ago when we learned the truth upon "meeting" the parents neither of us had ever known. I can't wait to talk with them again.

Molly's not in my next class but as Rigel, Tristan and I are on our way to lunch afterward, we see her up ahead in the hallway. Before we can catch up, Alan Dempsey comes out of a classroom she's passing.

Alan's one of our newer *Echtran* students, a senior. He's taller and blonder than Tristan, and nearly as handsome. But the moment he sees Molly, his expression turns peevish. He and Molly went out a couple of times pre-Tristan and he wasn't happy about her new relationship.

"Hey, grow any good plants lately?" Alan taunts, his back to us. "Guess your new *boyfriend* can't help you with that, huh?"

With an indignant exclamation, I hurry to Molly's side. "Wow, Alan. What kind of jerk makes fun of a girl for something that's not even her fault?"

His pale blue gaze snaps to me and he sucks in a breath, clearly embarrassed that I—the Sovereign—overheard him. "Um, sorry. I, uh, yeah. That was out of line," he says. To me.

"It's Molly you should be apologizing to," I point out, glaring at him. "Guess you're not up on the latest news?"

He blinks at me in confusion. "News?"

"Maybe you should give your parents a call over lunch," I suggest, turning away.

The four of us leave him stammering and continue toward the lunchroom.

"Why did you do that?" Molly whispers the moment we're out of earshot. "Once he calls home, he'll tell everyone else and—"

"Sorry. He ticked me off, talking to you like that. I'd have lambasted him for it even if you weren't, y'know, my sister." I give her an apologetic smile.

She frowns at me uncertainly for a moment before returning it. "Thanks. I guess it doesn't matter, since everyone will know by tonight anyway. I may as well start getting used to it."

After getting our lunches, the four of us go to our usual table. A moment later my *Duchas* friends Bri and Deb join us, giggling together—again—over what happened at Trina's Halloween party Friday night. Rigel and I share a smile at the memory, too.

While I eat, I keep an eye on Alan a few tables away. He and several of the newer *Echtran* students still sit together, even though I've repeatedly encouraged them to spread out more. The exact moment Alan hears the news is obvious. He puts down his phone, his expression stunned, then stricken, as he looks toward our table.

Freshman Jana asks him something and after a moment's hesitation, he answers. Immediately, all the other *Echtran* students at the table lean forward, bombarding Alan with more questions.

"Word's out," I mutter to Molly.

She sucks in a panicked breath and convulsively grabs Tristan's hand. As she turns to look at the other table, the four youngest *Echtrans* jump up and rush our way.

Crap! Now it's my turn to panic.

"Is it true?" Kira's little sister Adina squeals as they reach us, her short blonde hair bouncing.

Then the others chime in. "We just heard—" "Alan told us—"

"Not here!" I hiss, making frantic shushing motions.

They all freeze, belatedly coming to their senses.

"Sorry, sorry!" Sophomore Erin's face turns as red as her hair. "We didn't— That is— Sorry!" Abashed, apologetic and scared, they all scurry back to their table.

But now my *Duchas* friends are curious. Deb, petite and blonde, looks questioningly at me. "What was *that* about?"

"Something to do with NuAgra?" Shaking her dark, curly hair out of her eyes, Bri frowns over at the *Echtran* table. It's no secret that all the newcomers' parents work at the top-secret facility on the outskirts of Jewel. "Why would they ask *you* about it?"

To my relief, Molly steps into the breach. "I think it was me they were asking. The cheerleaders are putting together a special routine for when the football team goes to State and we want to do a demo at NuAgra. But it's still in the planning stages, so we're not supposed to talk about it yet."

"But you knew about it?" Bri asks me suspiciously. She's become kind of sensitive about me being more popular with the "in" crowd this year, though I keep telling her that's only because of Rigel being Jewel's star quarterback.

"I, ah—" I stammer.

This time Tristan comes to my rescue. "Molly told me and I told Rigel here, and I guess he told M. Probably won't happen anyway, tight as security is out there."

That seems to satisfy my non-Martian friends. For now. Keeping our secret has become harder since the recent influx of *Echtrans* into Jewel. We need to do better.

As we're all leaving the cafeteria a little later, Alan hurries to Molly's side. "I, uh, heard that you— I mean, my parents told me about— I mean, I'm really, *really* sorry for...for everything, Molly. I never would have— That is—"

Molly shrugs, looking nearly as embarrassed as he does. "It's okay. You didn't know."

"No, it's not okay," I inform Alan with a frown. "Being rude is never justified, no matter what *fine* someone's in." I have to speak softly because of all the *Duchas* students around, but that doesn't keep the disapproval out of my voice.

Alan flushes. "Sorry. You're right. I only meant... Anyway, I'm sorry, Molly."

With a quick, respectful nod to me, then another to Molly, he hurries on to class. Tristan, I notice, looks amused.

"I've been looking forward to that," he admits, grinning after Alan. "He gave us nearly as much flak as my father did for dating outside our *fines*."

"Not something *you* two should need to worry about now." I can't keep a trace of irony out of my tone.

Molly notices. "Maybe soon you and Rigel won't, either. Or Sean and Kira—even Mum's come around on that one. All those old, entrenched attitudes are bound to change before long."

I smile at her. "Hope so. I'm working on some ideas for articles I can write for the *Echtran Enquirer* to help that process along."

By the end of the day, every *Echtran* student and teacher at school has discreetly told Molly and me how happy they are about our news. Some of them seem a little uncertain how to act toward her now, but I keep assuring her they'll get over that.

"Don't worry," I repeat before she heads off to cheerleading practice after the final bell. "By next week things will be back to normal. You'll see."

.⁺₊

That evening, I go to Molly's house after dinner. Our boyfriends are meeting us here in an hour to walk to Dream Cream, the local ice cream shop. When she greets me at the door, I sense she's still stressed.

"Everything okay?"

Molly lifts a shoulder. "Oh, it's just Mum and Dad. Since Saturday night, they've been—" She breaks off and glances toward the kitchen, where I can hear Mr. and Mrs. O'Gara talking together quietly.

I nod in sympathy. "Want to go up to your room? I came early on purpose, hoping we might have time to…you know."

It was such an incredible gift to discover our parents' stored images, memories and personalities in a Martian Archive Molly had kept for years without realizing what it was. We haven't had a chance to talk to them again since our first conversation Saturday evening.

"Yes!" she eagerly agrees. "I've been dying to do that, too." Grinning at each other in anticipation, we hurry up the stairs together.

Once in her bedroom, Molly locks the door before fetching my Royal Scepter out of her closet, along with the blue crystal that contains our parents' Archive. I swap it out with the main Archive—an identically-sized pink crystal embedded at the top of the Scepter.

"*Chartlann rochtana,*" I say, to activate it.

Instantly, two incredibly lifelike holograms appear in the room with us—the birth parents Molly and I met for the first time two days ago.

"Hello, Malena, Emileia," our mother, Galena, says, smiling at us both. She's beautiful, her gray eyes exactly like Molly's. "It is lovely to see you again."

The strong emotion I sense off Molly matches my own. Like me, she was probably starting to wonder if we'd merely imagined Saturday's momentous discovery.

I swallow the sudden lump in my throat. "It's great to see you both, too. We wanted to let you know that after we talked on Saturday, Molly —Malena, I mean—was officially certified by the Council as my sister. But neither of us are sure what will—should—happen next."

"Yes," our father, Mikal, agrees. His eyes are green, like mine—and like Sovereign Leontine's. "This situation is unprecedented, so it stands to reason that it may take time to settle the specifics. Fortunately, you are both still quite young, so there should be no hurry."

Molly radiates relief. "That's good to hear. I should remind the O'Garas of that. Especially since the Council only sent the announce-ment about me out to our people today."

"I'm sure that was very happy news for them." Galena smiles at Molly. "I imagine soon you'll have prospective Consorts lining up. Or has one already been designated?"

Molly and I exchange a startled glance.

"Er, not officially," she says, "but I do have a boyfriend. Tristan Roark. I think you knew his parents?"

"Why, yes," Galena replies. "Teara and I were quite close, particularly before her marriage. She is still on Earth, then?"

Molly nods. "She and Tristan live here in Jewel. They moved here because of Connor being on the Council, but plan to stay even though Connor got kicked out yesterday."

Galena's eyebrows rise. "Connor Roark was removed from the *Echtran* Council? For cause?"

"He shared classified information outside the Council," I explain. "About Molly's identity, among other things. That nearly got her killed." I tell them about yesterday's assassination attempt and what followed.

"Connor always was ambitious," Mikal comments dryly. "His and Teara's bloodlines are impeccable, however, so Tristan should be acceptable to our people as a future Royal Consort. What of you, Emileia?" He turns to me. "I assume yours was chosen some time ago?"

I hesitate, biting my lip before answering that awkward question. "Sort of? I mean, it was *supposed* to be Sean O'Gara, Molly's brother, but by the time he and I met I was already *graell*-bonded with Rigel—Stuart, I mean. So I obviously couldn't break up with him to be with Sean, no matter how much the Council wanted me to."

Both of our parents look rather taken aback.

"*Graell*-bonded?" Galena echoes. "I always understood the *graell* to be a myth."

"So did almost everybody else," I agree. "But it's not. Earlier this fall, some of our Scientists verified our bond by running a bunch of tests on us. We get sick when we're apart too long, we can create electrical charges, speak to each other telepathically—all the classic *graell* stuff from the storybooks."

Molly nods emphatically. "It's true. They even used their electrical power to save the whole Earth from... Well, I guess that's too long a story to tell right now. But it's definitely real. Even though Rigel's not Royal. Apparently *fine* doesn't matter much to the *graell*, because it looks like Sean and his girlfriend Kira may have it, too, and she's an Ag. Like we all thought I was, until a couple days ago. I, ah, also think Tristan and I might be bonded."

I stare at Molly in amazement. "You once hinted about you and Tristan, but I didn't know about Sean and Kira. Really?"

She shrugs. "They haven't actually *told* me so, but from some stuff Sean's said... Anyway, we can talk about that later."

"Oh. Right. Where were we?" I look back at our parents.

"In the process of exploding some of our people's long-held beliefs." Mikal's amused smile reminds me of the one his father Leontine sometimes gets while talking to me. "I'm curious, at what point after Faxon's overthrow were you Acclaimed Sovereign?"

Unfortunately, a complete answer will take way more time than we have now. I've barely started recapping the events of last winter, spring and summer when the doorbell chimes downstairs.

"Oops, that'll be Rigel and Tristan," I interrupt myself. "We can tell you more later, but right now we'd better go if we want to keep these Archives secret. Love you!"

Molly echoes that, then I deactivate the crystal. Sticking the Scepter back in the corner of her closet, she unlocks her door and we both hurry downstairs to greet our boyfriends for the walk to Dream Cream.

.⁺₊

Fifteen minutes later, the four of us claim a table as far as possible from the gaggle of *Duchas* teens on the opposite side of the ice cream shop. We're just sitting down when Sean and Kira walk in. Spotting us, they come over.

"Mind if we join you? Mum said you might be here," Sean tells Molly. "Don't blame you for wanting to get out of the house." He pulls up a chair for Kira, then one for himself.

"Yeah, Mum and Dad are stressing me out a little," Molly admits. "Going on and on about what kind of leadership position I should have, no matter how many times I say I don't want one."

Does she mean that? Rigel sends silently, startling me.

For now she does, I reply. *If she changes her mind later, I'll be fine with that. After all, she has as much claim to the throne as I do.*

He quirks an eyebrow. *Aren't you older?*

Only because her embryo was in stasis for three months. Anyway, Nuathan succession hasn't always gone by chronological age. Psychological profiles are just as important when evaluating potential Sovereigns.

"Will you guys stop that?" Sean interrupts. "You're being a little obvious, you know."

"You're right, that was rude," I apologize. "Just because you know we can do this, doesn't mean we should shut you out."

Rigel looks sheepish, too. "Yeah, I guess old habits die hard." He stands up. "What does everyone want from the counter? Mint chip ice cream, M?"

"And some water. Thanks, Rigel."

Sean and Tristan ask Kira and Molly what they want, then the three boys head to the front to order. A few minutes later we're all digging into our various ice cream treats.

"You know what I just realized?" Molly says when her hot fudge sundae is nearly gone. "Sean and I got to Jewel a year ago this week, the first week of November. So much has changed since then!"

"No kidding," I agree. "The six of us hanging out together is proof of that."

I actually fantasized about exactly this last November—that someday Rigel and I would come to Dream Cream with Sean and Molly, all of us friends. At the time it seemed impossible, considering how hostile Sean and Rigel were toward each other.

Like most of our people, Sean only accepted the fact of Rigel's and my *graell* bond in September—and the last of his lingering resentment didn't disappear until he and Kira got together last month.

"*Efrin*, I couldn't *imagine* becoming actual friends with all of you when I first got here," Kira quietly agrees. "I was still trying to get dirt on you for Allister and Lennox. Of course, I had no idea they'd stuck a *bomb* in my neck…"

I sense an echo of her remembered fear as Sean puts an arm around her. "Don't remind me," he murmurs. "It's terrifying how close I came to losing you."

Kira smiles tenderly at him. "I was more terrified my stupid mistake would kill you, too, than I was for myself, when you refused to leave me."

The love passing between them is palpable, emphasizing just how thoroughly Sean is over me. Thank goodness.

Tristan looks around at the rest of us. "Sometime you guys need to catch me up on all the stuff that happened before I got to know you all—before my life took a huge turn for the better." He and Molly exchange a look similar to the one Sean and Kira just shared.

Suddenly giddy, I grin around the table. "Guys, I can't tell you how happy I am right now! It's so wonderful we can all—" I'm interrupted by my omni-phone vibrating in my pocket.

Pulling it out, I frown at the message displayed. "Hm. This doesn't sound good. Kyna's calling an emergency Council meeting—right now. I'd better go. Molly, you should probably come, too."

She sucks in a startled breath. "Me? Do I have to?"

I shrug, getting up. "Since it'll be at your house, you might as well. Besides, it might have something to do with you."

Rigel and Tristan stand up, too.

"We'll walk you back," Rigel says. "I know Cormac's out there some-where, but he's only one Bodyguard for the two of you—or have they assigned someone to Molly?"

"I don't think there's been time," I reply. "I'm sure they will soon."

Though Molly's clearly startled again, Tristan takes her hand in his. "Until they do, I'll stick close," he promises.

Carrying our drinks and leaving Sean and Kira to finish theirs, the four of us head for the door.

"Oh, I meant to tell you," Rigel says as we head down Diamond Street, "my parents both need their cars tomorrow, but I'm sure one of them can drive you to school first. It would probably look weird for Cormac to do it."

I snort. "Yeah, it would." My Bodyguard, Cormac, is also our school's Vice Principal.

"She can ride with us," Molly volunteers. "Right, Tristan?"

He nods. "So, M, you think they might let me train to become Molly's Bodyguard, like Rigel is for you?"

"We can ask." I glance at Molly, who seems pleased by the idea. "Tonight, if there's a chance."

Rather than stress about the upcoming meeting, I try to focus on the wonderful sensation of Rigel's hand clasping mine as we walk. It works until he asks, "Any idea what this emergency is?"

"Not yet. Maybe they got info from that assassin they want to act on right away."

Rigel tightens his grip on my hand. "Like another attack?"

"The guy did say there were lots more like him," Tristan reminds us. "If he provided names, maybe the Council can round them up before they try anything else."

"I hope so," Molly and I say simultaneously. Despite our worry, we flash a quick grin at each other. Sisters!

When we get to the O'Garas' house, I call my Aunt Theresa to say I might be late coming home. She must guess it's to do with "that Martian business" she prefers to ignore, because she doesn't ask any questions, just reminds me it's a school night.

"I'll call you later, Tristan, okay?" Molly says, her earlier apprehension creeping back.

"You'd better. Especially if it sounds like you're still in danger."

She promises, going up on her toes to give him a lingering kiss.

Rigel pulls me to him and we indulge in our own delicious goodnight kiss. *You want me to stick around out here?* he sends silently.

No, I'm sure if there was any immediate threat, Kyna would have said so. Go on home and I'll fill you in on everything as soon as the meeting ends.

"See you guys tomorrow," I add aloud as Molly opens the door.

.⁺⁺.

Mrs. O'Gara meets us in the front hall carrying a tray with tea, cups and cookies. "Ah, good, you're both here. Kyna and Nara have already holo-ed in and the locals should arrive any minute. I don't suppose you know —?" She directs a worried glance at me.

I shake my head. "We probably all got the exact same message."

"Ah, well, we'll know soon enough. Oh, I forgot the napkins. Molly, will you— That is, if you wouldn't mind terribly—"

"Mum! I've asked you not to go all formal on me. Please? I'm the exact same person I was last week."

Mrs. O chuckles but I can sense her conflicting feelings. "Yes, of course you are, but it still seems—"

"We know," I interrupt, smiling. "Come on, Molly, we'll both go get the napkins."

When we're alone in the kitchen, Molly sighs. "I wish Mum would stop doing that."

"She will, once she's more used to the idea of you being…who you are," I assure her. "It's only been two days. Aunt Theresa acted pretty weird at first, too, after learning the truth about me, but she's mostly back to normal now. And she had a whole lot more to absorb—not just me being Sovereign, but the whole concept of Martians on Earth."

Grabbing a stack of napkins, Molly manages a smile. "You're right. It's not like I'm used to the idea myself yet."

"You'll get there. Let's go see what this meeting's about."

The six remaining members of the *Echtran* Council—down from seven, now Connor's gone—are waiting in the O'Garas' small living room. When Molly and I enter, they bow in unison—Royals Breann, Malcolm and Mrs. O, as well as Science *fine* representatives Kyna, Nara and Rigel's father, the newest member.

Molly and I incline our heads in response, Molly carefully mimicking me, then we take seats next to each other.

"I'm sure you are all busy, so let's get right to business, shall we?" Council leader Kyna suggests once we're seated. She's a NASA astrophysicist and always seems to have something time-sensitive going on. Both she and little Nara, a pediatric specialist and microbiologist, are here holographically from Washington, DC.

"I apologize for the unexpected nature of this meeting," Kyna continues, "but given the sensitive and rather frightening nature of the news I received today, I considered any delay unwise."

Not surprisingly, I immediately sense anxiety from everyone physically in the room, Molly and me included.

"First the good news," Kyna says. "Our efforts to track the source of the antimatter used for the explosive implanted in Kira Morain have finally borne fruit. This evening our investigators in Dun Cloch discovered which secure microchamber was compromised—and precisely how much antimatter was taken. It has now, of course, been secured against further intrusion."

My worry spikes higher. "Then…more *is* missing than what they put into Kira?"

Kyna nods, her mouth pressed into a grim line. "That's the bad news. It appears that attempt on your life used only a fraction of the total amount stolen. If our Scientists are correct—and believe me, our antimatter stores are *very* closely monitored—nearly half a milligram is yet unaccounted for."

There's a long silence. Then Breann hesitatingly says, "That's…that's not very much, is it?"

I'm surprised—again—by how little science most Royals seem to remember from their school days. I open my mouth to correct her but Kyna beats me to it.

"It is more than enough to be concerning," she replies. "For context, less than one picogram—one trillionth of a milligram—was used in that previous explosive. While not enough to pose a global threat, half a milligram of antimatter could certainly destroy several city blocks…or a town the size of Jewel, Indiana."

2

Disruptive selection

THERE'S a moment of shocked silence at hearing the magnitude of the threat laid out in such stark terms, even among those of us who already understood the math.

"There must be some way to locate that missing antimatter before the thieves can deploy it?" Malcolm exclaims, his fear palpable.

"We certainly mean to try," Kyna assures him. "However, keep in mind that the amount used in the bomb the traitors implanted in Miss Morain was the size of a small bacterium, virtually undetectable. Even a containment capsule five hundred billion times larger would be absurdly easy to conceal."

More fearful looks are exchanged.

"What about the memories of the man who attacked Princess Malena yesterday?" Mrs. O'Gara asks. "Do we have those yet? That might help."

"The extraction should be performed by the end of the week," Kyna tells her, "though he may know nothing of this. Van, I don't suppose you've picked up any more messages from those rogue settlements?"

Mr. Stuart shakes his head. "None since the signals abruptly stopped two weeks ago. If they've switched to another method of communication, I haven't found it yet. I did discover that there were four, not three, locations sending messages. One in rural Idaho, another in Nevada and two in Montana—Dun Cloch and another site within fifty miles of it. My triangulation algorithm did not originally distinguish that one from Dun Cloch itself. I am still working on pinpointing it."

"Ah. Please make finding that location a priority," Kyna says. "The antimatter might well have been taken there. Any progress deciphering the messages you intercepted earlier?"

"Enough to rule out any innocent purpose," Mr. Stuart replies. "The timing alone suggests orders and responses to those orders. I'm working on a new decryption program now and should learn more in time."

Kyna raises a brow. "Time is something we may not have in abundance. We don't know how far along these people are in their planning. While we hope the traitor Enid was the only one in their ranks with the expertise to create an antimatter bomb, she could have created others prior to her capture and subsequent suicide. If so, the most likely targets are the Sovereign, her sister and this Council."

Rigel's dad glances uncertainly at me, which I take as my cue to speak up.

"Mr. Stuart is working on some extra safeguards, both in Dun Cloch and here in Jewel, based on the security system in the Royal Palace on Mars," I tell Kyna. "We didn't mention it sooner because we suspected a leak on the Council. But since that leak was Connor and he's gone now, the rest of you may as well know."

Kyna nods approvingly. "Van?"

"Yes, the Sovereign provided me with some extremely sensitive technical specifics for the creation of far more robust security systems. I've already begun installations at NuAgra, as it is to become our primary Earth-based government facility. I plan to do the same for the Sovereign's house and Princess Malena's."

"What about members of the Council?" Malcolm asks.

Mr. Stuart gives him a reassuring smile. "Yes, I believe I will also be able to provide personal protection for each of you."

Malcolm and Breann, another Royal, both look relieved.

"Molly will be assigned a Bodyguard, too, won't she?" I glance sideways at her, remembering my promise.

Mrs. O nods vigorously. "At once, I should say, given this news. That should be—"

"Can't Tristan be trained for that, like Rigel was?" Molly interrupts. "He offered."

Eyebrows go up all around the room.

Sensing general disapproval, I quickly add my support. "I think that's a great idea. At school, Rigel's my main Bodyguard, since it would look weird for Cormac to stick close to me there. That will be true for any adult Bodyguard you assign Molly, too. Tristan's already in most of Molly's classes, so he's in a perfect position to keep her safe there."

Kyna now looks thoughtful. "You make a valid point, Excellency. I suppose Tristan could be a supplemental *Costanta*, as under the circumstances, the more protection both of you have the better. Can Tristan be trusted in such a role, however? He *is* Connor's son."

"Absolutely," Molly affirms before I can reply. "I...I've gotten to know him really well these past couple of weeks. Believe me, he's *nothing* like his father. And he, um, cares a lot about me."

"Very well, I'll see what can be arranged," Kyna concedes. "We'll also assign an experienced, adult Bodyguard immediately." She glances at Mrs. O, who nods her approval. "Meanwhile, Van, I suggest you give your new security systems a higher priority than deciphering those old messages or implementing our new *Echtran* communication network."

He readily agrees.

Kyna thanks him, then turns to the rest of us. "I'm sure I needn't caution you all to keep tonight's revelations private. We don't wish to spark a panic. As it is late and a weeknight, I suggest we postpone further discussion until our regular meeting on Saturday—though it is likely to be a long one. Quite a few items have accumulated on our agenda due to recent, unexpected developments." She smiles at Molly, who blushes.

With that, Kyna adjourns the meeting and winks out. Nara lingers for a few minutes to again tell Molly and me how happy she is about our newfound relationship, then her hologram disappears, too. Breann and Malcolm are already headed for the door, both looking distinctly rattled by tonight's revelations—not that I blame them.

"Did you get everything you need from the data chip I gave you?" I ask Mr. Stuart before he leaves.

"I believe so. If I or my colleague have questions, shall I bring them to you?"

I nod. "If I don't know the answers, I should be able to get them for you." I don't say how, since it would involve my ancestors in the Scepter Archive, which is supposed to stay super secret.

Once he's gone, I turn to Molly and her mother. "I should probably get home. Aunt Theresa will be getting antsy, what with it being a school night and all."

My house is just around the corner, so I walk, my Bodyguard Cormac following a short distance behind. Along the way, I telepathically relay the high points from the meeting to Rigel.

Not surprisingly, he's immediately worried. *Should I come over to help Cormac keep an eye on your house?*

No, don't be silly. What would you do, camp out in my back yard? No way I could explain that to my aunt and uncle without scaring them half to death. We don't even know that the bad guys, whoever they are, actually have a bomb. Without Enid, they might not be able to make another one at all. Even if they did, what could you do except get blown up along with me?

He doesn't chuckle, like I hope. *I'd rather do that than nothing at all. But if you're sure you're safe for tonight—?*

I'm sure. Kyna will let me know if they discover a local threat. Tomorrow you and I can do our distance thing to detect any enemies before they get close enough to Jewel to be dangerous. Okay?

Okay, he reluctantly agrees. *See you in the morning. I love you, M!*

Ditto, I think back. Smiling, I go up the porch steps to my front door. *G'night, Rigel.*

.+.

"So, did you tell Rigel about...everything?" Molly asks when I join her on her front porch the next morning to wait for Tristan.

"Last night. Did you tell Tristan?"

She wrinkles her nose. "Only a little. Our phones aren't as secure as your omni, so I said I'd fill him in on the rest in person. I know Kyna said to keep it secret, but—"

"Boyfriends are exceptions." I give it the authority of an edict. "Especially when you think you might be *graell*-bonded," I add with a grin.

"I never said I was *sure*—" She breaks off as Tristan drives up.

Over both of their objections, I climb into the Porsche's tiny back seat so they can sit together in front. "You guys are doing me the favor, remember?"

They give in and Tristan pulls away from the curb. "So, can you give me more details about the meeting now?"

Molly glances back at me. I give her a thumbs-up, so she recounts most of what we learned last night. To his credit, Tristan manages to keep his eyes on the road through the whole rendition.

"So there's enough antimatter out there to blow up the whole town, but they don't know who stole it, where it is, or who's behind it all?" he summarizes when she's done.

"Basically, yeah," Molly says. "In better news, Kyna agreed you can train to become my Bodyguard...if you're sure you want to?"

"Are you kidding?" He can't hide the excitement in his voice. "When can I start?"

I laugh. "She didn't say, but probably soon. Do you think your mother will be okay with it?"

"Probably. She was completely okay with Molly and me even before anyone knew who Molly really is. I'm sure Mother will want her kept safe, and for me to help with that if I can."

We're nearly to school now, so I mentally reach out to Rigel. I tried first thing this morning, but he must have still been asleep.

Good morning, I send.

Hey, he replies immediately. *Everything still okay?*

Everything's fine. I hope you didn't stay awake worrying.

Only for an hour or so. Did you manage to sleep okay after hearing all that scary stuff at the meeting?

Mostly, I reply. *Molly just told Tristan everything. He's super excited to train for—*

I break off, belatedly realizing Molly asked me something when she turns around to look at me.

"Sorry, what? I was, er, talking to Rigel."

Her brows go up. "Whoa, I didn't know you two could do telepathy from *that* far away! I wish we could."

"It, ah, keeps improving. Anyway, I think his bus is only a little way behind us."

Sure enough, by the time Tristan parks his car, Rigel's waiting for me on the sidewalk. I hurry to him, eager for our first hand-clasp of the day after being separated overnight. Strength and vitality course through me at his touch. His kiss is even better, making me temporarily forget all of last night's worries.

At the warning bell, we reluctantly part to head inside, only to be waylaid by my friends Bri and Deb.

"So, Rigel, are you ready for Sectionals next weekend?" Bri asks excitedly. "According to my dad, our football team has never even *been* to State, but he thinks the Jags have a shot at actually *winning* this year! If anyone can make that happen, you can."

"He's not the only player on the team, you know," I remind her, like Rigel often does.

She grimaces. "True. Our defense, especially, will need to step up their game. But nobody can deny we have a real chance. Right, Molly?"

Because Molly's a cheerleader, Bri tends to assume she's also obsessed with sports. Molly usually plays along.

"Sure—though even Rigel can have an off game sometimes."

She knows the Council's been concerned about his level of play attracting unwanted *Duchas* attention—though I wonder if Mrs. O gave Sean that hard a time last year, when he was such a phenom on the Jewel basketball team he *did* take them to State.

"Not during playoffs, he won't," Bri declares confidently. "Rigel's only off games are when the two of you are on the outs. No chance of that this year. Right?" she challenges us both.

Though I grin, I feel a tingle of alarm. Bri's not the only non-Martian to notice the correlation between Rigel's football skills and the state of our relationship. It's because of our *graell* bond, but they don't—can't—know that.

"Things have never been better between us," I tell her truthfully, shoving away a superstitious worry my words might jinx us. Last fall everything seemed perfect, too, before…

"So, did you hear?" Deb pipes up, clearly bored by the football talk. "Jennifer said she saw Ms. Kowalski at the Lighthouse Cafe over the weekend with some man…*holding hands*."

That successfully diverts Bri's attention. Speculation about our Government teacher's love life lasts until we're all inside the school.

When do you want to do our scanning thing to look for bad guys? Rigel asks silently as we're walking hand in hand to lunch later on. *Since it only works when we're touching, it might be tricky at school.*

How about now? Lunch in the courtyard? I don't mind having a legit reason to touch for a while every day. Do you? I slant a suggestive glance at him.

Rigel laughs out loud, drawing a few curious glances from passing students. *Not when you put it that way. Lunch in the courtyard it is.*

After grabbing sandwiches and drinks from the lunch line, we head outside. It's chilly enough that the courtyard is empty, so once we're settled on the stone bench with our lunches, we clasp hands.

Reaching out with my emotion-sensing ability, I carefully probe the area around us, radiating outward from the school. I pause every time I pick up anything negative, which is fairly often. By pushing my sensing a few miles past Jewel, I discover several other *Echtrans* in nearby towns but none that feel like a threat.

"I think we're good for now," Rigel says. "Don't wear yourself out." Then, to rejuvenate me, he leans in for a kiss that I eagerly return. After three or four lovely minutes, he pulls back and hands me my drink and sandwich. "Now eat some lunch."

Nodding, I take a big bite. Scanning like that *is* draining. "We'll try again before school tomorrow, if you can drive me," I suggest.

"Sounds like a plan," Rigel agrees, unwrapping his sandwich. "I should be able to borrow Mom's car."

.⁺.

By the end of the day, the other *Echtrans* are acting noticeably less weird around Molly, as I predicted.

"See? The newbies aren't treating you that much different than the *Duchas* are now," I comment to Molly as she and I walk together to the football stadium. She has cheerleading and I'm going to watch Rigel's practice. I do that at least once a week to help him compensate for the way our bond enhances his playing.

As though to demonstrate how clueless the *Duchas* are, Trina Squires, head cheerleader and all-around mean girl, makes one of her cracks as she passes us on her way to the field. "I hope you'll be less distracted today than you were at last week's practices, Molly."

"I'm sure she will be," I say, which predictably earns me a glare from Trina.

"How would you know?" she snarks. "You'd be the worst cheerleader ever, Marsha—not that you ever had the guts to try out. Good thing for us."

Instead of snapping back, I just smile, knowing that'll piss her off more than any retort I could make. Molly opens her mouth to defend me, but I stop her.

"Don't. She's not worth it."

Trina shoots me another poisonous look and marches off.

Molly frowns after her. "Why do you let her treat you like that? If she had any idea—"

"She doesn't, and she can't," I remind Molly. "Not about either of us. Honestly, her crap hardly bothers me anymore, after everything else I've had to deal with. Trina's been like that since way back in elementary school."

"That doesn't make it any better."

I shrug. "I figure she must be an awfully unhappy person to be so mean all the time. Realizing that helps me ignore her insults."

We separate then, Molly to the track and me to the bleachers to watch Rigel and do homework.

Tristan promised to swing by later to give the three of us a ride home, so Molly, Rigel and I head to the parking lot an hour and a half later. Tristan's talking to Sean and Kira, next to the blue Toyota Sean got for his eighteenth birthday last week. None of them look happy.

"What's going on?" Molly asks before I can.

"This week's *Echtran Enquirer* came out right before I left NuAgra," Tristan quietly replies. "Can you call it up on your phone, M? There's an article I think you'll all want to see."

Nodding, I pull out my omni and log into the super-secure app. "Let me guess," I say, skimming the contents of the secret weekly newspaper. "Gwendolyn Gannet's piece?"

"Yup. You're not going to like it, Molly."

Judging by the title, I doubt I will, either.

"Our New Princess—Who Is She Really?"

Cringing in anticipation, I quietly start reading aloud while the others lean in close.

By now, I'm sure all of you have read that bombshell MARSTAR Bulletin the *Echtran* Council sent out yesterday. I imagine you're also as frustrated as I am by how few details they shared about our new Princess. Like me, you must all be wondering:

—How does the former Molly O'Gara feel about her sudden change in status?

—How does Sovereign Emileia feel about suddenly having to share the stage—and perhaps power—with her former Handmaid?

—How do Sean O'Gara and his parents feel, knowing they've had a potential Sovereign in their midst all these years? Will Sean's fledgling romance with that Ag girl survive this discovery, or will he now be tempted to transfer his affections to his adopted sister?

—What, exactly, were those "long-hidden" records? Where were they hidden, and why were they only discovered now? Could the timing of that discovery indicate an agenda on someone's part?

Rest assured, yours truly is already working to bring you answers to these and other questions. Be sure to check this space regularly over the next few weeks to see what I've learned!

"Ugh, seriously?" I exclaim. "I can't believe this woman has such a big readership when half the stuff she prints isn't even true."

Sean shakes his head. "Sensationalism sells, that's what Dad says."

I hand my omni-phone to Molly so she can read it herself. She scowls at the screen.

"Aye, Gwendolyn Gannett has a gift for making the most innocent things sound awful. She'll probably claim I made the whole thing up to get attention."

"How can she?" Tristan gives her shoulders a squeeze. "The Council made you take the traditional blood test and announced the result. If she's going to accuse anyone of making stuff up, it'd have to be them."

Molly doesn't look convinced. "She'll find some way to get people upset about it—about me. You wait. She loves stirring up controversy."

I elbow her in the ribs. "Aren't you the one always telling *me* not to borrow trouble?"

That makes her smile, since Molly saying that was what led to me telling her about the Archive in my Royal Scepter—which led to us discovering the truth about her.

"Still, be super careful if you give her an interview, Mol," Sean cautions.

"I'd rather not talk to her at all," Molly says, shuddering. "But she's bound to make me look even worse if I don't."

"Get your dad to help," I suggest. "He did a great job running interference with all the Nuathan reporters when we first got to Mars and the news about Rigel and me broke. He went over talking points with me and everything."

Molly's alarm fades slightly. "Good idea. He doesn't like Gwendolyn either, especially after the stuff she wrote about Sean."

"There you go, then," I say bracingly. "Seriously, don't sweat it. In the grand scheme of things, Gwendolyn Gannett is a minor annoyance."

Even so, it's one more thing to worry about, when we had way more than enough already.

3

Selective pressures

THE NEXT MORNING Rigel picks me up early, so we have time to run another "scan" before school. I stretch my senses farther than yesterday and find more *Echtrans* in north-central Indiana, but still no "bad guy" vibes.

"Maybe tomorrow we should try to reach Indianapolis," Rigel suggests after recharging me with some welcome kissing. "Or even Chicago."

I shudder, remembering how icky Chicago "felt" that first time we tested our range—the day we discovered the Grentl in orbit. But then I nod, since it's important. "If I can somehow filter out all the *Duchas* negativity, it might not be so bad."

"If you can't, we'll stop," Rigel promises with another quick kiss before we get out of the car and head into the school.

In Pre-Cal, Molly tells us she heard from Gwendolyn Gannett and reluctantly agreed to talk with her on Sunday. "She asked to meet tomorrow but I wanted more time to prepare." She wrinkles her nose in disgust.

"You'll do fine. Remember how well your dad prepped me for all those press conferences and interviews in Nuath? People were already prejudiced against me because of Rigel, plus I had a huge secret to keep, but that turned out okay."

"Dad did promise to give me some talking points, but since I can't tell him exactly how we learned the truth about me, he won't be able to help with *that* question. You know she'll ask."

I frown. "Just tell him—and her—it's classified. That for security reasons I've asked you not to talk about it. She won't like it, but she can't *force* you to tell."

Tristan looks curiously at us from Molly's other side. "Does that mean you can't tell us, either?" he whispers, with a glance at Rigel.

Regretfully, I shake my head. "Sorry."

You told me about your Scepter, Rigel silently reminds me.

That's different, I think back. *We're bonded, and you're my Bodyguard. You needed to know. I told Shim, too, since he's my Regent, but nobody else—except Molly.*

Isn't Tristan going to become Molly's Bodyguard?

I shoot Rigel a frowning glance. *Supposedly. But he and Molly haven't even been dating for two weeks yet. Plus, he's Connor's son and those Archives are supposed to stay super secret.*

So you still don't trust Tristan? He seems like a good guy now.

I can't deny that, but...I'm not ready to take such a big step yet. Maybe if it turns out Molly and Tristan have an actual *graell* bond, I'll change my mind. Though I can tell Rigel thinks I'm being a bit paranoid right now, he doesn't push it.

That night, during our usual bedtime "chat," Rigel tells me his parents will need both cars Thursday and Friday. *But I already messaged Tristan and he's fine giving you a ride both days.*

Though touched, I'm also a little irritated by his over-protectiveness. *I'm sure I'd be perfectly safe on the bus...but okay.*

I snuggle under the covers then so Rigel and I can send loving thoughts back and forth to each other as we fall asleep. It's not quite as good as actually being together, but still a wonderful way to end each day.

The next morning Tristan runs a little late, so Rigel's already in the parking lot talking to Sean and Kira when we get there.

"Any more news?" Sean asks quietly as we join them. "You know, about that...matter?" In other words, the missing antimatter.

I shake my head. His reminder makes my insides contract since we still have no idea what to do about that looming threat. Then, looking around at our group of three couples, I'm struck by an idea.

"This will sound weird," I say quietly, "but have you guys started noticing any, um, changes since getting together?"

The other couples exchange startled glances. Then, cautiously, they all nod. Rigel looks surprised, too, so I send a quick, silent apology for not running this past him first.

"A while back," I continue, "when Rigel and I discovered how much more our bond could do, we joked about someday becoming crime-fighting superheroes. But what if it could be more than a joke? And more than just the two of us?"

They all stare at me but before anyone can say anything, the warning bell rings.

"No time for details now, but let's get together someplace, um, discreet soon, so we can talk about...stuff."

"Good idea," Rigel agrees, picking up more from my thoughts than I've said aloud. "Maybe we can come up with a time and place over lunch."

Everyone agrees to that and we hurry to first period.

During Pre-Cal, I silently share my theory with Rigel—and what it could mean if I'm right.

You're not worried you'll freak them out with a lot of graell *talk? What if Molly's wrong? What if they don't even have it?*

That's the first thing we need to find out, I think back. *For their sakes, too. If they really are* graell *bonded, the sooner they know for sure, the better.*

All six of us do sit together at lunch, but there's no chance to talk privately. Along with Bri and Deb, a few of Rigel's teammates are also at our table, all buzzing about the upcoming playoff game in Kokomo. Then Liam and Alan, who both recently made the basketball team, come over to ask Sean about the practice schedule. Alan, I notice, avoids Molly's eye.

Not till we're all on the way to Government class afterward does Rigel get a chance to whisper, "My parents will be gone most of Saturday afternoon, if we want to get together then to talk about M's idea. Mom has a shift at the hospital and Dad'll be working out at NuAgra."

"Great. Are you all okay meeting at Rigel's Saturday, after Kira and I finish our noon Taekwondo class?" I ask the others.

"Absolutely," Sean whispers as they all eagerly nod, clearly intrigued.

Just think, I send to Rigel. *If they can develop powers too, we won't be our people's only last line of defense. Wouldn't that be a relief?*

He can't disagree.

Rigel and I don't get another chance to check for bad guys until Friday. During seventh period, while pretending to work on the school newspaper website, we manage a discreet scan. We still don't sense anyone threatening within ten miles of Jewel, so when class ends I tell Rigel I'm going to take the bus home.

"What? Why?" he demands, startled.

"I've been feeling like a third wheel in Tristan's car all week. They're such a new couple, they're still getting to know each other."

Rigel scowls. "You can wait here while I go home and borrow a car to come get you. Mom should be back from her rounds by now."

"Don't be silly. If there were any baddies nearby, we'd have detected them just now. Anyway, I promised Aunt Theresa I'd wash all the bed sheets, plus I want to get started on my first article for the *Echtran Enquirer* before tonight's game. The bus will get me home sooner."

"I still don't like it," he grumps.

I go up on my toes to give him a quick kiss. "Cormac will follow the bus to my house, like he's done all semester," I assure him. "I'll be fine."

Finally he relents. "Okay. But let me know once you're home safe, so I don't worry."

I promise and we head to our separate buses. I'm nearly to mine when I see a woman who looks unpleasantly familiar talking with *Echtran* sophomores Erin Campbell and Grady Quinlan. Sharpening my gaze, I confirm that it's *Echtran Enquirer* reporter Gwendolyn Gannett.

She and the two sophomores are standing a bit apart from the milling crowd, their heads close together. Making sure I'm out of the reporter's line of vision, I casually move a little closer and focus both my hearing and emotion-sensing ability.

"—news?" Gwendolyn Gannett is saying.

"It's pretty exciting," red-haired Erin replies. "My parents are really happy about it."

Grady nods. "Mine, too. Especially since Molly's already dating Tristan Roark."

The reporter's sudden interest is obvious to me. "Connor Roark's son? Are you sure?"

"Oh, yeah. They've been together for—" Grady breaks off. "Uh-oh, the buses are about to leave, sorry."

Though I can sense Gwendolyn's frustration, she smiles. "Of course. Perhaps we can talk again soon. Thank you both for your time."

The two younger *Echtrans* head to their buses and I have to hurry to mine, wishing I had time to ask them what they told that prying reporter. A glance shows her now walking briskly toward the school parking lot, her phone already in her hand.

Her satisfied smile makes me even more determined to get my own side of the story out there as soon as possible.

.✦.

By the time Rigel and his parents pick me up to ride with them to Kokomo, I've got a decent first draft of my article. Getting into the back seat, I scoot closer to Rigel for the hour-long drive. He feels wonderful.

So do you. He puts an arm around my shoulders. Then, aloud, "Sorry I went all protector on you earlier about the bus."

"No, I get it, but I was fine."

"I know. Still, after what happened to Molly Sunday..."

In front of us, his father clears his throat. "I'm afraid I agree with Rigel, Excellency, particularly until I can add a personal security app to your omni."

Something else he's developing based on those specs I gave him from the advanced security network at the Royal Palace on Mars. Warmed by their concern, I promise not to take the bus again anytime soon—even if it means cutting into Molly and Tristan's alone time.

We stop for dinner along the way, which reminds me of the first time the Stuarts drove me to an away game—the day I learned that not only was I born on Mars, I was heir to the Martian throne.

Shortly after we get back in the car, Mr. Stuart clears his throat again. "Rigel, I should warn you that some on the Council have asked me to remind you—again—to be, ah, circumspect during tonight's game."

Rigel grimaces. "Are they still giving you grief about that one game back in September? I only played like that because M's life was on the line. I haven't done that since."

His father sighs. "I know, son. Still, I recommend you pull back even more tonight than you have lately. The Council heard from concerned *Echtrans* all over the country after that game. It drew national attention, you know, with clips airing on more than one cable sports channel. They were fearful it heightened the chance of discovery for our people."

Rigel's mom turns around to give him a sympathetic smile. "There will likely be a fair number of *Echtrans* at tonight's game, possibly including reporters from the *Echtran Enquirer*. The more you distinguish yourself compared to the *Duchas* players, the more criticism we're likely to hear."

"Exactly," Mr. Stuart agrees. "The Council feels strongly that Jewel High winning the State championship for the first time in history would draw far too much attention to both you and the school. With so many *Echtran* students enrolled there, they consider the risk too high. I...have to admit I agree."

"Are you saying you want me to actually *throw* a game?" Rigel demands, outraged.

His father hesitates for a moment before saying, "I'm sorry, Rigel, but if that's what it comes to...yes."

Did you know about this? The waves of anger and frustration coming off of Rigel make me flinch.

No! I silently insist. *I heard some grumbling the night after that game when I was kidnapped, but I thought I talked them out of taking any drastic action. Someone on the Council must have talked to your dad privately later. Are...are you okay?*

Yeah, he thinks back resignedly. *It's just...I know how much the playoffs mean to the rest of the guys. I already feel like I'm letting them down whenever I hold back. They're all so pumped to make it to State...*

Maybe they still can? I offer hopefully. *The whole team's better than they were last year.*

Maybe. I can tell he doesn't believe that any more than I do.

"What if some Jewel alum who's bet on our team accuses me of shaving points?" Rigel asks aloud after a moment. "Doesn't the Council realize *that* could draw attention, too? Maybe even worse attention?"

When Mr. Stuart doesn't answer right away, Rigel and I both hope he'll relent, but then he shakes his head. "I'm afraid the only alternative is to remove you from the team entirely, son—which a few on the Council have already suggested."

Rigel doesn't respond out loud, but to me he seethes, *I hate this! No matter what I do, I'm a jerk. Either I let down my teammates or I risk our people. If it really is a risk...*

You're not a jerk, Rigel. But...you saw what happened with Mr. Farmer, and he claimed to have friends who believe the same stuff he does. What if a bunch of those nut jobs got together to threaten our people, or got the media to pay attention to them. Things could get ugly in a hurry.

He scowls. *Yeah, you're right. I know you're right. I just...hate it.*

"Rigel seems off tonight," my friend Bri observes during halftime. "He's not sick, is he? If our offensive line hadn't improved so much this season, I'd be worried about this game."

Now that Jewel has advanced to Sectionals, we're playing better teams than those in our district. Even so, the game would easily be a blowout if Rigel were playing his best.

"Um, yeah. On the way here he said he thinks he has a stomach bug or something," I lie. "Hopefully just one of those twenty-four hour things. He hardly ate anything when we stopped for dinner."

Bri's expression becomes sympathetic, even though I'm not nearly as good as Molly at coming up with stories on the fly.

"Poor guy. Guess he won't want to go to the after-party tonight, even if we win by a lot."

"Probably not. He almost never does anyway."

Mostly because of me. We did both go to Trina's Halloween party after our first playoff game last week, but that was such a fiasco I doubt Trina will ever let *me* in her house again.

During the second half, Rigel keeps Jewel's scoring under control by throwing to our mediocre receivers, sometimes intentionally too hard, rather than running the ball himself. That results in a lot of dropped passes that don't look like his fault.

Even so, Jewel wins 24-14 and our fans mob the team the moment the game ends—especially Rigel. As always, head cheerleader Trina makes a point of hugging him when she's sure I'm watching. Not that it bothers me like it did before Rigel and I finally re-bonded in September.

I've just received my delicious, post-game kiss when Bri runs up. "Great game, Rigel, even if you're not feeling so hot today. By the end I could hardly tell."

Before he can reply, I quickly think to him, *I told her you have a stomach bug when she commented you weren't playing as well tonight.*

Great. I feel his brief exhilaration from the game souring. *Now you have to lie for me.*

Just a little fib. Nothing compared to all the other stuff we have to keep secret.

That gets a smile from him, but it's halfhearted.

During the drive back to Jewel, Rigel is quieter than usual. A few times I try silently to draw him out, but he insists he's fine. His emotions aren't, though, and probably won't be until the season ends.

Which I can't help looking forward to now. Not only is Rigel's mood likely to improve, he'll have more time to spend with me after school—assuming the bad guys don't blow up the town before then.

4

Group selection

TOWARD THE END of Taekwondo class Saturday, I get to spar one-on-one with Kira. That's always fun for both of us, since it means neither of us have to hold back. Afterward, I have time for a shower and a quick lunch at home before Tristan and Molly pick me up for the ten minute drive to Rigel's house.

"Happy anniversary, you two," I say as I climb into the back seat. "You've been official for two weeks today, right?"

They grin at each other.

"Yup. Best two weeks of my life," Tristan replies. "Thanks for remembering.

"Um, how is your mom doing, now it's been almost a week since... you know?" I ask a moment later.

Tristan's father was hauled off to Dun Cloch in Montana for more questioning Sunday, after the Council forced him to admit he'd spilled secrets to the elusive Devyn Kane.

After a moment's hesitation—my question *was* kind of personal—Tristan replies, "Mother's doing a lot better than I expected. With Father gone, she's already getting out more. She even went to NuAgra this week, said she might start doing some work out there."

"What kind of work?" Other than the *Echtran* government center being set up there, most of NuAgra's research is agricultural and Tristan's mother is pure Royal.

"Consulting, I think. She's...kind of an expert on government structure, Nuathan, *Echtran* and Terran. It's pretty much been her life's work. Now she's digging deeper into Nuath's political history, says that might help you and the Council plan for the future here on Earth."

I blink. "Wow, I had no idea. But yeah, that probably will be helpful. I'm glad she's adjusting so well."

Of course, Tristan and his mother did testify against Connor at the Council meeting, confirming he'd been up to something. Between that and other things I've heard about Connor, his leaving Jewel was probably a relief to both of them.

We're just getting out of Tristan's Porsche at Rigel's when Sean's car pulls into the driveway. We wait for him and Kira to join us before trooping up to the front porch.

"So what's this really about, M?" Sean asks as I ring the bell. "I hope it's not actually a surprise party for Rigel's birthday. We didn't bring presents."

I laugh. "No, he was adamant he didn't want a party this year. His birthday's not till next weekend anyway. Maybe Rigel's right that my idea is crazy, but—"

Rigel opens the door before I finish my sentence. "Hey, guys, come on in." He greets me with a quick kiss. "It's just us, like I said. Mom and Dad both left half an hour ago."

We all go into the Stuarts' living room, comfortably but tastefully furnished and more than twice the size of mine or the O'Garas.'

"Sorry for the, um, healthy snacks." Rigel nods toward a bowl of popcorn and a plate of grape clusters. "All I could find to put out." He and I take the loveseat and the others all sit on the couch, facing us expectantly.

"I want to know what M meant the other day, about superheroes," Tristan says before I can start explaining.

I bite my lip. "Okay, that might have been a slight exaggeration. But it occurred to me that if you and Molly—and Sean and Kira—turn out to have *graell* bonds, too, we could maybe…team up somehow. Put any extra abilities you guys develop to good use. To, er, stop any bad guys who try something."

They all stare at me with varying degrees of incredulity, just like they did Thursday morning.

Molly finds her voice first. "I can't speak for Sean and Kira, but Tristan and I definitely haven't shot off any lightning bolts."

"Neither have we," Sean confirms.

"None of you have been bonded all that long," I point out. "You did admit you've noticed changes, though. What kind?"

Molly shrugs. "Mostly what you'd expect, if it's the *graell*. We both feel better when we're together, stronger and more focused, that sort of thing. And I think maybe I've got some Royal 'push' after all, not that I ever tried to use it before finding out who I am."

"I'm sure you do," I tell her. "But you may also have something that goes beyond that. Remember how you got that fib past your mother a couple weeks ago? And I noticed a while ago that I can't sense your emotions like I can most people's—at least, not when you're trying to hide them. Blocking other Royals' abilities isn't quite the same as the regular 'push' but I can see it being useful."

"Aha! Then you *can* read emotions?" Her tone is accusing. "You never told me, though I suspected."

Oops. "Um, yeah. I first started noticing it when we were on our way to Mars last spring, but Rigel thought it would be more useful if I kept it secret. Then, after we re-bonded in September, I discovered that with Rigel's help I could extend it to sort of...scan for negative vibes in the area. That's how we found Gordon, two towns away."

"Who's Gordon?" Tristan looks confused.

"Another guy who was in cahoots with Allister and Lennox," Rigel explains. "He hacked the security cameras on the *Quintessence* last spring and nearly kept M from getting Acclaimed, among other things. Anyway, once we'd located Gordon we decided to test our limits. First we pushed it all the way to Dun Cloch, in Montana. Then we *tried* to reach Bailerealta, in Ireland, but—"

"But they found the Grentl, instead," Sean finishes for him.

Tristan stares at us. "Whoa, seriously? Molly told me you somehow sensed the Grentl before they attacked, but not exactly how."

"It was totally an accident," I admit. "On our way to Montana we ran into Chicago and it was awful—tons of negative emotion. I was afraid New York would be even worse, so I tried to direct our focus up and over but I, um, went way higher than I meant to. Which turned out to be pretty lucky."

"Lucky is right," Rigel agrees. "Otherwise, we wouldn't have had enough warning to come up with a counter-strategy before the Grentl zapped Earth back to the Stone Age."

Molly quirks an eyebrow. "Which involved a whole different *graell* ability you two have. You can't honestly think the rest of us will ever be able to do stuff like *that*?"

"We won't know till you try." I grin at her, then turn to Sean and Kira. "You two said you've noticed some changes, too?"

"That same thing of feeling better, stronger when we're together," Sean says. "We've also started picking up each other's emotions, at least when we're touching. Plus recently, we, uh..." He glances at Kira.

She returns his look uncertainly. "Should we tell them that part? It's not like we're sure."

I look from one to the other. "Tell us what?"

"Maybe we just imagined it, but Sean and I think we might be able to, well, move things without touching them."

"It's happened twice now," Sean confirms. "The first time, a cup I dropped somehow sort of...stopped before it hit the floor and broke."

My eyebrows go up. "Was Kira with you when that happened?"

"Yeah, it was at her apartment, in the kitchen. I leaned over to, um, kiss her while I was helping carry dishes to the sink and...yeah. It freaked us both out, then we tried to rationalize it—that maybe our eyes just played a trick on us."

"And the second time?" I prompt.

They exchange another glance. "We were shooting hoops in the gym a couple evenings ago, just the two of us," Kira says. "It's the only time we can both play full out, y'know?"

I nod. "Like when you and I spar together in Taekwondo." Sparring with *Duchas* students gives me an inkling of how Rigel must feel on the football field, using only a fraction of his abilities.

"Exactly. Anyway, Sean blocked a shot of mine and the ball went flying to the other end of the court. We both started toward it and then it...took a funny bounce and came back to us. It was weird, I'd never seen a ball do that before. But again, we weren't positive it was something *we* did."

"Cool!" I exclaim. "Definitely worth finding out, right? If it *is* a new ability, who knows how far you might be able to take it? Rigel and I can't do anything like that, but the things we *can* do have gotten stronger as time goes on."

Sean frowns. "Yeah, but you two had been bonded a whole year before you could do the stuff you were just talking about, right? Even if the rest of us do eventually get there, it won't be in time to stop any bad guys."

"Hey, every little bit might help," I say encouragingly. "It's not like we knew any extra abilities would develop at *all*—though I guess the first lightning thing happened early on."

That was my first clue something seriously weird was going on, before I had any idea there were Martians on Earth.

"Maybe if we'd actually *tried* to strengthen that, or develop other abilities sooner, we could have," I add.

"I dunno," Rigel says. "The times our bond got noticeably stronger was when we got back together after being separated. Not a strategy I particularly recommend," he tells the others with a grimace.

"Even if it means we'd all get superpowers?" Tristan asks. "Just think if we could *all* do the kind of stuff you two do. Maybe it would be worth it?"

Rigel looks at me. "You say that, but—"

"None of you have been apart much since bonding, have you?" I ask the others.

Sean and Kira shake their heads but Molly and Tristan both wince.

"Only for a weekend, but yeah, it kind of sucked," Tristan admits, slightly deflated. "I take it that gets worse the longer you're apart?"

"A lot worse," I tell them. "Sean and Molly saw how sick I got when Rigel and I were apart for a week and a half over Thanksgiving last year."

They both nod. "It was pretty bad," Sean confirms. "But that antidote thing they developed in Nuath worked, didn't it?"

"It kept us both functioning," I allow, "but definitely not at the same level as when we're together. Anyway, it's not like we can ask for more of it without telling them why we want it. Are you guys ready to come out and tell people you think you have *graell* bonds?"

Kira looks positively alarmed by the idea. "Think what your mum—and mine—would do," she says to Sean.

"It's not like there isn't precedent," he replies rebelliously, nodding toward Rigel and me. "But I guess the less people suspect, the bigger the element of surprise we'll have if we need to use any *graell* abilities against bad guys."

"Yeah, like shooting lightning bolts." Tristan's getting excited again. "Even the old fairy tales mention that being a *graell* thing—and it's what you guys used to stop the Grentl's electromagnetic pulse, right?"

Rigel and I nod.

"If all of us can figure out how to do *that*, we'd have an actual weapon to use against anyone else who comes after Molly," Tristan says. "Or, um, you or anyone else."

I'm relieved they seem to be taking my idea seriously. "True, though it only works if we at least pretend we're in danger. We found that out when the Scientists were trying to measure our, um, voltage. But our first step should be to confirm whether you guys are *graell* bonded or not, and that's as good a way as any. Rigel, do you still have that multimeter, or did the Scientists take it?"

"I think the little one we maxed out is still here. Let me check."

He goes into his dad's office and a moment later comes back with a small gray box. "Found it!"

Sean regards the device dubiously. "What do you want us to do? The same thing you two did when they were measuring to see if you could produce enough to stop the Grentl?"

"Well, when the Scientists did their original *graell* tests, they had us each touch it separately first," I explain. "Then when we did it together without imagining a threat, we actually produced *less* electricity than either of us did alone. That's what gave us the idea to try making a dampening field, like the one we did to keep that bomb in Kira's neck from exploding. Which, come to think of it, will be super useful if whoever stole that antimatter is planning more bombs!"

"For sure," Rigel agrees. "We should practice that more. Now, though, let's see what these guys can do. Here, I'll set it up."

He does something with the dials. I wonder how he knows what to do, then remember he has his dad's Informatics talent with computers and stuff.

"Okay, I think it's ready," he says after a moment. "Sean, why don't you go first. Just move a finger slowly toward that red dot."

Sean does, and just before he touches it, a spark jumps to the machine.

Rigel looks at the readout. "Not bad. You produced half a joule, which is about what I do alone—roughly twice what most *Echtrans* create, according to those Scientists. M does twice *that* much, by the way. Kira, you try now."

She nervously approaches the device. "I just…touch it?"

"Slowly," I caution her. "You saw how it sparked before Sean actually made contact."

Nodding, she approaches her finger to the red dot and again a spark skips to it before she touches it.

"Only a tiny bit less than Sean's," Rigel says. "Also well above our people's average—maybe because of your bond? Now together, without imagining a threat—maybe even try to suppress it. Think...happy thoughts, I guess?"

Clasping hands, they grin at each other and reach toward the device with their free hands. This time they have to actually touch it before it registers and, sure enough, it's a lot less—no more than the average *Duchas* would produce.

"Cool," Sean exclaims. "Should we pretend we're being threatened now?"

At Rigel's nod, they briefly discuss what to imagine and decide to pretend they're back in that empty apartment with Allister's and Lennox's holograms, when they both expected to die. Definitely scary stuff.

Hands clasped, they again reach for the multimeter. They're still more than an inch away when a spark arcs to it, much brighter this time.

"Wow, that's really good," Rigel says, checking the readout. "Especially for not being bonded very long. Over seven joules, enough to give someone a serious shock, though maybe not knock them out. Molly? Tristan? You guys want to try?"

Eagerly, they both step forward. Tristan produces a solid half joule, about what Sean and Rigel manage. Then, to everyone's surprise but mine, Molly sparks nearly a full joule, only a teensy bit less than my first test.

"Just in case you needed any more proof that we're sisters." I grin at her.

Her momentary alarm fades and she smiles back. "Cool. Together now, with happy thoughts?"

Nodding, I motion them back to the machine. They don't dampen it as much as Sean and Kira did, more like the usual *Echtran* amount. And when they imagine they're in danger, their spark gives a reading of three and a half joules.

"Considering you two have only been together two weeks, that's really promising," I tell them excitedly. "It proves you guys are definitely *graell*-bonded—and both your output and control should improve over time. If we can find out exactly what our enemies are plotting, we should be able to come up with specific ways to use this against them."

They all seem pleased about that prospect.

"Now that we've established that you all have actual *graell* bonds, let's try some other tests," I say then.

"Tests!?" Molly squeaks. "What kind of tests?"

I laugh at her. "Nothing scary. I probably should have said 'experiments,' like what we just did with the multimeter, but for other abilities. For a start, I'll try using 'push' to make you do something you don't want to do."

"Oh. Sure. Okay." She still looks nervous.

"Molly," I say after a moment's thought, making sure to put plenty of 'push' behind my words, "I think you should tell Tristan exactly what I said about him after his first day at Jewel High."

She doesn't even hesitate before shaking her head. "Not a chance. Even if it was sort of true at the time. I want you two to stay friends." Then she frowns curiously at me. "Were you even trying to use 'push' when you said that?"

"I was. You didn't feel it at all?"

"Nope. But probably your heart wasn't in it."

Not true. "Hm. Have you ever felt 'push' from anyone? Like your mother?" I ask.

Clearly startled, she blinks. "Of course. I must have. I'm sure she used it all the time on Sean and me both, when we were growing up."

Sean nods, but I keep my focus on Molly. "Can you remember a specific time you actually felt it, though?"

"I... Not at the moment," she replies after several seconds, frowning. "Do you really think—?"

"Yeah, I think you might always have been resistant—probably way more so now. Interesting. Okay, let's try something different," I say then. "Tristan, you have different kind of 'push,' don't you?"

He turns slightly pink. "Um, sort of, I guess?"

"There's no 'sort of' about it," Molly says. "He's got this charm thing he does. It's especially devastating when he uses it on *Duchas* girls—he can even make Trina go all nonverbal, believe it or not. Is it stronger now, have you noticed?" she asks him.

"I, ah, haven't tested it on anyone lately. Not since you and I... You know."

"Guess I should be glad of that." She winks at him. "Hey, Sean, will you get mad if he tries it on Kira? Or you could try it on M, for an even harder test."

Tristan looks more embarrassed than ever. "I don't think—"

"Go ahead." I'm honestly curious now. "Try it on me."

"It won't work," he insists. "I tried like crazy when I first got here and you never felt it then, did you?"

"Did you? Huh. I thought you were just over-the-top flirting. But maybe it's stronger now you've bonded with Molly. Try again—just as an experiment."

Still looking acutely uncomfortable, he takes a deep breath. "Okay. I'll try. Give me a sec."

His brow furrows for a long moment and I can feel him trying to subdue a combination of embarrassment and guilt, gradually replacing it with determination. Then, with a quick, apologetic glance at Rigel, he turns to me, his eyes holding mine like I remember from his first week in Jewel.

"That sweater looks great on you, M," he says, his voice smooth as silk. "Has anyone told you that? What do you say we get together tonight, someplace we can be alone?"

Involuntarily, I swallow—because this time I definitely feel something. In fact, if I weren't sitting right next to Rigel, I'd almost be tempted to… Blinking, I give myself a mental shake.

"Um, yeah. Definitely stronger. I don't even want to think what you could get Trina to do now."

Everyone laughs but I notice Molly and Rigel both frowning a little.

Quickly, I turn to Sean and Kira. "Okay, how about you two? Have you tried affecting objects on purpose?"

They both shake their heads.

"We were too freaked out when it happened before," Kira admits. "But if it's real, and if we can learn to control it—"

"It could become really useful," I finish for her. "We'd better start with something harmless, since you probably *can't* control it yet." I glance around the room. "How about a piece of popcorn?"

Plucking one out of the bowl, I hand it to Sean. "Keep holding hands. Now drop it and see if you can keep it from hitting the floor—or at least slow it down."

Clearly skeptical, he stretches out his arm and lets go of the popcorn. It immediately bounces on the hardwood floor. "So much for that idea," he says.

"Were you both concentrating?" I ask.

Guiltily, Kira shakes her head. "I wasn't. Can we try again?"

Sean picks up the popcorn piece. "We weren't concentrating those other times, either. But...maybe it mattered more? I mean, neither of us wanted that cup to break. And the basketball was no big deal, but it would have been a pain to chase it down."

"Hm, good point. Rigel and I were able to generate a much stronger lightning bolt when those Scientists were testing us by imagining a threat. Can you pretend that something bad will happen if that piece of popcorn hits the floor? Like it'll set off an alarm or something?"

"Let's pretend if it touches the floor, your mum won't let me come over to your house anymore," Kira suggests.

A legit fear, since Mrs. O only recently withdrew her opposition to Sean and Kira as a couple—her present to Sean for his eighteenth birthday.

"Good one," he agrees. "Ready?"

When she nods, he drops the fluffy popcorn kernel again. It falls like before until it's about halfway to the ground. But then, as we all watch, it slows and then stops. For a full two seconds it hovers in midair, then finally drifts the rest of the way down to the floorboards.

Kira lets out a breath. "Whew, that was a lot harder than it probably looked."

"Yeah, I had to really concentrate, too," Sean agrees. "But...we did it!"

"We did!" Kira grins at Sean, then at the rest of us. They both look slightly boggled.

To be honest, I am, too. What they just demonstrated is a totally different kind of ability than anything Rigel and I have ever done.

"Wow, that was...amazing," I tell them. "And you're sure to get better and better at it the longer you're together, especially if you practice. You've only been bonded how long? A month?"

Sean exchanges a glance with Kira. "That depends on when you count from. It's probably been a good six weeks now since we first touched."

"I don't claim to be an expert or anything," I tell them, "but I think forming a *graell* bond is more of a process than an instant thing, and the first touch or two sort of...primes it. Like priming a pump."

They all look confused—even Rigel.

"Wait," he says. "You don't think our bond formed that first time I touched you?"

I shrug. "I used to, but now I'm not so sure. Touching definitely wasn't enough to *re*-establish our bond and give you your memory back, because I tried that after we both got back to Jewel." Remembering what *did* work, I stop, embarrassed.

Rigel's brows go up in sudden understanding. "Oh. Right. Yeah, I guess that *is* a critical component."

"What?" Molly demands, still looking mystified. "What's a critical component?"

Though I feel my cheeks warming, I grin at her. "Kissing."

Now understanding breaks across everyone else's faces, along with a bit of embarrassment.

"I dunno, though." Rigel looks thoughtful again. "We hadn't kissed yet when we accidentally shocked Bryce Farmer last year. That happened less than a week after we first touched, remember?"

He's right. "Hm. So maybe touching does create the bond and kissing just strengthens it?"

"Too bad there's not a manual or something," Molly says half-jokingly. "There's those articles Regent Shim has written, but it's not like anyone's done much research on the *graell*. Not in the last century or two, anyway."

"Maybe we should write one," I suggest and get a general chuckle. "Anyway, you're all bound to get better at everything you can do, the longer you're together."

I'm about to elaborate when I hear the garage door opening. Rigel hurries to put the multimeter back.

"Molly and I weren't supposed to tell anyone about the threats out there yet, so let's keep this between the six of us for now, okay?" I say when he rejoins us. "Our, um, bond squad."

That gets another laugh from the others.

"The Bond Squad. I like it," Tristan says, grinning. "Makes us sound like real superheroes. And who knows? Maybe we will be, once we get better at everything."

5

Linkage disequilibrium

THAT EVENING I go to Molly's house well ahead of the Council meeting, so she and I can spend some more time talking with our parents in the Scepter Archive. I wonder what they'll think of today's developments?

When I call up their images, they again seem delighted to see us, making Molly and me feel almost like they're really here in her room with us.

"I thought maybe we could pick up where we left off," I suggest after we exchange greetings. "There's a Council meeting soon, but we have a little time now."

"Yes," Galena agrees. "We may be able to advise you both better once we know more about the current state of affairs."

There's still nowhere near enough time to tell them everything, I realize. "I don't suppose you can access all the stuff I've added to the main Archive?"

"Leontine may know how to transfer those records to this Archive," Mikal says, "but at the moment, I'm afraid not."

"Then we'll try to at least give you the basics now."

Taking a deep breath, I relate how Faxon was deposed last December...on the same day Rigel and I ran away from Jewel to keep the *Echtran* Council from separating us. That leads to explaining more about our *graell* bond and how nobody wanted to believe in it until we used it against those super-aliens, the Grentl, in September.

"Let me get this straight," Mikal says at one point. "Allister Adair, ranking Royal on the *Echtran* Council, actually conspired to kill this young man, Rigel Stuart?"

I nod. "He and Governor Lennox, after Rigel and I were caught on the road and they hauled him off to Dun Cloch. Allister got kicked off the Council for that, but I had to make a super awkward deal with the Council to pretend I was dating Sean instead of Rigel before they'd let him come back to Jewel."

"I never did care much for Allister," Galana comments with a grimace.

"Neither did I," Molly and I say together, then grin at each other.

After a second, I continue. "Even though Allister and Lennox were both locked up in Dun Cloch, last month they tried to kill me, too, by planting an antimatter bomb in Kira's neck. Sean's girlfriend we told you about last time."

"I see," Mikal says. "And who are those Grentl aliens you mentioned?"

Taking turns, Molly and I quickly describe last spring's hurried trip to Mars to get me Acclaimed so I could respond to a message from the non-human aliens who originally created the colony of Nuath—while keeping their existence a complete secret. With a shudder, Molly recounts how close they came to destroying Nuath by cutting the power.

I go on to explain how I appointed Rigel's grandfather, Shim, Regent, then still had to persuade over four thousand Martians to move to Earth because of Nuath's dwindling power supply before I could come home, too. Because time is getting tight, I gloss over Rigel's memory being erased, then restored when we re-bonded in September and skip to the part where the Grentl showed up in Earth orbit.

"She and Rigel were amazing," Molly tells them. "They used their *graell* electricity to turn the Grentl's EMP back on itself by boosting a positron particle emitter. That kept them from zapping this whole planet back to the Stone Age."

"Please do ask Leontine how we can access all the details you clearly had to leave out," Mikal says, shaking his head, as we finish. "I confess I'm now quite curious to hear the *entire* story!"

I promise to do that, and then have to regretfully deactivate the Archive so Molly and I can hurry downstairs for the meeting.

By seven the whole Council is here, and at one minute past Kyna calls the meeting to order, right on time for a change. Connor used to arrive late more often than not—one more reason I'm glad he's gone.

"As I mentioned Monday, we have a lengthy agenda tonight, so we'll get right to business," Kyna begins. "I'll start with a few brief updates in order of importance."

She glances at her notes. "First, I regret to report that no real progress has been made thus far on tracking down that missing antimatter. Our Mind Healers were fortunately able to perform the promised memory extraction on Waylan Carney, the man who attempted to assassinate Princess Malena last weekend, but nothing useful has yet been gleaned from those memories."

"Fortunately?" I echo, sensing an odd mix of frustration and relief from Kyna.

She nods. "As you suggested, Carney was thoroughly scanned and searched on his arrival in Dun Cloch Sunday night. Embedded in his thigh was a capsule containing a highly toxic substance. Had it not been removed, he almost certainly would have died prior to yesterday's memory extraction."

"Like Enid and the man who attacked me two months ago," I say.

"Precisely. The remains of the ampule he attempted to use on Princess Malena revealed traces of the same compound. Had he done so, it would have been almost immediately fatal."

My stomach clenches and Mrs. O'Gara sucks in a quick breath that sounds almost like a sob.

"What *did* the Healers learn from his memories?" I ask then. "Anything implicating Devyn?"

"No. He remembered receiving a message instructing him to neutralize Princess Malena, but not who sent it," Kyna replies. "It's possible he never knew, though our Mind Healers cautioned that Carney is mentally unstable, throwing the accuracy of his recollections into doubt. We can only hope more details will emerge as his memories are further examined."

I try to rein in my own frustration. "Devyn *had* to be involved. He's the only person Connor told about Molly. Even before that, he was obviously up to something. Why else would he ask Connor to keep their conversations secret from the Council?"

Malcolm responds, "Perhaps, as Connor suggested, Devyn simply did not wish to be brought to *your* notice, Excellency, given your prejudice toward him."

"Prejudice?" I glare at him. "You make it sound like I took some random dislike to him. After nearly keeping me from getting Acclaimed Sovereign—which would have destroyed Nuath—he conspired to wipe Rigel's memory and lie to me about it. So excuse me if I don't share your faith in his good intentions. Besides, we know he was closely connected with Allister and Lennox from *their* memories."

"True," Kyna agrees. "In addition, as Council head I've received quite a few messages urging us to appoint Devyn Kane as *Echtran* Regent to Sovereign Emileia. Though they've come from widely disparate locations and *fines,* all contain suspiciously similar wording. It appears Devyn has been actively cultivating support across numerous demographics."

"That's hardly a crime," Malcolm insists.

"Also true," Kyna admits, though her irritation is evident. "We still have no *direct* evidence that Devyn is involved with those malcontents out west—which brings me to my next update. Allister's and Lennox's trials for the attempted assassination of our Sovereign are now scheduled to start this coming week, after being delayed due to various, ah, unexpected events." She smiles at Molly.

Mrs. O speaks up then. "Did that assassin's memories give any hint of who those 'others' were that he mentioned might go after my Molly?"

"I'm afraid not," Kyna tells her, "though the conspiracy does appear more extensive and organized than we originally believed." Then, to me, "You believe this man was originally an adherent of Faxon's, Excellency?"

"Yes, he attacked me last year, right in downtown Jewel, also with some kind of ampule. Then he was with that little army of Faxon followers who came after me in the cornfield later that same day—the ones supposedly mind-controlled by an Ossian sphere."

Kyna grimaces. "We'd hoped the destruction of that Sphere, combined with Faxon's overthrow, would persuade his radical *Echtran* adherents to give up and move on. Unfortunately, the recent arrival of Faxon loyalists from Mars appears to have reenergized them. Amid his ravings, the assassin spoke of dominion over the *Duchas,* which we all know was one of Faxon's ultimate goals."

"Surely that negates the Sovereign's theory that Devyn Kane is involved?" Malcolm exclaims. "Whatever else he may have done, Devyn is no Faxon sympathizer."

"Probably not," I agree. "But that doesn't mean he's not using them for his own ends, the way Allister and Lennox pretended to be Populists to convince Kira to help them. The assassin they sent after me at that football game also claimed to be a Populist—though I guess we'll never know for sure."

Malcolm still looks skeptical. "We don't know for certain that they were behind that."

"Actually, we do," Kyna corrects him. "It was in the transcription of Allister's and Lennox's memories I sent you all on Tuesday. With the help of Gordon Nolan, they twice targeted the Sovereign prior to their most recent attempt with an antimatter bomb."

"Does that mean the leaders of this current Anti-Royal movement have support from more than one faction of malcontents?" Nara asks fearfully.

Kyna glances at her. "So it would seem. Worse, what little we've learned so far indicates the malcontents are attempting to foment unrest among those recently relocated to Earth."

"That would fit with those messages I intercepted," Mr. Stuart says. "Overturning the established order was a recurring theme in those communications, based on what I've deciphered so far. That, of course, was Faxon's original agenda, a goal apparently shared by the radical fringe of the Anti-Royals—or Populists, as they prefer to be called."

"But where would traditionalists like Devyn Kane come in?" Malcolm demands. "Or Allister Adair or Lach Lennox, for that matter? None of them would want the Royal *fine* exterminated, as they are all high-ranking Royals themselves. What can they possibly have in common with lower-*fine* rabble like Faxon followers or Anti-Royals?"

I give a little snort before stating the obvious. "Me."

"I'm afraid she's right," Kyna wryly agrees. "All three groups *are* somewhat united in their opposition to Sovereign Emileia, though each for different reasons."

There's an uncomfortable silence, broken by Molly. "When we were in Nuath campaigning for M's Acclamation, Traditionalists *were* the first ones to speak out against her."

"That was different," Breann protests. "That was solely due to some of her more, ah, unorthodox choices."

"In other words, my relationship with Rigel." I can't keep the edge from my voice. "That video Gordon leaked of us kissing is what turned the Traditionalists against me. And now Gwendolyn Gannett's doing her best to keep their grudge alive on Earth, with her hit pieces in the *Echtran Enquirer*. You'd think Rigel helping to save this whole planet would've made our people grateful enough to stop attacking him."

"Entrenched attitudes, like old habits, take time to change," Mr. Stuart gently reminds me. "Barely two months have passed since you two averted the Grentl attack. Some people did apologize once Rigel's involvement was revealed—those who know us personally, anyway. But with so many new *Echtrans* on Earth, and in Jewel, perhaps it's not surprising—" He breaks off.

Something in his expression alerts me. "Have you received more threats?"

"Not threats, precisely. Just some strongly worded…suggestions. Some apparently believe Ariel and I should be doing more to discourage your relationship, for the good of our people."

I fight down a spurt of anger.

"The good of our people? Or the good of their comfortable traditions? You say to give them time, but as Kyna pointed out Monday, we don't know how much time we have. We need to start swaying *Echtran* support in our direction ASAP, before those anarchists, or whatever they are, get organized enough to blow Jewel off the map!"

"I agree, Excellency," Kyna says. "Are you perhaps willing to play a role in shifting those opinions? You were quite persuasive in Nuath, by all accounts."

I'm both startled and flattered by this evidence of how much I've risen in her esteem as a leader over the past year. Fortunately, I have an answer ready.

"More than willing. In fact, I was already planning to write my own series of articles for the *Echtran Enquirer*. You know, to counterbalance the stuff Gwendolyn Gannett is printing."

Kyna's brows rise approvingly. "An excellent idea. Until we have a real news network here on Earth, that weekly publication is the best way to reach as many *Echtrans* as possible. Nor can I imagine the *Enquirer* refusing to publish anything you send."

She then turns to Mr. Stuart. "Speaking of that network, Van, how soon do you expect it to become generally available?"

"I hope to deploy it planet-wide by the end of the year. We're already using it internally at NuAgra, as a beta test."

"You've said this will be a sort of *Echtran*-only internet?" Nara asks.

"Essentially," he confirms. "Though far more secure than even the most sensitive *Duchas* networks. Access will require retinal scans, along with our people's unique identity codes."

That reminds me of a question I meant to ask last week. "How will you get those for every single *Echtran* on the planet?"

There's a startled silence, broken by Kyna. "We already have them, Excellency. Raised on Earth as you were, perhaps you were not aware? Those metrics are entered into the *Echtran* database for every new arrival from Mars. That's been true for over a century."

"Really?" I glance at Molly, who nods.

"I thought you knew. Everyone in Nuath gets an identity code as soon as they're born," she explains. "Sort of like Social Security numbers, but a lot more complicated. We used them for everything—enrolling in school, riding the zippers, you name it. For more sensitive stuff, like accessing credit balances, we had to confirm with a retinal scan, which is basically unhackable. It's how they checked us in when we landed on Earth."

Kyna raises a brow. "Won't this new network make it easier for those with questionable agendas to communicate?" she asks Mr. Stuart.

"I suppose so," he admits. "However, unlike our current MARSTAR system and the weekly *Echtran Enquirer*, which are view-only, this network will collect data every time it's accessed. Anyone using it will reveal both their identity and their whereabouts—much like the polling and voting systems in Nuath."

"In that case, those with ill intent may choose not to use it at all," Kyna points out.

Mr. Stuart smiles. "Only if they understand what they're revealing. As with the Nuathan *grechain*, that information will be buried deep within the terms of use all must agree to when first logging in. I, ah, doubt most will take the time to read it thoroughly."

That draws a general chuckle.

"Once the network is up and running planet-wide," Mr. Stuart continues, "we'll also be able to stream news. Our small news crew at NuAgra is quite eager to begin wide broadcasts."

"Do you mean we'll eventually have something here like the news feeds in Nuath?" I ask, startled.

"Not on that scale, but yes," he replies. "Given our limited staff, we initially plan just one daily broadcast covering the latest *Echtran* and

Nuathan news. Over the next few launch windows, we hope to scale up to something closer to what our people enjoyed in Nuath."

I cringe, remembering the garbage I saw on some Nuathan news feeds—especially those incessant polls. "I hope they'll stick to real news. It would be nice for our people to have an alternative to the *Echtran Enquirer* that's more, ah, fact-based. Especially with Gwendolyn Gannet still trying to stir up division. Did you all see what she wrote about Molly?"

Everyone in the room nods.

"I've been contacted by numerous people since Tuesday, demanding more details," Breann tells us. "If we don't give the people additional information soon, they'll start concocting their own theories—which could conceivably play into the hands of those traitorous conspirators."

"That reminds me," I say. "Gwendolyn Gannett was hanging around the buses after school yesterday, asking some of the newer *Echtran* students about Molly. Can she be banned from the school grounds?"

"Absolutely. I'll put in a call to the *Enquirer's* managing editor in the morning," Kyna promises in a voice that assures me she'll be listened to.

"Moving on," she continues, "I do have some slightly better news to share. Our investigators unearthed Enid's private files—encrypted, of course, so we don't yet know what they contain. Van, perhaps you'd be willing to assist there?"

Mr. Stuart immediately agrees. "Let's hope she used the same protocol as those other messages."

"Indeed. The next item I'd like to address tonight is Connor's vacated Council seat," Kyna says then. "This afternoon I sent you all a few names I thought we might consider for the spot, but feel free to offer suggestions of your own."

I clear my throat. "I have one that wasn't on your list."

Instantly, all three Royals on the Council tense. I can guess why.

"Don't worry, it's a Royal," I quickly assure them. "We should probably maintain the usual balance of *fines* for now, since the Traditionalists are upset with me already."

"That...is good to hear, Excellency," Breann says, perceptibly relaxing. "You know the Royal *fine* is specifically adapted for governance. That's why we've always held a majority of the seats on this Council, as well as in the Nuathan legislature, prior to Faxon."

I concede her point with a smile even though I don't completely agree. Now isn't the time to make extra waves.

"You have a particular Royal in mind, Excellency?" Kyna's surprise is understandable. I adamantly opposed adding any of their suggested Royals to replace Shim after he resigned from the Council. But unlike Connor, Shim wasn't Royal.

"I do. Strange as it may sound, I believe Teara Roark, Connor's wife, would be a good choice. She's apparently one of our leading experts on the history of Nuathan culture and government, and is also well informed on the various Earth governments. That sort of expertise would be very useful as we set up a more extensive *Echtran* government here on Earth."

All three Royals seem pleased by my suggestion. The three non-Royals on the Council nod, as well.

"After Connor was removed for cause, I reviewed Teara's record from the time she left university in Cleirach," Mr. Stuart informs us. "I was concerned she might also pose a threat to our security, but quickly concluded she does not. In fact, she appears to have been a close friend to Royal Consort Galena, the Sovereign's mother. I quite agree that Teara's experience could be of assistance."

"I must concur," Kyna says. "Many traditional duties of this Council must be farmed out to various local authorities, as we are too few to adequately govern our increasingly numerous and scattered people. Indeed, every *Echtran* enclave of any significant size will need its own legislative body in addition to their current governors and mayors. I intended to introduce that topic next, but if Teara is going to join us, I'd like to table that discussion for now. All in favor of adding Teara Roark to this Council?"

The vote is unanimous. Molly looks especially pleased. I'm sure she can't wait to give Tristan the news.

The last few items on the agenda include appointing an adult Bodyguard for Molly and filling Connor's vacated roles at NuAgra. After discussion, Breann is appointed as Immigrant Liaison and Malcolm accepts the post of *Echtran* Minister of Terran Obfuscation. It's nearly midnight when we finally adjourn.

"I will of course let you all know if anything new comes to light about our current emergency," Kyna says before blinking out. "Barring new developments, I will see you all next Saturday."

I spend the night with Molly, like I often do when Council meetings run late. Because I promised Rigel a recap, I mentally "ping" him when she goes to brush her teeth, but he's clearly half asleep.

I've been trying to stay awake till I heard from you. Anything big?

Nothing that can't wait till tomorrow. Go to sleep. I love you!

He sends back a sleepy *Love you, too.* Then silence.

The next morning during church, I silently fill him in on the essentials from the meeting.

So no more bombshells, he thinks back when I'm done. *I always feel like I'm waiting for another shoe to drop. How many have there been now?*

Way too many, I think back wryly. *But I'm sure someday they'll all finally be on the floor.*

Though he chuckles, I sense his frustration at the current situation mirrors my own. *Arboretum later?* he asks. I eagerly agree.

A freezing mist is falling when I leave for the arboretum after lunch. I'm glad, since it means we'll likely have the place to ourselves. Turning up my coat collar, I start walking. I haven't even gone a block when Rigel pulls up beside me in his parents' silver Audi.

"Hey, cutie, want a ride?" He leers playfully at me through the open passenger window.

Grinning, I hop in. "How long do you have the car for?"

"As long as I want." His grin gets even wider. "It's mine now."

My mouth falls open. "Seriously?"

Rigel nods, clearly enjoying my reaction. "Early birthday present. My folks planned to give it to me next weekend, but after hearing you took the bus, my dad moved up delivery of *his* new car—which I didn't even know he'd bought. He also added some cool Martian security features to this one, since I'll be doubling as your chauffeur from now on."

Parking in the arboretum's little gravel lot, Rigel leans over for a kiss, which I eagerly return.

"Mmm," he murmurs a few blissful seconds later. "We should build in even more extra time before school now. After school, too."

"I like the sound of that." I snuggle against him.

Even though no one's *officially* trying to keep us apart these days, we don't get nearly enough time truly alone. Rigel's parents have become as strict as my Aunt Theresa, insisting someone else has to be home whenever we visit each other.

My aunt's just prudish, but the Stuarts claim it's because we never know who might be watching their house. While I get they want to avoid even more criticism, sometimes I wonder if it's worth it. But now...

I tilt my face up for another kiss and for the next few minutes nothing else matters. It's tempting to spend the next hour or two doing only this but after a few cars drive past, we decide we'll be more private —if less comfortable—in the arboretum.

Since it's as deserted as I hoped, I activate my omni app to ward off the chill drizzle, even though I'm plenty warm at the moment after fifteen minutes of quality kissing. I twine my fingers through Rigel's, reveling in the contact as we head to "our" bench in the back corner.

"So they still have no clue at all who sent that guy after Molly—*or* who stole the antimatter?" he asks as we walk.

"No. Apparently the guy's so crazy, his memories are a mess. Kyna hopes we'll learn more as they pick everything apart. They did find Enid's files, though, so if your dad can decrypt them we may know more soon." I don't mention how all the different groups with grudges against me seem to be joining together, but of course he picks up on my unspoken thought.

"So you're still a target, maybe to lots of people?" he demands. "I knew I should've—"

"You're probably as much a target as I am," I counter. "Why didn't you tell me your family is still being hassled by the Traditionalists?"

That halts him in mid-tirade. After a brief, uncomfortable silence, he says, "I didn't want you to worry. It's not like anyone's actually *done* anything to me or my folks."

"But they've threatened to?" I prod, even though Mr. Stuart denied that last night.

Rigel's emotions answer me before his words do. "Just vague hints. Nothing specific enough to report."

"Or to tell you who or what to guard against?" I challenge him. "Rigel, you *have* to keep me in the loop on this stuff!"

He pulls me to him. "I will. I do. But you already have so much to deal with—"

"None of it's half as important to me as you are," I insist. "Maybe these articles I'm writing will move the needle of public opinion back our way. Meanwhile, I'm really glad your dad put those security upgrades in your car."

"They're mostly for you," he reminds me with that crooked smile I love. "But if it keeps you from worrying about me so much, that's good, too."

I smile back, leaning in for another kiss.

"Do you think your dad can put security in Tristan's car, too?" I ask a few moments later.

"Probably. Good idea." The slight edge to his voice puzzles me. "Maybe the O'Gara's minivan and Sean's car, too, since we don't know who they might go after next."

I watch his face, trying to decipher what I just sensed off him. "You're...you're not still bothered by that charm thing Tristan did yesterday, are you?"

His brows shoot up. "I wasn't—!" At my look, he breaks off and huffs out a breath. "Okay, it bothered me a *little*. Because I couldn't help picking up an echo of what you felt when he did it. I know it's stupid."

Smiling, I shake my head. "Not stupid, but totally not necessary. He's bonded with Molly now. He only tried it because I insisted. You saw how embarrassed he was."

"I know. You're right. I just couldn't help remembering how he flirted with you when he first got here, right up until a couple weeks ago. And he's Royal. So many people have tried to come between us over the past year, I guess I'm still a little paranoid."

I lean my head on his shoulder. "Don't be. Even when they kept us apart physically, they never for an instant made me doubt how I feel about you, Rigel. Never. I don't think anything could."

Rigel's brief uncertainty vanishes as he lowers his lips to mine. *Good. Because nothing will ever matter to me a fraction as much as you do, M. I love you.*

Kira

6

Genetic distance

IT'S STILL DARK when I wake from a vaguely disturbing dream. For a moment I try to recall the details, but they're already fading. Rolling over, I grab my cellphone from the nightstand. My alarm will go off in half an hour, so there's not much point trying to get back to sleep.

With a yawn, I get out of bed and start dressing—quietly, since Adina is still sound asleep. As I leave our bedroom for the equally dark living room a minute later, something white flashes past my ankles—Adina's puppy, Aggie. I make a grab for her, but hampered by the laptop tucked under my arm, I miss. I know if I try to catch her she'll think it's a game, so I give up rather than risk her barking.

"Fine," I whisper. "You can stay out here as long as you're quiet."

Going to the kitchen table, I open my laptop. Might as well catch up on email and some school work before breakfast. But before I even click on my browser, Aggie gives a little yip and runs to our apartment door.

"Shh!" I admonish her. "Settle down. Adina will take you outside when she gets up."

Too excited to mind me, the little dog starts scrabbling at the bottom of the door. She must really need to go out. With a sigh, I get up and find her leash, then hook it to her collar.

"Let's be quick about this, okay?" I open the door and pause, frowning down at a cardboard shoebox at my feet. "Huh."

During our first week or two here, a few neighbors left little welcome gifts of baked goods or flowers at our door—examples of "Midwest hospitality," Mum claimed. But we've been here nearly two months now, so this is a surprise. Shrugging, I pick up the box and carry it inside. Maybe it's something we can have with breakfast.

I'm about to set the box down when it occurs to me that whatever it is might need to be refrigerated. Keeping my hold on Aggie's leash, I lift the lid to check—and nearly drop the box.

Because what's inside isn't pastries or cupcakes. It's a dead animal.

Swallowing my distaste, I look more closely. Though I've never seen a real one before, I identify it as a rat—something most Terrans regard as vermin. Remembering a few other negative connotations from Earth television and movies, my distaste turns to horror.

This is a threat, no question. But from who?

Running back to the open door, I look wildly around the deserted landing and stairs before realizing the box could have been left hours ago.

"Come on," I tell Aggie, taking a firmer grip on her leash.

Carrying the box in my other hand, I hurry down to the apartment complex dumpster to dispose of the nasty little 'gift' before Adina or Mum can see it.

.⁺.⁺

"Aren't you tired of criticizing my personal choices yet?" I whisper to Alan in Physics class an hour and a half later. "Because I'm sick to death of it."

Shortly after Molly's news broke last week, Alan started needling me again. His comments bother me more than usual after finding that rat this morning.

"I just hate to see a friend going down what's clearly a self-destructive path," he stubbornly whispers back. "Didn't you read last week's *Echtran Enquirer*? I've told you what people are saying about you and Sean behind your back, that it reflects poorly not just on your parents but on our whole *fine*. I can't believe you're both so willing to throw off centuries of tradition when—"

The teacher clears his throat and Alan breaks off, belatedly realizing class has started. For the next few minutes he shoots me disgruntled looks that I pretend not to notice. Could he be the one who—? I doubt it. But I *do* wish, again, that Alan and I weren't stuck as lab partners for the rest of the grading period. Maybe the teacher will let me switch after the first of the year. I'd enjoy this class a lot more if I were partnered with Sean.

Which is exactly what pisses Alan off.

"That article implied that if Sean doesn't get back with the Sovereign, he might pair up with Princess Malena," he mutters to me when the teacher's back is turned. "Especially with his mother on the Council, everyone's going to—"

The teacher turns back around and he shuts up again. I'm glad since it stops me from informing him there's no chance of either of those things happening. M and Rigel are totally *graell*-bonded. And if they were right on Saturday, so are Molly and Tristan...and Sean and me.

After leaving Rigel's house on Saturday, I was exhilarated by the thought I might actually be part of a band of "superheroes" who could help protect the Sovereign and everyone else in Jewel. Now, between the rat and Alan, it's hard to recapture that upbeat mood.

"Maybe if you'd heard what people were saying out at NuAgra after last week's *Echtran Enquirer*, you'd take what I'm saying a little more seriously," Alan whispers near the end of class.

There's no question the nasty cracks my parents and I have received since I started dating Sean got worse after Gwendolyn Gannett's article last week. That dead rat was an even more forceful reminder that Sean is way out of my league, according to our traditions.

I swallow as a new worry occurs to me. What if criticism aimed at Sean takes an uglier turn, too?

Alan's parting words at the bell don't help. "I just don't want to see you hurt—or Sean, either. I'm only trying to help...but I guess it's your life."

"You're right. It is. Bye, Alan."

Refusing to let my anxiety show, I head toward Sean, who's waiting for me near the door. Smiling, he laces his fingers through mine. As always, his touch chases away my fears, giving me a wonderful sense of well-being. Of rightness.

But then his smile falters. "What's wrong?"

Flach. Mostly I love the way we can now sense each other's emotions when we touch, but sometimes it can be awkward.

"Oh, it's just Alan. He's making snide remarks to me again, now that your sister's no longer an option."

Sean snorts. "Molly was already done with Alan before she learned the truth. Said he was a real jerk the couple times they went out."

I give him a wry smile. "Guess it's not just me that brings that out in him, then. Hard to believe I used to like him back in Nuath."

"Like him?" Sean slants a glance down at me. "You mean...*like* like?"

Quickly, I shake my head. "No! We never— I mean, I knew him at school. He was a year ahead of me and kind of good looking, so I thought he was, I don't know, sort of cool. Until I got to know him better."

"Whew. You had me worried there." Sean gives my hand a playful squeeze.

I laugh, but realize I never told Sean about Brady, the guy I really did have a crush on back home. No real point now, since nothing ever came of that, either. Brady made it perfectly clear he considered me too young for him.

"Penny for your thoughts," Sean says, startling me again. Maybe it's good we haven't developed real telepathy like M and Rigel have. Yet?

"I'm impressed how well you've adopted Earth sayings we never used back home," I say instead of answering. "I'm still working on that."

"I do have a couple of years on you there," he reminds me. "It'll come. But what's up? A second ago you looked like you were on another planet."

He'll know if I dodge, unless I let go of his hand first—which I don't want to do. "You're close. I was thinking how intense things got just before I left Nuath."

"Intense? With Alan?"

I stare at him. "Huh? No! With *caidpel*, mostly."

Now his expression becomes sympathetic. "Yeah, it must still bother you that you had to leave right when the Ags made the playoffs. Their next best player—what was his name? Brady?—pulled them through the first round game, at least, but that was the best they could do without you."

His mention of Brady, immediately after me thinking about him for the first time in weeks, jars me.

"Next best?" I force a grin. "Brady's at least as good a player as I am, probably better. Unfortunately, the guy they brought in to replace me wasn't ready to play at that level and the team didn't have time to compensate."

I'm not sure why I'm defending Brady, especially after realizing the only reason he ever flirted with me was to recruit me to the Populist cause. Though Sean knows I was briefly part of that group, I never told him how I first got into it. In retrospect, it's kind of embarrassing.

"At least you have basketball now," he says, giving my hand another squeeze. "I'm looking forward to your first game tonight. Maybe it can't compare to being a famous *caidpel* star, but you'll easily be the best player on the team. Shoot, the whole state."

He knows the fact I was a sort of celebrity in Nuath made coming to Earth, where I'm a nobody, that much harder.

"Thanks, but that reminds me. I need some pointers on how to play more like a *Duchas*. I mostly managed it for tryouts, but it's harder during practice, even the drills. I'm bound to have even more trouble during the game tonight, even if it is just a scrimmage."

"Can't turn off the competitiveness, huh?" He winks at me. "Trust me, I get it. I find it helps to think about my teammates and how they'll feel if I make them look bad by comparison. They're all good guys and I don't want to do that."

"I'll try to remember that. Once I get to know the other girls better, it'll probably get easier. How are Alan and Liam handling that in your practices?"

Sean grimaces. "I'm constantly having to remind Liam not to be quite so gung-ho out there. Alan's worried enough about the rules—*our* rules, I mean—to be more careful. Let me know if you want me to tell him to back off, by the way."

"I think I can shut him down on my own, but thanks." I grin, even though that reminder has me worrying again that some of what Alan says might be true.

Sean and I reluctantly separate then, to go to our second period classes. When I get to French, which I share with both M and Molly, M gives me a quizzical look.

"Something wrong, Kira?"

Ugh. It's awkward enough sometimes when Sean picks up on my emotions without the Sovereign doing it, too.

"Just thinking about my first game tonight...and Alan being a pain," I add, in case M can tell it's more than that.

Molly looks past her at me. "Don't tell me he's started coming on to you again, now he knows I'm not...you know."

"Sort of. I appreciated you giving him another focus for a while, but now he's back at it. I can't even flatter myself he actually likes me. I'm just the only Ag near his age in Jewel and he's so tradition-bound he refuses to date outside his *fine*."

Molly clicks her tongue in disgust. "Yeah, he made it obvious that was the only reason he asked me out, too, after you and Sean got together. He'll give up eventually if you ignore his flirting."

I don't correct her, but in fact flirting wouldn't bother me nearly as much as the stuff he says about Sean and me—and his reminders that a lot of other people are saying the same things.

"Believe me, I'm doing my best. He's surprisingly persistent."

When class starts, my thoughts revert to those last weeks in Nuath and how hard I fought against leaving. Ironic, since my life on Earth has turned out a thousand times better than I expected. Despite the challenges, I definitely don't regret coming here now.

That'll be even more true if I can make a difference here after all, maybe even become a "superhero" someday, with Sean's help.

. . .

I'm increasingly nervous about tonight's basketball scrimmage during the drive to nearby Elwood. My family's coming tonight, too, but because I have to be here early, Sean offered to drive me separately. That gives him a chance to calm me before my first test of playing well but not *too* well with an actual game on the line.

"You'll do fine, seriously. Just remember not to hog the ball—because you'll be tempted. Trust me, I know. Especially if your teammates flub a lot of shots. It helps if I make a game out of how evenly I can spread out the points between everyone on our team. Try that."

"That's a really good idea. Thanks, Sean."

He parks the car in Elwood High's lot, then gives me a long, fortifying kiss before we get out of the car. I throw myself into it, drawing all the strength and confidence from him I can.

Elwood's gym is no bigger than Jewel's but by the time the game's about to begin, it's still more than half empty. Proof of what I've already heard, that girls' sports on Earth don't get anywhere near the same support as boys' sports. That definitely wasn't the case in Nuath. Just one more way the *Duchas* are backward compared to us.

I smile up at my family and Sean, sitting together in the small wooden bleachers and they all wave to me. Scanning the small crowd,

I'm fairly sure they're not the only *Echtrans* attending. Which only adds to the pressure.

The other girls on my team aren't bad, for *Duchas*. But they're still *Duchas*, and Jewel is a small school. Not much of a talent pool.

We go to shake hands with the other team before the game starts and I'm startled to discover Elwood also has an *Echtran* girl on their team. She gives me a secret smile when our hands touch, acknowledging the *brath* we both feel. From her frankly admiring expression, I assume she's aware of my *caidpel* fame in Nuath.

As the game gets underway, I realize it only makes sense there'd be *Echtrans* in Elwood since the town is barely five miles from Jewel and slightly bigger. Because of Jewel's current housing shortage, I've heard some NuAgra workers are having to live in nearby communities. I'll bet there are also a few people who didn't make the cut for Jewel that figured settling here would be the next best thing.

Unfortunately, having an *Echtran* to compete against makes it that much harder to rein myself in, though I'm clearly better than she is. At the end of the first period, I guiltily realize I've scored every single one of Jewel's 13 points—not good.

When the second quarter starts, I try harder to give my teammates opportunities to score when I get the ball.

"Sarah!" I call, bouncing it to our next-best player, who's under the basket. Carefully, since our practices have taught me that I can only use a fraction of my strength and speed if I want a pass or bounce caught.

Sarah takes advantage of her position to lay up a two-pointer and I breathe a little easier.

Remembering Sean's suggestions, for the rest of the game I'm careful to hang back and pass the ball more—though it chafes my competitive spirit to see Elwood catching up on the scoreboard.

We still win easily—a little too easily. I realize I didn't do a great job with Sean's "game" of spreading out the points. Two-thirds of the successful shots and all of the three-pointers were mine. I'll definitely need to hold back a lot more next game, if I don't want to attract the Council's attention.

After the final whistle, the other team gathers to congratulate us. While the spectators are still making their way down the stands, Elwood's *Echtran* player grabs a quick word with me.

"Wow, I can't believe I actually got to play against Kira Morain. I'm

Glynnis, by the way. I, um, could tell you weren't really trying all that hard, especially after the first period. Am I right?"

I lower my voice so no *Duchas* can overhear. "It's really not safe to. You know that, right? The *Echtran* Council already takes a dim view of us playing sports."

"How do you know that? Oh, right. You're going out with Sean O'Gara these days, aren't you?" Her gaze suddenly becomes more critical than admiring. "My father says that's—"

She breaks off as the small crowd from the stands converges, then moves off with a frown. Good. I really didn't want to hear whatever her father said about Sean and me. Judging by her tone, it wasn't complimentary.

Sean himself reaches me then, throwing an arm around my shoulders. "You looked great out there," he congratulates me. Then whispers, "But not *too* great. Good job."

"Thanks." I return his grin. "Don't know if you noticed, but Elwood has, ah, one of us on their team, too."

"Yeah?" He looks over the crowd. "Hm, must be number 20. I thought she was awfully good for a—you know. Even more props to you, then. I know I'd find it harder to tone it down in that situation."

I give him a crooked smile. "It was. Need to do better next time, though, if I don't want an ultimatum like Rigel's."

"Nah, you were fine." He dismisses that concern with a wave. "I'm way more worried about *our* first scrimmage on Thursday. Alan and I both talked to Liam at practice today, but—"

We drop the subject as my parents and Adina join us, but I worry my —all *Echtran* students'—days playing sports may be limited. Sean told me the Council has threatened to forbid it completely, if Rigel takes Jewel's football team to State. Even if Rigel loses, that could still happen if *Echtran* athletes aren't careful.

In contrast to the fans at every football game I've attended since getting to Jewel, ours disperse fairly quickly. Ten minutes after the final buzzer, nearly everyone has left the gym.

"Thanks for coming, Mum, Dad," I say again to my parents as we walk out, my hand securely clasped in Sean's.

My mother almost never attended my *caidpel* games back in Nuath, the crowds bothered her so much. Of course, this crowd was a fraction the size of the ones I used to play in front of. Still, she seems to be a lot less nervous overall since moving to Earth—to Jewel.

As we cross the parking lot, I notice a small group of *Echtrans* watching Sean and me, their expressions ranging from critical to outraged as they whisper among themselves.

"That's so wrong!" I overhear one of them say. Another woman gives me such a venomous glare it makes me flinch.

I try to hide my reaction from Sean, but he notices anyway.

"Ignore them," he whispers to me.

"Easier said than done," I mutter back.

I'm careful not to make eye contact again as we accompany my family to their car.

"Is it okay if Sean takes me home, too?" I ask. The girls' team doesn't rate a bus for away games, like the boys do.

"Oh! Of course, if he prefers that," Mum says, with a deferential little dip of her head toward Sean. I've asked her not to do that, but she apparently can't help herself, her reverence for Royals is so ingrained.

He smiles down at her without a trace of the arrogance I used to imagine in him before I got to know him. "I'll bring her straight home, Mrs. Morain, not to worry."

"I wasn't— That is— Thank you," she stammers and I stifle a sigh.

I wait till we're in Sean's car to say, "I'm sure she'll get used to you soon and stop acting like that."

"It's fine." He slants an amused glance my way. "Gives me a better idea of what M has to deal with, though. She's always hated the way people defer to her, since way back last fall."

Something I truly believe now, unlike the first time he told me that, when I was still clinging to all of my misconceptions about M. It's embarrassing now to remember how rude I used to be to her—and how I worried my attitude might get my family in trouble.

"I do wish certain *other* people would show you more respect, though," I tell him then. "Some of the stuff they say—"

He takes one hand off the wheel to put it over mine. "Seriously, Kira, ignore them. They'll get used to us being a couple eventually. They'll have to. Just like they've had to get used to M and Rigel being together."

I don't point out that not everyone's reconciled to that, either, judging by opinion pieces I've seen in the *Echtran Enquirer* recently. Or some of the things I've heard from fellow *Echtrans* at school, or out at NuAgra during my seventh period work-study shifts.

"You're right," I say, even though I don't fully believe it. "We just need to give them time to come around."

"That's the spirit." He squeezes my hand and I can feel his confidence.

I just wish I shared it.

.⁺⋅

"Have any of you had a chance to work on your, um, powers since Saturday?" M quietly asks the rest of us at lunch the next day, before any *Duchas* get to our table.

Sean and I exchange an uncomfortable glance. "Not really, sorry," he says. "We haven't had a chance."

When we got to the gym after church Sunday, most of both the boys' and girl' basketball teams were there. Afterward, when we'd planned to go for a walk, it started raining. Yesterday Sean had basketball practice after school, then I had my game in Elwood.

"Neither have we," Molly admits. "I had that interview with Gwendolyn Gannett Sunday afternoon and I've been obsessing about what she'll print ever since. It's sickening how she pretends to be so nice, then writes such awful stuff!"

"Tell me about it." M rolls her eyes, then turns to Tristan. "Do you want to try testing your suggestion thing on Trina?"

He looks startled. "I thought you were kidding about that. Should I?" he asks Molly. "What should I try to make her do?"

She ponders for a second, then nods toward the cashier, where Alan is having his card scanned. "How about you convince her to go after Alan?" She winks at me. "Kira says he's started pestering her again, now that I'm permanently unavailable."

Tristan chuckles. "Sure, worth a try."

He takes a big sip of his drink, then casually strolls over to the cheerleader table. Trina instantly jumps up to talk to him. As we all watch, her eyes widen and she swallows visibly, then looks over to where Alan is setting his tray down next to some other basketball players.

Tristan says something else and she nods. Then, snatching up her lunch tray, she heads toward the other table, a determined smile on her lips.

When Tristan rejoins our table a moment later, he's grinning. "That was kind of fun," he says quietly to Molly. "Maybe you should try the same thing on Alan, about Trina. Convince him tradition is overrated."

She giggles, drawing a curious glance from Bri, who's just sitting down. "Maybe I will," she mutters back. Then, to Bri, "So, did you hear? Trina apparently had a wardrobe malfunction at the after party Friday night and accidentally flashed half a dozen guys."

That immediately gets a laugh from everyone.

"I bet she did it on purpose." Bri scans the cafeteria for Trina. "Look at her over there, coming on to Alan Dempsey, that cute new senior, when two weeks ago she was all about Tristan. Typical."

While that bit of gossip dominates conversation for several minutes, I marvel at how quickly Molly came up with that cover story for laughing. It's not the first time I've seen her do that, but only now realize it's probably because she's Royal. Funny how many clues were there all along without anyone ever suspecting.

7

Adaptive logic

LIKE MOST DAYS, Sean and I only manage to snag a couple of minutes between our separate sixth period classes and me leaving for NuAgra.

"I was hoping we could try again for a walk tonight," he says, "but the guys want to get together to plan something for Pete's birthday. Maybe tomorrow?"

"I think it's supposed to rain again, but sure." Maybe if we go someplace private, Sean can use the weather app from his omni to keep us dry.

Grinning, he gives me a thumbs-up and a quick kiss, then hurries off to seventh period while I head to the office for my ride to NuAgra.

Now that both our basketball seasons have started, it's become harder than ever to find time to be together. My practice starts right after Sean's ends and we barely get time in between to exchange two words. With our crazy schedules, our only real chances to be alone during the week are before school and the occasional non-game evening when the weather happens to cooperate.

Maybe being barred from playing *Duchas* sports wouldn't be so terrible after all?

Because I never get home from practice before seven, Mum has recently moved dinner half an hour later than we used to eat. I appreciate that, since I'm usually starving by then and hate eating alone.

Unfortunately, that means even less after-dinner time I can spend with Sean.

We're halfway through a great meal of stuffed salmon and mushroom risotto Tuesday evening when Dad asks if any of us have read this week's *Echtran Enquirer* yet.

Mum, Adina and I all shake our heads.

"More nastiness from Gwendolyn Gannett?" I guess.

"Not much this time. Just another crack about how slowly things are moving at NuAgra." His glance at me is understanding. "But there's also a piece written by the Sovereign that I hope most of our people will read. It should put a few rumors to rest, maybe change a few minds."

M did mention Monday she'd sent in an article with exactly that goal in mind.

"I'll read it right after dinner." I start eating faster.

Once we've cleared the table, Adina and I run to our shared bedroom for our tablets. When we get back to the living room, Mum is already reading from hers.

"The Sovereign expresses herself so well," she comments while I'm still pulling up the *Enquirer* on my own device. "I'm always impressed by how articulate she is, given her youth."

A remark like that would have irritated me two months ago. Not now. Skimming the contents, I click first on M's article: *"From the Sovereign's Desk: first in a series"*

"Sounds like she plans to do more articles, now they've published this one," I comment and start reading.

So much has been written about me in this periodical over the past year, it seems only fitting that I use this space to share some of my thoughts with you directly.

As you know, I only learned of my true heritage a little over a year ago. Since that time, I have worked with numerous advisors and have also read extensively to prepare myself for the role I was told I would have to one day assume. That day came more quickly than I expected when Faxon was deposed last December. The ensuing uncertainty and threatening chaos in Nuath required me to travel there far sooner than I would have liked, considering my entire life at that point was on Earth.

Almost from the start, there was resistance to my association with Rigel Stuart, both in the *Echtran* Council and among the more traditionally-minded of our people. Even so, by December the Council had been convinced of the reality of our *graell* bond. They therefore acceded to my request to have Rigel appointed my Bodyguard so that he could accompany me to Mars.

There's no need for me to detail how a lapse in my own judgment endangered both Rigel himself and my Acclamation as Sovereign. However, I would like to lay to rest one misconception I understand is still circulating: that for many months I actively deceived Sean O'Gara about where my real affections lay. Sean will corroborate that I never did any such thing. When the O'Garas arrived in Jewel last November, I was already bonded with Rigel—something I made clear to Sean from the first. I was, however, persuaded by the Council to give the public appearance that Sean would one day become my Consort, as they felt this would be reassuring to our people after the upheaval caused by Faxon and his abrupt overthrow.

No doubt many of you saw video feeds of my time in Nuath in company with Sean, particularly before my Acclamation. This was all by design, and on the advice of those better versed than I in Nuathan politics. Appearances aside, I never once renounced my relationship or my bond with Rigel, not even when his memory of me was erased by those who misguidedly allowed their patriotism to prevail over their ethics.

I cannot deny that Sean's role throughout all of this was extremely difficult. From the outside, I'm sure it appeared that shortly after the O'Garas' arrival in Jewel, I turned my back on Rigel to be with Sean. Then, upon my return to Earth, it probably looked as though I jilted Sean to get back together with Rigel. That is not at all what really happened. From the start, Sean was no more than my good friend, fully aware that I would resume my relationship with Rigel as soon as it was politically feasible. This was absolutely necessary for both my optimal health and Rigel's, due to our bond, something Sean completely understood.

Now that I have laid out the truth of the matter for you, I hope everyone reading this will find it in your hearts to set aside any lingering disapproval of Rigel and his family over his association with me. Likewise, I hope to hear no more criticism of Sean, the O'Garas, or the Morain family now that Sean has formed a real relationship of his own. Instead, I would ask your best wishes for the happiness of all concerned as we follow the paths we have chosen.

No doubt you are also curious about my relationship with the girl we all knew as Molly O'Gara, but whom we recently discovered is in fact my sister. Long before the truth surfaced, Molly had become my closest friend, far more than a Handmaid to me. Learning that we are full sisters was an incredibly happy surprise for both of us and has only strengthened our bond of friendship. I can't imagine that ever changing, no matter how it is eventually decided Malena and I should share power in the future. In any event, you may rest assured that she will join me, along with the *Echtran* Council, in working toward the best possible future for our people, both on Earth and on Mars.

I look up. "Wow. This is...really good."

"Isn't it?" Mum smiles brightly. "It was extremely kind of her to include a mention of *our* family. I...I haven't wanted to worry you, but—"

"I know," I tell her. "I've heard the whispers, too, and Dad showed me some of the messages you've received." He's the only one I told about the dead rat. "Maybe this will help."

Mum nods vigorously. "Oh, I'm certain it will, coming from the Sovereign herself! How can it not?"

I wish I had her confidence but I suspect she's in the minority when it comes to blindly accepting everything M says. Still, this article is bound to change a few minds and I'm grateful to M for writing it.

Bracing myself, I next click over to Gwendolyn Gannett's column: *"Disarray at the Top"*

As I'm sure we all expected, the recent revelation that we have a second legitimate heir to Sovereign Leontine's throne has created confusion among our leadership. So far, the *Echtran* Council is staying mum on how they intend to incorporate our new Princess into the current governmental structure, though they have been quick to claim that those deliberations are proceeding in an orderly fashion—for now.

Then, as Dad said, she spends a couple of paragraphs criticizing how long it's taking to get the new governmental headquarters up and running at NuAgra and speculates that the news about Princess Malena has slowed things further, though I doubt that's true. Then there's a last bit that's sure to make Molly cringe:

Over the weekend I had a most enlightening chat with Princess Malena. I'll be sharing all of the juiciest highlights from that interview with you in next week's issue.

"Juiciest highlights?" I repeat aloud when I finish. "I swear she's not even pretending to be a serious journalist anymore. She's just trying to stir up controversy."

Sean's told me his dad claims sensationalism sells. Apparently that's true. Unfortunately.

.+.

The next day, I overhear a few other *Echtran* students discussing M's article as I'm passing their lunch table.

"That was pretty smart of the Sovereign to put her story out publicly like that, don't you think?" sophomore Erin is saying to some of the others.

"Do you really think it will do any good?" freshman Jana asks skeptically. "Anyway, my parents both think she probably didn't really write it herself."

At that, I step closer. "Yes, she absolutely did," I interrupt. "She mentioned last week she was working on it. I don't think she even ran it past the Council before sending it in."

"Sure, you'd say that," Jana retorts. "You're probably sick of people making cracks about you and Sean."

Jana may be Adina's best friend, but her snide cynicism often rubs me the wrong way. To my surprise, my sister actually calls her on it.

"You know, Jana, Kira's not the only one who's sick of people criticizing M and Rigel and Sean, after they worked so hard to keep us all safe. If you ask me, it was way past time for M to set the record straight after all the stupid rumors and gossip."

Since Adina is usually content to follow her friend's lead in everything, Jana's clearly startled, too. "I didn't mean— Okay, yeah. I guess you're right. Sorry, Kira."

With an approving smile for my sister, I nod graciously to Jana and continue to my table, where M, Rigel and Sean are already talking. Molly and Tristan join them just before I do.

"—still don't know any more?" Sean is saying quietly to M when I sit down next to him. "I guess they can't take any real precautions, then?"

"Not specific ones," M replies, "though we hope with Enid gone, they won't be able to weaponize the rest of the antimatter anytime soon. Meanwhile, Rigel's dad is designing lots of extra security for NuAgra and Dun Cloch. Also for my house and yours, though those might be trickier to install discreetly."

"Then the quicker I can get trained as Molly's Bodyguard, the better," Tristan says. "I got a call yesterday afternoon saying I can start tonight at NuAgra."

I blink, then turn accusingly to Sean. "You didn't tell me anything about—" I begin, but break off when M's friends Bri and Deb sit down at our table.

Giving Sean a look that says *later*, I take a bite of pizza and pretend to listen to Bri's rendition of today's gossip.

On the way to Government afterward, I pull Sean slightly aside and whisper, "So the Council's okay with Tristan becoming Molly's personal Bodyguard?"

"Yeah, apparently they didn't like it at first, but once M and Molly pointed out how hard it would be for an adult to stick close to her at school, they agreed. They're appointing an adult, too, but I guess they figure the more protection the better."

"That's true for you, too, isn't it?" I ask, frowning.

He's clearly startled. "Why? It's not like I've ever received death threats or anything. I seriously doubt I'm any kind of target these days."

"I still think you should have a Bodyguard," I say stubbornly. "Not only are you a super high-ranking Royal, a lot of people still think you ought to be Consort. Just last week, Gwendolyn Gannett implied you should pair up with Molly, if not the Sovereign."

Sean snorts. "Yeah, I couldn't believe she said that. Our mum hinted at the same thing the night we found out about Molly and we both let her know in no uncertain terms how gross that would be. Even if she weren't with Tristan and I wasn't ecstatically happy with you—" He gives my hand a squeeze— "I'll never think of her as anything but my sister. She feels the same way."

His vehemence totally extinguishes any tiny worry I might have had on that score. Even so, I'm still thoughtful when we reach the classroom.

I never told Sean about the dead rat left at our door, not wanting to worry him. But that was only the latest, worst veiled threat aimed at me and my parents. We've all received numerous rants via emails and texts, mostly anonymous, about me "presuming" to date a Royal.

Though I hope M's article will help, it can't possibly change such strongly-held views overnight. Which means Sean *could* become a target, since some *Echtrans* are obviously *really* opposed to us being a couple. There's no knowing what lengths those people might go to drive their message home.

.+.

When I'm out at NuAgra that afternoon for my seventh period work-study apprenticeship, I play close attention to any gossip I hear in the greenhouses. Though most of what I overhear about M's article is positive, Jana's not the only skeptical one.

"—think the Sovereign convinced Sean O'Gara to confirm everything she claimed?" a woman two stations away whispers to her research partner at one point.

"Maybe if he doesn't, she'll let the Council censure him and his new girlfriend after all. I've heard some of them already—" The man on the opposite side of the station notices me looking their way and breaks off.

They don't say anything else in my hearing, but that snippet of conversation makes me that much more determined to do whatever I can to keep Sean—and me and my family—safe while waiting for attitudes to shift. If they ever do.

I'm still wrestling with how to do that when M approaches me at the end of our Taekwondo class a couple of hours later.

"I've noticed your sparring just keeps getting better," she quietly comments as we're leaving. "Though I guess Sean should get some of the credit. I know I wouldn't do half as well if not for my bond with Rigel."

"Yeah, it does seem to be making a difference." Abruptly, I decide to share my concerns with her. "Speaking of Sean...considering who he is and all the crazies out there, wouldn't it make sense for him to have a Bodyguard, like you and Molly?"

She frowns. "A Bodyguard? Sean? Nobody's threatened him, have they?"

"Not yet, but that doesn't mean they won't. Like that guy who attacked Molly in their front yard. If Sean had stepped outside before she did, who knows what he might have done?"

When she still seems skeptical, I relate some of the veiled threats my parents and I have received because of my relationship with Sean, which makes her frown again. Finally, I tell her about the dead rat somebody left for us to find, which clearly alarms her.

"All the nastiness has been aimed my way so far, but who's to say Sean won't become a target, too?"

Now she looks angry as well as alarmed. "I guess I shouldn't be surprised, after all the pushback Rigel and I have had. Mostly aimed at him and his parents, same as what you've seen—cowards. I'm more worried now about you and your family than I am about Sean."

I force a laugh. "Yeah, but we don't exactly rate a Bodyguard. Rigel's family doesn't have one, do they?"

"They have Rigel himself," she points out. "His dad's working on a security system for Molly and me and I was going to suggest he install it at their house, too. Once the O'Garas' system goes in, Sean will also have some protection at home. You don't think Sean will feel insulted if I have a personal Bodyguard assigned to him, like I'm assuming he can't defend himself?"

That crystalizes the thought that occurred to me during our last sparring round in class today. "He probably would. Unless...what if *I* train to be his Bodyguard, like Tristan will for Molly? That would help me keep both Sean *and* my family safe."

Her brows go up. "Huh. That's actually not a bad idea. You're already really good at both offensive and defensive moves in Taekwondo, plus you were a famous athlete back in Nuath. I don't see how the Council can possibly refuse. I'll call Kyna when I get home. If she okays it, could you start training tonight with Tristan?"

Hearing myself called "famous" by the Sovereign startles me, but not enough to distract me from my goal.

"What time? I have basketball practice right after the boys' team is done, so I'll be heading to the school as soon as I get home and change."

"I'll check. If it's too early, maybe they can push it back to, say, eight or so? Give you a chance to grab some dinner in between?"

I grin. "That would be perfect...if the Council really will okay it."

"It'll be an awfully grueling day." She looks at me in concern. "Taekwondo, then basketball, then that?"

"Not an issue," I assure her. "I've been feeling lazy since getting to Earth after all the *caidpel* practice I was used to back home. This won't be any worse, trust me."

My only regret is that it will further delay Sean and me exploring our new powers—assuming we really have any.

"All right," M says. "I'll text you as soon as I hear back."

Her message is waiting on my phone when basketball practice ends —a thumbs-up emoji followed by, *Kyna says it's a go! Be at NuAgra at 8pm.*

There was no time—or privacy—to tell Sean about this plan during the two minutes we had together when he was leaving his practice and I was arriving for mine. Now I figure I might as well find out more tonight, then tell him in person tomorrow rather than in a text. Especially since I expect him to argue. Instead, I just send him a quick message saying I won't be able to get together after dinner tonight after all.

At home I grab a quick shower, then slap together a sandwich while telling my parents the plan. They're surprised, but once I explain my reasons they both agree it's a good idea. Ten minutes later, Dad lets me take the family car out to NuAgra for my first Bodyguard training session.

I put my palm on the scanner and enter the main lobby area, where I'm greeted by a petite blonde woman who reminds me slightly of M's little *Duchas* friend, Deb.

"Kira Morain?" she says. I nod. "I'm Gilda. This way, please. I've been asked to give you and Tristan Roark your initial *Costanta* instruction."

Blinking, I follow her into a long room with pale green mats on the floor, similar to the red and blue ones in M's and my Taekwondo *do jang*. Tristan is already there, also dressed in sweatpants and t-shirt. He looks wary and a little confused. So am I, but I hope I hide it better.

"I assume neither of you has ever trained or served as a *Costanta* before?" Gilda asks us, all business. We both shake our heads. "Any self-defense or martial arts instruction?"

"Football," Tristan says. "I'm a pretty good tackler, if that helps?"

Gilda gives him a thin, almost patronizing smile, then looks at me, her expression making it clear she doesn't expect much.

"I played colony-wide *caidpel* in Nuath," I say, in case she didn't know that. "I also learned some self-defense there and I'm taking Taekwondo here in Jewel."

"That should prove helpful," she allows. "Tonight I'll mainly be evaluating your current skill levels, so I can map out an instruction plan. Tristan, stand just there, please. I will attack and you will attempt to render me helpless. Nod when you are ready."

He looks almost amused as he moves into position and nods, probably because he's nearly twice Gilda's size. But with two quick steps she closes the distance between them, and an instant later he's on his back blinking up at her.

"How...how did you do that?" he gasps, winded from hitting the mats so hard.

"I plan to teach you. Get up and we'll try again."

By her fourth attack, he's able to evade her long enough to turn it into a brief wrestling match before she sweeps his legs from under him with her foot and puts him on the ground yet again.

"That will do," she says as he clambers back to his feet. "I believe I can place your level now. Kira?"

As she moves back to her starting place, I go to the same spot Tristan just vacated and nod. Again, she's lightning-quick, but because I had the advantage of watching her moves with Tristan, I'm better prepared. Sidestepping as she closes, I half-turn and deflect her initial attack, then make a grab for her wrist as she adjusts direction. Though I miss, she has to change tactics, lashing out with a foot to trip me like she did Tristan.

I avoid her first effort at that, too, but on the second our legs get tangled. I think we're both going down, but somehow when I hit, she's still standing.

"Not bad," she says approvingly. "You do know a few moves, don't you? Let's try something a bit different."

She goes for my throat with both hands, but I instinctively use a Hapkido move I learned in Taekwondo class last week, countering with a knife hand to *her* throat—which she easily avoids—followed by a quick back kick to her midsection. That forces her to skip back, but she immediately returns to the attack, this time coming in low.

Calling on my *caidpel* skills, I wait till she's about to touch me, then leap straight up, twisting in the air as I go and landing off to the side. Before she can adjust, I follow up with a low backspin kick, my hands on the mat, and sweep her legs the way she did Tristan's. Rather to my surprise, she goes down.

Only for a second, though. Smiling, she bounces right back up and accords me a little bow.

"Nicely done. I believe I can place your hand-to-hand level now. Any weapons experience?"

"No, sorry."

Nodding, Gilda goes to a small table in the corner I didn't notice before and types into a tablet. When she finishes, she turns back to us.

"That will do for tonight. You'll hear from me once I've prepared a course of training for each of you."

That should give me time to convince Sean.

"I'll do my best to work around your schedules," she continues. "I understand you are on one of the *Duchas* sports teams at school, Kira?" She sounds disapproving.

"Er, yes. Girls basketball. I have practices most days, but any time after seven-thirty should be doable, except when there's an actual game."

She taps a note into her tablet. "Very well. I understand time is of the essence for you, Tristan."

He nods. "Molly, er, Princess Malena, is finally getting an adult Bodyguard this week, but I can stick a lot closer to her at school—and she should have constant protection now."

"The Council agrees. Accelerating your training will also allow me to more quickly assume my role as Princess Malena's *Costanta*."

Tristan and I both blink at her in surprise. "*You're* the Bodyguard they're appointing?" he asks.

"I am. Others will therefore assist in your instruction, though I will be overseeing it all." She turns to me then. "As you already have the basics, Kira, you can join the training in progress when Tristan moves on to weapons and more advanced moves. Under the current circumstances, the Council attaches far less urgency to assigning Sean O'Gara a *Costanta*."

I assume she means because M is with Rigel instead of Sean. Her phrasing makes it sound like a temporary condition. I almost ask if she agrees with those who think it should be.

But I'm not sure I want to know.

8

Isolating mechanism

SEAN HAS DRIVEN me to school every morning since his father gave him a car for his birthday. I appreciate that more than ever now our schedules are so full. It's become our only guaranteed time to talk privately, except on the phone. Today, I take advantage of it to tell him about the Bodyguard thing.

"So," I begin, trying for a casual tone, "I did a bit of training out at NuAgra last night."

"Training? What for?" He slants a curious glance at me.

"Um, to become your Bodyguard."

Sean visibly tightens his grip on the steering wheel. "You're kidding. Who asked you to do that? Are they nuts?"

"Actually, it was my idea. I mentioned it to M yesterday after Taekwondo. She ran it past the Council and they signed off on it. You're still an important person, no matter how much you try to downplay it—even if you haven't been directly threatened. This way I'll be ready if you are."

At his frown, I quickly add, "I'll also be better able to protect my parents. They've been receiving the same kind of flak the Stuarts have, because of us dating. Only verbal so far, but what if it escalates?"

As I hope, that undercuts his objection. "They have? You didn't tell me that."

"I didn't want you to worry. But I do, and not only about them. We know there are crazies out there, and not all of them are Faxon sympathizers. Some people have gone to pretty extreme lengths to keep M and Rigel apart. What if they do the same to us?"

Though he clearly still doesn't like it, he slowly nods. "Okay, I see your point. But wouldn't it make more sense for you and your folks to have a proper Bodyguard?"

I bite back a laugh. "Right. What are the odds the Council Royals will waste a Bodyguard on a nobody Ag family? Not a chance. You, however..." I trail off and let him think about it.

Finally, as he pulls the car into a space in the school lot, he says, "Fine. I guess I can live with having a Bodyguard if it means keeping you and your family safer. But why does it have to be you? Won't that put you at even more risk?"

"Why should it? If I'm officially appointed your Bodyguard, people will *expect* me to be with you as much as possible. Didn't Rigel become M's so they could still spend time together while M was pretending to be with you?"

"It was," he agrees, grinning now. "*That* part I'm totally on board with. I guess my male ego can take being protected by a girl if that means more time with you."

"A girl? Really? How can you—"

He silences my indignant protest with a kiss—and after token resistance I melt into him. But only for a moment, because the warning bell rings, forcing us to jump out of the car and hurry into the school.

Frustrated, I fervently hope we can schedule a serious chunk of time alone soon.

.+.

Because the boys' first basketball game is that evening, the girls' practice is cut fifteen minutes short so they can set up the gym. Even so, I barely have time to get home, shower and wolf down another sandwich before heading back to the school to watch Sean play.

Unlike our game, the boys' first scrimmage draws a capacity crowd. I try to rein in my irritation by reminding myself that not only is this a home game, the Jaguar boys went to State for the first time ever last year, so they're bound to be popular locally.

Needless to say, with three *Echtrans* on the team, Jewel trounces tonight's competition. I can tell Sean and Alan are both pulling most of their shots, but Liam definitely isn't. Midway through the third period, he actually launches himself into the air from behind the foul line to dunk the ball.

It's a move no *Duchas* could possibly have accomplished. When he sinks the ball, nearly all of the spectators, on both sides, cheer wildly.

Not all, though. Sean's parents, I notice, are frowning. Two other Council members who live in Jewel, Malcolm and Breann, don't look happy, either.

At the final buzzer, the score is a lopsided 82-39, Jewel over Blackford. I celebrate our victory by running out to the court to give Sean a big hug and kiss, despite my certainty there'll be a reckoning of some sort. Definitely for Liam, and maybe for all of us.

"You looked great out there." It's even more true than when he said the same to me after my game. "I didn't see you lose control once."

His smile holds a trace of bitterness. "I didn't dare."

We both glance across the court at Liam, who's surrounded by admiring fans. Among them, only his twin brother Lucas looks like he's aware Liam's performance tonight might be a problem.

"It *was* his very first game," I remind Sean. "I guess he couldn't help himself."

"Alan did," he points out, scowling. "I don't think Liam even tried, though we warned him more than once. He's going to ruin it for all of us if someone can't get through to him."

Stepping back to allow others to congratulate Sean, I see the Council members I noticed earlier making their way toward Mr. and Mrs. Walsh, Liam's parents. Yep, there's definitely going to be a reckoning.

Sean confirms that when he calls just before bedtime, as he often does.

"Yeah, the Council came down hard on the Walshes. On all of us, really. They asked Alan and Liam and their parents to come back to our house, then said if we have another game like this one, they'll yank all three of us off the team. I think—I hope—Liam finally gets it. His parents definitely do."

Though I expected something like that, I wince. "That doesn't seem fair to you or Alan."

"Yeah, well. Like my dad says, it's not always about what's fair. Especially when there's so much at stake—like blowing our cover wide open."

I can't disagree. "Did they say anything about other sports?"

"Not directly, but I imagine they'll be paying a lot more attention now—and not only at Jewel. I just hope they won't issue some kind of edict."

So do I, but it's sounding more and more likely.

The odds of that seem greater than ever when we get to school the next day. Sean and I are still in the parking lot when Pete Griffin, Sean's teammate and best *Duchas* friend, comes over to talk.

"Wow, what a game last night! Those two new guys are awesome, aren't they?"

Cautiously, we both nod.

"You know, it almost makes me wonder if there really is something in NuAgra's water," he says then. "I mean, they're both out there two or three times a week."

I force a chuckle and Sean says jokingly, "Oh, yeah, right, that must be it."

Pete doesn't laugh. "Seriously, guys, I'm not the only one saying that. You're doing work-study there too, Kira, and my sister tells me you're easily the best player on the girls' team."

Andrea Griffin is a teammate of mine, so no big surprise she and her brother have discussed this.

"We all did play before we got here, you know," I tell him. Okay, technically we played *chas pell*, not basketball, and only when we were kids. But it's really similar.

He frowns. "Yeah, somebody else mentioned that. I guess the competition was a little stiffer back in—where was it? New York?"

"Upstate, right. We were all in a lot bigger school there, and in a really tough district." This part, of course, is complete fabrication.

"Then I guess all of you being so good isn't a *huge* coincidence. The NuAgra angle is still kinda weird, though," he says with a shrug.

We go inside the school building then and since Pete's not in our Physics class, he turns down another hallway.

"Okay, that was a little disturbing," Sean whispers as soon as he's out of earshot. "And it sounds like he's not the only one making that connection."

"You're an amazing player, too, and you're not spending any time at NuAgra," I point out.

His mood doesn't lighten. "No, but my parents are out there a lot.

Rigel's dad, too. And we're *all* going out to NuAgra Sunday for the monthly meeting. Eventually, people are going to connect the dots."

We're holding hands now and his worry comes through loud and clear—a worry I share, though I try to suppress it.

"You said last night you think Liam finally wised up," I remind him. "So maybe it'll be less of a problem from now on?"

Judging by his emotions, Sean doesn't believe that any more than I do.

"Yeah. Maybe," he says as the bell rings.

As the day goes on, I overhear other *Duchas* talking about the basketball team's incredible performance last night, particularly Liam's.

"I told my dad when I got home that no normal person could have pulled off that flying jump shot," one boy in my third period Statistics tells another. "But then he showed me an old video of Michael Jordan in his prime making practically the same move. Of course, that guy was a professional NBA player—and according to my dad, the best there's ever been. Liam Walsh is just a high school junior."

"Yeah, it was pretty freaky," his friend agrees. "Even Sean O'Gara never made a shot like that. But hey, if Liam Walsh can help get us to State again, I'm not going to complain."

In Lit class next period, I worriedly mention that exchange to Sean and suggest telling M and the rest of the "Bond Squad," as Tristan jokingly calls our group of six.

He agrees. "Maybe the other *Echtrans*, too. We all need to do what we can to counter this before it goes any further."

At lunch, I quietly share our concerns with M, Molly and their boyfriends in the cafeteria line while Sean corrals Liam and Alan. Then we all carry our trays to the table where most of the newer *Echtran* students still sit together.

"Have you all heard what everyone's talking about today?" Sean asks them all as he sits down. "Not just last night's game, but some of the theories people are coming up with?"

Some nod, though others seem puzzled, so Sean quickly repeats what Pete said to us this morning. Now everyone looks alarmed.

"Crap. And it's all my fault," Liam says, red-faced. "I know you guys told me to chill, but once the game started, I got carried away." He shoots an apologetic glance at Sean and Alan. "Sorry, guys."

"That definitely didn't help," Rigel admits, "but I was the one who first soured the Council on us playing sports. Did you see our first football game after you got here?"

Now every head nods.

"You were amazing," Liam says. "Probably one reason I went a little over the top last night."

Rigel looks chagrined. "I don't normally play like that, but there were...special circumstances that night. Even so, the Council came down hard on me and my parents, like they did you."

"Because they're rightfully concerned about the *Duchas* getting too suspicious," M says. "Hardly anyone knows this, but the night of that game I was kidnapped and threatened by a local, because he was convinced I'm an alien."

That gets gasps from around the table. The four youngest students look positively scared.

"A *Duchas* actually kidnapped you?" Erin asks, wide-eyed.

M nods. "It's a long story, but he thought keeping me away from Rigel would make him have a bad game. So the only reason Rigel played like that was to prove him wrong."

Adina's friend Jana leans forward. "So...what happened?"

"I escaped, with some help from Rigel and a few others. Then Rigel's mom gave the man something to confuse his memory, so he'd think he just drank too much and passed out. But I'm afraid if he starts talking again, more people will listen, what with these latest rumors floating around."

Sean must send my growing nervousness, because he puts a hand over mine. "It doesn't help that there's been resentment from the start about NuAgra not hiring locally," he says. "Not to mention all the speculation about what's really going on out there. The secrecy alone is enough to spark conspiracy theories. Unfortunately, some are getting a little too close to the truth."

"Luckily the guy who kidnapped me already had a reputation for being kind of crazy," M says, "but in this case he wasn't completely wrong. He's not the only conspiracy theorist around, either. If they start organizing, things could get ugly in a hurry."

"What do you think they'd do?" Adina asks fearfully.

M lifts a shoulder in a half-shrug. "I'm not sure, but they might start asking a lot more questions and press harder for answers. I'd better address that at the NuAgra meeting this Sunday."

There's some muttering, then Liam's brother Lucas speaks up.

"We can stick to the excuse that the secrecy at NuAgra is just to guard against corporate espionage. But we also need to have our personal histories down pat—the ones we were supposed to memorize before moving here. It'll be extra important to sound and act as, er, normal as possible."

"That especially goes for those of us in the NuAgra work-study program, since that's the most obvious connection," Tristan says to me, Alan and the Walsh twins. "It, uh, might help to socialize more with *Duchas* students, make a few friends."

That's greeted by a few grimaces—but also a few nods.

"Most of them are pretty nice," M insists. "Shoot, before Rigel and his family got here, my only friends were *Duchas*. And we're still good friends."

"I've made friends with most of the cheerleaders, too," Molly volunteers. "So have Sean and Rigel, with their teammates. The trickiest part is not getting so comfortable you let something slip. Honestly, it's no wonder if they're getting resentful that you've kept them all at a distance since getting here. And it's a pretty short step from resentment to suspicion."

M looks over her shoulder at our usual table, where Bri and Deb are shooting curious glances our way. "Speaking of which, we've probably congregated long enough for now. Guess we'd better come up with a good reason we've all been talking together. Molly? You're always good at that."

Sean's—no, M's—sister chuckles. "You always say that, but this one's easy. Alan's in our same Government class next period and there's a test tomorrow. We'll tell Bri and Deb the teacher told him what the focus will be and he offered to share—and we'll share with them, too. I just need to figure out what that is."

"Which I'm sure you'll do." M shakes her head fondly. "You should be the one in charge of convincing the *Duchas* there's nothing odd going on."

Molly laughs. "I'll work on it." But as she heads back to our regular table, she looks thoughtful.

.⁺.

Because Sean and I have had so little alone time this week, I'm really looking forward to our drive to Muncie for tonight's football playoff game. But half an hour before Sean's supposed to pick me up, he calls.

"Mum's asked us to ride with them in the van tonight, along with Molly and Tristan. She *claims* it's to save gas, even though it's only half an hour away."

From his tone, I assume it has more to do with keeping an eye on both couples.

Mrs. O'Gara only withdrew her opposition to our relationship two weeks ago, so I don't argue--but I'm disappointed. Because Molly has to be there a little early for cheerleading, they come by ten minutes later.

Unfortunately, Molly and Tristan have already claimed the bench seat in back, leaving the separate middle chairs for Sean and me. That makes even holding hands discreetly problematic, though he grabs mine anyway as soon as I climb in. The frustration I feel from him matches my own—which helps a tiny bit.

"You'll have to ride the team bus to away games next year, won't you?" Molly asks Tristan as we're leaving Jewel, already sounding wistful about it. I'm sure they'd rather be driving separately, too.

"Assuming I'm allowed to play at all. Will the Council really make Rigel quit the team if the Jaguars win tonight?" he asks the O'Garas.

Sean's dad hesitates a moment before answering. "Possibly, if it's too obvious that Rigel's playing is the only reason they win." He looks at his wife, who nods.

"The Council is rightfully concerned about attracting too much *Duchas* attention, particularly after last night's basketball game," she says. "Not only have there been suspicious rumblings here in Jewel, we've had reports of similar talk in other towns. It's important to quell as much speculation as possible before the next launch window."

"But...that's a whole year and a half away!" Sean protests, startled. "You don't think the Council will ban *all* of us from sports if the Jags win tonight, do you?"

His mother gives him a quelling look over her shoulder. "There are far more important things at stake than sports, Sean, you know that."

Her wording jars me. It's exactly what *my* mother said when I argued I was too important to my Nuathan *caidpel* team to leave Mars right before the playoffs.

"Even before last night's game, some Council members were concerned about three *Echtran* players on the Jewel basketball team,"

Mrs. O'Gara continues. "You really should have cautioned the others not to stand out so much."

"I did!" Sean insists. "And I talked to them again today. Liam gets it now. He swears he won't play like that again."

I can tell from his voice—and touch—that he's afraid it's already too late. For the first time, I'm glad I'm the only *Echtran* on the girls' basketball team.

"It puts Rigel in a really tough situation tonight, though," Tristan points out. "I totally get why he's so torn up about it. He's caught in the middle. If he throws tonight's game, he lets down the team. But if he doesn't, he could mess things up for every *Echtran* athlete at Jewel High, maybe even on Earth. It doesn't seem fair he has to make a choice like that."

"No, it's not fair," Mr. O'Gara agrees. "But life frequently isn't. In order to achieve the most important things, we're often required to sacrifice lesser ones, even if they matter desperately to us personally."

I wonder if he's talking about how he and others justified what they did to Rigel and M back in Nuath—or abandoning his own hopes of becoming M's Regent. Maybe both?

Thankfully, Sean and I don't have to sit with his parents once we get to the stadium in Muncie. We do end up near M and her closest *Duchas* friends, but at least we can openly hold hands now and kiss when our team scores—which isn't nearly as often as usual.

By the end of the first quarter, it's obvious Rigel isn't playing anywhere close to his best. We *Echtrans* aren't the only ones who notice, either.

"What's wrong with Rigel tonight?" Bri demands as the teams switch ends of the field. "He's not sick again, is he?"

M hedges. "He was feeling better most of this week but he told me last night his stomach is bothering him again. I guess it was more than just a twenty-four hour bug after all. Poor guy."

The emotion she puts into those last two words underscores the awful dilemma Rigel's facing tonight, caught between two duties. She must be hyper-aware of it, since she can hear Rigel's thoughts and sense his feelings even at a distance.

As the game progresses, I can tell Rigel is doing all he can to maximize his teammates' contributions on the field. He throws gentle, easily-catchable passes, makes super-secure hand-offs and even helps block for the running backs.

It's not enough.

Now they've progressed to Regionals, Jewel's team is up against the toughest competition they've faced so far. They only got this far because of Rigel's exceptionalism. Without it, they're not up to the challenge.

Late in the fourth quarter, Rigel seems to revive out there, playing more like his usual self. I wonder if he's decided to win after all, but at the final whistle the score is Westbrook 28, Jewel 24.

Bri is in tears as the clock runs out. "I thought sure Rigel was going to pull off another last-minute comeback," she wails. "He was looking so much better right there at the end."

"Yeah, you could see he was really trying," Deb agrees. "He must have started feeling better after halftime. But isn't this still the furthest Jewel has *ever* gone in the playoffs?"

Glumly, Bri nods. "My dad says this is only the second time Jewel's ever even *made* the playoffs, much less Regionals. But with Rigel at the helm, I thought we had a real shot at State this year."

"He's just one player," M reminds her. She looks cautiously relieved, so maybe Rigel isn't beating himself up *too* badly.

"I know. You're right." Bri manages a tiny smile. "And he's brought up our whole team's level of play this year. Maybe next year we really will make it to State."

I doubt that'll be allowed, either, but M pats her friend on the shoulder. "That's the spirit. Come on, let's go console our guys."

The three girls head down to the field. Tristan's right behind them, eager to reach Molly on the sidelines where she's been cheering. Sean and I follow more slowly.

"Well, he did it," he whispers to me. "Made it look pretty good, too. Nobody's likely to accuse him of throwing the game after that fourth-quarter surge. Still, it's gotta sting."

"Yeah." I glance up at him. "I just hope it's enough. You took the basketball team to State last year, didn't you?"

He nods, his brow furrowing. "It'll be hard not to do it again, and I don't just mean how it'll feel. With Alan and Liam on the team, too—"

"I know. You'll—we'll—all have to pull way back, which won't be much fun."

"It won't. But I'll warn Liam and Alan we need to cool it in practice, too, or it'll be too obvious when we hold back during games."

I give Sean's hand a sympathetic squeeze. "Just remind them that *not* holding back will mean not playing at all. Surely that'll give even Liam enough motivation to dial it down?"

"Hope so. It might help if we could sometimes play full-out without any *Duchas* around, like you and I did before the season started."

"Yeah, that was fun. It's too bad—" I break off at a sudden memory. "Back in Dun Cloch, after we were selected for Jewel, Alan mentioned starting a NuAgra *caidpel* league. I figured it was just a ploy to get me to spend more time with him, so I shut him down. But maybe it's not such a bad idea after all? Could be a good outlet for people like Liam."

Sean nods thoughtfully. "Maybe for all of us. I'll suggest it to my mum," he whispers as we reach the crowded sidelines. "See what the Council thinks."

We join the others then, commiserating with and congratulating the team. Rigel, I'm pleased to see, seems in reasonably good spirits. With any luck, his performance tonight will convince the Council to let both him and Tristan play next year. Either way, he's done being pulled in two directions for the season, which has to be a relief.

Because his mother is watching, I get a disappointingly brief good night kiss when the O'Garas drop me off at my apartment complex an hour later. Again, I sense Sean's frustration, too. I haven't even reached my apartment when I get a text from him.

Can we get together tomorrow?

Yes! I immediately send back. *I don't have anything after Taekwondo.*

Great. I'll call in half an hour and we'll plan something, just us.

Sounds perfect!

I hope we can arrange for a good long makeout session, since we're *way* overdue. Also somewhere we can safely work on our supposed *graell* powers.

If we aren't allowed to be basketball phenoms, we should get started on becoming superheroes, instead.

9

Concerted evolution

I'M FEELING POSITIVELY itchy by the time I head to the arboretum late Saturday afternoon. It would have been earlier, but as we left Taekwondo class, M mentioned she was going to meet Rigel there. They probably need alone time even more than we do, so I texted Sean to reluctantly push our own meeting back.

Hurrying along Diamond Street, I wonder if this weird, unpleasant tingling, like my skin doesn't quite fit, is a side-effect of our bond? That question is answered a moment later.

Sean is already waiting in the arboretum, both of us a few minutes earlier than we'd agreed on. We grin at each other in greeting and the next instant we're in each other's arms, kissing like there's no tomorrow.

The moment Sean's lips touch mine, my itchy feeling disappears, along with every doubt or worry I've had over the past week. This, *here*, is absolutely where I belong.

"Mmm. I've missed this," he says when we finally draw a little apart. "Almost makes me wish they *would* make us both ditch basketball so we can spend more time together."

"I can't say that idea hasn't crossed my mind," I admit, smiling up at him. I'm tall for a girl, but he tops me by more than a head.

The day is cold and overcast, but I don't mind since it gives us the whole arboretum to ourselves. Even though Sean didn't take time to activate the climate control app on his omni, I feel toasty warm after several minutes of kissing him.

"So, um, have you thought as much as I have about what happened at Rigel's last weekend?" he asks then, breaking the mood.

"Of course." Though I don't let go of his hands, I put a tiny bit of distance between us so I can think more clearly. "Even if I hadn't, M mentioned it again before Taekwondo class today. I told her we still hadn't had a spare minute this week to, um, work on that thing we did. If we really did?"

Ever since leaving Rigel's house, I've found it harder and harder to believe it was really *us* controlling that piece of popcorn last Saturday. It seems way more likely a draft from the next room—or something—kept it from hitting the floor when it should have.

"If?" Sean echoes. "Who else could have? M's never mentioned having any powers like that and I'm positive Molly doesn't. I'd know by now."

I shrug. "I guess. But...have you *ever* heard of anyone being able to move things with their minds? It's not in any of the *graell* fairy tales."

Sean flinches slightly at the word *graell*. Which I completely understand.

"I'm still not a hundred percent convinced we—" he begins, then snorts, more at himself than at me. "Well, if we are, it won't help to pretend we're not. Anyway, I was thinking since we have the place to ourselves, we should use this time to experiment a little more."

"Now that we're not quite so distracted?" I'm grinning now. "But yeah, they're predicting snow later, so getting together outdoors might not be an option tomorrow. And the gym will probably be too crowded to try there."

His grin is half grimace. "Count on it. The other guys are great but I'd much rather play one-on-one with you."

"You really have become friends with some of the *Duchas,* haven't you?" I ask almost wonderingly.

"Well...yeah. I mean, until your group got here, the only other *Echtran* guy at Jewel was Rigel, and we weren't exactly going to be friends last year. Not when—"

"When you both wanted to be with M," I finish, trying to ignore the tiny cold spot that forms near my heart when I think about that.

He looks a little sheepish but doesn't contradict me. "Yeah. I was kind of a jerk about it, which of course made Rigel a jerk right back. We nearly got into fights more than once—M and Molly were constantly having to play peacemaker. Of course, we're totally cool now." He reinforces his words with a lingering kiss.

I know I can't change the past. It makes sense that Sean was desperate back then to fulfill his supposed destiny as M's Royal Consort. Still, I can't help wishing, in my heart of hearts, I could have been Sean's first love. Because he's definitely mine.

"So," I say briskly, again thrusting away that niggling but persistent doubt. "Like you said, we should make good use of our privacy here. To figure out just what our bond can do, I mean," I quickly add.

"Right," he agrees. But the way his eyes crinkle reassures me he's thinking the same thing I am: that the *best* use we could make of this time would be more kissing. "Duty and all that. What do you think we should experiment on?"

I look around. "There are a lot of dead leaves. Those should be safe to play with."

Nodding, he leads me to the very back corner of the arboretum, where we'll have plenty of warning if anyone else shows up.

"Okay, let's focus on that red leaf there." He points. "We already managed to slow something down that was falling. Let's see if we can lift up something that's already at rest."

Linking hands tightly, we both stare at the designated leaf, willing it to rise from the ground. Nothing happens, even when I scrunch up my face in concentration. Not to the leaf, anyway, though I'm more acutely aware of Sean's feelings—*his* concentration—than I've ever been before. I can almost swear I hear a faint echo of his voice in my head saying, *C'mon. Up. Up, you stupid leaf!*

Breaking my concentration, I glance at him in surprise. He immediately feels the change in me and meets my eyes. "What?"

"Were— This is going to sound stupid. But were you just thinking, "Come on. Up, up, you stupid leaf?"

He blinks. "I...yeah. Those exact words. Do you mean—?"

Slowly, I nod. "I heard you. Your thoughts. That's never happened before."

"Whoa. Screw the leaf, let's work on that!"

I start to agree, then hesitate. "We won't need total privacy for that, and somebody else could show up any time. Let's try this again first." I gesture toward the leaf. "Make up a reason we *need* the leaf to rise. That made a difference before, remember?"

"Oh. Right. Why didn't I think of that?"

"Neither did I, till just now." Sean's nearness—and especially kissing him—likely clouded my thinking. "How's this? We can pretend the leaf is covering something sensitive, like a bomb trigger. We have to get it off without touching it, because that would make it detonate."

His sudden grin makes my heart turn over. "Good one. Have you been watching more TV dramas with your folks lately? That sounds like a classic plot device."

I grin back, nodding. "Mum claims watching Earth TV helps with assimilating, so sometimes she insists. Anyway, the leaf?"

"Right."

Again, we focus. This time, I imagine an antimatter bomb, like the one in my neck last month, will explode if we can't get that leaf off the trigger in time.

Nothing happens at first. Then, like with the popcorn last weekend, it does. The leaf starts to quiver, then slowly, slowly, it rises above the other leaves on the ground. One inch. Two inches. Three.

By now, I'm shaking with the effort. Beside me, I feel Sean doing the same. Still, we manage to keep the leaf in the air for a full five or six seconds before we break focus.

"Whew!" we exclaim together, then look at each other. Though we're both grinning, I'm sure my face reflects the same amazement Sean's does. I put voice to it first.

"We really did do that, didn't we? We really *can* move physical objects with our minds."

He swallows visibly. "Yeah. Wow. And we did it for longer this time, though it was at least as hard as before. Maybe lifting something takes more effort than stopping something? But M seems to think it'll get easier with practice."

"I hope so. I don't feel this wiped after an hour shooting hoops. Maybe we should wait a few minutes before trying again?"

"Yeah. I'm pretty wiped, too." But then his blue eyes warm as he looks down at me. "I have an idea what might cure that."

I don't protest a bit when he lowers his lips to mine. Sure enough, I'm immediately infused with new strength and vitality. Within moments I feel supercharged, like I can do almost anything. Sean's kisses always have a rejuvenating effect but now, after that draining experience, the sensation is even stronger. Curious, I decide to try something.

I hope we get more time alone soon, I think as hard as I can while still kissing him. *Don't you?*

Sean jerks back to stare at me, breaking all contact. "Did you just—?"

I nod. "What did you hear?"

"Your voice. In my head. Asking if I hope we get more alone time soon."

"That's exactly what I thought to you!" I tell him excitedly. "I didn't expect it to work, but—"

"But it did!" His excitement matches my own. "Okay, let me try." Both fists clenched by his side, he presses his lips tight together and shuts his eyes to concentrate.

I listen for all I'm worth, but don't hear anything. After several seconds, he opens his eyes.

"So? What did I say?"

Unfortunately, I have to shrug. "No idea, sorry. Maybe we have to be touching for it to work?"

He frowns, deflated. "Oh. Maybe. Though M and Rigel can—"

"They've been bonded for more than a year," I remind him. "And she said their abilities didn't really ramp up until after they were separated."

"Oh. Right." After a couple of deep breaths he says, "Okay, let's try that again, touching this time."

We clasp hands and he once more closes his eyes to send me a mental message. This time I hear him.

Do you want to get together after church tomorrow?

I squeeze his hands and think back, *Yes! Two o'clock?*

It's a date. He opens his eyes and looks at me again. "Did I imagine that? Or did we just make plans?"

"We did," I assure him, grinning. "For two o'clock tomorrow. You didn't say what you want to do, though."

He laughs and I feel his surprised delight through his touch. "More of this, if we get a chance! Or maybe the other thing, if we manage some privacy again."

"You mean kissing?" I slant a glance up at him.

"That, too." He leans down to capture my mouth, again convincing me that together we can do anything…even if it takes a while.

A few minutes later, both of us feel rejuvenated enough to work on our fledgling telekinesis some more. With our next effort, we manage to levitate a leaf an inch or two higher than before, and hold it there for a few seconds longer. Still not exactly useful, but definite progress.

"See?" Sean says excitedly when we relax and let the leaf fall. "M was right—like usual."

Stifling a momentary spurt of resentment, I nod. "With enough practice, who knows what we'll be able to do?" Then I glance up at the sky and realize with dismay that the light is already fading. "I told my parents I'd be home before dark," I reluctantly tell him.

"Yeah, so did I. But first—" He pulls me to him again.

Finally, after several more minutes of rejuvenating kissing, we head for the exit. The rose canes gracing the archway were still blooming when we first came here together last month. Now they're gray and leaf-less. *Not* an omen, I tell myself. Just a reflection of the fact there are real seasons here, unlike Nuath.

As we leave the arboretum, something white lands on my sleeve, making me flinch. Then I notice more flakes falling, all around us.

"Is that—?" I gasp.

"Snow," Sean confirms. Though he's smiling, I sense a trace of nervousness through his touch. "Your first, right?"

I nod. "I read about it, but…"

"My first snowfall kind of freaked me out, too—which was embarrassing, since M was with me at the time and I was still desperate to impress her."

Again, that tiny twinge at my heart. "Did she laugh at you?"

"Not until Molly did."

"Molly was there, too?" That makes me feel a little better. Until his next words.

"Yeah, we were just leaving the winter formal. My first sort-of-date with M, after she made that deal with the Council."

I try—hard—not to think about Sean and M slow dancing together. "I, ah, can see how that would have been embarrassing, then. Glad I don't have to feel that way with you, since you get why this—" I gesture at the now rapidly-falling snow— "bothers me."

"Definitely. But I hope you'll never feel embarrassed around me, about anything."

He kisses me then, which keeps me from thinking about anything else for several wonderful seconds.

I'm nearly home when I realize I *would* feel embarrassed if Sean knew I still occasionally obsess about him and M. Not that I ever plan to tell him.

.⁺⁺

Sean and I practice our new telepathy some more during church the next day. Because both of our mothers would frown on us holding hands here, we settle for touching wrists. It works, though not quite as well.

What? I think to him more than once.

"Nothing important," he whispers back. "Just testing."

Frustrated, I press the whole back of my hand against his. *Shouldn't we be getting better at this?*

We will. Give it time. He smiles sideways at me. *We just need to be patient.*

Patience has never been my strong suit, but M told us the same thing, so I refrain from elbowing him in the ribs.

When we stand up after the service, he gives my hand a squeeze. It feels wonderful. *We're still on for two o'clock, right?*

That comes through loud and clear. *You bet!* I send back. *Arboretum again?*

Sure. His mum comes up to us then, so we release hands. She *claims* she's okay with us being a couple now, but we both know better than to push it, especially in church.

At ten till two, I pull on my jacket to leave for the arboretum, which is less than five minutes away.

"Going to meet Sean again?" my thirteen-year-old sister, Adina, asks in a teasing sing-song.

I stick my tongue out, which makes her grin. "Maybe. Not that it's your business, Sprout."

Mum, puttering in the kitchen, overhears. "Have fun. Don't forget we have the monthly NuAgra meeting tonight, so we'll be eating dinner at six."

She's smiling but I also see a trace of concern in her eyes. Though she's mostly thrilled I'm dating Sean, the criticism from other *Echtrans* has bothered her a lot. The way Mum reveres Royals, I suspect she also worries being with me will lower people's opinion of Sean.

It's a worry I share, no matter how often he insists he doesn't care. I hope M's recent article will make a noticeable difference soon.

The sun is out, though it's still cold, making the light dusting of snow on the ground sparkle. I'm startled by how beautiful it is, and say so to Sean when he greets me at the arboretum entrance.

His handsome face breaks into a smile. "Not as beautiful as you, but yeah, it is." His kiss is quicker than I'd like because other people are here today, taking advantage of the sunshine.

"No trouble getting away?" he asks as we walk through the archway hand in hand.

"Just some ribbing from Adina." I glance around. "Looks like this isn't the best place for what we had in mind today after all. Though we can still—"

I break off as M and Rigel enter the arboretum.

"Hey," Sean greets them as they reach us. "Didn't know you two planned to be here today, too."

They exchange a glance. "We come here when we can, which isn't very often, lately," M says. "This place is…kind of special to us."

"Us, too," I admit. Ever since our first kiss, just outside the entrance.

Rigel grins. "It *is* one of the few places to get any privacy in downtown Jewel. Sometimes, that is." He gives a mock glare at the half dozen or so *Duchas* strolling the paths.

"Oh, hey, happy birthday, Dude." Sean punches Rigel playfully on the shoulder. "How does it feel being seventeen?"

"No different." He shrugs. "The guys on the team threw me a little party last night. Made me feel even worse about the way I let them down Friday."

M gives him a quick hug. "You didn't have a choice, you know that."

"And the rest of us really appreciate your sacrifice," Sean tells him. I nod my agreement.

Rigel's smile doesn't quite reach his eyes. "Thanks. Hope it was enough."

"The Council hasn't lowered the boom yet," M says encouragingly, "though Malcolm made more noises about it at last night's meeting." Then, to us, "Have you two found time yet to work on…you know?"

She starts moving toward the least crowded corner of the arboretum and we all follow. Sean waits till we're well away from the nearest *Duchas* to reply.

"Finally, yesterday afternoon, when this place was deserted. We managed to levitate a couple of leaves. But only for a few seconds, and it took total concentration. Still nothing we can use to stop bad guys."

"Give it time." M echoes what Sean thought to me in church. "The stuff we can do took a whole year to develop."

Squashing down a spurt of annoyance, I say, "We did make one breakthrough yesterday. We can hear each other's thoughts now, if we're touching and both concentrating."

"Wow, really?" M's brows go up gratifyingly. "Rigel and I had been bonded at least twice as long as you guys before we managed a single word."

Rigel nods. "Though we didn't actually try earlier. We had no idea it could even be a thing until that Ossian Sphere was about to kill us—and like M said, it was just one word. Even after that, it took so much focus we only used it when we were desperate."

"How long before you could do it without touching?" Sean asks.

They frown at each other, thinking. Then Rigel gives a mirthless laugh.

"Exactly a year ago today. Remember, M? My birthday party, after Allister made his big announcement about Sean and the whole Consort thing."

I glance at Sean but he's not looking at me.

"Oh, right," M says. "When I was leaving and they wouldn't even let us touch to say goodbye. Then we did it again the next day in church."

"Yeah, talk about desperate!" Rigel says. "Our folks wouldn't even let us get close enough to talk the normal way. Though considering how things turned out, we might have been better off if our telepathy *hadn't* worked that time."

I look from one to the other. "What happened?"

"We agreed to meet here at midnight, but got caught." M winces visibly. "It was the angriest I ever saw my aunt."

"My parents were almost as pissed," Rigel says. "Endangering the future of our people and all that. Then they dragged me with them to DC for ten whole days. It nearly killed us both. But when I got back—"

"Our telepathy was suddenly way, way stronger," M finishes. "Not only did it take less effort, we could do it from a lot farther away."

Sean looks thoughtful. "So separation really is what fast tracks it? Gotta say, I'm not a huge fan of that strategy."

"Oh, yeah, it totally sucks," Rigel agrees. "But it definitely makes a difference. There was another noticeable boost after they hauled me off to Dun Cloch for a few days, then brought me back."

"After we were apart all summer and re-bonded in September, our range *really* ramped up," M adds. "And it keeps getting better. We can communicate across serious distances now. Like, miles."

Boggled, I shake my head. "How about the lightning thing? Did the separations make that stronger, too?"

"It did, though we couldn't exactly test it without frying things," M says. "Especially since it only seems to work when we're threatened, or at least pretend to be."

Sean and I exchange a glance.

"Same thing's true for our telekinesis thing," he admits. "We couldn't levitate any leaves yesterday until we pretended we *had* to."

"But the electrical thing even shows up in the fairy tales," I point out. "Maybe that's what we should mostly be working on? Us newer couples, I mean. It's a way better defensive weapon than our lame telekinesis."

Rigel frowns. "You'd need a safe place to practice to avoid, um, accidents. Maybe my back yard? It's pretty isolated and you can aim at rocks and stuff that won't matter. Finding a time when my folks won't be home and nobody has school or sports conflicts will be tricky, but let's aim for that."

"Sounds good," Sean says.

After that we separate into couples to enjoy the rest of the time we can spend here today.

"Want to work on our telepathy thing again?" I ask Sean after a few minutes of silently enjoying just holding hands. "It's about all we can do with so many people around."

Unfortunately. Telepathy alone won't stop bad guys, including whoever left that dead rat.

"Might as well," Sean agrees. Then, apparently sensing my impatience, he adds, "I wish we could progress faster, too, but I'd rather not have to go through the kind of stuff M and Rigel did to get there."

"No, I guess I don't, either. Still, it can't hurt to practice, right?"

"Right. Okay."

He grips my hand a little more tightly and I hear, *Sometimes it's good to be a nobody after all.*

True, I think back. *The more I hear about everything M and Rigel had to deal with, the less I want to be in the public eye.*

Sean looks at me, the warmth in his eyes driving away the chill. *It's hard to believe how desperate I was to be important—until I met you.*

We both were, I remind him, working to maintain my focus. *I was way more stupid about it than you were.*

Not stupid. You just got bad information.

For a long moment I hesitate, then broach the subject that's been niggling at me for the past half hour. Aloud, because the concentration required to talk silently is still more draining than most physical activities.

"Was it... It must have been weird when your uncle told everybody about your and M's supposed destiny for the first time?"

He takes so long to answer, I think he's not going to—that it's something he doesn't want to talk to me about. Which I kind of get. If I'd been as hung up on a guy as he was on M, I probably wouldn't want to talk to Sean about it either. I haven't even told him about Brady, and that was just a fangirl crush.

Still, I really want to know. I'm about to repeat the question silently when he responds.

"Not so much weird as super, super awkward," he says heavily. "Because M had no clue before that—obviously. I wanted to break it to her gently, after she got to know me better, but Uncle Allister wasn't willing to wait. She was...pretty upset."

"Weren't you sort of glad to have it out in the open, though? I mean, that's why you came to Jewel in the first place, right? To connect with M, take your place as her destined Consort?"

I don't know why I'm so determined to make him say something I really don't want to hear, but I can't seem to help myself.

"It was. At least, I thought so at the time. But having it dumped on her like that... Let's just say diplomacy was never Uncle Allister's strong suit. The way he told her pushed her further away from me than ever. Not that I'd been making much progress in that direction anyway."

There's more self-deprecation in his voice than pain. I take some comfort in that.

"I guess I still don't fully get why she was so determined to flout tradition once she knew what was at stake." Not that I'm sorry now, of course.

"I didn't either—then." He pulls me a little closer. "Now I totally get why she refused to give in, when everyone insisted she should be with me instead of Rigel. Now I'm really, really glad she held firm. If she hadn't—" He smiles down at me with an expression that makes my heart speed up.

Swallowing, I return his smile—but I still need to know. "I'm glad, too. Obviously. But...don't you wonder sometimes how things might have turned out if, um, if Rigel hadn't been in the picture?"

He frowns. "Why are you—? I mean, sure, I used to think about it a lot, but not since meeting you. Anyway, if it weren't for Rigel, she'd probably still be missing, since he's the one who found her. Where would we be then? Probably with somebody like Devyn Kane as Sovereign, who only cares about the power that comes with it. Oh, except the Grentl would have wiped out Nuath and probably Earth by now. So, no. I don't ever wish things had turned out differently. Not anymore."

Heedless of any *Duchas* still around, he leans down and kisses me and my lingering doubts dissolve again.

For now.

10

Recombination

MY PARENTS SEEM a little nervous when we arrive for the monthly NuAgra meeting that night. Because of the recent *Echtran* criticism of our family.

Or maybe they're remembering September's meeting, when M called out everyone who'd given her uncle gifts or dinner invitations—which my parents had. Even though she didn't mention them by name, they were mortified. I'm about to reassure them when Sean motions to me from the front row of the big auditorium.

"C'mon," I tell my family. "Sean's saved us seats."

My mother frowns worriedly. "Do you think that's...appropriate? The front row is generally reserved for members of the Royal *fine* and the *Echtran* Council, isn't it?"

"I don't think it's an actual rule." I hope. "Anyway, it would be rude not to go down there now he's saved the seats."

Though she clearly still has misgivings, Mum accompanies me, Dad and Adina down the sloping floor to the front.

"Hey," Sean greets us. The look he gives me is almost as intimate as a kiss.

"Hey," I respond, moving to his side. "You sure there's room for all of us? We can sit behind, like before."

Turning, he mentally counts the chairs in the front row. "Nah, it's fine. There are still enough seats for the local Council members who aren't here yet."

Reassured, my parents and Adina all sit down. Mrs. O'Gara nods politely as we pass her, but with a slight frown I hope Mum doesn't notice. I take my seat next to Sean and he covers my hand with his, sending warmth and strength flowing through me. If anyone behind us disapproves, I refuse to worry about it right now.

When nearly everyone's seated and the babble of voices is dying down, M appears through a door near the front of the room and walks to the podium.

Applause breaks out, along with a few cheers and chants of *"Faoda byo Thiarna Emileia!"*

She smiles and waves, then touches the tiny mic button on her collar and clears her throat. Instantly, the room quiets.

"Thank you all for coming tonight," she begins. "Last month's meeting was primarily a social occasion, as there wasn't much business to cover. Next Sunday's picnic will be another one, but tonight I need to address a more serious topic—evidence of growing suspicion within the local *Duchas* community."

Even those on the front row exchange nervous glances.

"We knew from the start that the necessary secrecy surrounding NuAgra, along with the rather sudden arrival of so many newcomers, might give rise to speculation. We've tried to answer questions as they arose, both face to face and in media interviews. Lately, however, they're becoming more pointed—and more dangerous.

"Last night I learned that a few local *Duchas* attempted to scale the fence surrounding this compound, apparently hoping to discover details about our operations. Fortunately, our security system spotted them before they succeeded. The Council and I will discuss ways to avoid similar incidents in the future and to allay *Duchas* suspicions. However, if you hear anything of concern along those lines, please let us know.

"In addition, please report any *Echtrans* you encounter in town who are *not* Jewel residents, particularly if they do or say anything suspicious. We've recently uncovered evidence of *Echtrans*, outside Jewel, who seek to undermine our current leadership—in other words, me and the Council. We believe that group is still small, but they may be trying to grow their numbers. If anyone approaches or messages you with propaganda to that effect, let us know at once. Though there appears to be no immediate cause for concern, it never hurts to be cautious.

"Now, are there any questions?"

Several hands go up and the Sovereign points to someone a few rows back. "Yes?"

"What should we do if the *Duchas* attack us?" the woman asks. "Are we allowed to defend ourselves?"

Though she looks a little startled by the question, M answers without hesitation. "I seriously doubt it will come to that. If you are directly threatened, of course you may defend yourselves. But try not to use any, ah, abilities that might appear super-human—speed, strength, et cetera. Maintaining secrecy is extremely important, particularly now. The personal safety of our people is an even higher priority, but the Council and I will try very hard to make sure no one ever has to make that choice."

Another hand goes up, off to the left.

"What's going to happen about Princess Malena, your sister?" a man asks when M calls on him. "Do you plan to share power, or will she only ever be a Princess? Is it possible we'll end up with *two* Sovereigns?"

M smiles at Molly, further down the front row. "We only discovered Malena's identity a couple of weeks ago, so it's too early to predict what will happen. She's already reading up on Nuathan and *Echtran* government, our people's history, the same things I had to study after learning about my heritage. As my *Chomseireach*, she was constantly with me before and after my Acclamation last spring and now attends the weekly *Echtran* Council meetings. Rest assured that if the time comes for her to take a leadership role, she'll be well prepared."

A few more questions follow, mostly wanting to know how much of a threat the local *Duchas,* or those *Echtran* factions M mentioned, might be. After half an hour of soothing their fears, M calls a halt.

"Tonight's a school night for me and all the other students here, so I think we'll end for now. As always, feel free to bring any additional questions to anyone on the Council, or to one of the Stuarts or O'Garas. I look forward to seeing most of you back here next Sunday for our picnic. Let's hope the weather cooperates!"

With that, she taps off her mic and steps away from the podium. As everyone starts getting up, she steps down to the front row, going first to Rigel.

"See?" I hear her saying. "Not a single question about our relationship this time. I guess people did read my article."

I don't hear his answer because Sean leans close and whispers, "I was a little worried people might panic when they heard about two different potential threats. Glad that didn't happen."

"Me, too, but I'm not surprised," I say. "M's getting better and better at this sort of thing."

"Yeah, she is." He smiles over at her, but she's not looking our way. "She's growing into a great leader. Smart, confident, compassionate— exactly what our people need right now."

As he says it, I not only watch his expression but focus on the emotions I sense through his touch. Though I don't detect even a trace of longing or regret, I still can't help wondering if he sometimes wishes he were—

No. That's just my own insecurity talking. I'm almost sure of it.

⁺⁺

M and Rigel are next to Tristan's car talking to him and Molly when Sean and I get to the school parking lot the next morning. As we get out of the car, M motions us over.

"We were just discussing the highlights from Saturday night's Council meeting," she tells us. "I was saying we probably don't need to panic *just* yet. The most recent transcriptions from Allister's and Lennox's memories prove how dependent they were on Enid for technical expertise. They didn't have *any* of their own, and didn't remember anyone else who'd know how to create a bomb."

"But still no clue where that antimatter is," Sean says. "Or who stole it, unless it was Enid herself?"

M shakes her head. "Kyna says she couldn't have, that she never had access. And the antimatter could be anywhere—except Dun Cloch. They've done enough scans now to mostly rule out it being hidden there. Still, turning it into a weapon without blowing themselves up will take some pretty special know-how. Breann is sifting through everyone who's gone off-grid, so we'll at least know which *fines* are represented. So far, they've mostly been Mining and Maintenance, plus a few Ags. No one who's likely to know how to build bombs, thank goodness."

"Meanwhile, my dad's about done beefing up NuAgra's security system," Rigel tells us. "He says it'll be trickier protecting M's house and yours—" he nods at Sean and Molly— "but he thinks he can get it done before those malcontents become a credible threat."

I raise a skeptical brow. "Antimatter bombs aren't necessarily the only thing we need to worry about. It only took one determined assassin to nearly kill Molly. Until we know more, we all need to be hyper-vigilant."

"Agreed." M gives me an approving smile. "That's why I'm keeping you all in the loop. Nobody else outside the Council knows about the antimatter or that Molly was attacked. Let's keep it that way. The last thing we need is a panic."

The warning bell rings then, so we all head to the school, everyone else looking as thoughtful as I am.

"Hey, you want to come over after dinner tonight?" Sean asks when I arrive for my basketball practice that evening, right as he's leaving his.

"Sure, if you think your family will be okay with it. I don't start my, ah, special training till later this week." Gilda messaged me earlier we'll begin weapons instruction then.

He grins. "Cool. I mean, Saturday was great, but that was two days ago. We didn't get a chance to be really, y'know, alone yesterday."

In other words, no makeout session.

"You think we will tonight?" I ask skeptically. His mother never allows us that kind of privacy.

"We can try. Okay, you better get in there—not that the coach will kick you off the team if you're late to practice."

He's probably right, but I don't want to act like I expect preferential treatment. "Yeah, I'd better. See you around eight?"

I go up on my toes for a quick kiss, then hurry into the girls' locker room.

Three hours later, I ring the O'Garas' doorbell. A delicious fragrance wafts out when Molly opens the door.

"Hey, Kira! Come on in."

I sniff the air appreciatively. "Hi, Molly, what smells so good?"

"Mum made pumpkin bread. Sean told her you were coming over and Tristan'll be here any minute, too. Are you and Sean going to stick around this time?"

"I think so. It's too cold to go for much of a walk tonight."

That's what he and I usually do when we both have an evening free, since we can never be very alone at my place or his.

"I told Molly you'd say that, this being your first Indiana winter," Sean says, coming out of the kitchen with a stack of dessert plates.

"My first Earth winter," I remind him. "I'm just glad I'm not in Dun Cloch—they got their first snow back in September. My parents still keep in touch with friends there."

Molly shivers. "At least we got to ease into it by going to Ireland first. It doesn't get nearly as cold there, and never snows in Bailerealta. Not that snow bothers me as much as it does Sean." She winks at him and he glares back.

"Sean was fine when it snowed on Saturday," I inform her. "I'm definitely not there yet myself, though. I—"

The doorbell interrupts me and Molly practically drags Tristan inside.

"Hi, guys," he greets us. He's leaning toward Molly when Mrs. O'Gara appears, carrying a plate with two loaves on it.

"Well, here you both are and just in time. Come into the living room, do, and help us eat some of this while it's still warm." Though I'm still a little wary around her, the smile she gives me appears every bit as welcoming as the one Tristan receives.

"That smells amazing, Mrs. O'Gara," I say as we follow her into a living room only a little bigger than the one in our apartment.

It still seems odd that such high-ranking Royals don't have a nicer house. Maybe its proximity to the Sovereign's house makes up for it? Sean and I sit together on the couch while Molly pulls Tristan down next to her on the smaller love seat.

"It *is* amazing," Molly promises. "Mum got the recipe from M's aunt. We didn't even have pumpkins back in Nuath."

Sean cuts a slice and hands it to me on a napkin. I wait until Sean and Molly start eating theirs before I take a bite.

"Wow. It's even better than it smells." I quickly consume the rest of my piece. "I'd love to give this recipe to my mum," I tell Mrs. O'Gara.

"I'll be happy to copy it out before you leave." Again, her smile looks totally unforced.

My lingering tension abates. I still keep half-expecting her to revert to her earlier attitude toward me, but so far she's sticking to the promise she made on Sean's birthday. Prior to that, she went out of her way to make it clear she did *not* approve of inter-*fine* dating—especially between us.

Sean cuts himself a third slice. "Mrs. Truitt makes great pumpkin pie, too," he volunteers. "We had it at their house last Thanksgiving."

Before I have time to obsess about Sean enjoying a holiday meal at M's house, Mr. O'Gara joins us and the conversation shifts to the progress out at NuAgra. Finally, Molly stands up.

"If we're going to do any work on our Government projects, we should probably get started." She stacks several slices of pumpkin bread on a napkin. "We can take some of this upstairs with us."

Now Mrs. O'Gara does frown. "You'll all be studying in one room." It's a statement, not a question. "Otherwise, you can stay down here."

Molly rolls her eyes. "Yes, Mum. Though none of us are exactly kids anymore, you know?"

Mrs. O quirks an eyebrow. "If you were, I wouldn't worry. Sean may legally be an adult in this country, but the rest of you aren't. Nor is there any harm in observing Nuathan customs about such things when it comes to our own people."

In Nuath, none of us would be considered adults before the age of twenty-five. It was interesting to learn that the age of majority on Earth varies by both country and the activity in question—mostly ranging from sixteen to twenty-one.

"Let's go to my room," Sean suggests. "It's bigger, plus I actually cleaned it this weekend. I'd hate to have all that effort wasted."

Laughing, the three of us accompany him upstairs.

It's my first time in Sean's room—his mother is still strict about that, claiming we have to set a good example for Molly. So once inside, I look around with interest.

He's clearly not much into decorating. The only things adorning the walls are a big map of the United States and a wall calendar. On his desk is an Earth-style photo of his family and another of M—which he casually turns face-down almost before I see it. I swallow but don't say anything. It's not like he even *has* a photo of me.

"So, how far along are you two with your project?" he asks a little too quickly, sitting down with his back to the desk and gesturing me to the only other chair, next to his.

Molly closes the door, then sits next to Tristan on the bed, facing us. "I thought first we could talk some about this, um, bond thing. There's a lot we don't know, we're still so new at it."

Sean and I exchange a glance, then he takes my hand, soothing away my momentary discomfort.

"We only know what M and Rigel told us and you were there for that," he says. "We're only what, three weeks further along than you guys?"

"Then you haven't experimented any more with that telekinesis thing?" Molly sounds disappointed.

"A little, on Saturday," I admit. "It was the first chance we'd had—and we only saw a tiny bit of improvement. At this rate it'll be a year or ten before it's much use, especially as any kind of weapon. What are we going to do? Say, 'Stop right there or we'll throw a piece of popcorn at you'? Not that we can even do *that* yet."

Everyone laughs.

"See?" Molly says to Tristan. "I told you we can't expect to do much of anything, um, real yet."

"I guess." He shrugs. "At least their power has the potential of becoming useful at some point, especially once they can practice enough to get better at it. You can only practice resisting someone else's 'push' if they use it on you. And it seems kind of unethical to practice my charm thing—except maybe on Trina."

That gets a chuckle from all of us.

"It was great when you got her to go after Alan. Maybe next you can charm her into being nice to M for a change," I jokingly suggest.

By now I've heard about some of the awful things Trina did to the Sovereign over the years. I never liked Trina, even before that, but now I know what a truly nasty piece of work she is.

"You can always work on the telepathy thing," Sean suggests. "Can you sense each other's emotions yet?"

Molly nods. "Just when we're holding hands, but we can usually make a good guess even without that, we're so tuned in to each other."

"That'll probably get easier and easier." I sneak a quick glance at Sean. Did he pick up on my discomfort a few minutes ago when I noticed M's picture? I hope not, it seems so...petty.

"You'll probably also get to where you can hear each other's thoughts," Sean tells them. "We finally managed it for the first time on Saturday. Only when we're touching so far, and it takes a lot of concentration, but it's already getting a little easier."

"Definitely easier than levitating things," I agree. "Though until we can do it over at least short distances, it's not a lot more useful than whispering."

Tristan looks excitedly at Molly, then back at us. "It's cool you can do it at all. We'll definitely start working on that, at least."

"We will," Molly promises him. "But speaking of work, we should probably do a *little* on our projects, in case Mum asks."

We all pull out our notes then and start talking about our Supreme Court cases. Sean and I are analyzing Plessy v. Ferguson and how it evolved, while Molly and Tristan discuss the ramifications of the Korematsu decision.

"Isn't Alan on your team, too?" I ask Molly when we're packing up our notes later.

"Yeah, and it's even more awkward now than when he was still trying to get me to go out with him. Other than in class, he only works with Tristan and me by email now."

I shake my head. "Poor Alan. First I shoot him down, then you do. Then he finds out you were never even an option."

"He deserved it," she says with a snort. "He was rude and sulky, even before Tristan and I got together. Then he spent like a week groveling and apologizing after my news broke, which was almost as irritating. Is he still pestering you?"

"Not much." I don't mention how he keeps needling me about my 'inappropriate' relationship with Sean—though thinking of it makes me glance involuntarily at M's face-down picture on Sean's desk.

My hope that he didn't notice is dashed half an hour later, when he's walking me home.

"I can tell something's bothering you tonight. Want to talk about it?" he asks, his hand firmly around mine.

"It's...nothing important."

Because it really isn't. I've never once seen him so much as flirt with M, or vice versa. This whole thing is completely in my head.

"Hey, if you're bothered, it's important to *me*," he insists.

He watches my face for a long moment and I'm sure he's trying to decipher my thoughts—or at least my feelings. Successfully, unfortunately.

"It was that picture of M, wasn't it? I...saw your face when I flipped it over, but hoped I imagined it, that I was quick enough. Honestly, I totally forgot it was even there. It's been sitting on my desk so long, since way last year, I don't even see it anymore. I'll get rid of it tomorrow, I promise."

Startled, I stare up at him. "What? No! You do *not* have to do that.

Seriously. I was silly to let it bother me, even for a moment. I'm not so insecure that I can't handle an occasional reminder I wasn't your first love. It's what we have *now* that matters."

To my surprise, he stops walking and turns me to face him.

"Okay, I obviously need to clear something up right now. Kira, you *are* my first love. Totally my first love. Now and always."

I frown uncertainly. "You...don't have to say that. I know how desperate you were last year to get her to accept you as Consort, you told me so yourself. And M and Molly have both mentioned how jealous you used to be of Rigel, and how hurt you were when— Anyway, you're eighteen years old! Of course you've been in love before."

"You're seventeen. Have you?"

Caught off guard, I gape at him for a moment, then shake my head. "Um, no. I went out with a few guys back in Nuath, and had a little bit of a crush on another member of my *caidpel* team, but—"

"Brady?" he asks, grinning.

I laugh self-consciously. "Yeah. Along with half the girls in Nuath. But he never— I mean, it was never more than a crush, and a brief one at that. So...no. I've definitely never been in love before."

"Neither have I." His bright blue eyes hold my gaze so I can't look away, can't deny the sincerity I see there—nor do I sense the tiniest bit of ambivalence through his touch.

"Really?" It comes out almost as a sigh.

Smiling tenderly, he nods. "Really. I'll admit at one point I *thought* I was in love with M, but that was before I met you. Before we bonded. That's when I realized what I'd felt for her was never love at all."

"How can you be sure?" I ask, still slightly skeptical.

"Because now I know the difference. What I felt for M was a mixture of jealousy and possessiveness and thinking we were *supposed* to be together because of Nuathan tradition. Plus...okay, this part's kind of embarrassing...I used to fantasize about her when I was a kid, years before I ever met her. So when I met her for real, I convinced myself it was, I don't know, fate or something. But the girl I imagined myself in love with was never M at all, just a made-up fantasy version of her."

I blink up at him for a long moment while all that sinks in, then lick my lips nervously. "It, uh, sounds like you've given this a lot of thought."

"I have." His grin is sheepish now. "It was...sort of an epiphany for me when I realized how much more I wanted to be with you than I'd ever wanted to be with M."

"When was that?"

"Two days after we first kissed. You were pulling away, not talking to me—because of what was going on with Uncle Allister and Lennox. I was terrified you were planning to break things off with me before they even got started. Like, really, really terrified."

The remembered anguish in his eyes makes me melt. "No risk of that now," I assure him, stepping closer.

"You don't know how happy I am to hear that." He gathers me into his arms for a long, satisfying kiss.

Kissing him back with all my heart, my last, lingering doubts about where I belong finally dissolve—for good.

Molly

11

Contrivance

I CAN BARELY CONCENTRATE during cheer practice on Tuesday, I'm so nervous about this afternoon's *Echtran Enquirer*.

Oh, aye, Gwendolyn Gannett acted all nice and friendly while interviewing me, but I've seen how she can create scandal out of nothing. The other *Echtrans* at school are finally behaving normally around me—even Alan. Will they all hate me tomorrow?

Now that football season is over, we spend as much time coaching the JV squad as practicing ourselves. I'm glad of that today, since it makes my screwups less obvious. When we're done I don't bother to change, just grab my bag out of the locker room and hurry to the parking lot.

Tristan's waiting for me, as I expected, but so are M and Rigel. Their expressions tell me they've already seen the article.

"How bad is it?" I ask.

"It's not awful," M says, "but..."

She lets that hang, which doesn't reassure me a bit. She hands me her omni-phone, Gwendolyn's article already open on the screen.

I read the title. *"Exclusive Interview with Princess Malena: An Exposé"*

"Exposé?" I read aloud, appalled. "I didn't tell her anything that... gah!" Shaking my head, I continue reading.

Our newest Princess was gracious enough to invite me into her home—that is, the O'Garas' home—for this interview. As luck would have it, that

117

privacy allowed me to learn even more juicy details than I'd hoped. Today I'll be sharing some of the more notable exchanges from our conversation, slightly paraphrased and abridged for the sake of brevity. Read on!

GG: Tell me, Princess, how did it feel to learn you are a legitimate heir to the Nuathan throne, after believing yourself a member of the Agricultural *fine* your entire life?

Princess Malena: I was of course delighted to be suddenly elevated from one of our lowest *fines* to our very highest! Along with my rise in status, it's quite a relief to no longer be at the Sovereign's beck and call as her Handmaid.

I look up. "Relief—? I'm sure I never said that. Not even close!"

Tristan puts an arm around my shoulders and gives me a squeeze. "We believe you. But…keep reading."

GG: Speaking of the Sovereign, how is your sister taking the news? At the very least, she must find the loss of her *Chomseireach* inconvenient. Has she said how she feels about sharing her status with you?

PM: She doesn't seem interested in handing over any power to me, at least not yet. As for status, she's been the center of attention for a long time, so it's an adjustment for her to have people focusing on me for a change. If she finds my true identity inconvenient, she hasn't said so, at least not directly.

"Not directly?" I repeat, outraged. "I never even implied any of this. How can she—?" With an exasperated snort, I look at the screen again.

GG: What about the O'Garas? I imagine they're treating you much differently now than when they thought you were just an Ag foundling.

PM: (Laughing) That's an understatement! They still sometimes order me around out of habit, but now they immediately apologize. It's great being deferred to for a change. I'm sure they'll all get used to that eventually.

I wince. "Okay, maybe I said something a *little* like that. But I definitely didn't put it that way, just that it's taking my parents time to… Ugh."

GG: I recently spoke to a few of your *Echtran* classmates, who say you're now dating Tristan Roark, son of Council Member Connor. Tell me, are you two becoming serious?

PM: It's too soon to say, but I hope so. We get along so well, I can imagine us being a couple for a long time, maybe permanently.

Now I feel myself blushing. Even though those weren't my words, I can't deny thinking—hoping—exactly that. I dart a quick glance at Tristan before finishing the article.

And there you have it! Though the Princess's fellow students claimed she and Tristan began dating before her true identity was known, I'm sure I'm not the only one who finds the timing suspicious. More likely the Council, at least, knew the truth earlier. That would certainly explain why Connor, one of our more ambitious Council members, might nudge his son her way. Motives aside, however, should she and Tristan become serious, their pairing will surely lead some to wonder whether Malena might be a better choice for Sovereign than her sister, given Emileia's refusal to break things off with Rigel Stuart. It will be interesting to see whether the supposedly close relationship between the two sisters can survive what would seem to be an inevitable power struggle.

I will of course share more tidbits as I learn them, so keep watching this space!

"I can't *believe* her!" I exclaim, handing the omni back to M. "'Slightly paraphrased and abridged'? I mainly talked about how happy I am that M's my sister and she didn't even *mention* that. Most of this sounds like stuff she *tried* to get me to say, with all her leading questions. I knew I couldn't trust her."

Tristan gives my shoulders another squeeze. "It's okay, Molly. By now everyone knows how Gwendolyn Gannett exaggerates things for the sake of controversy. Nobody who knows you will believe any of this."

But I can tell he's bothered, too—probably because of that bit at the end, questioning his motives.

"Maybe," I say, "but what about all the people who *don't* know me? They'll have no reason not to believe I said all that stuff. That I actually want power and that M—" Glancing at her, I break off, embarrassed.

"She's just trying to stir up controversy, like she always does," M says soothingly, though she also looks troubled.

Rigel pulls her closer. "Hey, you knew she'd take another dig at you, after your article last week basically contradicted everything she's been saying for the better part of a year. I'm sure she—and maybe her editors—weren't too happy about that."

"Probably not." M gives him a reluctant smile. "I expect she'll like my next one even less, because I'm going to explain just how wrong she is with all *these* assumptions. So don't worry, Molly. Whatever people think after reading this, it'll be temporary."

I hope she's right...but I know from experience how people love to believe the worst.

.⁺⁺.

The moment I get home, it's obvious Mum and Dad have read that article, too. In fact, Mum greets me in the front hall, tablet in hand.

"Ah, you're home. You may want to read—"

"Already read it," I tell her before she can finish. "What a load of garbage! I never should have agreed to talk to her."

Dad joins us from the back of the house. "I'm sure she'd have done worse if you hadn't. But I can't deny she's demonstrated a terrible lack of journalistic integrity."

"That's putting it mildly," I sourly agree. "Not only did she make me sound like some power-hungry brat, she implied Tristan is only interested in me because I'm M's sister."

"Aye, her phrasing was unfortunate," Mum says. "Still, she made a good point at the end. Many of our people will likely expect you to take a prominent leadership role eventually. Even more so now word is out you're dating another high-ranking Royal, unlike our current Sovereign."

I stare at her, because *her* phrasing is nearly as bad. "*Current* Sovereign? You make it sound like M's position is temporary."

She lifts a shoulder, not quite looking at me. "There's no knowing what will happen in the future. Should circumstances—or opinions—shift substantially, it might be safest if you are prepared."

"Prepared? For what?" I ask suspiciously.

"For whatever may be required of you. We saw last year how quickly things can change."

Now I'm frowning. "What, you think M might suddenly be deposed, like Faxon was? She's *nothing* like Faxon! Our people love her."

"Most do, yes, but there are still those who disapprove of some of her choices."

"Like dating Rigel, you mean." I don't say it as a question.

"That's the main one, yes," she concedes. "*I'm* certainly not suggesting she step down for that reason, but now that our people know there is a viable, ah, alternative, it's possible—"

I cut her off. "Forget it, Mum! I've told you all along I don't want to take M's place or even share her authority, so please don't try to convince people I should. You're not, are you?"

She just looks at me for a long moment, clearly conflicted. "I...no. Not beyond a question or two during Council meetings, which you were there to hear. Of course, there *are* those in Nuath who worry Emileia is perhaps too focused on Earth since leaving Mars. They might be open to—"

"What? No! We don't need *two* Sovereigns," I exclaim, alarmed now. "M was properly Acclaimed by the people of Nuath and officially Installed and everything. Not to mention the next launch window to go there isn't for another year and a half."

"Which gives you a year and a half to prepare," Mum says complacently. "Far more time than Emileia had. As she herself frequently reminds us, with more and more of our people transitioning to Earth, many of our old traditions will need to change. It could be we will eventually discover a need for a second leader after all."

I stare at her, aghast, and she quickly adds, "I suppose it's not something we need to discuss just now, however."

"No," I tell her. "We don't. If I ever change my mind, I'll let you know, okay? Until then, *please* just let M and me continue as we are."

She nods, but with obvious reluctance. "Very well. I simply think— No, never mind. I'd best start making dinner."

I'm still frowning as she heads to the kitchen, because I know from long experience how stubborn she can be. Despite what she just said, I know I haven't heard the end of this.

.⁺.

Sure enough, all during dinner Mum continues throwing out oblique hints about my future, though I do my best to ignore them. We've just finished eating when I get a text from Tristan.

Hey, Molly! Can you come over tonight?

I'll ask, I text back, my spirits lifting at the thought. *Just a sec.*

"Mum, Dad, is it okay if I go over to Tristan's once I clear the table? I won't stay late."

Mum's indulgent smile reminds me unpleasantly of the end of that article. "Certainly, dear. Shall I drive you, or will he pick you up?"

"He'll come get me." He didn't actually say, but I assume so. Almost the only time Tristan and I ever get to be alone is in his car.

"Will his mother be there?" Mum asks then, clearly as an afterthought. Usually that's the very *first* thing she'd want to know.

"I'm sure she is, but I'll ask."

I text Tristan back to let him know I can come and to make sure his mom really is home. She is, so I pass that on to Mum—not that she seems as concerned about it as usual.

When he drives up, I hurry out to his car before he can come to the door.

"Thanks for letting me escape," I say, buckling myself in. "That stupid interview has Mum more determined than ever to make me take on some leadership role."

"Don't let her bully you into something you don't want to do." Leaning over, he gives me a quick kiss. "By the way, I told *my* mother I'd be running a few errands before picking you up, so she won't expect us for an hour or so. Want to go for a drive first?"

Our first date involved some completely unplanned parking because of a rainstorm and traffic jam—which led to a whole new understanding between us, followed by our first makeout session. Ever since, I've thought of Tristan's car as our "special" place.

"Sounds perfect," I tell him, thrilled at the idea of some guaranteed alone time. "Any particular place you want to go?"

He smiles over at me. "Anywhere we can be private is fine with me."

"Me, too. We haven't had many chances lately, between my cheer-leading and your Bodyguard training."

"I've noticed. Not to mention how people—*our* people, anyway—always seem to be watching us these past two weeks, ever since the news about you broke. It'll be nice to have you to myself for a change."

We head in the direction of Tristan's house, but partway there he points to an office park set back from the road. Since it's after business hours, the lot is completely empty. "What do you think?"

Grinning, I nod. He turns in, then drives around back where the loading docks are, out of sight from the road. Pulling into a parking space, he turns off the car and reaches for me. I meet him halfway and we spend a blissful ten minutes just kissing.

"Mmm. I definitely needed this," Tristan murmurs when we finally come up for air. Then, after a pause, "So, um, since we're alone, do you want to try practicing that telepathy thing Sean said he and Kira can do now? I'm already picking up on your feelings better than I could just a week ago."

"Same here. That's a long way from actually hearing each other's thoughts, but I'm willing to try…if you're sure you're ready to go there?"

Shortly after we first touched, before I was sure I even *liked* Tristan, it sounded like the worst "ability" ever. Now I definitely see the appeal, though the idea still unnerves me a little.

Tristan doesn't even hesitate. "Totally ready. Anything that could help against the bad guys is worth developing, right?"

His enthusiasm overcomes my reservations. "Of course. Right."

Taking both of my hands firmly in his, he holds my gaze. "Okay, what am I thinking?"

As Tristan's chocolate brown eyes smolder into mine, a delightful warmth swirls through me. I gaze back, trying to tap into his thoughts… which are all too obvious.

"When you look at me like that I can make a good *guess* what you're thinking," I say after a long moment. "It's making me think about the same thing, but I'm not picking up *words*."

Tristan chuckles, a delicious sound. "Good guess, though." He leans in for another lingering kiss that I eagerly return. "Want to try one more time before we head to my house?" he asks several minutes later.

"If you insist, though I'd rather do this." Smiling up at him, I grip his hands like before. "This time you try to tell what I'm thinking."

I mentally recite a line from poem that I memorized a while back, willing him to hear me. After thinking it at Tristan half a dozen times without even a flicker of response, I give up. "Nothing?"

"No." I can feel his disappointment through his touch. "But I guess we should get going."

"It's probably too soon to expect real telepathy anyway," I say as he reluctantly releases my hands to start the car. "Sean said he and Kira only managed it this past weekend and they've been together nearly a month longer than we have."

He huffs out a frustrated breath. "Yeah, I guess. Though that depends on when we count from, right?"

"Our first kiss was just one day after our first touch," I remind him, grinning. "Or shouldn't we count that one?"

"Um." He slants a look at me. "It *was* pretty…dramatic. So maybe?"

We *definitely* didn't like each other yet, the night that happened. In fact, we were hurling insults at each other and Tristan only kissed me to shut me up. But he's right the effect was dramatic—equal parts terrifying and thrilling. By contrast, our first *real* kiss, just three nights later, was completely wonderful.

"Whichever we count from, we've been bonded less than a month," I remind him again. "Only half as long as Sean and Kira."

"I know. But we should still keep trying. Not just telepathy but the other stuff, too. The sooner we can become superheroes, the better."

That gets a laugh from me. "Rigel did say we can work more on the electrical thing as soon as there's a convenient time when his parents won't be home."

"Yeah, that's right." Tristan's also grinning now. "It'll be seriously cool if you and I can learn to shoot actual lightning bolts!"

Sounds kind of scary to me, but I don't say so. Time enough to worry about becoming a superhero once I've gotten used to being a Princess.

When we arrive at Tristan's house, his mother greets me with a full, formal bow, her right fist over her heart.

"Welcome, Princess. I'm so pleased to see you again. Tristan said you two plan to work on a school project?" Her smile seems sincere, if tentative.

"Some," Tristan says. "It's nearly finished. Mostly we just wanted to hang out, since we never have time at school."

Her smile broadens. "No, I imagine not. Why don't you both have a seat while I go get you a snack?" She motions toward their elegant living room, more than twice the size of ours. Then, with a slightly smaller bow to me, she hurries off to the kitchen.

"Haven't you asked her not to—" I whisper to Tristan.

"More than once," he assures me. "I'm not sure she can help herself."

Sighing, I nod. Hopefully once she gets to know me better she won't be quite so nervous and respectful around me.

Tristan flips on the TV. "I guess we don't have time now for a movie?"

"Not really—though I don't regret the reason for that." I scoot closer to him and he covers my hand with his.

"Neither do I." He leans over for a quick kiss that makes me yearn for more than we dare with his mom in the next room.

Less than a minute later, she comes back with a tray of brownies and two glasses of milk—the same thing she served us my very first time here, with M.

"I believe you enjoyed these before, Princess?" she says, setting down the tray. "Amazing how only three weeks ago, no one even suspected your true identity. Though honestly, I should have guessed. You look so very much like your mother."

Since hearing my news, several people have said that. I find it funny —though not surprising—no one ever noticed before.

"It's a shame you never had a chance to know her, Princess," she continues. "Apart from the physical resemblance, you share several of her mannerisms, particularly in the inflection of your voice. I'm sure she would have been very proud of the young woman you're becoming."

"Er, thanks," I say. Tristan gives my hand a little squeeze. He knows how weird this sort of thing makes me feel. "I wish I'd had a chance to know her, too."

Of course, neither of them knows I *am* sort of getting to know my mother, via her stored persona. Every time I talk with my real parents, it's like a hole inside me becomes a little less empty. M probably feels the same. I sometimes wish I could tell Tristan about it. Rigel knows...

"Please feel free to ask me anything you'd like about her, Princess," Mrs. Roark says then. "As I told the Sovereign, I'm more than happy to share my memories of her. The two of us spent much of our time together when we were young, though we occasionally got into a bit of mischief."

That immediately sparks my curiosity. "What kind of mischief?"

She smiles reminiscently. "There was the time I helped her elude her chaperone so she and Mikal could slip off to the Royal gardens alone. We would all have been about your age then, so several years before their joining. Both of us would have received quite a scolding had we been found out, as tradition was still quite strict then."

Tristan and I exchange a slightly embarrassed glance.

"We also both loved exploring places we weren't technically allowed to go," his mother continues. "Galena was usually the instigator, but she never had trouble convincing me to go along. Far more than I, she dreamed of one day venturing beyond Nuath, something we both did later. I…wish she'd had time to experience more of life on Earth."

She and I both get a little choked up over that. I always felt bad for M that she lost her parents before she could know them. I'd felt the same about the Ag couple I believed were my parents. Now I know M's and my stories are remarkably similar—both of us orphaned twice, first by our real, then our adoptive parents.

"What…" I clear my throat, suddenly tight. "What else did the two of you do together when you were young?"

Tristan's mother wipes an eye and smiles. "Quite a lot. There was a time when we were ten years old…"

Though I'd originally hoped for more private time with Tristan, I'm eager to hear more and Mrs. Roark seems equally eager to answer my questions. By the time I have to leave, she's given me a much more complete picture of the young girl my mother was—one who rescued hurt or abandoned animals and found them new homes, and who frequently chafed at the restrictions placed on her, as destined Consort.

Finally, regretfully, I stand up. "I should go, but this has been grand, Mrs. Roark. I need to tell M some of these stories. Or, better yet, maybe you can sometime? I know she'll enjoy hearing about the two of you as girls every bit as much as I have. Thank you."

"Thank *you*, Princess, for letting me relive such happy times. It will be my honor to do so again with the Sovereign."

Rising, she gives me another formal bow, making me cringe slightly. Tristan, holding my hand, senses my discomfort immediately. "Mother," he begins, but this time I speak up myself.

"Please, Mrs. Roark, I'd rather just be Molly when I'm here. If that's okay?"

"Of course," she quickly says, looking embarrassed. "Tristan has told me you would prefer that, but I'm finding it more difficult than I expected to set aside tradition."

Now I feel bad for embarrassing her. "No, it's okay. Maybe when we get to know each other better, it'll come more naturally?"

She smiles, clearly relieved. "I'm sure it will. Good night…Molly."

During the drive home, I think over all the stories she told me, trying to reconcile them with the woman I'm getting to know from the Scepter Archive. M and I never thought to ask about our parents' childhoods.

"I'm glad you and my mother get along so well," Tristan comments as he turns onto my street.

"I'm glad, too. Sorry if you felt a little left out tonight."

He shrugs, pulling the car to a halt in front of my house. "I had you to myself earlier. Honestly, I loved seeing how well you relate to each other." Leaning over, he gives me a lingering kiss.

I respond wholeheartedly, trying to absorb enough strength and vitality from him to last till morning, when we can be together again. If anything, being apart, even overnight, seems to be getting harder instead of easier.

An hour later I settle into bed, planning to read myself to sleep with one of the files I'm supposed to be studying because of my new status. Dad mentioned over dinner he'd be testing me on some of that new material soon. I have trouble focusing, though, because I can't stop thinking about everything Mrs. Roark told me tonight about my mother—and wondering if her archived self recalls those incidents the same way?

Finally, I set aside my Nuathan scroll-book and get out of bed. I open my closet door, but then hesitate. I've never attempted to activate a Scepter Archive without M, though I've watched her do it plenty of times. Do I dare? Will M mind if I do? I suppose I could call or text her to ask...but it's pretty late.

Stepping into the closet, I stare at the Scepter for a long moment, chewing my lip. The last time M and I used it was to talk to our parents, so it already has the blue stone installed at the top. Which means I wouldn't even have to swap out the Archives...

12

Acquired trait

MOVED BY A SUDDEN, overwhelming need to talk to my mother—my *real* mother—I reach out and grab the Scepter. As always, it feels warm in my hand, very…"mine."

Back in Nuath, when M described that sensation to me, I didn't tell her I'd experienced the same thing those few times I carried it, because she'd forgotten it for something official. Then, I'd chalked it up to my imagination. Now, I know it's because we share the same bloodline.

Not that it means I should be a Sovereign or anything… Something else I'd like to ask my real parents about. Firming my resolve, I grip the Scepter a little tighter.

"*Chartlann rochtana*," I say aloud. Immediately, the Scepter vibrates in my hand, then the images of Prince Mikal and Consort Galena appear before me.

"Hello, Malena," my father says, then looks around. "You are alone this time?"

"Er, yes. M…Emileia isn't here right now, but…I wanted to talk to you. If that's okay?"

Though I know Galena is a technological artifact and not a real person, her smile warms me. "Of course, my dear. This record was primarily left for you, though it's wonderful Emileia also has access to it. What did you wish to talk about?"

I'd planned to ask for stories about her girlhood, but belatedly realize

M would enjoy hearing those stories, too. Surely it makes more sense to use this opportunity to talk about things I might not, if M were here.

"Um, well, I'm still having trouble adjusting to being a Princess, after thinking I was an Ag all these years," I confess. "And now my mum— Mrs. O'Gara, I mean—is insisting I should become some kind of leader, even though M—Emileia—is already doing a great job as Sovereign. I don't *have* to, do I?"

"I can't imagine anyone will force you into a leadership role you don't want," Galena replies. "Perhaps you should take time to become used to your new identity and status before making a decision of that magnitude, however?"

Her words make me even more glad I decided to do this. "Thanks. I'll do that. Even if I did want to somehow become a...another Sovereign, I don't see how it could ever be worth messing up my friendship with M. Er, Emileia. I'd hate for her to think I don't believe she's all the leader our people need—because I do. Believe that, I mean."

My father Mikal nods. "I understand. It isn't as though our people have ever had—or needed—more than one Sovereign at a time, though judging from all you and your sister tell us, these appear to be rather unusual times. Barring that, I should think there are other roles you might fill. While serving as your sister's Handmaid, you were also a confidante and counselor of sorts, were you not?"

I shrug. "I guess? Though she also had other, better counselors, like Regent Shim and my dad. Quinn O'Gara, I mean." It feels weird to use his first name.

"Even so, I imagine Emileia still finds you an important source of advice and support. Perhaps instead of *Chomseireach*, you could assume a more active role as her *Priomh Comhairlea*? Most Sovereigns have had one, and that person was generally seen as second in authority only to the Sovereign him or herself."

"Chief Advisor? I don't know nearly enough for that yet! I'm only sixteen. Isn't a Sovereign's *Priomh Comhairlea* supposed to be a lot older than the Sovereign?"

Mikal smiles. "Traditionally, yes. But that is because Sovereigns often designate someone who previously served as his or her mentor during youth. Have you not acted in that capacity for Emileia as she adjusted to her status?"

"Well...yeah, sort of. But that doesn't mean—"

"It is simply an idea for you to consider," Galena quickly assures me, her expression sympathetic. "A mere suggestion. You need not share it with anyone, even Emileia, if it makes you uncomfortable."

Swallowing, I smile back. "Thank you. It's at least something to think about. Someday."

After that, I do ask her a couple of questions about when she was young, mentioning Teara Roark, who she remembers fondly. Twenty minutes later, I deactivate the crystal. Setting the Scepter back in its corner of my closet, I fleetingly wish again I could tell Tristan about it.

✦

"They've *finally* finished the jury selection for Allister's and Lennox's trials," M tells the rest of our "squad" before school the next morning. "Apparently it took so long because their Royal lawyers kept raising new objections. It's pretty obvious they're trying to delay this trial as long as possible."

"Probably because nothing will go public until it actually starts," I tell her. "I know Mum is dreading that. Probably other Royals are, too."

M shoots a sympathetic glance at Sean and me. "Sorry. I keep forgetting how it will affect your family when the news breaks about what they did."

Sean shrugs. "The sooner they get what they deserve, the better, as far as I'm concerned."

I doubt he'll ever forgive Uncle Allister for what he almost did to Kira…and to M. I'm also looking forward to the trial starting, but for a more selfish reason—because it's bound to overshadow all other *Echtran* news for a while, including speculation about me.

As we head into the school, the three boys and Kira all start talking sports so I hang back a little with M to quietly tell her about the stories Tristan's mom shared with me last night, about our mother.

"She said she's more than willing to talk to you about her, too."

"Oh, I'd *love* that," M exclaims. "I'll ask her at Saturday's meeting when would be a good time."

"Maybe this afternoon, before Sean's game?" I don't have cheerleading practice today, and Tristan's Bodyguard training at NuAgra has been moved to right after school, to accommodate Kira's schedule.

M bites her lip, then shakes her head. "No, I need to finish my next

130

piece for the *Enquirer* today if I want them to include it in next week's issue."

"Oh, right. I definitely don't want to keep you from doing that." Especially if she's planning to debunk some of Gwendolyn Gannett's insinuations about me.

I don't say anything else for a moment, but then I blurt out, "So, um, would you be mad if I told you I also talked to our parents last night?" I've been feeling slightly guilty about that since waking up this morning.

Her brows go up in surprise. "Mad? No, of course not. Were you worried you weren't allowed to do that without me?"

I shrug. "I just thought maybe I should have asked you first."

"They're as much your parents as mine, Molly. It's fine. I'm actually kind of impressed you remembered how to activate the Scepter. What did you—? Oh, there's the bell. We'd better hurry."

I gladly drop the subject, since I'd rather not tell her about that Chief Advisor idea our father suggested. Especially after Gwendolyn Gannett implied I'm somehow angling to share M's power.

Which I'm absolutely not.

.⁺⁺
.⁺

Last night I had enough distractions to keep me from thinking much about yesterday's *Echtran Enquirer* interview but once school starts I can't help worrying again, since by now everyone will have read it. By lunchtime, though, no one's said anything to me about it.

That changes halfway through Government class, when the teacher sends us to work in our project groups.

"Nice to have the mystery finally cleared up," Alan quietly comments as the three of us gather in our usual back corner.

"Mystery?" Tristan repeats. "What mystery?"

Alan gives him a knowing look. "Why a Royal suddenly started acting all interested in an Ag. Your dad obviously found out the truth about—" He nods my way— "and told you. It all makes total sense now."

"That's not true, though I'm sure it makes you feel better to believe that," I angrily whisper back. "When Tristan and I first started dating, *nobody* knew yet—not even M and me."

Alan's mouth twists unpleasantly as he looks from me to Tristan and back. "Uh-huh. And I'm sure it makes *you* feel better to believe that. Less gullible, anyway. Or maybe you were in on it, too? Part of a plan to undermine the Sovereign? So much for you and her actually being *friends*."

I suck in an outraged breath, but he's not done.

"Would have been nice if you'd told me, too," he adds. "That way I'd've known not to waste my time even trying."

Upset as I am, I'm also determined to set him straight. "Seriously, Alan, there's no possible way *anyone* could have known in advance. Not me, not Tristan, no one."

"Yeah, you're way off base, dude," Tristan tells him. "Molly only told me the day before that bulletin went out, and I was as shocked as anyone. My father may be ambitious, but he definitely didn't—"

A couple of people from the closest group look our way and he breaks off. "Never mind. How about we work on the project?" he suggests, rather than continue arguing.

I'm glad. Not only were we getting too loud, I'm abruptly eager to drop the subject now that Alan has put my biggest worry about that interview into words—that people will assume I really do want to take power away from M.

What Tristan just said also made me realize it was barely an hour after learning the truth that he first told me he loved me. Not that it had anything to do with that. Of course it didn't. But it's kind of odd I never even thought about it before.

"Alan, you were going to watch that old TV interview with Korematsu himself. Did you take any notes from it?" I ask before I can dwell on such an unimportant detail.

Grumbling under his breath, Alan opens his notebook and lets the argument drop—for now. I sneak a glance at Tristan, who also looks slightly troubled. Is he also remembering the unfortunate timing of his first use of the L word?

Seriously, though, it's no big deal. I *know* Tristan loves me now, whether he meant it deep down the first time he said it or not. And that's what's important.

Right?

.⁺.

"You know Alan has a vested interest in attributing base motives to us getting together after the way we hurt his pride," I remind Tristan—remind both of us—on the way to Psych class. "Probably more than anyone does."

"Maybe. But Alan's not the only one who'll believe I found out ahead of time, after reading what Gwendolyn Gannett wrote. She did make it sound awfully plausible."

I can't refute that, since I've been thinking the exact same thing. "We'll just have to convince them otherwise." I make my voice more upbeat than I'm feeling.

Unfortunately, he can sense my emotions as well as I can sense his. "Maybe the ones we actually get a chance to talk to—though we obviously didn't convince Alan just now. And what about all the ones we'll never even see?"

We get to sixth period Psych before I can reply...not that I have an answer.

I spend most of the class obsessing over what Alan said about *my* motives, not Tristan's. So when he leaves for NuAgra right afterward, I intercept M on the way to seventh period.

"Hey," I say, suddenly feeling more awkward than I normally do around her. "Has anyone, um, said anything to you yet about yesterday's interview article?"

"Not *to* me, but I overheard Liam and Lucas talking about it in Lit class. I let them know you didn't actually say most of that stuff."

I nod jerkily, cautiously relieved. "Which part were they—?" I start to ask when the warning bell rings.

"Yikes, I'd better run," M says. "Angela, our editor, has been on the warpath this week. I'll give you a call if I hear anything else, okay?" She hurries off to Publications.

I frown after her for a moment, then shrug and continue on to Chorus.

For the next few hours, I do my best to put the interview—and Alan's comments about it—from my mind. But when Tristan picks me up for that night's basketball game, he brings it up himself.

"Has your mother stopped hassling you about the stuff in that interview?" he asks when we're halfway to the school.

"For the moment," I reply. "Though I didn't give her much chance today. I was in my room doing homework till dinner, which we rushed through so Sean could get to the school early."

I pause for a moment, then voice the worry that's been niggling at me since Government class.

"M insists no one who knows me will believe I said all those things, but...what if *she* does, at least a little? There was something in her expression when I talked to her earlier..."

"Molly, relax. Please." Tristan puts a hand over mine which does calm me down—again. "M can read emotions, remember? She knows when you mean what you say."

I want to believe that, but— "She also knows I can shield my emotions from her," I remind him. "Guess that's the big downside of being a good liar—nobody knows for sure when I'm telling the truth."

"I do. Maybe you can hide your emotions from M, but I almost always know what you're feeling, especially when we're touching." He gives my hand a squeeze.

I smile over at him. "Thanks. That helps."

"Good."

He doesn't say anything else until we reach the school, but despite reassuring me, I can tell he's still troubled. Sure enough, after parking the car he turns to me with a worried frown.

"Remember I said Alan wouldn't be the only one to assume I knew the truth before we started dating? That I only wanted to be with you because you're the Sovereign's sister? Well, a couple people at NuAgra came up and asked me point blank today."

Now it's my turn to reassure him. "I assume you set them straight?"

"Yeah, but the more I denied it, the less they seemed to believe me. I wish—"

I put a finger against his lips, silencing him. "Hey. As long as *I* know it's not true, does it really matter what other people think?"

He's still frowning. "*Do* you know for sure it's not true? You said you and M found some old records, but...what if someone on the Council found them before you did?"

We're on dangerous ground now, so I choose my words carefully. "The, um, records were in a box of stuff in my closet that I'd had since I was adopted. I just never knew what they were. M was the one who figured it out, once I showed them to her. The Council had no idea until she told them, that same night."

That's essentially the truth, except the "records" were an Archive stone with our parents' holo images and memories in it.

But Tristan doesn't look convinced. "Isn't it possible your mother looked through them years ago, when you were little? She could have guessed what they meant and said something to others on the Council."

"Nope. No way. *Nobody* could have seen them before M and I did. We—" I break off, realizing I almost said too much.

Unfortunately, Tristan senses my jolt of alarm at that near-slip. "You what?"

I shake my head. "Sorry. I'm…not allowed to tell you that part. It's classified."

Though I sense a trace of hurt, he nods. "No, it's okay. You *shouldn't* tell me anything classified. I completely get why M wouldn't want you to, considering my father was the one leaking Council secrets."

"You're not your father, Tristan. I know that and so does M," I assure him, resolving to ask her *soon* if I can tell him the whole truth. "Anyway," I hurry on, "if you'd seen Mum's face when M told the Council, you'd know she was as shocked as everyone else. Plus, the way she acts around me now is totally different from how she used to. She definitely had no clue, and neither did my dad."

"You don't think they—?"

"No." I grip his hands in mine so he'll know I'm telling the truth. "Trust me, there's no possible way your father or *anyone* else could have found out before M and I did."

He relaxes slightly. "Okay, if you're sure. Though it'll still be a trick to convince everybody else."

"We will." I say it with more confidence than I feel. "Everyone at school already knows you asked me out a whole week before the news broke, when everyone—including me—still thought I was an Ag. I told Gwendolyn Gannett that, too, though of course she didn't include it in her column."

I smile, remembering the stunned look on Tristan's face when I told him…but then my smile slips a little as I also remember it was only an hour later that he first said *I love you*. Snatching my smile back, I add, "I'll ask M to emphasize that again in her next column. That should help."

Despite my attempt to cover, it's clear Tristan picked up on my brief moment of doubt. "Is there something—?"

I yank the car door open before he can finish. "Yikes, look at the time! Trina will have my hide if I'm late again. I'd better get inside."

.⁺₊

During the game, I pay more than usual attention to our cheer routines, determined not to obsess any more over the doubts sparked by that interview. In between, I also watch the game. Liam's doing a much better job of holding back tonight, I'm pleased to see. Sean and Alan must have finally gotten through to him.

A conversation over halftime underscores just how important that is.

"Did you hear?" Donna says to the rest of the cheer squad as both teams run off to the locker room. "Alexandria's new player—the super cute one who's so good—also moved to our area because of that NuAgra place. I heard him telling one of our guys his dad works there. I'm going to introduce myself after the game."

"You can if you want, but I'm totally over those NuAgra guys," Trina responds with a scowl. "They all act like they're too good for us home-grown Indiana girls. Why would anyone want to go out with someone that stuck up?"

Donna looks over at the opposing team's bench. "Okay, sure, some of them are a little stand-offish, but I always thought you liked a challenge?"

"My dad thinks there's something suspicious about all those NuAgra people anyway," Ginny Farmer, one of our JV cheerleaders, pipes up.

With a start, I realize her dad is the same guy who kidnapped M and her aunt back in September. Because her parents are divorced and she lives with her mother, I hadn't thought much about it before.

"Why, just because they're not from around here?" I ask, hoping to deflect the girls' speculation from veering into dangerous territory. "Most of them seem pretty nice so far."

Ginny rolls her eyes. "Sure, you'd say that, Molly. You've dated two of them so far and your brother's dating one, too. How about *you* tell us what's really going on out there?"

I glance over at Kira's sister Adina and her friend Jana, also on the JV squad, a short distance away. Their parents all work at NuAgra, too. Though no *Duchas* likely would have heard what Ginny said over the crowd noise, I suspect they did, judging by both girls' expressions.

"I haven't heard it's anything different from what they claim to be doing, research on how to develop better crops—you know, feed-the-world type stuff. I do know Tristan, Kira and Alan all had to sign non-disclosure agreements to be in the work-study program there. So even if they do know more, they wouldn't be allowed to tell anyone. You know how those big tech companies are, always worried about corporate espionage or whatever."

"Tristan's seriously never even talked to *you* about what his dad does there?" Trina sounds skeptical.

I don't hesitate. "Nope. Though his dad doesn't seem like the sort who'd talk about work at home anyway." It's not common knowledge yet that Connor was voted off the *Echtran* Council and forced to leave Jewel. "Alan definitely never said a word, and if Kira's told Sean anything, he hasn't shared it with me."

Ginny glares at me through narrowed eyes. Except for not being rich, she sometimes reminds me of Trina—whom she clearly idolizes.

"Yeah, well, my dad thinks it's not just plants they're experimenting on out there. He thinks they're giving something to their kids, maybe something illegal. Look at those two new guys on our basketball team, Alan and Liam. They're already nearly as good as Sean. I hear Kira's really good, too."

"Good by Jewel standards, sure, but that's a pretty low bar," I scoff. "They all played for some huge school back east in a tough district, a whole different level from dinky Jewel. So of *course* they're way better than most of our guys." That's the explanation Sean said they're using.

Ginny still doesn't look convinced. "If you say so."

To my relief, Amber chimes in then. "You can make up whatever theories you want, but there's no denying these new guys are all super cute—including the one on Alexandria's team Donna wants to make a play for. And Liam's really nice. He's my lab partner in Chem class now, so I've gotten to know him pretty well. In fact, I think he *might* be planning to ask me out soon."

"If he does, see what you can find out," Trina says, looking even more disgruntled. None of the new guys have acted the least bit interested in *her*, something she's not used to. "C'mon, girls, halftime's almost over. Let's get into our positions."

⁺₊

When all six of us again gather briefly in the parking lot the next morning before school, I tell them about last night's conversation, especially what Ginny Farmer said.

"M definitely wasn't wrong when she told everyone at NuAgra Sunday about the local *Duchas* getting suspicious."

"Yeah, it does seem to be getting worse," Kira agrees. "Yesterday, at the end of Econ, Nate Villiers flat-out demanded I tell him what I really do out there."

"Kira totally kept her cool, though," M says with an approving smile. "Gave him the party line and made it sound completely logical. I'm not sure he was convinced, though. The Council will have to figure out *some* way to satisfy people without giving them the whole truth."

I agree, then go on to repeat all of last night's halftime conversation, including what Donna said about Alexandria's new player. "Apparently his dad works at NuAgra, too? She heard him say so to one of our guys."

"He told all three of us," Sean confirms. "We talked to him for a couple minutes right before the game started, after Alan picked up on his vibe and gave Liam and me a heads-up."

"You know," I say, "until last night, I never even thought about all the *Echtrans* who must live near Jewel but not in it. Would the Council even know if any are anti-Royals or neo-Faxists or whatever?"

M frowns. "I'm not sure. Maybe not? Everyone who was allowed to move *to* Jewel had to go through special screening, but I don't think anyone else did. They must not have kept very close tabs on who went where, or they'd have known about all those radicals who disappeared."

My insides go cold. "So...they might already be in places like Alexandria or Elwood? Or am I just being paranoid?"

"Paranoid?" M echoes. "It's not paranoia if someone really is after you, and both of us have been attacked now. I'll ask Kyna if there's any way to find out who's living within, say, a fifty mile radius of Jewel."

"Why didn't somebody keep track of that sort of thing?" Tristan demands as the warning bell rings. "Especially with Molly's—and your —safety on the line?"

M raises an eyebrow at him. "Somebody was supposed to. Your father. Maybe Devyn convinced Connor it wasn't necessary?"

Paling slightly, Tristan blinks but doesn't reply. Irked by the hint of accusation in M's tone, I squeeze his hand reassuringly.

"This isn't good," Rigel's saying. "One of those messages from last month my dad's been decrypting mentioned little towns close to Jewel. Referred to them as 'opportunities.' Maybe that's what they meant."

We all exchange uncomfortable glances but there's no time for more discussion if we're going to make it to first period.

As we head inside, everyone agrees we should get together away from school soon, to do some brainstorming and maybe practice those new powers we're developing. Sounds like we may need them.

13

Reinforcement

TRISTAN'S unusually quiet on the way to class.

"You okay?" I can sense his disquiet through our clasped hands.

He shrugs but doesn't answer.

"M wasn't implying you should have known about whatever your dad did or didn't do," I tell him before we go into the classroom.

At least, I don't think she was.

"Maybe not," he mutters. "Still, it's one more thing I wish I'd paid better attention to when it mattered. I just— Never mind." Stepping through the doorway he lets go of my hand, still frowning.

All day, I do my best to reassure him, quelling any doubts of my own as they arise. Alan's snide cracks at the start of Government class don't help.

"You should have heard what people were saying at NuAgra yesterday," he whispers as he passes us. "About you two, I mean. Looks like I'm not the only one who—"

"Shut up, Alan," I snap, startling him. "Unless you want me to mention your disrespect to my sister?"

At that, he shoots me an alarmed glance and scurries to his seat. Good.

"Thanks for defending my honor." Tristan gives me a twisted smile, but if anything he seems more bothered than before.

. . .

That evening after dinner, he and I go for a walk, since Mum frowns on driving for its own sake, probably guessing what we'd end up doing. If anything, she's become even stricter about that sort of thing now I'm a Princess. Our walks are now shadowed at a distance by Gilda, my new Bodyguard, but we make the best of it.

"I like parking better, but this is still nice," I say as we walk hand in hand down my street. It's clear tonight, though a little colder than it's been lately.

"It is," he agrees, but then lapses into silence. I detect a trace of the same anxiety I sensed from him at school.

I wait until we're nearly to Diamond Street before saying, "You've been down ever since this morning. Want to talk about it?"

"I'm not— Okay. Sure." He glances back to make sure Gilda's not within earshot. "I really can't blame M—or anyone—for thinking I might be like my father. Up until a few weeks ago, I spent my whole life trying to be."

I tighten my grip on his hand, trying to soothe his anxious uncertainty. No question that particular gossip bothers him a lot more than it's bothering me.

"I don't think she does, not now. Maybe a few weeks ago, but you were practically a different person then," I remind him. "It's obvious to anyone who knows you how much you've changed since then."

He looks down at me, a worried crease between his perfect brows. "You think? I didn't even *start* changing until a week or so after I got here. What if it doesn't stick? How can *I* even know it will?"

I sense some relief from him as he voices what must be his biggest fear aloud.

"It will stick because once you realized what kind of person your father is, you decided you didn't want to be that kind of person yourself," I tell him with complete certainty. "You can't possibly think you'll ever change your mind about that?"

Swallowing visibly, he shrugs. "Maybe not, but you know what they say about old habits…"

I stop walking to face him, taking both of his hands in mine to help me convey all the love and trust I can through that link.

"Tristan, you won't. If you ever even started to revert to your old ways, I'd know…and I'd smack some sense into you." I say it jokingly, but he doesn't smile.

"You sometimes have doubts about me, too, though, don't you?"

"What? Of course not!" Okay, I guiltily realize, maybe I did *briefly* fret about the timing of his first declaration of love, but—

"Even though I never told you I loved you until after I found out who you really are?"

I stare at him, stunned. "How—? Did you just—?"

His answering smile is more of a grimace. "Nope, not telepathy. Just a lucky guess—because after Alan's cracks, I realized it, too. Now I wish I hadn't edited that email."

"Huh? What email?" Now I'm totally confused.

"The first one I sent you the day you were attacked. *Before* you told me your news. I actually typed 'Love' but then erased it, because I wanted to tell you in person."

The emotion I sense from him, even more than his expression, proves he's telling me the truth.

"And you did, the very first chance you got." I squeeze his hands to show I believe him. "I admit the timing bothered me a little, too, when I first thought about it. But then I decided it didn't matter, because I know for sure you love me now."

"I do." He squeezes my hands back. "So much. But...even that can't change how big a jerk I was when I first got here last month."

"No, it can't," I agree. "I'm still not the least bit worried you'll turn back into one, because if you'd *really* been a jerk, deep down, you never could have changed in the first place."

"You honestly think so?" His worry is now tinged with hope.

Holding his gaze, I nod emphatically. "Absolutely. Maybe your father had you convinced you were like him, but you never were. Not in any way that mattered."

Now, finally, he smiles for real. "Thanks. I only wish I could be as positive as you are. I want so badly to deserve your trust, Molly—even if I'll never, ever deserve *you*."

My heart melts.

Because we're right next to the entrance of the arboretum, I drag him into the shadow of the archway. There, I wrap my arms around him for a long, satisfying kiss, determined to somehow erase his doubts about himself—doubts instilled by a lifetime as Connor's son.

.⁺+

The next day at lunch, I wait till Tristan and Rigel are discussing football to whisper to M, "Do you think you'll have time to talk today after school?"

"Sure, if you want. What's up?"

"Just…a couple things we can't talk about at school."

One of her brows goes up, making me realize that sounded kind of evasive, but she doesn't push. I'm glad, because this isn't the time or place to share the epiphany I had last night—that telling Tristan the truth about the Scepter Archives would prove to him that both M and I consider him completely trustworthy.

"I'm supposed to holo in for some kind of pre-trial conference in Dun Cloch tonight," she says when I don't elaborate, "but not till after dinner, since it's earlier there. Do you want to come over? Or would you rather talk at your house?"

"If your aunt won't be home, your house will be more private. Thanks, M. I'll explain when I get there."

As I eat my lunch, I start mentally lining up my arguments for the case I want to make to her this afternoon.

When I ring M's doorbell a few hours later, I'm more determined than I am nervous. I think.

"Hey," she greets me, smiling. "C'mon in."

I follow her to the kitchen table, the place she and I always seem to have our most important talks. At least, the ones I initiate. She sets out a plate of her aunt's pecan cookies and two glasses of milk, reinforcing my sense of *déjà vu*.

"So," she says, plunking herself down across from me. "What did you want to talk about?"

"I…um…your Scepter?" That's *so* not how I'd planned to start this!

"Oh, right!" she says, like she knows. "You never did tell me what you talked to our parents about the other night."

Not what I actually planned to bring up, but now I realize this is as a good time as any to lay to rest any worries she might have that I secretly want to share her power. Maybe then I can stop fretting about what she suspects.

"Yeah, that, too." I swallow. "You know how Mum's been bugging me to take on some kind of…role? I, uh, wanted to see what they thought about that."

She nods. "That was probably a good idea. What did they say?"

"That nobody can *make* me do that if I don't want to—and that even if I did want to—which I don't—there's no rush. Which was a huge relief."

Her smile makes me wish I could read emotions, too. Does she believe me?

"They're right, of course," she says after a tiny pause. "At the very least, you need to give yourself time to get used to being who you are. I know from experience that can take a while. If you decide later you do want to help with some leadership stuff, let me know—because I sure wouldn't mind sharing!"

I can tell she's not kidding. I hadn't thought about it as helping her out instead of grabbing power. That thought prompts me to admit, "Our father did suggest that someday—not right away!—I could maybe become your *Priomh Comhairlea*."

M blinks in surprise, then looks thoughtful. "That's actually not a bad idea at all. I mean, it's totally not appropriate for you to still be my Handmaid, considering you're every bit as high ranking as I am. Becoming my Chief Advisor instead would make perfect sense."

"Whoa. Seriously?" Not what I was expecting.

Looking slightly embarrassed now, she shrugs. "Kyna—and your mom—insist I should appoint another Handmaid, but I've put it off. Partly because I don't really need one here, but mostly because I...didn't want to give up that excuse for keeping you close. I know it's selfish, but I still depend on you a lot, Molly—more than you probably realize."

My breath catches, I'm so incredibly touched. "Thanks, M. You always know just what to say."

That gets a laugh from her. "Not always, trust me! But practice helps. Was that all you wanted to talk about?"

"Um...no."

Now I'm reluctant to bring up my real reason for coming over, for fear it will spoil what turned into a wonderful new level of understanding between us. But I owe it to Tristan to try.

"Back to the Scepter Archives," I make myself say before I can change my mind. "You told Rigel about them, right?"

"Yes, right after we re-bonded back in September, when I caught him up on everything he missed after they wiped his memory. He knows not to tell anyone else, though. Other than Rigel, the only people I've told are you and Shim. Why?"

"I, um, wondered if it would be okay for me to tell Tristan. I'd swear him to secrecy too, of course."

Like I was afraid she might, she frowns. I hold my breath for the several seconds she hesitates before finally answering.

"I'm....not sure that's a good idea, Molly. You two haven't been together all that long yet and...he *is* Connor's son. I know he's nothing like his father," she quickly adds when I open my mouth to protest. "Not anymore. But he was, mostly, up until a few weeks ago."

"But he's totally changed now, you know that. Anyway, he was never like Connor, not really," I tell her, just like I told Tristan last night. "Even when he tried to go along with his dad's plan to...to seduce you or whatever, he only did it because he believed it would be for the good of our people, not because he wanted power or anything."

Her frown doesn't go away. "Don't he and his father still talk, though? What if Connor somehow gets the secret out of him? We know *he* can't be trusted."

"But Tristan can," I insist, offended on his behalf. "Besides, I think he's only spoken to Connor twice since he was sent off to Montana, and only because his mother insisted. He'd *never* tell him anything that's supposed to be secret."

She still doesn't look convinced. "Connor's only been gone a couple of weeks. He hasn't even been formally charged with anything yet, so they might let him come back to Jewel—though not to the Council, of course. I have to take the long view about something like this. I'm sorry, Molly."

"I can't imagine he'd come back to Jewel," I say, refusing to give up yet. "Why would he? Even if he did, I doubt Tristan and his mother would let him in the house. Remember it was Tristan himself who first told you what Connor had been up to—and he hasn't so much as hinted since then he still feels any loyalty to his dad. At all."

But M is still shaking her head. "Sovereign Leontine made it super clear from the start that I'm supposed to keep knowledge of the Archive to as few people as possible. I didn't even tell Rigel's dad where I got the specifications for the security system he's designing. *No one* should know unless they absolutely need to."

"You told me," I remind her.

"That's different. You're my sister. The Sovereigns in the Archive are as much your ancestors as mine."

I smile grimly, trying not to look smug. "You didn't know that yet when you told me. Neither of us did. I was still just your Handmaid."

Her expression tells me she'd forgotten that detail. "Well…it turned out to be a good thing I did, though, right? Otherwise we never would have found out your blue crystal was an Archive, too, or that we had the same parents."

"True," I concede. "I'm just pointing out that when you told me, I didn't have an *absolute* need to know. Neither did Rigel when you told him, did he?"

"He can read my mind," she says, though there's now a trace of doubt in her eyes. "It's not like I could have kept it from him for long anyway. Besides, he's my Bodyguard."

Aha! I have her now.

"Tristan is going to be *my* Bodyguard, as soon as he finishes his training," I point out. "And if you're right that he and I are *graell* bonded, he'll probably be able to read my mind eventually, too. I don't see that there's any difference at all."

"That's not—" She breaks off, frowning. "Okay, the situation is sort of similar, but there's still the issue of Connor."

I raise an eyebrow at her. "So you're condemning Tristan simply on the basis of his birth? You sure don't like it when people do that to Rigel. Tristan's Royal, at least."

M sucks in a breath and I immediately regret saying that.

"I'm sorry, that was out of line. You know *I* don't think that way about Rigel," I assure her.

"You used to," she reminds me, swallowing. "I remember when we sat right here at this table and you tried to convince me I couldn't possibly be bonded to Rigel, or continue my relationship with him, because of his *fine*."

The hint of betrayal in her expression undoes me. "I should never have— I promise I haven't believed that for a long time. How could I, when it was your bond with Rigel that saved us all from the Grentl? Even before that, way before that, I knew your bond was real, that you two had to be together for…for all sorts of reasons."

"I know," she whispers. "I just get…defensive, I guess, when anyone disses Rigel."

"Which I totally, totally get," I say, desperate to repair the damage I just inflicted. "I was just pointing it's also not fair to judge Tristan because of his father. I swear I wasn't criticizing Rigel."

For a long moment, she looks at me uncertainly. But she must sense how much I mean it, how sorry I am, because she suddenly relaxes.

"No, I guess you weren't. It…only makes sense you'd also get defensive, since it probably did sound like I was badmouthing Tristan. But you're right, he's nothing like Connor now—except in looks—and I'm sure he never will be. Not with you to keep him straight." She manages a little smile.

Relief floods me. "Then…can I tell him? Please?"

Slowly, she nods. "I guess so, since it means so much to you. Just make *sure* he understands it's super, *super* important he never even hints about it to *anyone* else."

"I will, I promise. Thank you, thank you, M!" Jumping up, I run around the table to hug her.

She hugs me back, tight. "I'm sorry I gave you such a hard time, Molly. It's just…I'm always afraid I'll screw up and make some decision that will come back to bite me. It's not like I haven't before."

"Hasn't everyone?" I laugh, thankful to have our first quarrel as sisters behind us. "But don't worry, M. Letting me tell Tristan about the Archives won't be one of those."

I'm sure of it.

.⁺₊

Weirdly, now that I've convinced M it will be perfectly safe for me to tell Tristan the truth about her Scepter, I start having second thoughts myself.

All through dinner I keep hearing M's arguments in my head, now sounding slightly more reasonable than when she actually said them. What if Connor *can* somehow trick Tristan into sharing the secret with him? Unlikely, but maybe not impossible?

By the time Tristan comes over for another evening walk like we'd planned, I'm so conflicted I invite him inside instead.

"It's even colder than last night," I say, going up on my toes for a quick kiss. "How about we wait till tomorrow afternoon, when it'll be warmer?"

"Guess I should've brought my omni, though Mother doesn't like me carrying it around." His obvious disappointment makes me feel guilty for my earlier doubts. "How come you don't have one of those cool phone ones, like M does?"

I shrug. "I don't really need one. It's not like I have any, y'know, official duties."

"Yet."

Though he's grinning, at his qualifier I'm abruptly reminded of the comment he made immediately after I told him my big news: *I guess our people have another leader now, huh? If you're the Sovereign's twin, you must have as strong a claim to the throne as she does.*

More unsettled than ever, I grab his hand and tug him toward the living room. "Come on, let's see if there's anything good on TV."

An hour later, I feel guilty for passing up what would have been a perfect chance to tell Tristan about the Scepter. *I'll tell him during our walk tomorrow,* I promise myself, tightening my clasp on his hand.

Unfortunately, Tristan texts me shortly after breakfast to say he has to spend the next few hours at NuAgra, for more Bodyguard training.

It's the first chance Kira's had for a longer session. Our instructor said if we do well enough today, we'll get officially certified in just a couple of weeks!

That'll be great, I text back, stifling my disappointment. *We can still get together later on.*

But then as soon as we finish lunch, Dad tells me he wants to spend the afternoon quizzing me on all the Nuathan government stuff I've been studying. Crap.

I text Tristan, explaining.

Maybe if I ace all the questions, there'll still be time for a walk before tonight's Council meeting.

Two hours later, even though I feel like I've answered everything pretty well, Dad's not satisfied.

"This isn't just a class for school, Molly," he reminds me. "You need to know more about our laws and traditions than the average Nuathan student, even at university level. If you should be called upon to lead our people—"

"I won't." Why does everyone keep saying stuff like this? "C'mon, Dad, what makes you think that'll ever happen? Why should it?"

He gives me a stern look. "We cannot know what the future will hold. You should be prepared for all eventualities. No doubt that is why you were kept safely hidden all these years, so that Nuath would never be left without a viable successor to the throne. Now. Again. Tell me the names of all twenty-seven ministries and what functions they serve."

It's *another* two hours before Dad finally seems satisfied I've regurgitated everything I know, after which he sets me an accelerated course of study for the next two weeks. By then it's nearly time for dinner—a quick, early one because of the *Echtran* Council meeting and Sean's out-of-town basketball game tonight.

"I'm useless at these meetings anyway," I grumble as I help Mum clear the table afterward. "Sean got to go to his game. I ought to be there to cheer."

Trina gave me a hard time about that, even though the varsity cheerleaders aren't technically required to go to the away games. More importantly, it would have been a chance to see Tristan. I wish more than ever I hadn't chickened out of going for a walk with him last night. Not only could I have told him about the Scepter, it would have been a chance to make out.

"Sean isn't an heir to the Nuathan throne," Mum reminds me. "Your sister told everyone at NuAgra last weekend that you now attend the Council meetings. How would it look if you missed the very next one, just to play cheerleader?"

I nearly snap at her, I'm feeling so grouchy after a whole day without Tristan, but I don't. Because she's right, whether I like it or not.

Fifteen minutes later the doorbell rings and I welcome Tristan's mother, the newest member of the *Echtran* Council.

"I'm not too early am I?" she asks anxiously as she follows me into the living room.

I assure her everyone else will be here any moment and sure enough, Kyna, the Council leader, materializes just then, immediately followed by Nara—both holograms from Washington, DC.

"Good evening, Princess," Kyna greets me with a formal bow. "I trust all is well with you?"

"Pretty good. Er, I mean yes." I'm glad Dad went with Sean, so he didn't hear my slip. I have a much better appreciation now for how awkward M must have felt early on, after being raised as a *Duchas* nobody.

She's the next to arrive, then Rigel's dad and finally the other two Royals on the Council, Breann and Malcolm, who always seem to arrive together. I wonder, not for the first time, if something's going on between those two.

Once everyone's seated, Kyna says, "Before we begin, I'd like to welcome Teara Roark to her first *Echtran* Council meeting. I assume you've had a chance by now to read some of the materials I sent, detailing our more important recent business?"

Tristan's mother nods, still looking nervous. "Yes, Council Leader. I, ah, actually read through it all twice to make certain I hadn't missed anything. Thank you so much."

"You're welcome." Kyna's smile is as warm as I've seen from her. "And just 'Kyna' is fine going forward. We don't stand on much ceremony during these meetings, at the Sovereign's request."

She then becomes all business. "Tonight's first item involves the ongoing investigation in Dun Cloch, where we've had a small breakthrough."

14

Diffusion

EVERYONE LOOKS SUDDENLY hopeful but Kyna regretfully shakes her head. "No, we haven't yet found the missing antimatter."

We all deflate slightly as she continues.

"However, our investigators believe they may have discovered the identity of the thief. Enid, the woman who created that first antimatter explosive had a friend," she says. "She and Scanlon were reportedly very close at one time, but hadn't been seen together at all in recent months. We now suspect that may have been by design, to disarm suspicion. Also a highly-skilled Informatics technician, Scanlon oversaw the antimatter containment system until he disappeared—the day of Enid's untimely suicide. That makes him our top suspect, particularly as he possessed the clearance to carry out a theft undetected."

"And probably the expertise to make more bombs," M adds. "I'm not seeing the good in this news, Kyna. I assume we don't know where this guy is?"

"I'm afraid not," Kyna admits, "though his name and likeness can now be circulated to all of our people, with a request to report any information or sightings to this Council. That might possibly yield results."

M looks skeptical. "Only if he tries to deploy a bomb or bombs himself. That's not how these people have operated so far. They use lies to recruit others to do their dirty work, so it can't easily be traced back to them. Like the man they sent after me at the start of the school year, and the one who attacked Molly three weeks ago. And like they tried to do with Kira."

"A bulletin warning our people against this man may undercut that strategy somewhat," Kyna points out. "Until we learn more, I don't know what else we can do. Van, how close are you to implementing those security systems?"

"I'm putting the finishing touches on the one out at NuAgra," he tells her. "The new perimeter sensor was already able to give us early warning when those *Duchas* tried to scale the fence last week, and when another group attempted the same thing two days ago. Both times, the gate guard was alerted in of time to stop them well before they reached the top."

I exchange an alarmed glance with M.

"They tried again?" she asks. "Sounds like they're getting bolder. Was one of them Mr. Farmer, by any chance?"

"I don't believe the guard got their names. The first group were teens but the second was a pair of adults. I suppose one of those might have been Farmer. The man who kidnapped the Sovereign in September," he clarifies when a couple of people look puzzled.

M frowns. "If so, he'll probably keep trying. He's not only nuts, he's apparently pretty stubborn. And now his daughter is spreading rumors at school, too. Molly, tell them what she said to the other cheerleaders."

I repeat the gist of what Ginny Farmer said at Sean's basketball game, which has everyone looking concerned.

"She didn't say anything about aliens, at least," I say, "but a lot of kids at school are wondering what's actually going on at NuAgra. I doubt we can keep rumors from spreading unless we give them some kind of plausible explanation."

Mrs. Roark surprises me then by raising a tentative hand. "Suppose we offer to give some of the local *Duchas* a tour? A very, very limited one, of course, after making certain nothing of a, ah, sensitive nature can be observed. We did exactly that back in Colorado to allay suspicions about the perceived secrecy around Fiarway, and it worked quite well."

Kyna gives her an approving smile. "Not a bad idea, Teara, thank you. Malcolm, suppose you and Breann look into the logistics of arranging such a tour. It might go a long way toward addressing the locals' suspicions."

They both agree to do that, though Malcolm looks dubious.

"Quinn can likely help with that as well," Mum offers. "I'll mention it to him when he gets home—he's at one of Sean's basketball games right now."

"Speaking of that," Malcolm says, "in light of these new suspicions, I feel we should reconsider allowing *Echtran* school students to play on *Duchas* sports teams. Otherwise we risk drawing even more *Duchas* attention to our people, as happened at Jewel High School last week."

A couple of heads nod in agreement.

"But just last week you said you *weren't* going to stop them from playing," I blurt out, remembering how relieved Sean was to hear that. "It seems unfair to suddenly change your minds."

Little Nara unexpectedly supports me. "I must agree with Princess Malena. As I pointed out last week, our young people have already given up a lot by emigrating to Earth. Many have had their studies set back by months, even years. It does seem unfair to deny them this one outlet for their energies. Weren't their parents told back in Nuath that one benefit to relocating would be the competitive advantages our people's superior abilities would give them here?"

"Yes, I used that argument repeatedly," M confirms. "I'd hate to be proved a liar. Rigel even lost his last playoff game last weekend for the sake of all the other *Echtran* athletes, though it killed him to let his team down like that. And Liam, the boy who, um, overdid it at that basketball game, toned it down a lot at the next one, just like he promised. If you pull the plug now, those sacrifices were for nothing. Let's please hold off on any edicts for now, and see how things go."

There's a lot of muttering, but finally Kyna nods.

"Very well, Excellency. I am willing to table that discussion for the moment, but we should reexamine the issue regularly. Perhaps we should explore the idea of a NuAgra *caidpel* league, as you suggested. However, Jewel's student athletes may not be the only ones we need to consider in this context."

Which reminds me of the other concern I brought up when we were talking about that *Echtran* basketball player from Alexandria. Gathering my courage, I speak up again.

"Do we know how many *Echtrans* live in this area other than the ones actually in Jewel?" I ask. "Nobody had to be, er, approved to live in nearby towns, did they?"

Kyna looks startled, then thoughtful. "No, I don't believe so." She turns to Breann. "Do you have Connor's notes on our newest immigrants?"

"Yes. Just a moment." Breann pokes around in her tablet for a moment, then her brows go up. "Hm. Princess Malena raises a valid concern. Of those who applied but were not chosen to live in Jewel, more than a hundred appear to have settled within a twenty mile radius. It might be wise to take a closer look at why their applications were declined."

"I should say so!" Mum exclaims. "Why, we could have a whole group of Anti-Royals the very next town over and not even know it."

Kyna nods. "That does appear to have been an oversight—one we'll rectify as quickly as possible. Thank you, Princess," she says to me. Then, to Rigel's dad, "Given the possibility of *Echtrans* with, ah, worrisome political leanings living near Jewel, you may also want to accelerate your plans for improving security for the Council, our Sovereign and her sister."

"I agree," Mr. Stuart says. "I'd like to install a system similar to NuAgra's at the Sovereign's residence, as well as here at the O'Garas' house, as soon as possible."

My mum raises an eyebrow at him. "How disruptive will that be, Van? With Thanksgiving coming up…"

"Er, yes, I hadn't considered that. I'm afraid it will require giving my little crew access to every part of the house at some point, though now that we have the basics down, it shouldn't take more than a few days. We can wait until after the holiday weekend, if you prefer."

She looks thoughtful, then shakes her head. "No, I'd rather it be set up as soon as possible. It might make sense for our family to clear out for a few days so you can work more quickly—have our Thanksgiving somewhere else. Somewhere safe."

"Breann, you haven't sold your house in Kentucky yet, have you?" Nara suddenly asks.

Breann blinks, then shakes her head. "No, the market in that area is rather depressed. I've considered renting it out over the summer, as it's furnished, but it's unoccupied right now. The O'Gara family is more than welcome to stay there for the holiday weekend, or for the whole week if they'd like."

A week? Much as I want us all protected, I recoil at the idea of being away from Tristan for that long. Twenty-four hours apart has been bad enough.

M also looks startled, but gives me a tiny smile and nod before turning to Mr. Stuart. "Would it be easier for you to do this house and mine at the same time? My aunt and uncle talked about going some-where for Thanksgiving too, but never made any plans."

"My Kentucky house has four bedrooms," Breann volunteers. "It can accommodate all of you, if the Sovereign and her sister don't mind sharing a room."

"No, we don't mind at all," she assures Breann with another smile at me. "I already spend the night with Molly most Saturdays, when these meetings run late. Do you want me to suggest it to Aunt Theresa?" she asks Mum.

"I can invite her myself," she replies. "If you're sure you don't mind, Breann?"

"Not at all. In fact, it will be my honor. I'll drop the keys by tomor-row, along with detailed driving directions—it's about five hours south of here."

Mum smiles her thanks. "Very well. I'll speak with the Sovereign's aunt at church tomorrow."

While I'm still struggling to hide my panic over leaving Jewel—and Tristan—Kyna goes over a few other minor administrative matters and then concludes the meeting.

"We won't meet next Saturday, as it will be during the holiday week-end. Any updates can be sent to me and I will forward them to the rest of you, along with anything new I find out. Should something arise that requires discussion, we can meet holographically. Adjourned."

Everyone again bows to me as they leave, but I'm too distracted by worry to be as bothered by that as usual. I incline my head to each one automatically, just trying to keep my composure until I can unload my fears to M.

⁺₊

When Nara winks out, the last to leave, Mum carries the tray of coffee cups to the kitchen. I immediately turn to M.

"Are you sure—?" I start to say, when Dad and Sean walk in.

M, clearly sensing my near-panic, puts a calming hand on my arm before turning to them. "How was the game?"

"Good—on both fronts," Dad answers. "Jewel won, but by only six points."

"We were all extra careful," Sean confirms. "Even Liam didn't look much better out there than Pete, our best *Duchas*."

"Glad to hear it." I pretend more enthusiasm than I feel. "Malcolm pushed again tonight to ban *Echtrans* from playing sports. Luckily M and Nara convinced the Council to hold off for now, but if anyone's too obvious they may change their minds."

"Yes, under the circumstances, Sean missing a game will be no bad thing," Mum says, coming back from the kitchen just then.

When Dad and Sean look confused, she explains about the Thanksgiving plan. I detect a flash of alarm in Sean's eyes, but he quickly conceals it.

"Yeah, maybe you're right." Then, with a significant look at M and me, "Want to catch me up on everything else while I get a snack?"

While Mum and Dad go into the living room to talk, we follow him to the kitchen, where M gives him a quick recap of tonight's meeting, to include Enid's Informatics friend and the fact that an unknown number of un-vetted *Echtrans* might be living within an easy drive of here.

"Still," Sean says, pulling sandwich fixings out of the fridge. "I guess you realize what this Thanksgiving trip will mean?"

M nods. "We'll all be away from our significant others. It definitely won't be fun, but if a separation strengthens your bonds the way they have Rigel's and mine, it could be worth it. Might give us all an extra edge."

I hadn't thought of that angle. Even so, the thought of going days and days without Tristan makes my stomach clench. "I remember how sick you got over Thanksgiving last year."

"Trust me, I haven't forgotten. But this won't be for nearly as long," M reminds me.

Mum pokes her head in then to remind us we all have to be up early for church tomorrow, so M and I head upstairs while Sean scarfs down the rest of his sandwich.

I haven't talked to Tristan since last night, except for a few texts today, so as soon as M goes into the bathroom to brush her teeth, I message him.

Can you talk?

Instead of texting back, he immediately calls me. "Hey, what's up? Mother didn't tell me much when she got home, just that the investigators have another clue to follow."

"She didn't mention Thanksgiving?"

"No. Should she have?"

I hesitate for a second before saying, "I guess not, since it doesn't exactly involve you. Unfortunately."

"What do you mean?" Now there's an edge to his voice.

"Mr. Stuart wants to install a new security system at our house and M's, so my mum suggested we leave for a few days to let them work. The plan is for my family and M's to spend the long weekend in Kentucky, five hours away."

There's a brief silence. "And it's already a done deal?"

"Pretty much. So it looks like we'll be testing that separation thing M talked about sooner than we thought."

"I guess if it ramps up our bond it'll be cool." He doesn't sound particularly excited, though.

Neither am I. "From what we heard tonight, an extra line of defense might be necessary. Being apart will suck, but—"

"But maybe worth the trade-off? I sure hope so. We've barely been apart a day and I already miss you something fierce, Molly."

I swallow at the intensity in his voice, an intensity I share. "Ditto. Let's try for some time alone tomorrow, before that picnic out at NuAgra. Are you and your mother going?"

"That's the plan. Mother even seems to be looking forward to it. But we should have time to do something before that, just us. Sound good?"

"Really, really good. Can you come by around noon?"

He agrees and we continue talking until M comes in.

"Sorry, should I leave again?"

"No, we're done," I tell her. "See you tomorrow, Tristan. Love you."

"Love you, too, Molly. G'night."

I click off and turn to see M grinning. "I didn't know you two had progressed to the L word. When did that happen?"

I'm tempted to fudge, afraid of what she'll say if I tell her the truth, but I hate lying to M.

"Right after I was attacked, actually," I confess.

"Wow," she says, her brows going up. "You'd only been together what? A week at that point?"

My cheeks get warm. "Yeah. I did wonder later if he—we—only said it because of that close call."

"Or because you'd just told him who you really are?"

I shake my head. "I admit that occurred to me later, but we talked about it and I totally don't believe that now. We…can't lie to each other when we're touching."

"Because of…right. I get that. And now you're sure it's really true?"

I nod, still half expecting her to chide me for being gullible, like Alan did. Instead, she sighs.

"That's so romantic! It's like a rom-com movie, falling in love after the way you two clashed when Tristan first got here. Remember me teasing you about keeping him away from me by flirting with him yourself, and how disgusted you were by the idea? It was obviously fate."

She grins and I stick my tongue out at her, even though I've thought the same thing.

"Go brush your teeth," she tells me then. "It's after midnight and your mom will have us up early for church." Still chuckling, she tosses my toiletry bag to me.

Absurdly relieved, I head to the bathroom.

.⁺₊

By the next morning, I'm missing Tristan worse than ever. Being apart this long has me feeling…unbalanced, along with grumpy and a tiny bit achy. Which doesn't bode well for Thanksgiving. He's only ever come to church once, when Connor tried to set him up with M, but I find myself hoping he'll show up today.

He doesn't. I guess his mother still isn't completely comfortable mingling, especially when it's a mixture of *Echtrans* and *Duchas*. I hope she'll be okay at the all-*Echtran* picnic this afternoon.

Though I'll be seeing Tristan in less than three hours, right now it feels like a long time to wait. M's reaction last night to learning when Tristan first said he loved me solidified my resolve to tell him the truth about the Scepter first chance I get—which should be today. I've even rehearsed what I want to say…assuming I can keep my mind on it once we're together.

Stifling a sigh of impatience, I try to focus on my hymnal.

After the service, my family walks home with the Truitts, like we usually do when the weather's halfway decent. The temp is near freezing today, but the sun is out and there's hardly any wind.

Mum takes the opportunity to invite M's aunt and uncle to join us in Kentucky for the upcoming holiday weekend.

"Why, that's extremely kind of you, Lili!" Mrs. Truitt exclaims. "Isn't it, Louie?"

M's uncle bobs his head up and down enthusiastically. "The place is on Lake Herndon? I've heard the fishing is great there. Wonder if my license is good in Kentucky?"

"Are you sure we won't crowd you?" Mrs. Truitt asks then.

"Not at all," Mum assures her, then lowers her voice. "The truth is —" She breaks off and glances at M.

"Aunt Theresa, do you remember what I told you about getting more security set up for our house?"

Suddenly looking nervous, Mrs. Truitt nods.

M continues. "Well, they're ready to do that, and it'll be easier for them and for us if we're out of the house for a few days. Same with the O'Garas—they're getting extra security, too, because, well…"

She looks over at me and I wonder if she's finally going to tell her aunt about us being sisters.

"Because that's where the Council meetings are," she finishes. "Among other things."

When our two families separate in front of M's house, she leans in close to me and whispers, "I didn't think out on the street was the best place to spill the beans about us, but we can tell her over Thanksgiving. Just don't be surprised if she treats you weird."

I was starting to feel a little hurt she hasn't told her aunt and uncle about me, but she's right. *Echtrans* treating me like a Princess is bad enough. The Truitts could be even worse.

At five minutes to twelve, Tristan rings the bell and I greet him at the door.

"Hey. Want to go for that walk now?" I tilt my face up for the kiss I've been longing for and he instantly obliges me.

For a long moment I'm lost in that kiss, absorbing strength and well-being, my mood improving by the second. I can tell Tristan's feeling something similar. But since one of my parents could appear any second, we keep it briefer than either of us want.

Raising his head, Tristan's deep brown eyes melt into mine. "It's still pretty cold today. Maybe another drive would be better?"

"Definitely better." A walk can't guarantee enough privacy for the makeout session I suddenly crave.

"Mum, Dad, I'm going for a drive with Tristan," I call, pulling on my jacket. "Back soon."

Mum hurries out of the kitchen before we can escape. "Wouldn't you both like a spot of lunch first?"

I shake my head, chafing at the delay. "I had a peanut butter sandwich when we got home from church, remember?"

"And I ate at home before coming over," Tristan says. "But thanks, Mrs. O'Gara."

"Aye. There'll be plenty of food at the picnic, anyway. Where do you plan to go?" Even during the day, she's not a fan of us driving without a specific destination.

Luckily, I've lined up a few for times like this. "We thought we'd check out that new outlet mall that just opened between here and Kokomo."

Also luckily, she doesn't focus her lie-detector on me. "Ah, all right, then. Be sure to keep an eye out for anyone suspicious and be back by two-thirty, as we plan to leave for NuAgra before three."

"We will," I promise and whisk Tristan out of the house.

"Three weeks ago we weren't even allowed to talk to each other," he reminds me with a chuckle, accompanying me down the front porch steps. "Kind of amazing."

The feel of his hand around mine is divine after two days apart. "Yeah, this is so much better. We don't actually have to go to that outlet mall, by the way. I only said that so Mum wouldn't assume we just want to go make out somewhere."

"Don't we?" he asks, opening the passenger door for me with a wink that makes me tingle all over.

I return it. "Only if you can find a good parking spot."

Grinning, he gets into the car and starts the engine.

Five minutes later, he pulls into the same little office complex as before—deserted again, since it's Sunday—then around back to the exact same space.

Turning off the engine, he gives me a toe-curling smile. "This spot worked pretty well last time."

"Good point." I unbuckle my seatbelt and lean toward him.

His arms come around my back and then we're kissing—*really* kissing. My worries about our upcoming separation and everything else dissolve while I focus on nothing but Tristan.

After a blissful twenty minutes or so, I pull slightly away with a happy sigh. "I feel at least two hundred percent better than I did an hour ago. I wish we could stay here all day."

"Mm," he agrees, but then his smile gets wistful. "You'll be gone how long? Five days? It's going to feel like forever."

"Four nights, but if we get back late Sunday we won't see each other till Monday morning. And yeah, it will."

For a long moment I just stare at him, memorizing the perfect lines of his face so I'll have a mental picture to sustain me while I'm gone. Tristan gazes back like he's doing the same thing...and then we're kissing again, which is even better.

After several more wonderful minutes, we finally release each other again and I snuggle against his shoulder. "I'm going to miss you so much."

"No more than I'll miss you." He rests his cheek on the top of my head. "I sure hope it'll be worth it."

"Me, too." Then, before I can get too distracted again, I say, "So, um, do you still talk to your dad sometimes? How's he doing these days?" I figure I owe it to M to at least ask before sharing anything classified.

Not surprisingly, Tristan seems startled by the abrupt change of subject—and not particularly pleased. "Why would you care how *he's* doing? You were nearly killed because he—" He breaks off with a shudder.

"He's still in Dun Cloch, of course," he continues after a moment, "but he seems okay. Mother calls him every few days but they never talk long. All he ever wants to do is complain and blame everybody else and she gets tired of it in a hurry. So do I, if she makes me take the phone. He still insists he didn't do anything wrong." Tristan shakes his head, scowling now.

"I'm sorry I brought it up," I say—truthfully, since it totally spoiled the mood. "You hadn't mentioned him for a while so I was just curious."

"No, it's okay. I just try not to think about him if I can avoid it."

"Sorry," I repeat, squeezing his hand so he'll know I mean it.

Through that touch, I sense his lingering anger at his father but definitely no sympathy for him, or any trace of admiration. M was definitely wrong about *that* being a reason I shouldn't tell Tristan the truth.

Reassured, I say, "So, you know how you've been wondering how M and I found out about being sisters?"

"Yeah, along with everyone else. But it's okay, Molly. You made it clear M doesn't want you to tell me."

"That *was* true but I, uh, convinced her to change her mind."

A little frown forms between his perfect brows. "Convinced? Do you mean you used…'push' on her?"

I blink, because that possibility never even occurred to me. "I…I don't *think* so. Definitely not on purpose! Anyway, she said I can tell you and I want you to know."

But he shakes his head. "No. Not if it's classified. Is that why you asked about my father?"

"Well…yeah. M was a little worried about that, but since—"

"No, she's right. As long as I'm in contact with him, it *is* safer not to tell me anything he shouldn't know. I get it. Let's…talk about something else, okay?"

At his pleading expression, my determination to tell him about the Archives wavers. The idea was to make him feel better about himself, not stress him out.

"Are you sure?"

"I am." There's no compromise in his tone—or in what I sense from him. "What do you say we work some more on the telepathy thing until we have to go back?"

15

Coevolution

BECAUSE I'D PLANNED to use this time alone to finally explain everything to Tristan, I'm disappointed. But he's so very determined to keep me from doing that, I capitulate. "Okay. Sure. We can try our telepathy again instead."

His smile is sympathetic. "I'm sorry, Molly. If I could be absolutely sure—"

Leaning over, I cut off his words with a kiss that I hope conveys all the love and trust I feel for him. As he responds, I can feel his uncertainty fading. Still, this probably isn't the best time to push it.

A minute or two later, I pull back with a smile. "So, telepathy?"

Though his gaze is still smoldering, he nods. "Maybe we should try not looking at each other this time, so we don't get so...distracted?"

That gets a chuckle from me. "Good idea. How about we both stare at something boring, like that loading door, so we can *just* focus on picking up each other's thoughts?"

Like Tuesday night we clasp hands, but this time look straight ahead, through the windshield.

I "listen" for a minute or so but don't sense anything except Tristan's mounting frustration, which I share. Then I try sending a brief thought to him.

What color is that "no parking" sign?

He stiffens slightly, then turns to frown at me. "Did you—?"

"What did you hear?" I ask excitedly. "Did it work?"

He's still frowning. "I…thought I heard *something*. The word 'color,' maybe?"

"I did think that word to you! I asked what color that sign is. I didn't hear anything at all from you, though."

"Oh. Um, maybe because I was too busy listening for *your* thoughts to try sending one."

I laugh. "Same here, until right at the end. No wonder neither of us picked up anything at first. Okay, now I'll listen and you try sending a thought to me."

Nodding, he faces forward again, brow furrowed. For a full minute or more I don't hear anything but my own heartbeat. I'm about to give up when I detect a faint echo of Tristan's voice in my mind saying, *probably stupid.*

"It's not stupid," I retort out loud.

His brown eyes snap to mine. "You heard that?"

"Barely, and only the words 'probably stupid.' I'm guessing there was more?"

"Yeah, a whole lot more. Those were just the last two words I thought." He's clearly discouraged.

I'm not.

"Hey, this is real progress! Even that tiny bit puts us *way* ahead of Sean and Kira *and* M and Rigel, considering how long we've been bonded."

"Oh." His brows shoot up. "I guess you're right! Should we—?"

Before he can finish, I glance at the clock on the dash. "Oh, crap! We told my mum we'd be back by two-thirty and it's nearly that now. We'd better go."

Tristan's frustration echoes my own, but he releases my hands and starts the car. "We should keep practicing, every chance we get. It would be great if we could get to the point of talking over distances before you leave Wednesday, but I guess that's pretty unrealistic."

I laugh. "I doubt even M and Rigel can talk from *that* far away yet. The most she's ever told me about was less than ten miles, when she was kidnapped."

"Okay, super unrealistic, then. At least we'll have our phones."

"And I'll be sure to set aside time every day when we can talk privately," I promise. "We'll get through this, Tristan. M and Rigel have dealt with a whole, whole lot worse. With any luck, when I get back we'll suddenly be way better at telepathy and…everything else."

He smiles over at me. "That'll be cool. Hope it works that way."

"Let's assume it will, okay? Maybe that will make it easier."

.⁺⁺

Even though I know I'll see him again in less than an hour, it's a wrench to say goodbye to Tristan when he drops me off. Again, it makes me worry how I'll handle our Thanksgiving separation.

When my family gets to NuAgra half an hour later, I immediately look around for him and spot him across the big atrium-style lobby, talking to M, Rigel and Kira. Sean and I head over to join them.

"We just need to focus on the possible benefits," Rigel is saying when we come up.

"Talking about our Thanksgiving plans?" I ask quietly, taking Tristan's outstretched hand.

Kira nods. "It'll be the first time Sean and I have been apart for more than twenty-four hours." They clasp hands, too. "Sure hope it'll be worth it."

"I'll bet it will be," Tristan says encouragingly. "Molly and I were apart for not quite two full days this weekend, then this afternoon we managed actual telepathy for the first time."

"Already?" M's clearly startled.

"Just a word or two," I admit. "But when we tried last week we couldn't even do that, so it was a definite improvement."

Sean and Kira look both impressed and hopeful. "If a separation that brief can make a difference—" Kira begins.

"A longer one should make even more," Sean concludes. "Let's remember that if things are…bad next weekend."

At that moment there's an announcement inviting everyone to continue through the main lobby to the rear courtyard for the picnic.

"Brr, it's going to be cold out there," Kira says, reminding me again that this is her first winter on Earth.

When we step outside, though, it's perfectly comfortable, even though the temps are hovering around freezing today.

"Wow, I didn't know they could climate control an area this big," Tristan says, gesturing around the huge courtyard behind the greenhouses, between the back wings of the main building.

"My dad said they were hoping to get it operational in time for the picnic," Rigel tells us.

M looks around appreciatively at the long tables and benches, easily enough to seat everyone. "Nice." Then she turns to the rest of us. "So, I was thinking that as soon as we get back, we should—"

She breaks off as several more *Echtran* teens join us. All but one are Jewel High students.

The one who isn't steps forward. As he bows to M, then to me, I recognize him as the basketball player the other cheerleaders were talking about at the Alexandria game on Wednesday.

"Excellency, Princess," Alan says. "This is Eric. His parents just started working at NuAgra last month."

The tall, dark-haired boy nods. "I met Alan, Sean and Liam at our basketball game against Jewel a few days ago. They, ah, warned me I should probably be more careful about playing too well."

"We all should." Sean grimaces sympathetically. "Otherwise the *Echtran* Council might ban us from sports completely. Right, M?"

Eric's eyes widen—probably at Sean's use of her nickname—as she nods. "They've seriously considered it already. If there are any others at your school, maybe pass that warning along."

"I will. Um, thanks...."

"M is fine," she tells him, smiling. "It's what I've gone by for years, since way before I knew...anything."

Kira touches Sean's arm. "Didn't you say you were going to talk to your mum about some kind of *caidpel* group or league here?"

"Yes, Kyna mentioned it at last night's Council meeting," M says. "I'm afraid I have no idea what would be involved, though."

"Kira does," Sean volunteers. "How big does the field need to be?"

Liam jumps in to answer. "120 meters by 75 meters. Right over there would be perfect." He points, grinning. "All we'd need are goalposts."

"And balls and *camman*," Kira adds. "But yeah, if the Council is on board, we could probably make that space work." She's clearly getting into the idea, too.

"Let's go pace it out now!" Alan exclaims, heading that way. "If they say we can use that area, maybe they can get all the equipment we need from Dun Cloch."

Kira and Sean follow him, as do most of the other teens. M and Rigel hang back, as does Tristan.

"Not interested?" I ask him.

He shrugs. "Maybe later, if anything actually comes of it—especially if they decide not to let me or Rigel play football next year."

"Yeah, if that happens, maybe I'll learn to play, too," Rigel says, then glances off to the side, where several people appear to be waiting to talk to M. "Hm. Guess you should do the Sovereign thing for a bit," he murmurs to her.

She quickly hides a grimace. "Guess so. Ah, well."

Pasting on a smile, she turns and the small group surges forward, a couple of them frowning at her and Rigel's clasped hands. If M notices, she doesn't let on. She did say she plans to keep throwing their relationship in everyone's faces until they finally accept it.

I hope it works.

"C'mon," I whisper to Tristan, tugging him in the opposite direction. I don't want anyone to think I expect them to pay court to me, too.

Tristan doesn't argue, though his slightly amused look tells me he knows why I want to be elsewhere.

Soon people start coming up to me anyway, probably because it's the first big *Echtran* social occasion since the news about me broke. Most just want to introduce themselves—even if we've already met—and congratulate me. But a few make comments that bother me.

"It's nice to see you taking a more *traditional* path than your sister has, Princess," one woman says, glancing over her shoulder at M and Rigel a short distance away. "I know I'm not the only one who finds that very comforting."

Before I can think of a way to defend M without being rude, she smiles broadly at Tristan and moves away.

A moment later a man hints that I'm wise to defer to M until I can consolidate support of my own. "Particularly as there's no real rush."

"I'm not—!" I begin, but he immediately steps back and bows.

"Of course not, Princess. Just know that many of us will be behind you, when the time comes." With another bow, he moves off as quickly as the woman did.

I turn worriedly to Tristan. "Is that what most people think I'm doing? Biding my time and trying to build some...some faction of my own?"

"Only those who put too much stock in that interview article," he assures me.

"Exactly like Gwendolyn Gannett wanted them to do. Ugh. If M doesn't set the record straight in her next *Echtran Enquirer* column, I just might write one of my own."

He gives my hand an encouraging squeeze. "That's the spirit."

But then an older couple approaches, focused on Tristan more than me.

"You're Connor's son, aren't you?" the man asks.

Tristan nods, looking wary now.

"Any truth to the rumor he was removed from the Council because he leaked the truth about our new Princess to you before anyone else was supposed to know?" He flicks a curious glance my way.

"What? No!" Tristan replies. "Of course not. Where did you hear—?"

"Sorry, sorry." Though he takes a step back, a smirk still plays about the man's mouth. "Just a rumor, as I said. By the way, congratulations, Princess."

He and his wife both bow to me, then walk away whispering together.

Now I'm the one reassuring Tristan. "It's just that interview again, and her stupid insinuations," I tell him. "Guess it's common knowledge now your father left Jewel?"

Tristan nods glumly. "But not why. Mother said the Council thinks it would scare people to know you were attacked. More may come out in that trial, though."

"If so, we'll just—" I start to say when there's an odd whirring sound overhead. At the same time, I hear startled exclamations all around us.

Looking up, I see what appears to be a small, white drone hovering twenty feet or so above our gathering. Then, almost before I can get a good look at it, a thin beam of light hits it and it falls like a stone, people on the ground hastily jumping out of the way.

Before anyone can approach it, Rigel's dad hurries forward, accompanied by two other men. Leaning down, he examines it briefly, then nods to one of the others, who scoops the fallen drone into a small crate. Then they all head toward the main NuAgra building, though Mr. Stuart pauses briefly for a quick word with M.

A moment later she and Rigel come over to us, looking slightly shaken. I also see Sean and Kira racing our way from the hoped-for *caidpel* field.

"What was that?" Sean demands as they reach us, keeping his voice low.

Before M can answer, at least half the people at the picnic converge on her, all asking the same thing. With a tiny shrug, she touches a button at her neckline I hadn't even noticed till then and turns to face the worried crowd.

"No need for alarm," her suddenly-amplified voice assures them. "I'm told it was a drone of the sort readily available to *Duchas*, but that NuAgra's security system jammed its signal before any video could be sent offsite. I did warn you they're becoming more curious, though the Council is working on ways to allay their suspicions. Again, please let us know at once if any of your *Duchas* neighbors say or do anything that seems concerning. And now, I believe it's time to eat!"

She taps off the mic and turns back to our little group. "Hopefully that'll avoid a real panic. Mr. Stuart will know more once his men have had a chance to analyze the thing."

We disperse to fill our own plates then, not wanting to spark more rumors by continuing to whisper together. Not surprisingly, the food is both excellent and abundant. Mum's not the only one who brought enough to feed a small army.

An hour or so later, as everyone's mostly done eating, M makes another brief address, this one obviously scripted in advance, mostly thanking everyone for coming—though she concludes by promising to let everyone know if they discover anything important about that unexpected drone. I'm impressed again by what an awesome leader she's become over the past year.

Once nearly everyone has left, Mum pulls M and me aside to say the Council wants us to stick around while they discuss what to do about that drone. I give Tristan a quick kiss goodbye before joining the others in one of NuAgra's conference rooms.

"If nothing else, this has been an excellent test of our new, enhanced security system," Mr. Stuart tells us once Kyna and Nara holo in from DC. "It was able to detect and disable that *Duchas* drone quite efficiently, after confirming it did not contain antimatter. A different protocol would have been used if it had."

Everyone seems pleased by that.

"What should we do with the drone now?" Malcolm asks. "Apparently NuAgra has already received a few rather hostile calls from its owner asking to have it back."

"Who are they from? Do you know?" M asks.

He glances down at his tablet. "A Mr. Farmer. Isn't he—?"

"The same person who kidnapped me back in September," M confirms. "The conspiracy theorist. And yes, he can be pretty hostile."

"In that case," Mr. Stuart says, "I would suggest we return the, er, remains of the drone after either erasing its flash memory or replacing it with our own footage. Perhaps a collision with a bird?"

M and I both snicker and a few others smile.

"Great idea," M tells him. "Better than wiping it, which he'd consider proof we're hiding something here."

"Hopefully the tour we discussed last night will help," Breann suggests. "Malcolm and I will start planning for it right away."

Mrs. Roark offers to help, too.

After that, Kyna adjourns our impromptu meeting. I accompany my family out to the van, already looking forward to seeing Tristan tomorrow morning.

.⁺+

On the way to school Monday morning, I sense the same sort of disquiet from Tristan I did at the end of last week.

"You're bothered by some of the stuff people said yesterday, aren't you?" I ask. "Especially the bit about your father."

"Some, yeah. I hate people thinking I only want to be with you because of…who you are. You were bothered, too," he reminds me.

"Only by what they said about you and me, versus M and Rigel. It's like they're trying to pit me against M, even though she's doing an awesome job as Sovereign. Way better than I could ever do—or would ever want to do."

He reaches over and covers my hand with his. "I think you underestimate yourself, Molly. But I promise to support whatever *you* want to do, one hundred percent. Always."

Gratitude wells up in me as his sincerity comes through loud and clear. Having Tristan fully in my corner is incredibly comforting… especially since I don't always get that feeling from Mum and Dad. I wish more than ever he'd let me tell him about the Archives, so I can prove how much I trust him.

I "check in" on Tristan's emotions periodically throughout the school day. Though he's not always as down as he was this morning, he never feels very *up*, either. After school I'll try again to explain about the Archives. Planning out how I'll convince him to listen helps to keep my mind off of *my* worries. Mostly.

"Are you picking me up after cheerleading practice today?" I ask as we're leaving sixth period, our last class before he leaves for NuAgra and more Bodyguard training.

"Sure. Our sessions never last more than two hours. I'm usually back here in plenty of time to do homework in my car while I wait. Which reminds me—do you have that worksheet from yesterday's Chem lab? I accidentally left mine at home."

The warning bell rings, so rather than page through my binder for it, I just hand him the whole thing. "Check the tab marked 'Chemistry.' It should be there."

"Cool, thanks. I'll give it back when I pick you up." He gives me a quick, discreet kiss and heads off, while I hurry to Chorus.

Tristan's waiting in the parking lot when I get out of cheerleading, just like he promised. Eager for a *real* kiss, I trot to his car and get in, smiling in anticipation.

Quickly shoving papers back into my binder, he hands it to me before leaning over to give me my kiss—but the second his lips touch mine, I can tell he's more upset than he's been all day.

"Uh-oh," I say, after too brief a kiss. "What's wrong? More ugly gossip out at NuAgra?"

He blinks, then shakes his head. "Not— That is— Why did you—? No, never mind."

Confused now, I cling to his hand, trying to figure him out. "Tristan? What is it?"

"It's...nothing." He smiles at me then, but it's clearly forced.

"It's not nothing, I can tell." When he only shrugs, I continue, "Maybe you'll feel better if I tell you the truth about how M and I found out—"

"No!" His forcefulness startles me. "Don't. Not when— Anyway, didn't you admit you might have cheated to get M to agree you could? With your 'push'?"

I frown. "No, I said I didn't think I had."

"But you weren't sure. I saw my father abuse his ability plenty of times. Hell, I did it myself when I first got here, or tried to. It didn't work, but not for lack of me trying. I'd hate to think—"

"Okay, okay!" I throw up my hands in surrender. "If you're that worried about it, I won't say another word. Though I honestly think it would be fine."

He just leans over and gives me another kiss, a longer one this time, before starting the car. "Thanks, Molly."

On the way home, he tells me every detail about today's training session. Probably to keep me from bringing up that other subject. When he drops me off, he says he'll see me tomorrow, since he has stuff to do at home tonight. I wonder if it's just an excuse, but I don't ask.

I'm still puzzling over what could have ramped up Tristan's anxieties so much when I sit down to do my homework after dinner. Frowning, I open my binder—and gasp.

There, stuffed roughly into the front pocket, is a sheet of paper I immediately recognize. Unfolding it with shaking fingers, I see I'm right.

1. *Arrogant*

2. *Prejudiced*

3. *Huge sense of entitlement...*

The day after our first, angry kiss, when I was desperately trying to purge Tristan from my mind, I made this list of all his very worst attributes—then. I totally forgot about it after he and I got together, or I would definitely have shredded it. I wish I had, since this is obviously what upset him so badly.

I only hesitate a moment before calling him.

"Hey, Molly, what's up?" He sounds wary.

"I just figured out what upset you, what you found in my binder," I say, then continue before he can interrupt. "Tristan, I made that list forever ago, when we were both still determined to avoid each other. I don't believe any of those things about you now, not even a little bit! I promise!"

There's a long silence at the other end before he asks, "Then why do you still have it?"

"Because I completely forgot about it! I've never even *looked* at it since I first made it, I swear I haven't. How did you—? I mean, it wasn't with my Chemistry stuff, I'm sure."

"Um, I was curious about what you'd written in Creative Writing, so I peeked...and then found that. Sorry. I guess that kind of crossed a line, almost like snooping in your diary, huh?"

I feel color creeping up my neck, thinking about some of the poems and stories I've written recently. "A little, yeah. I almost never look at my older efforts, which is probably why I never noticed that list still in there. Anyway, you need to know I haven't thought those things about you in forever. Definitely not since—"

"No, I get it. If I'd written anything about you then, I wouldn't want you to see it now, either. Sorry, Molly."

"It's okay," I tell him.

We chat for a few minutes then. I'm relieved to hear the tension is gone from his voice, though I wish I could touch him to confirm how he's feeling now. I'll do that first thing tomorrow.

Meanwhile, there's something else I need to clear up. Since it's only eight o'clock, as soon as I hang up with Tristan, I give M a call.

"Are you busy right now?" I ask her.

"Not very, just going over some files. What do you need?"

"Can I come over for a few minutes? I need to ask you something, and don't want to do it over the phone."

Though she's clearly curious, she immediately agrees. Leaving my homework undone on my desk, I hurry downstairs and grab my coat.

"Mum, Dad, I'm going over to M's for a little bit. I should be back before nine."

They don't object—they never do, when M's involved—so five minutes later I ring her doorbell. Guessing I don't want to be overheard by her aunt and uncle, she invites me upstairs to her room after pouring us each some milk and grabbing a stack of her aunt's chocolate pecan cookies.

"So, what is it?" she asks as soon as we're sitting cross-legged on her bed with the cookies between us.

"I...well...I wanted to make *absolutely* sure you're okay with Tristan knowing about the Archives. That you don't feel like I somehow...pressured you into saying I could tell him. Like, with 'push.'"

Her brows go up, then she focuses on me sort of like Mum does when she's trying to detect a lie. "You've really been worrying about that, haven't you?"

"Yeah. A little." I don't tell her it was Tristan who first mentioned it.

"Well, don't. There was no 'push' involved. I definitely would have known. You can stop worrying."

A rush of relief floods through me. "Thanks, M. I haven't told him yet, but I really, really want to. Mostly because once he knows about the Archives, he'll finally be convinced his dad couldn't possibly have found out about me earlier."

"Like Gwendolyn Gannett implied." M's smile is understanding. "I wish there were a way to prove it to everyone else without letting them know about the Scepter."

"Me, too!" I fervently agree.

"But I'm fine with Tristan knowing. Partly because it means so much to you—and also because your arguments made total sense, once I got past my prejudice against Connor and, um, the idea that what you and Tristan have could be as special as what I have with Rigel."

Because that confession obviously embarrasses her, I lean over and give her a hug. "What you two have is amazingly special. That'll be true even if hundreds of other couples develop *graell* bonds."

She hugs me back. "You're right. And…how cool would that be?"

.⁺₊

Tuesday, our last full day together before I leave for Kentucky, Tristan and I are nearly as inseparable as when his father was threatening to send him back to Colorado. Though we sit apart from the others at lunch, the school cafeteria doesn't seem like the best place to tell him about the Archives. I'm totally determined to do it before tomorrow, though.

That afternoon the *Echtran Enquirer* comes out, with M's next "From the Sovereign's Desk" installment. Just like she promised, she directly addresses the nasty distortions in Gwendolyn Gannett's column about my interview.

> Contrary to what you may have read here last week, there has never been even the slightest friction between Princess Malena and me. Nor do I "miss" having her act as my Handmaid, as I was never comfortable being waited upon anyway. Also, I will be more than delighted to share my duties with her in the future, if she's willing. Finally, I can positively assure you that absolutely no one could possibly have known Malena's true identity before she and I discovered it ourselves, then shared it with the *Echtran* Council.

"Good job! Thanks, M," I tell her after reading it on her omni-phone right after cheerleading practice.

"Thanks from me, too," Tristan says. "Of course, Gannett had to get another little dig in. Look." He reaches over and brings up her column.

Sure enough, though she spends most of it crowing about the job she expects to have when the new *Echtran* news network begins broadcasting, at the end she writes:

I've now had the opportunity to speak with a fair cross-section of our people and it seems I was right. Many express a sense of comfort on learning our newly-discovered Princess appears more traditionally-minded than her sister.

I snort and shake my head. "Guess she couldn't resist. Still, I think M wins this round."

Laughing, the others agree.

"So," Tristan says as he and I get in his car a couple minutes later, "okay if we take a little...detour on the way home?"

"Definitely." I grin across at him. "This will be our last chance for a bit of privacy until next week—practically forever!"

His mood is better than it's been in days after reading M's article, which makes me hope he'll be less resistant now to me finally telling him the whole truth.

Eager as I am to do that, when he pulls into a spot behind an ice cream place that's closed for the season, the *first* thing I want to do is make out. Which we do, for at least fifteen wonderful minutes.

Finally, knowing Mum will ask questions if I'm *too* late getting home, I pull away far enough to look at him.

"While we have this chance, there's something I really, really need to tell you."

Like I expect, he frowns. "*Need* to? Is this the same thing—?"

"Yes, but I talked again with M last night and she's positive I didn't use any 'push' when I convinced her you should know. She still thinks you should—though you have to promise not to tell another soul, not even your mom. Okay?"

"Of course. You know I'd never do anything that could get you in trouble."

I still sense worry from him, so squeeze his hand reassuringly. "I know you wouldn't, but I told M I'd make you promise. It, um, has to do with M's Royal Scepter."

His brows go up. "With her— What?"

"I know you've never seen it in person, but you've seen pictures of it, right?"

He nods, still looking totally confused.

"Well, it's not just a pretty staff. It's also an amazing technological device that includes an Archive reader that only the Sovereign bloodline can access."

I go on to explain that the main Archive includes the stored images and memories of all the Sovereigns of the past five hundred-plus years, and how interactive they are. Then I tell him about the blue crystal my real parents left me, and what led up to M and me realizing it was another Archive—one containing M's and my parents.

As the words tumble out of me, Tristan's confusion is gradually replaced by amazement, and then happiness…for me.

"Wow, that must have been wonderful, huh? Actually getting to see and talk to your parents?" he asks at the conclusion.

"*So* wonderful! For M, too. Mikal, our father, isn't in the main Archive, since he never had a chance to become Sovereign, so she'd never talked to either of them before. And it was that same evening, maybe two hours later, that she told the Council about me, so…"

He finishes my sentence for me, realization dawning. "So there really *was* no possible way anyone else could have found out sooner."

"Exactly. No matter what anyone else chooses to believe, M and I—and now you—*absolutely* know that."

Then we're kissing again and the relief I feel from him reassures me once and for all that I made the right decision by telling him. Sending back all the love and trust I can, I silently vow never to keep secrets from Tristan again.

Rigel

16

Genetic drift

"YOU'RE *SURE* this isn't just another ploy by the Council to separate us permanently?" I ask M as we walk hand and hand across the school parking lot at lunchtime Wednesday. Because it's the day before Thanksgiving, school let out early. "You'll definitely be back by Monday, right?"

"Yes," she promises. "We're *only* leaving to make it easier for your dad and his crew to install all that spiffy new security equipment in our houses. You've been pestering for me to have that."

Which is true. "I know. I just hate being without you, M."

"Ditto, but we've been through a lot worse."

I snort. "Yeah, like last Thanksgiving." When most of them did want to keep us apart for good.

M picks up my thought. *This is totally different,* she thinks to me. *Last year I wasn't Sovereign and hardly anybody believed in our* graell *bond yet. Plus that was ten days and this will be less than half that long. We'll be okay.*

"We will," I reply aloud, trying to sound upbeat. "Let's think of this as a shortcut to improving the others' *graell* powers, giving us the extra edge we'll need to counter whatever Devyn and his gang have planned."

As we approach my car, I focus on the wonderful way her touch makes me feel, enjoying it while I still can. "What time is your family taking off?" I ask as I open the passenger door for her.

"We'll probably just eat a quick lunch and head out. Mrs. O'Gara wants to get there in time to buy groceries before dinner."

Nodding glumly, I get in and start the car.

By mutual agreement, we stop a block away from M's house for a quick makeout session to help fortify us ahead of what are bound to be a sucky few days. It's way too brief, of course, but I'm in a slightly better mood when I drop her off a couple minutes later.

"Remember, we're going to test our range during the drive," I say, as she leans back into the car for one last kiss.

"Right. I'll text you once we're on the road. Love you, Rigel!"

"Love you, M. Always."

Despite our bracing words to each other, I can tell we're both on the verge of tears. I drive off before either of us can see the other one cry.

Half an hour later, I get M's text that they've left for Kentucky. Telling my dad I've got stuff to do, I take my second sandwich up to my room so we can talk telepathically without me being obvious.

Where are you now? I send to her as I sit down at my desk.

Just left Jewel, heading South. Then, a few minutes later, *We're about ten miles away now—we just passed a mile marker.*

I'm pretty sure that's a new record for us. *Keep pinging me every couple of minutes or so.*

Will do.

As expected, communicating takes more and more effort the farther away she gets. Finally, so faint I'm not positive I don't imagine it, I hear, *...loop around Indy.*

Wow, almost fifty miles, I think back, but she doesn't respond. A moment later, she texts me.

I think that was our limit, but wow, almost fifty miles!

I grin. *That's the last thing I tried to say, word for word.*

LOL, I didn't actually hear you, but good to know we're still on the same wavelength. Now I should probably stop being antisocial. Talk tonight?

You bet!

After that, I settle in for a boring afternoon of reading and home-work. At Dad's suggestion, I'm supplementing my regular school studies with some of the same stuff M has had to learn as Sovereign.

When I mentioned to M I was doing this, I could tell she was pleased, though she never suggested it herself—probably worrying I'd take it as criticism. But I've also heard the snarky things people are saying about how ill-prepared I am to be Royal Consort someday and the last thing I want to do is reflect poorly on M.

Opening the scroll-book Dad gave me, I start reading up on the various branches of the Nuathan government.

Shortly after dinner, M calls. Grabbing my cell, I head back up to my room so we can talk privately, wishing again I had an actual omni so this could be a holo-call.

"Hey, M. Guess you got there okay?" I ask as I leave the kitchen.

"Yeah, the drive was fine, though Molly and Sean spent a lot of it stressing over being away from their significant others. I did my best to talk them down. Oh! On the way here, we finally told my aunt and uncle about Molly being my sister. Needless to say, they were pretty boggled."

I laugh. "I'll bet. Think they'll act weird around her now?"

"Probably, but hopefully they'll get over it before we're back in Jewel. Uncle Louie tried to insist she call them aunt and uncle, but I explained how awkward that would be back home."

"Hope he remembers that." Her uncle's not the sharpest tack in the box, I've noticed. "What's the house like?"

"Nice! Kind of old-fashioned, but comfy. It's on a lake, so a pretty view, though of course it's too cold to swim. Even if it weren't, I found out Sean and Molly don't know how. We should teach them this summer."

That surprises me, though I guess it shouldn't, considering how scarce water is on Mars, where they grew up. "We should. So what *is* there to do there?"

"Not much, though Uncle Louie and Mr. O plan to do some fishing. Thanksgiving tomorrow, of course, then...mostly just hoping none of us get too sick."

"Yeah, how will Sean and Molly explain that to their parents? They haven't mentioned their bonds yet, have they?"

"Nope. They both worry how their parents will react, though for different reasons, I think. I'll try to help cover for them if it gets bad. Maybe it won't, since it's only their first separation. Ours have gotten worse each time so far."

She's right—which doesn't bode well for this one. We talk for another half hour or so, then she has to go join the others.

It's only been eight hours or so, but I already miss her like crazy. It's going to be a long four days.

.⁺.

"I'm glad to see you haven't lost your appetite yet," my mom says encouragingly as I finish my second slice of pumpkin pie the next evening. "I hope this means that antidote my mother created for you last Spring is still in effect."

"Yeah, I hope so, too." I don't tell her I'm already feeling the beginnings of a headache...and starting to regret those last few bites of pie.

Though this Thanksgiving has been way better than last year's, I can't claim I've enjoyed it much, knowing M is nearly three hundred miles away. Not as far as DC, where I was last year, but way too far to sense each other.

"What do you say we set up a holo call with M's omni in a little while?" my dad says then, with a sort of forced heartiness.

Guess I'm not hiding my low spirits as well as I thought. But his offer does perk me up. "Can we? That would be great."

At his suggestion, I text M half an hour later asking if this will be a good time to do that, and she instantly replies that it will. Dad fiddles with his omni for a few seconds, then she appears, just like she's here in our living room.

"Hey, Rigel! Hey, Dr. Stuart, Mr. Stuart. Happy Thanksgiving!"

We all return her greeting, but I'm drinking in her face, her voice. And wishing we were doing this privately, instead of with my parents. Then she does something at her end, and suddenly the O'Garas and M's aunt and uncle are all in our living room, too. So much for privacy.

Still, it's kind of nice. Once M's Uncle Louie stops geeking out over the whole holo thing, we all chat together for a while. It's almost like having M here with me—except I can't feel her *brath*, which I'm already longing for.

After twenty minutes or so, M asks if the grownups would mind if just we kids talk for a bit, so Mom and Dad leave me alone in Dad's office with the omni. Then the O'Garas and Truitts wink out, too.

M waits a moment, looking over her shoulder, then says, "Okay, it's just us now. How are you feeling, Rigel?"

"Mostly okay, so far. How about you? All three of you."

Sean shrugs. "Also mostly okay, though I miss Kira a lot, of course. Wish she had an omni, so we could do this."

"Tristan has one," Molly points out. "I'll ask if he and Kira can get together sometime tomorrow. Between his omni and yours, the four of us can do another holo-chat. It's not like we have anything else planned at our end."

"Oh, yeah. Great idea, Mol," Sean agrees. "We can check with both of them as soon as we finish here." Then he frowns. "How do you think we'll all be feeling tomorrow?" he asks M and me.

"You guys might be fine," M says. "The *graell* hasn't been studied enough to know whether the *tinnea* is universal when couples are apart. Maybe Rigel and I are an anomaly."

Something in her tone catches my attention. "Are you starting to feel something already?"

"I was okay when I sat down to dinner, but then the headache started and…" She puts a hand over her stomach.

Molly immediately looks concerned. "I noticed you barely touched dessert. I guess that antidote's not still doing the trick after all?"

"Guess not. Which is actually kind of a relief."

Sean and Molly both stare at her. "You *want* to get sick?" Molly asks incredulously.

"Not getting sick would mean I'd lost that part of my bond with Rigel," she explains, stretching a hand toward me.

I reach back and our fingers phase through each other—predictable, but frustrating.

"Not to mention losing our biggest argument for why we *have* to be together," I add and she nods.

Molly nudges Sean. "Let's give them a few minutes of alone time while we call Tristan and Kira about tomorrow." He immediately agrees and they wink out.

M waits long enough for them to leave whatever room she's in, then says, "I already miss you a lot. I love you, Rigel."

"I love you, too, M. But you were right yesterday, we'll get through this. I'm feeling about like you are, by the way. Little bit of a headache and wishing I hadn't eaten quite so much at dinner. So not too bad, yet. Everybody there getting along okay? Must be a little weird for your aunt and uncle, huh?"

She grins. "Aunt Theresa's definitely been weirded out a few times, and she gets so twitchy if Martian politics come up, we've mostly avoided that topic. Uncle Louie just thinks it's all impossibly cool. My aunt and I keep reminding him not to tell any of his buddies about it when we get back to Jewel."

"After what happened a couple months back, you'd think he'd get that."

"You'd think." Half worried, half amused, she shakes her head. "Mrs. O was up to her old tricks at dinner, seating me next to Sean. We just humored her, though Molly made a crack about it."

A year ago that would have bothered me. Not now. Sean clearly abandoned the last traces of his original agenda toward M as soon as he and Kira got together.

We talk for a few more minutes, then with several more "I love yous," we reluctantly sign off, promising to talk more tomorrow.

My parents are in the living room, where Dad's telling Mom about what still needs to be done tomorrow with those security installations.

"We got a good start today, so there's a chance we could finish by Saturday night."

I hand him his omni back. "Would that mean M and the O'Garas could come back early?" I ask hopefully.

"That would be up to them." Though his smile is understanding, I know he can't *really* understand.

Which abruptly irritates me. "I'm going to bed."

Mom looks at me in sudden concern. "Are you—?"

"Yeah, a little. Mostly just tired. See you in the morning."

.⁺.

Like I expect, I feel worse when I wake up the next day than I did last night...and it's only Friday.

Over breakfast, which I mostly pick at, I ask Dad if I can help with those security installations at M's and the O'Garas' house. Anything that might get M back to me sooner.

Though he looks surprised, he shrugs. "I suppose so. If nothing else, you may be able to assist my technicians by holding things steady, handing them tools, that sort of thing."

I do my best, but I feel progressively worse as the morning goes on, making me pretty useless. Dad clearly notices. When he and I go home for lunch—which I barely touch—he suggests I do something different that afternoon.

"This might be a good time for you to study up a bit more on the workings of our people's government," he begins, then takes a closer look at me. "Or perhaps a nap?"

Dully, I nod. "Yeah, okay. Thanks, Dad."

A nap sounds great, but I go upstairs fully intending to spend at least an hour reading more out of my book-scroll first. Once I reach my room, though, my bed is so inviting I succumb to that, instead.

I've only slept an hour or so when M texts me to say Molly and Sean are planning a holo-call with their significant others in an hour.

You want to be there, too? Might be better than borrowing your dad's omni again.

Sure, I text back. *Where?*

Tristan's house. He'll text you the address.

Thanks to that nap, I feel alert enough now to drive, so forty-five minutes later I plug Tristan's address into my GPS and head out. On the way, I swing by Kira's apartment complex, since Sean asked if I could give her a ride. She's waiting for me out front.

"Thanks, Rigel," she says, getting into the car. Though she's smiling, I can tell she's not feeling her best, either.

My return smile is sympathetic. "No problem."

We both lapse into silence for a minute or two, then she asks, "Is it as weird for you as it is for me, hanging out with so many Royals these days?"

I blink, startled. "I...hadn't thought much about it. I mean, M's the first *Echtran* my age I ever met. Nobody had ever explained *fines* to me, so I thought 'Royal' just meant a political party on Mars."

Now she's the one who looks startled. "Oh, wow. Growing up in Nuath, there's no escaping *fines* and all the expectations that go with them, but I guess it makes sense that's not as true here. Interesting."

"It matters more here than I used to think," I wryly admit. "Especially to some people. Hopefully that's changing, though."

"Yeah. Hopefully." She sounds wistful.

Following the GPS, I turn into a ritzy neighborhood, then park in front of the mini-mansion Tristan shares with just his mother now. Kira and I go up and ring the doorbell.

"Hey," Tristan greets us. He also looks a shade paler than usual. "Glad you could both come over."

He leads us past a huge living area to a slightly smaller room set up as a sort of library with a square table in the middle. "Mother's out at

NuAgra at the moment," he says as we all sit down. "Good thing, or she'd insist on bringing us snacks. Or do you feel more like eating than I do?"

We both shake our heads.

"When did it start hitting you two?" I ask, mildly curious.

"Not till this morning," Kira answers. "Last night I felt fine."

"Same here," Tristan agrees. "Not much appetite today, though. Head's a little achy. Molly said with you guys it's gotten worse faster every time you've had to be apart?"

I nod. "Seems like." I'm about to elaborate when Tristan's omni pings.

"Ah. Guess they're ready." He brings up the little holo-screen and touches some controls, and a moment later we're surrounded by trees. M, Molly and Sean are all sitting together on a big, fallen trunk, facing us.

"We figured we'd be a lot more private here than in the house," Sean explains. "Especially since M's uncle has a tendency to snoop."

It's a little disorienting to be sitting in a comfortable chair in the middle of the woods, but I can't argue with their reasoning. "Good thinking. I take it your parents haven't noticed anything 'off' about you yet?" I include Kira and Tristan in my question, along with the two O'Garas.

They all shake their heads.

"Though from what M says, that might be trickier tomorrow?" Molly asks.

"Could be," I agree. "Based on how our separations have gone, by tomorrow you might start getting a little fuzzy—so you might want to come up with reasonable-sounding explanations while you can still think clearly."

Sean makes a sound between a laugh and a snort. "Maybe just as well I'm missing tonight's basketball game. I'd definitely be off my form."

"Yeah, well, I have one tomorrow night," Kira reminds him. "I predict right now *that* will be a disaster."

We all wince.

"Want Tristan and me to come, for moral support?" I offer. "Tristan should still be up to driving by then, though I probably won't."

"That's awfully nice, but you don't have to," she tells us, clearly touched. "In fact, I'm thinking the fewer witnesses to the debacle, the better."

Tristan frowns. "Hm. What about our Bodyguard class tomorrow? Gilda's bound to notice something's up."

"You're right," Kira says, grimacing. "Guess we should start working on those excuses, huh?"

For the next half hour, the four who are determined to hide their bonds—for now—brainstorm stuff they can tell their parents to avert suspicion. Then, because there's nothing else any of us would rather be doing, we keep talking until Tristan's mom gets home.

"Let's can do this again tomorrow, if we're all feeling up to it," Molly suggests just before Tristan ends our transmission.

Kira and I chat for a moment with Mrs. Roark on our way out. I drop Kira off, then continue home, where Mom is making turkey tetrazzini from yesterday's leftovers. I normally love that, but right now the smell roils my stomach.

Because I don't want to hurt her feelings, I don't say anything except, "Okay if I just have a cup of tea or something?" Tea always makes me think of M. "Not hungry, sorry."

"Of course I can make you some tea." Her expression is sympathetic. "I'm sorry you're not feeling well, Rigel. It should only be two more days."

"I know. Thanks, Mom."

I go up to my room and ten minutes later she brings me tea and some toast. I'm grateful she doesn't pester me to eat more.

After that, I try to concentrate on that Nuathan book-scroll with all the government info, but mostly I'm just killing time till I can talk to M again.

Two hours later she texts to ask if I can talk and when I reply I can, she immediately calls.

"Hey, M," I answer. "How are you feeling? Better than I am, I hope?"

"I doubt it, but it's not terrible yet. We can definitely make it till Sunday. At least you and I don't have to hide it."

"Yeah, how did that go this evening?"

She manages a tiny chuckle—for my sake? "At dinner I played up how yucky I'm feeling to keep Mrs. O's attention off Sean and Molly while they played with their food. It worked, except she insisted Sean and I try holding hands to see if it would help. She seemed pretty disappointed when it didn't—not that I expected it to."

I'm guiltily relieved to hear that, but don't say so. "Do your aunt and uncle know why you're feeling bad?"

"Yes, I explained it all to Aunt Theresa back in September, when we had all that time together in Mr. Farmer's meat locker. Uncle Louie still tried to insist some grilled, fresh-caught trout would help. Uh, no."

That gets an actual laugh from me. "You said he's teaching Mr. O how to fish?"

"Trying, anyway. But they seem to be enjoying themselves." She pauses and I hear her yawn. "Sorry. I forgot how tired being away from you makes me."

"Same here. I'm planning to turn in as soon as we hang up."

We don't talk much longer, we're both so drowsy. As I get into bed half an hour later, I wonder if I can sleep away the rest of the weekend, until M's back in Jewel.

It's past noon when I wake up the next day, and that's only because I need to go to the bathroom. I'm tempted to go right back to bed, but drag myself downstairs so my parents won't worry *too* much about me.

"Good afternoon, sleepyhead," Mom greets me a little too cheerfully when I find her in the kitchen. "Are you feeling any better today?"

"No." It doesn't even occur to me to be diplomatic. "And before you ask, no, I don't want anything to eat."

She looks a little crestfallen, but not insulted. "I was afraid that might be the case. Shall I make you more tea?"

I nod. "Thanks, Mom. Something with caffeine this time." I'll need it if I'm going to get together with Tristan and Kira again for another holo-chat—the only way I can see M today.

"Where's Dad?" I ask as she puts water on to boil. "Working on those installations?"

"Yes, he got an early start. If he can finish by this evening, the Truitts and O'Garas will at least have the option of coming back early."

That gets a small smile from me, since I know he's rushing it for my sake...and M's. No point me offering to help again. I'd be even less use than I was yesterday.

A few hours later, Tristan texts to ask if I want to come over for another holo session. *I can pick you up,* he offers before I can ask.

Thanks, I text back. *That would be great.*

Soon the three of us are back in the library at Tristan's house. His mom is home today, so there's a plate of cookies in the middle of the table. Luckily she didn't argue when we all opted for water to drink instead of milk.

"Here, I'll ping Sean," Tristan says once his mother leaves us alone.

A moment later, M, Molly and Sean are in the room with us, apparently sitting in mid-air.

"Hm," Tristan says. "Just a sec and I'll move some chairs. I know it won't matter from your end, but from ours this looks...odd." He drags three chairs under their images, which does seem more natural. "Where are you this time?"

"Sitting on the dock of the nearest house," Molly tells him. "Nobody lives there this time of year and it's a lot closer. None of us felt like walking very far."

We all compare symptoms and as expected, M and I feel the worst, though we're all achy, tired and queasy. Kira is understandably worried about her game tonight, but I don't repeat my offer to attend. I doubt I could stay awake through it.

Conversation sort of peters out then, with all of us just looking wistfully at our absent partners. If anything, seeing M without being able to touch her makes me miss her even more.

"It's weird," Molly finally says, "but M seems to be handling this better than we are, even though I know she feels sicker."

"I've had more practice," she reminds them. "I guess this is the very first time the rest of you have ever been sick at all?"

They all nod.

"It sucks even more than I expected," Sean admits. "I feel sorry for the *Duchas*, having to go through this sort of thing all the time."

"Not all the time," M tells him. "I only remember my Aunt Theresa ever being sick once, when I was in middle school. But then there are people like poor Eloise Crenshaw—seems like she's out sick from school several times a month. The good news is, we'll all be good as new—probably better than new—as soon as we get back to Jewel."

That reminds me. "My dad's just about done with your security systems, so it would be great if you guys can convince your folks to come back sooner."

"We will," M promises, grinning. "I'll act extra pathetic if I have to."

• • •

Sure enough, that evening M calls to tell me the adults all agreed to head back first thing in the morning. "I'll text you once we're on the road, but we ought to reach Jewel by two or three."

My relief at hearing that seems to make my headache fade slightly. "That's awesome! Think you can get them to come directly here and drop you off? I'll see if Tristan and Kira can be here when you get back, too, so nobody has to wait any longer than necessary."

"Great idea," she agrees. "See you tomorrow, Rigel."

"I can't wait. I love you, M."

17

Evolutionary jump

I SLEEP LATE AGAIN Sunday morning and wake to a steady rain...and a text from M saying they're on their way back to Jewel. Blearily looking closer, I see it was sent more than two hours ago. That jerks me awake enough to quickly text her back.

Sorry, just woke up. That's great! Can you come straight here?

A minute later she texts again.

I'll try. See if T & K can be there, too.

Will do, I reply.

Though I still feel yucky, knowing I'll see M again in just a few hours gives me the impetus to get out of bed, brush my teeth and make my way downstairs. My parents are in the kitchen eating lunch and look up in surprise when I come in.

"How are you feeling?" Mom asks in concern. "Well enough for some breakfast?"

"Um, no. But M's on her way back, so we'll both feel a lot better soon."

Dad frowns. "I hope so. There was a brief, virtual Council meeting last night, but Lili O'Gara told us the Sovereign was already in bed. I'm sure she'll want to be apprised of the newest developments, though Kyna has likely sent her a report already."

"Anything I should know?" I ask, though already I'm considering another nap before M gets here.

He hesitates, looking closely at me. "Perhaps I'd best let M fill you in when you're a bit more alert."

"You're probably right. Not sure I could make sense of anything right now anyway."

Mom hands me a cup of tea I didn't even notice her making. I wrap my hands around it, smiling my thanks, and take a fortifying sip before carrying it up to my room. There, I message Tristan, then Kira, asking if they can come over in a couple of hours. They both promise to do their best.

While I finish my tea, I try to study a little more from my Nuathan scroll-book, but my eyes get heavier and heavier. Finally, I put my head down on my desk, just for a sec.

A ping in my ear wakes me an hour and a half later. I fumblingly grab my phone to read M's text:

We should be there in half an hour! Mr. O will drop us all off at your house. Molly & Sean pretending they're fine now.

Great! I'll tell T&K, see you soon!

I text Tristan and he says they'll be right over.

You okay to drive? I ask. I'm sure not.

Kira's dad will bring us. She told him my car's in the shop.

I go downstairs to let my parents know everyone will be here soon and discover Dad went out to NuAgra while I was passed out.

"Something to do with the new communication network," Mom tells me. "He said he'd be back in plenty of time for dinner. Meanwhile, I'll put some snacks together for you and your friends, since I imagine you'll have your appetite back soon after M gets here." She sounds happy about that—though not nearly as happy as I'll be.

"Thanks, Mom."

Tristan and Kira get here about ten minutes before the O'Garas do. They put on a pretty good front for my mom, though it's obvious to me they're both dragging. When we hear a car door, the three of us rush out to the porch—or as close to rushing as we can manage.

Already, M, Molly and Sean are clambering out of the maroon van's back seat. Mrs. Truitt has stepped out, too, to make it easier for them, shielding her hair from the still-falling rain.

"You're both sure you're feeling all right now?" Mrs. O asks Sean and Molly through the passenger window.

They both assure her they are, though even from here I can tell their smiles are a little forced.

"I hope this has been a lesson to you both," she says then. "Our people may be generally resistant to Earth diseases but apparently not to food poisoning. You never should have eaten at that grubby little burger place."

Molly nods. "Lesson learned, Mum, believe me. And thanks, Dad, for dropping us here. We all need to work on our Government projects. I know we should have done some over the weekend, but—" She shrugs sheepishly.

"I'll let you know if I won't be home for dinner," M tells her aunt as she gets back into the van.

"It's a school night," Mrs. Truitt reminds her. "So try not to stay too late."

M's uncle motions to his wife to shut the van door. "C'mon, Theresa, let's go. I can't wait to check out our new high-tech Martian security system!" He's grinning like a kid at Christmas.

Mrs. Truitt gives him a stern look. "You're not to mention it to anyone, Louie. Not at work, nor to any of those so-called friends you hang around with. Understand?"

Though he looks a little crestfallen, he nods. "I know, I know. Didn't I tell you I'd learned my lesson? Still—"

"*No* one, Louie," she snaps, pulling the sliding door closed.

As Mr. O'Gara backs the van around, Tristan, Kira and I converge on our significant others, heedless of the rain. My gaze locks with M's and I force my feet faster.

A second later we're in each other's arms, kissing. Like magic, my lethargy disappears as strength and vitality flood through me. Through her touch, her kiss, I sense the same is true for M. I assume the others are all experiencing something similar, but I can't be bothered to look. I'm too busy absorbing the incredible healing M is providing me.

"Oh, man," I hear Tristan muttering several moments later. "Rigel promised I'd feel better as soon as you got back, but I didn't expect…this!"

Sean and Kira mumble some kind of agreement but don't stop making out.

I haven't been kissing M for nearly long enough when our front door opens again and my mom clears her throat.

M and I reluctantly break apart but I keep an arm around her waist, she feels so good. Not till actually seeing her, feeling her again, did I completely shake my fear that the Council might not let her come back.

"I suspect you're all hungry." Mom sounds more cheerful than she did earlier—probably because she can tell I'm not sick anymore. "I need to go do my rounds at the hospital, but there's plenty of food laid out for you in the dining room."

The other two couples look a little embarrassed—they must have been lip-locked, too. As we all head inside, I realize I'm suddenly ravenous. Judging by how fast the sandwiches, cookies and chips start to disappear, I'm not the only one.

"If you guys weren't convinced you have real *graell* bonds before, I'll bet you are now," M says after a few minutes, grinning around at the others.

Sean gazes fondly at Kira. "Yeah, I woke up feeling awful, but now it's like the headache and queasiness never existed. In fact, I feel better than I have in my entire life!" Then he looks at M and me. "Makes me even more sorry I tried to keep you two apart last winter and spring. I finally, totally get how desperate you must have been to—"

M stops him with a look. "We know. I won't claim we didn't resent the heck out of you at the time, but I'm glad we're all on the same page now."

.⁺.

"Is it just us here?" M asks after several more minutes of steady eating.

"Yep," I reply. "Mom's rounds usually take at least a couple of hours and my dad's out at NuAgra."

Tristan grins. "Then let's do some tests! Find out if all that misery was worth it."

"We will," M agrees. "But first I should reread that report Kyna sent me, now I can think again. I barely got the gist earlier, I was so out of it, but it didn't sound good."

She pulls out her phone and brings up the report. The more she reads, the more I feel her tension mounting. Uh-oh.

"Like Molly suggested, the Council checked the records of all the *Echtrans* who didn't make the cut for Jewel but settled in nearby towns," she tells us when she finishes. "Sure enough, at least two dozen were rejected because of their political leanings."

Now everyone looks worried.

"Two dozen?" Sean repeats. "That's…a lot of potential bad guys."

Connecting the dots, I add, "Probably means those radicals out west have allies right here in Indiana."

"Almost definitely," M confirms. "And maybe not just *Echtran* ones. They've analyzed more of that assassin Waylan Carney's memories and found out he spent several months in a nearby *Duchas* mental facility. Crazy as he is, there's no knowing what he told people."

"No *Duchas* would have believed him, though, would they?" Tristan asks.

M glances back at her screen. "One might have. That facility also serves as the local rehab center. I've heard Ted Farmer has been in and out of there for years."

"The guy who kidnapped M back in September?" Kira asks.

"And who sent that *Duchas* drone to spy on the NuAgra picnic," I add. "If he and Carney got to know each other at that facility, no wonder Farmer's obsessed with aliens."

"Exactly," M says. "I'll ask Kyna if they can find out if they were ever there at the same time. Meanwhile, we should make good use of our time right now."

I agree. "How's everyone feeling?" I ask them all. "Physically, I mean. Great, I hope?" They all nod. "Then I'll go get the multimeter so we can see if your *graell* powers have improved. The more ammunition we can muster on our side, the better."

No one objects, so I fetch the device from Dad's office again and set it on the table. "Who wants to go first?"

"We will," Sean volunteers. "Ready, Kira?"

She nods, looking determined. "Together or separately?"

"Together, with an imagined threat," M recommends. "Even Rigel and I can't shoot lightning bolts separately."

Not so far, anyway, I think to her. *Maybe we should try sometime?* I'd feel a lot better if M had that defense whether I'm with her or not.

Maybe, she agrees, though she looks skeptical.

Sean and Kira get up and stand in front of the multimeter, hands linked. "Let's imagine the same thing as before, that you're still being threatened by Uncle Allister," Sean suggests.

Kira nods and after a moment of concentration they reach for the red dot. Well before they touch it, a bright spark leaps from their fingertips and the little gray box skids back an inch or two.

There's a general "Whoa!" and Sean and Kira look as startled as anyone.

"How much was that?" Sean asks.

I check the readout and my eyebrows go up, too. "Twenty-eight joules! Four times what you did last time."

They stare at each other, wide-eyed. "Wow," Sean says. "Maybe it *was* worth getting sick."

"Maybe," she replies. "Not that I'm in any hurry to do it again."

Molly jumps up. "Let us try!"

I move the multimeter back to its original position. "Sure. Just do the threat one, like they did, so we have time to move on to other stuff."

She and Tristan step closer to the device.

"The assassin again?" Molly asks. He nods. "Ready?"

"Ready."

They have to get closer than Sean and Kira did, but are still a couple inches from the red dot when a spark jumps from their outstretched fingers. The little box wobbles, but doesn't skid back this time. I check the dial.

"Twelve joules," I announce.

Tristan looks disappointed until M says, "That should be enough to knock someone out. Pretty impressive, considering you've barely been bonded a month."

She turns to Sean and Kira. "Why don't you two test your telekinesis next?"

Nodding, Sean snags a potato chip out of the almost-empty bowl. "Let's pretend if it hits the ground, the floor will be electrified and fry us all," he suggests. "Ready, Kira?"

At her nod, he drops the chip. It's less than halfway to the floor when it suddenly stops in midair. Two seconds pass. Five. Ten seconds, and the chip continues to hover, motionless. Impressed, I glance at M, then at the two of them, their brows furrowed with concentration.

"Let's try to put it back in the bowl," Kira mutters then.

Sean gives a tiny nod and frowns even more fiercely.

As the rest of us watch, amazed, the chip drifts slowly, slowly upward. Soon it's level with the table, then the rim of the bowl. By now their clasped hands are shaking noticeably. I'm sure they're about to lose it, when the chip slowly starts moving sideways. Two more breathless seconds pass, then the chip drops smoothly into the bowl.

"Wow," Molly breathes. "That was…incredible. How hard was it?"

"Hard," Sean admits. He looks and sounds wrung out.

Kira leans against him. "Yeah. Definitely harder than last time. But maybe only because it took longer?"

"Try something heavier," Tristan eagerly suggests. "Something that could do actual damage to bad guys."

They both give a tired chuckle. "Not just yet," Sean says. "Give us a minute, huh?" He tugs on Kira's hand and she follows him out of the room—probably to make out. I don't blame them.

M and I turn back to the other two.

"I know what you're going to ask," Molly says, "but whatever it is we can do is a lot harder to objectively test. Maybe we should try telepathy instead?"

"You can do that at school, since no one will notice," M reminds them. "Right now we ought to work on stuff we can't do around anyone else. Tristan, how about you try your charm thing on me again?"

Sean and Kira come back into the room just then, looking remarkably refreshed.

"Or maybe use it on Kira this time?" I suggest, since I'm not a huge fan of him using it on M again.

Looking distinctly uncomfortable, Tristan glances at Molly. "You two haven't re-tested *your* electrical power yet," he tells M and me.

"We can't. Not with that." I nod at the multimeter. "We'd just fry it—or maybe even vaporize it."

Tristan stares at us. "It's that strong?"

M nods. "See that scorch mark on the table?" She points to the blackened stripe across the middle. "We did that when our Scientists wanted to see if we could produce enough power to stop the Grentl, except they had to use a way bigger multimeter to measure it."

"So…how much was it?" Tristan looks like he's not sure he wants to know.

"Six point seven gigajoules," I tell him. "Though we had to generate more like eight to actually stop the Grentl's EMP."

Tristan's mouth drops open. "Holy crap," he breathes. "No wonder the Council wanted you two kept apart."

"We can only do it when we're threatened," M reminds him. "Like, *really* threatened. Remember how tiny the readings were when you guys didn't imagine a threat?"

"Right." I tighten my grip on M's hand. "There's no reason for anyone on *our* side to be afraid of what we can do. What any of us can do, assuming you guys keep improving."

Through M, I sense Tristan's alarm fading. "I guess that's a good reason to keep our bonds secret for now," he says. "We don't want the Council voting to keep us apart like they almost did with you."

"No kidding," Molly agrees. "Even after the Grentl left, Mum still argued M and Rigel should be separated, supposedly 'for safety.' Even though it was their electrical ability that saved us."

Sean nods. "Not that that was her real reason. Anyway, Tristan, go ahead and test your charm thing on Kira," he says then. "M said she felt it last time."

Tristan reddens slightly, looking even more uncomfortable than before. He clearly doesn't want to.

Molly glances at him, then frowns at her brother. "You can't want him to do that. What if it works?"

Sean gives her a superior smirk. "Hey, *our* bond is totally strong enough to handle it. Are you worried yours isn't? Will it bother you too much to see Tristan flirt with Kira? Let's find out. C'mon, Tristan, give it your best shot."

"Shut up, Sean," Molly snaps.

Sean's eyes widen, his head rocking back. For a long moment his mouth opens and closes soundlessly, then he finally whispers, "Whoa."

"What?" She looks confused. We probably all do.

"That...what you just did," Sean says. "It was stronger than any 'push' I've ever felt. I *literally* couldn't make a sound for a few seconds."

Molly regards him doubtfully. "I've never been able to do anything like that before. Are you sure—?"

"You hadn't done the separation-reunion thing yet," Sean reminds her. "Try it again. Order one of us to do something we normally wouldn't, like M did to you last time."

Though she still looks skeptical, she shrugs. "Sure, okay. Let's see..." After moment's thought, she turns to me, her expression set. "Rigel, dump the rest of the crisps on M's head."

Without the slightest hesitation, I pick up the nearly-empty bowl of chips and upend it over M.

"Hey!" M glares at me, shaking chips out of her hair. "That wasn't funny. Did she really make you do that?"

I stare at her, horrified. "Oh, man, I am so, so sorry, M! I...I didn't even think, I just did it."

She turns to Molly. "He's not joking, I can tell. How did you do that?"

Molly looks as horrified as I am. "I...I don't know! I just...tried to make it a command, like it mattered. I *totally* didn't expect it to work."

M watches her probingly for a moment, then smiles grudgingly. "I'm just glad you didn't tell him to dump the milk on me. I'd have been seriously pissed." She brushes the last few chip crumbs off her shirt.

"I wouldn't—!" I start to protest, then stop. "Or...maybe I would have. That's kind of scary, Molly."

"I...I doubt I could do it without Tristan, if that helps," she says, still clearly rattled herself.

"Maybe you should try?" M suggests.

Molly's eyes go wide with alarm. "I don't— Though I guess we should find out." Standing, she lets go of Tristan's hand and puts some distance between them. Then, "Kira, go stand in that corner," she orders, pointing.

Kira blinks at her and twitches slightly, but doesn't get up. "I felt a little something, but I wasn't compelled or anything. Maybe if I weren't touching Sean?"

"Try that," I suggest, also curious about the limits of Molly's new power.

Kira lets go of Sean's hand and scoots a few inches away. Molly repeats her command, even more forcefully. This time Kira gets up and takes two quick steps toward the corner...then stops, shakes her head and turns around.

"That felt stronger, but still not like I *had* to obey. More like it was a completely logical suggestion—until I realized it wasn't. Even without touching Tristan, you've definitely got something there, Molly. I'll bet it would work really well on a *Duchas*, or even an *Echtran* who isn't bonded."

"Especially if you make it sound like a reasonable request," M agrees, grinning at Molly now. "That's something you were already good at, so it kind of makes sense you'd develop that kind of power— and it'll almost certainly keep getting stronger, the longer you're bonded. I can see that being really useful at times."

Tristan reaches for her hand and she takes it, tentatively returning M's smile. "Something to work on, anyway."

After that, Sean and Kira do their telekinesis thing again, this time using my Pre-Cal book. They manage to lift it an inch or so off the table and move it slightly to one side before dropping it with a thud.

"That's huge progress," M insists when they both look discouraged.

"Maybe—" Just then we hear the garage door opening. "Oops. Better pretend we're doing homework."

We all scramble for our backpacks and by the time my dad walks in, our Government notes are spread all over the table like we've been working on them for the past hour.

After an hour or so of actually working on school stuff, I offer to take everybody home—though I wish M could stay a whole lot longer.

"Yeah, we should get back," Molly agrees, "especially since our parents all think we've been sick."

"No worries about that now." Tristan gives her a sideways hug. "Though I guess we should pretend to get better a *little* gradually, huh?"

Kira nods. "Right. Maybe that'll help throw my sister off the scent."

We all head toward the garage. Passing the kitchen, I see Dad's back, helping Mom make dinner. They both turn and smile at us.

"Ah, I was just going to suggest your families might want you all home soon," Mom says. "Are you all right to drive now, Rigel?"

"Of course." I give M a wink. "Okay if I take the SUV?" It's our only car big enough for all six of us.

She nods, but with a slightly concerned glance at Dad.

M apparently notices. "I know our bond has caused you some... unpleasantness. I'm doing my best to put a stop to that."

"And we appreciate it, Excellency," Dad tells her with a little bow that makes M wince. "I'm sure in time people will get used to the idea."

"Meanwhile, how's *your* security?" M asks him. "I think you should have a system here like the ones at the O'Garas' and my house. Maybe Kira's apartment, too. She and her parents are getting similar criticism and we know there are some real crazies out there."

"Hm, good point," Dad says. "I'll run that past the Council. Breann and Malcolm have expressed concerns for their personal safety, as well, so I've been working on an omni app that would generate a personal security shield of sorts. Once it's ready, we can see about making it available to anyone likely to need protection."

M thanks him and we continue out to the garage.

"Does that mean I'll get my own omni?" Molly asks as we all pile into the SUV. "I haven't wanted to ask Mum, for fear she'd think I'm okay with her push to give me equal status with M."

Personally, I'd be fine with Molly having your status, I think to M as I back out the car. *Might give you a break...and us more time together.*

M just smiles, then turns to Molly. "Actually, I think she ordered one for you before we left. It may already be at your house."

"Ooh, can you drop me off first, Rigel?" Molly practically squeals. "I want to play with it!"

Though I laugh along with everyone else at her excitement, careful to hide my sudden jealousy. I've wanted an omni ever since learning about them a few years ago, but my folks always insisted teens on Earth weren't allowed to have them.

Unless they're Royal, apparently.

18

Adaptive strategies

I DROP everyone else off before M, so we can snag a little alone time before I take her home.

"Think it's too late to hang out in the arboretum for a bit?" I ask on the way back from Tristan's.

M glances out the window at the failing daylight. "Maybe, but let's do it anyway. I can tell you need to talk."

"I'm fine," I say—too quickly. At her knowing look, I shrug. It's almost impossible to hide anything from her these days. "Okay, I guess I was a little jealous when I heard about Molly's omni, which is dumb."

"Not dumb. Cormac has one. I'll tell the Council that as my other Bodyguard, you should, too."

"You don't—" I begin, then break off. Because I do want one. Even if it feels a little like she's throwing me a bone. "Thanks."

I park in the arboretum's tiny lot and we both hop out to hurry through the archway. The moment we're out of sight from the street, we put our arms around each other and start kissing.

After a fabulous couple of minutes, M pulls back a tiny bit and looks up at me. "Is that all that was bothering you?"

I can't lie to her. "It just reminded me—again—how not-Royal I am."

"You *know* that doesn't matter to me. At all."

"Yeah, I know. But it does matter to a lot of other people. Devyn might even be using it to recruit uber-traditionalists to his cause, turning them against you."

She pulls my face down to hers for another long kiss that can't help but make me feel better. Finally, she says, "Rigel we've been through this before, more than once. I know you worry you'll somehow make me a target, but just being Sovereign is enough to do that. Without you, I'd be a mess. We both would. But with you? Together we can handle anything. Remember?"

"You're right." It was our mantra when we risked our lives, using our combined powers to save the entire Earth—and it worked. At her reminder of that, my vague worries dissolve.

Gathering her more tightly into my arms, I again lower my lips to hers, absorbing as much of the wonderfulness that is M as I possibly can over the next few minutes.

✦

M and I are just getting to school the next morning when she gets a message from Kyna on her omni.

"Anything bad?" I ask as I park the car.

"Maybe." Frowning, she looks up. "Looks like the others just got here, too, so I can fill all of you in at once."

Stifling my impatience, I get out of the car and follow her over to Tristan's car, where he and Molly are chatting with Sean and Kira.

"Hey," M greets them. Then, more quietly, "Remember what I told you yesterday about Carney and that mental facility? Kyna just got back to me and sure enough, one of Ted Farmer's stays there overlapped with Carney's by more than three weeks."

"How did they find out?" Tristan asks.

M takes my hand. "Rigel's dad hacked into the facility's file, at Kyna's request."

"So that's what he was doing last night." I remember now he shut his office door to work on his computer after dinner, something he rarely does.

"Probably. Kyna also says the NuAgra folks returned that drone to Mr. Farmer over the weekend, with a video of it hitting a bird. He was apparently pretty obnoxious about it, claimed he'd been warned the drone might get shot down...and hinted about some plan to take care of the 'alien menace' once and for all."

The alarm I feel is reflected on everyone else's faces.

"What plan? And whose?" Sean demands. "Didn't they make him say?"

"How?" I ask, also irritated. "He's a *Duchas*—we have no authority over him. We can't haul a *Duchas* in for questioning or memory probes or anything. Our secrecy guidelines are super clear on that. What if someone called the cops? What would we tell them?"

Sean just glares, since he knows I'm right. "Can't we at least have him followed or something?"

"I'll get Cormac to put someone on that, if he hasn't already," M promises, still worried. "If it turns out these malcontents are compromising secrecy to convince *Duchas* to do their dirty work, it could be at least as big a problem as antimatter bombs. Whatever they're up to, we need to figure it out ASAP and put a stop to it."

"Agreed." I pull M a little closer, knowing she's likely to be a target for whatever they're planning. Since I can't protect her myself 24/7, like I'd prefer, I pray her new security system works as well as Dad claims.

An hour later, I hear something that makes me worry even more.

"Yeah, my dad's been asking around and almost nobody except those newcomers has ever even been allowed inside the gates," Nate Villiers is telling Pete Warner when I get to Spanish class second period.

"Almost?" Pete says. "Who else has been in there, do you know?"

Nate shakes his head. "There was some meeting or something out there a while back. Supposedly a few people who don't work there were invited, but Dad couldn't find out who. I don't think anybody heard about it until it was over."

"Huh. If they have another one, we should stake it out. Watch the entrance, see who shows up. Do you think your dad would let us borrow that super telephoto camera he's got?"

"I can ask. You know, both of the O'Gara kids are dating newcomers. Maybe their family's involved somehow? I mean, they're pretty new, too, only got here a year ago. Could be they were like an advance guard or something."

Pete glances my way, probably because I'm a relative newcomer, too, by Jewel standards. The bell rings then, so I pretend not to notice.

The moment class starts, I reach out to M. *Sounds like more people are getting suspicious about NuAgra...and about all of us.* I go on to share what I just overheard.

You're right, that's getting too close for comfort! she answers from her French classroom, at the other end of the hallway. *I wonder if Nate's dad has been talking to Mr. Farmer?*

I wouldn't be surprised, I think back. *Malcontents seem to be drawn to each other—*Duchas *as well as* Echtran.

Which gives me an idea.

As soon as class ends, I casually move toward Nate and Pete as they're packing up their stuff.

"I heard you guys talking about that new NuAgra place earlier. What d'you want to know about it?"

They both look at me, startled.

"Why? Do *you* know what's going on out there?"

I shrug. "They hired my dad to help set up their computer system, so he let me come inside with him once. I saw a bunch of greenhouses out back, some labs where they test new strains of seeds, stuff like that. Nothing all that interesting. Unless you're a farmer."

On that last word, I watch Nate closely and sure enough, he twitches a little.

"My dad heard there's more going on there than just research on plants," he says after a slight hesitation. "Like, secret experiments and stuff. Maybe even on people."

"Huh. Who told him that?" Might as well just ask.

He hesitates a little longer this time. "Just somebody he's friends with online, I think. Or maybe more than one, some group on the internet talking about it—not that I've paid much attention."

I force a grin. "Yeah, well, you can't believe every crazy thing you read on the internet. Guess it makes for a good story, though. See you, guys." With a nod, I head to my next class.

During Chemistry, I silently catch M up on that exchange. Then when class ends, we quietly clue Molly and Tristan in as we all leave the room.

"I'm going to do some digging online tonight," I tell them. "See what I can find out about this group."

That night after dinner, I ask Dad how he got into the files of that rehab center. He gives me a long look before answering.

"Fairly standard hacking. Their system was surprisingly easy to penetrate, considering the sensitive nature of what they do."

"Can you show me some of those tricks? I know a few basics, but I'd like to help with what you're doing, if I can. Especially since it involves M's safety."

Another long look, then he nods. "Yes, I suppose as part of her security detail you might make good use of skills like that. Already, you're showing a fair bit of talent in Informatics, though I think your mother was hoping you'd lean more toward her *fine*."

It *would* be pretty cool to heal with my hands, like Mom can, but right now I'm a lot more interested in the computer stuff.

"So, can you show me?" I ask again.

Dad spends the next hour demonstrating more and more advanced hacking techniques, starting with simple password-breaking, then walking me through buffer overflows and container escapes on increasingly more secure systems. I'm a little surprised by how easy it all seems.

"You appear to already know more than I realized," he comments after I take a turn at doing it myself. "I hope you haven't been putting that knowledge to less than ethical use?"

"No, honestly, I'd never seen most of this before." Which is true. Maybe my bond with M is helping? "Guess I do take more after your side of the family."

Now he smiles. "Hm. So it seems."

Closing the browser, he regards me thoughtfully for a moment. Then, turning back to the computer, he pulls up a folder full of obscurely-named files.

"It might be interesting to see if you can make anything of these."

I examine the first file he opens, comprising a couple dozen lines of gobbledegook—random letters, numbers and symbols, including a bunch I've never seen before, probably Martian. There are a few English words in brackets sprinkled in, but not enough to make sense of the whole. Most have question marks after them.

"Is this from those secret messages you were picking up for a while, a month or so ago?"

He nods. "The computer algorithms I created were able to unlock the message files, but decrypting the contents has proved trickier, even after adding dozens of Earth languages to the dictionary. At first I thought I was making fair progress, but I clearly missed some key element—or more than one. Maybe a fresh set of eyes can catch something I haven't. Mind you, no one outside of the Council is supposed to know about these, but as M keeps you apprised of all our dealings anyway, you may as well take a look."

I'm flattered he thinks I might figure out something he hasn't. Determined to merit his faith, I give all my attention to the seemingly haphazard collection of characters. At first I think I see a pattern, but then it gets away from me. After several minutes focusing, then refocusing, I feel like my eyes are starting to cross.

Finally, Dad reaches over and closes the window. "I don't expect you to crack it tonight—or ever, to be honest. I merely wanted to give you a look. As soon as I finish that omni security app, I'll attempt another algorithm to do the heavy lifting on this."

"Yeah, sorry. I got a little sucked in there." I've always liked puzzles, but this is easily the most complicated one I've ever encountered. Which also makes it the most fascinating. "Is it okay if I play with it some more later?"

"Be my guest." He rattles off the seventeen digit password to open the folder and I instantly commit it to memory. "Of course, by now much of the information in those files may be obsolete, but they could still give us insight into what those groups are up to. In addition, I believe Enid used a similar encryption for her files—in which case solving it would be immensely helpful."

Though I nod, already my thoughts are drifting back to the hacking methods he showed me earlier. So when I go up to my room, instead of doing homework I flip open my laptop and start poking around online.

A simple search yields a metric crap ton of conspiracy groups scattered across various forums and message boards. Even limiting my search to alien conspiracies leaves me hundreds of sites to comb through, some password-protected, some not.

I only poke around in a few before going to bed, since it'll take hours —or days—to figure out which one or ones the locals frequent. Tomorrow I'll check out a bunch more.

For some reason, the idea of contributing to the cause using abilities separate from the ones M and I have together, appeals to me a lot. After all, M can use her emotion-sensing thing even when I'm not around to enhance it. And her 'push.' Maybe this can be my own special power.

I become even more determined to keep at it when Kira shares another new development before school the next morning.

"I found out yesterday that being apart from Sean and getting back together improved my Ag skills, too," she whispers when the six of us again gather briefly in the parking lot. "When I was out at NuAgra yesterday, some seedlings I was working with shot up so quickly, I had to hide them before my mum noticed."

"How quickly?" Molly asks. "I thought what you could do already was pretty impressive."

Kira gives her an understanding smile. I remember she tried to help Molly grow plants when everyone still thought she was an Ag.

"Last week, Mum and I planted a bunch of hybrid tomato seeds," Kira replies. "When I got to the greenhouse yesterday, her flats and mine looked exactly the same, most of the plants about two inches tall. But an hour later mine had more than tripled in size, while she'd only coaxed hers to grow another inch. When I looked closely, I could actually *see* mine growing!"

That gets a startled murmur from all of us.

"So Kira's, like, Super Ag now," Sean says proudly. "How about the rest of you? Has anyone else noticed—?" He breaks off as a few *Duchas* classmates approach.

I think my computer skills might be better now than they were before, I think to M, silently answering the question Sean didn't finish. *Have you checked to see if your emotion-sensing has improved?*

No, but I will, she thinks back before her friend Bri demands her attention with the latest gossip.

I glance around at the other bonded couples, wondering what the limits will be for all our new powers, individually and synergistically. Maybe it's not just a joke that we could someday become superheroes.

That intriguing idea alternately amuses and concerns me off and on for the rest of the school day. Then, as we're leaving seventh period that afternoon, M quietly asks what I meant about my computer skills improving.

"Because I wanted to check out that online group Nate mentioned yesterday, I got my dad to show me some hacking tricks. He seemed kind of impressed by how quickly I caught on, so he also let me take a look at those encrypted messages he's been working on. I didn't make any real progress there, though, so...maybe not so much improvement after all?"

"What, did you expect you'd just magically crack a code your dad's had some computer algorithm working on for more than a month?" she asks, grinning.

I shrug. "Okay, maybe not. I just…" I trail off, embarrassed, but of course M figures out what I don't say.

"Want a special ability of your very own?"

"Well…yeah. Kira has her super-Ag thing now, and you've got your emotion-sensing—"

"Which I can only use long-distance with *you*, Rigel," she reminds me. "It's not like I ever did anything special before we bonded. Without you, I doubt I'd be able to do much more than the average *Duchas*."

I start to shrug, then I'm struck by an idea. "Hey, you want to come over and, um, boost me while I work on that code?"

She blinks. "Sure. Though my total *lack* of computer savvy might make things worse. I'm pretty hopeless at that kind of thing."

Now I'm the one grinning. "You're not hopeless at anything. But I'd like to see if having you there—"

"Makes as much difference to your natural ability as you do for mine. Definitely worth a try," she agrees.

We're exiting the building when Molly hurries over to us.

"I have to get to cheerleading practice, but have you two seen this week's *Echtran Enquirer* yet?" she whispers, steering us well away from other students heading toward the parking lot.

We shake our heads. M starts to get out her omni but Molly's quicker. "No, let me use my new one! It's so great not having to borrow Mum's or Sean's anymore. I've already let my friends back on Mars know I can keep in touch for real now."

She starts to pull up the little holo screen but M stops her. "Not here, Molly!" she hisses. "You know better than that."

"Sorry, sorry, you're right. Okay, here." She angles the regular phone screen for us to read. "Top story is about Allister and Lennox's trial, which won't make Mum happy."

We read through that report, but it's all stuff I already knew.

"I guess you didn't have a chance to write anything for this week, M?" Molly asks, going back to the list of contents.

"No, I felt too crappy. But every two weeks is probably often enough. What does you-know-who have to say?"

Molly clicks to Gwendolyn Gannett's column and we start reading.

"A Change You'll All Appreciate," it's titled.

I'm sure my faithful readers have been as frustrated as I've been with the dearth of news coming out of Jewel lately, but worry no more! You'll be pleased to hear that I am in the process of moving to Jewel myself, to fill an important role in the new *Echtran* News Network that will shortly begin broadcasting. I'll be able to bring you all the latest happenings in real time, directly from the heart of what is becoming our people's main hub of activity. Already I'm receiving tips from Moya, who most of you know from the highly-regarded Nuathan News Network back home.

Until the ENN is up and running, continue watching this space for updates. Among other things, I've heard an interesting rumor about NuAgra that I'll share with you next week. As they say in the streaming media biz, stay tuned!

M and I groan in unison.

"At least she's banned from coming onto school property, right?" Molly asks.

"Right," M says. "And I'll have Cormac enforce it if she tries."

Molly clicks off the omni. "You'll have to read the rest on your own— I need to run. Bye, guys!"

"Is Gwendolyn Gannett really going to become a news anchor on your dad's new network?" M asks as we continue on to my car. "Why would he allow that?"

"It's not 'his' network," I explain. "He's just creating the framework for it. Once it's operational, I don't think he'll have much say in how it's used, other than recommendations to the Council."

But I remember stuff I saw on the news in Nuath last spring, some of it twisted, even vicious. M's opponents used it to badmouth her while she was trying to get Acclaimed Sovereign. And some networks almost literally called for my head on a pike, once that video got out of us kissing on the way to Mars.

I don't see how M writing a couple articles a month for the *Echtran Enquirer* can possibly counter that sort of thing, if it starts up here. Once we're in the car, I tell her that.

"That's one way to look at it." Smiling, she puts a soothing hand on my cheek, which feels amazing. "But I'd rather think of it as an opportunity. I mean, if they're willing to hire Gwendolyn Gannett as a reporter, surely I can get airtime, too? That would be a great way to amplify what I'm already trying to do with my 'Sovereign's Desk' columns."

"Would you be okay going on camera regularly?" I remember how she hated that kind of thing when she was still getting used to the idea of being Sovereign.

She gives a cute little snort. "You didn't see what I had to do back in Nuath after you were gone, to convince people to move to Earth. I made on-air appeals and public appearances constantly. It definitely wasn't fun, but it gave me a ton of practice. So that sort of thing doesn't freak me out the way it used to. If that's what I have to do to get people to finally accept us as a couple, I totally will."

"Not to mention undercutting any messaging Devyn Kane's trying to do. Keeping those insurgents from blowing up Jewel is probably a *little* more important, don't you think?"

"Maybe a little," M agrees, laughing. "But *only* a little—at least to me. That problem is temporary, but you'll always be my *top* priority, Rigel. You know that, right?"

The love coming through her touch on my cheek makes my breath catch. "Ditto. Always." I pull her to me for a lingering kiss before starting the car.

On the way, she leaves a message for her aunt in case she gets back before M does. Then I belatedly call home to make sure someone's there, since my folks have made it clear I'm not allowed to have M over otherwise. Luckily, Dad's home. He joins us in the kitchen when we stop there first for snacks.

"Is it okay if I take another crack at those encrypted messages?" I ask once he's greeted M and chatted for a minute or two. "M's going to help."

His brows go up. "Oh? I didn't realize that was an area you're familiar with, Excellency."

"I'm not," she says, "but Rigel thinks having me here might help him while he works on it. Because of our bond."

"Ah." He nods. "I suppose there could be something to that. Good luck."

We carry our milk and a plate of peanut butter cookies to his office. There, I type the password into his computer to bring up the folder full of coded messages and click one open.

"Huh." M points at one of the brief English phrases in brackets. "I guess these are the bits your dad's already figured out? 'Recruiting going well.' I don't much like the sound of that."

"Yeah. I'm actually the one who figured out the word 'recruiting,' last night," I tell her. "But hey, you actually know a fair bit of Martian, right? Maybe you can help with more than—you know."

I put my hand over hers and we both feel the familiar boost in energy and clarity.

"I don't see any whole Martian words," she says, squinting at the screen. "Just bits. I can tell you what the individual characters are, though. This one, here and here, is a 'th' sound. Like in 'Thiaraway.' And this is hard C, with a K sound."

"Hm, yeah, that helps. Let me see..." Still gripping her hand, I focus on the screen. "I wonder..."

As I concentrate, the puzzle pieces start to sort themselves in my mind. Slowly, in stages, a pattern emerges.

M stays quiet for at least ten minutes, then finally whispers, "Well? Anything coming clearer?"

"I think...I think so. Maybe. This character here—" I point. "Is that a Martian L?"

"Yes! I thought you didn't—?"

"I don't. But an L would make sense there. Which means... Yes! I *think* what they've used is mix of Martian, Latin, and Greek alphabets, plus a fourth code using regular keyboard symbols to substitute for letters. Those are all jumbled together to spell out words that alternate between English, Martian, Irish, Spanish and Greek in a repeating arithmetic pattern. I'm surprised Dad's algorithm didn't catch that."

She looks at me, brows raised. "I'm not. It sounds *crazy* complicated. Does this mean you can actually read it?"

"I...yeah, sort of. Just a sec." With growing excitement, I run a finger along the screen, tracing the text line by line. Then I release M's hand so I can type, quickly adding more English to what's already inside the brackets.

A couple minutes later, the first paragraph reads: *Recruiting efforts are going well. 37 Populists, 55 former Faxon supporters and 12 Traditionalists now embrace our cause. Expect numbers to grow in coming months. Reaching out to settlements closer to Jewel to find potential staging area.*

M turns to stare at me. "You just now got all that? From this?"

Triumphant now, I nod. "Last night, I once or twice thought it was right on the verge of making sense, before it escaped me again. But with you here to sharpen my focus, I finally, really got it! Too bad these messages are all like a month and a half old, so won't have much about what they're planning right now."

"Still, this is huge, Rigel! I'm going to go tell your dad." Jumping up, she hurries out of the office.

I continue transcribing the open message into English and a moment later M's back with my dad. He peers over my shoulder and gives a low whistle.

"Very well done, Son! Kyna will be delighted. Or..." He leans closer, reading as I type. "Maybe delighted is the wrong word. It looks as though they were far more organized than we suspected, even before the messages stopped."

"We need to let her know ASAP," M says. "Maybe now she can finally get the Council Royals to take this movement seriously."

Already, Dad is pulling his omni out. "I agree. This should convince them we're not merely dealing with a small handful of malcontents, as they keep insisting."

"I should probably get back," M tells me then, with obvious regret. "Unless there's more you need me here for?"

Glancing at the screen, I shake my head. "Now that I've figured out their system, I should be able to decrypt the rest of the messages on my own. C'mon, I'll take you home."

Since she didn't tell her aunt a specific time she'd be back, we take advantage of the gathering dusk to park around the corner from her house. Like always, her kiss, her touch, makes me feel like I can do anything. The rest of those messages will be a piece of cake after this.

When I drop her off a few minutes later, I'm in a better mood than I've been since way before our Thanksgiving separation. Mainly because I now have reason to hope I can eventually become worthy of M, the one and only love of my life.

Royal or not.

Sean

19

Directional selection

"HEY, HOW WAS PRACTICE?" I ask when Kira arrives at my house Tuesday evening. Then I lean in for a quick kiss since we may only be alone for a moment.

She responds to my kiss enthusiastically before answering my question with a grin. "Which practice? Both basketball and Bodyguard training were fine, though holding back is even harder now. Not that I will if I ever have to actually protect you, of course."

That idea still weirds me out a little. "Did you ask if I can come watch your certification test Saturday?"

"Yep, you and Molly can both come. Your parents, too, if they want. My family and Tristan's mum plan to be there."

The doorbell rings again and Molly comes clattering down the stairs.

"Wow, Mol, very Princessy," I tease her.

She makes a face at me. "Don't you start. I get enough of that sort of stuff from Mum. She and Dad aren't back yet, are they?" she asks, yanking open the door.

"No, but she messaged they're on their way. Hey, Tristan."

"Hi, Sean, Kira," he manages before Molly practically attacks him with a kiss.

Rather than watch—not that Molly seems to care—I turn to Kira. "Mum and Dad have been helping sort out all the government offices at NuAgra."

"Yeah, I've seen them there a couple of times as I was leaving."

Finally breaking her lip-lock with Tristan—who looks embarrassed—Molly grins. "Did you do any more super-Ag stuff today?"

Laughing, Kira shakes her head. "I didn't have time. Gilda made us spend the whole two hours Bodyguard training. She seems to think it'll reflect poorly on her if we don't totally ace our certifications."

"Is that why she's pushing us so much harder?" Tristan flexes his shoulders. "I'll be glad when this week is over—I think my bruises have bruises."

Molly grabs his hand and tugs him toward the stairs. "Poor baby. Want me to give you a back rub?"

"Mum will go ballistic if she catches you two alone in your room," I warn, though I wonder if she really would. Mum seems a lot less strict about that rule with Molly and Tristan than she is with Kira and me.

Even more irritating, she claims the reason Kira and I can't be alone in *my* room is that it would set a bad example for Molly.

"Fine, why don't you two join us?" Molly gives me another grimace. "Maybe Kira can show off her super Ag chops with my poor plants."

I'm curious to see that, too. "Okay, let's get snacks first."

"Seriously?" Molly follows me to the kitchen. "You ate a huge supper barely an hour ago!"

Shrugging, I grab the open milk carton, four glasses and the rest of the apple crumble while Molly gets plates and forks. Then we all troop up to her room.

"Down to just three now, huh?" I gesture at the pitiful collection of houseplants on Molly's windowsill.

"Yeah, I finally had to toss my asparagus fern and my African violet, even though they're both supposed to be impossible to kill. Probably the only reason these are still alive is the boost Alan gave them a few weeks back. So Kira, show us your stuff, yeah?"

Kira gives an embarrassed laugh. "I hope I didn't oversell it at lunch today," she says, going over to the three drooping plants. "Poor things. Don't you ever water them?"

Molly turns pink. "I do, on the exact schedule all the websites recommend. I just...suck with plants. I'm like the Anti-Ag."

With a chuckle, Kira reaches for the one on the left—a peace lily, I think? Not that I'm particularly into plants.

"Okay, let's see what I can do with you," she murmurs to it, gently running her hands up two of the stems.

As the three of us watch, the plant not only straightens up but I swear it gets at least an inch taller.

"Whoa," I breathe. Then I have a thought. "Hey, want to try that again with us touching? Just to see what happens?"

At her nod, I put my hands on her shoulders—love that tingle!—and she repeats what she just did, on two different stems. This time, the whole plant gives a tiny shiver, then suddenly shoots up to more than double its original size.

"Yikes!" Kira jumps back. "I didn't expect *that* to happen. Yesterday my seedlings grew faster than usual, but not *instantly*. Or by nearly that much." She glances apologetically at Molly. "Sorry. This, um, might be a little hard to explain to your parents."

Molly's still staring at the plant, her mouth open. Closing it, she shakes her head. "That...was amazing! Tell you what, why don't you just take all three plants home with you? I'll help you smuggle this one out without our folks seeing it. I have no business owning houseplants anyway."

"All...all right." Kira's still obviously a bit shaken. She looks up at me. "Sorry if I scared you."

"You didn't—" But of course she felt my spurt of alarm. "Okay, startled, maybe. But that's a seriously cool power you've got there."

"No kidding," Tristan agrees, clearly still awestruck. "I wonder if there's a way to use it as a weapon? Maybe make a hedge of thorn bushes spring up to trap the bad guys in a maze?"

We all laugh.

"Yeah, I'll get right on that," Kira jokes. "I'll just ask if I can co-opt one of the NuAgra cornfields for a reason I can't explain. Then we only have to lure the bad guys there...once we figure out who they are, when they're coming and what they're planning."

Tristan looks sheepish. "Okay, fine. But what if—?"

He's interrupted by Mum's voice floating up the stairs. "Molly? Sean?"

"Up here, Mum," Molly calls back. "Doing homework with Kira and Tristan."

We all scramble for our backpacks while Molly rushes over to the now-huge peace lily to snatch it off the windowsill and shove it in her closet. She shuts the door just as our mother walks in.

"Ah, so that's where the rest of the apple crumble went. Do save a bit for your father and me—he's making us a spot of tea now."

I quickly spoon a generous portion out onto each of our plates and hand the pan to Mum. Taking it, she starts to leave, then pauses.

"Oh, Molly, you'll be happy to know I've arranged for you to have an office at NuAgra equivalent to the one Emileia will be getting."

"An office?" Molly echoes blankly. "Why do I need an office?"

Mum gives her a *duh* look. "So you'll have a proper place from which to conduct business. This room is all well and good for homework and such, but you can scarcely hold audiences here if you want to be taken seriously in the leadership hierarchy."

"*Audiences?* Even M's not 'holding audiences' here on Earth. What makes you think anyone will ever expect *me* to?"

"One never knows," Mum replies evasively. "As it's a school night, I suggest you all wrap up whatever you're working on over the next half hour or so. We can talk more about the future later."

Casting an approving eye over Molly's homework-strewn bed and how we're all spaced out from each other, she heads back downstairs.

Molly frowns after her. "Ugh! I love having M as a sister, but I hate how Mum keeps trying to push all this other stuff on me." Shaking her head, she opens her Pre-Cal book.

Our parents really are nagging Molly to death these days, I think to Kira as she and I get started on our own homework. Only this morning, we discovered we can now share thoughts without touching, if we're close enough. *Still, I can't help being grateful Mum's finally quit pestering me.*

Kira smiles back but doesn't reply.

Just as well. I'd rather not try to explain the vague resentment I sometimes feel about Mum's recent shift in focus.

Now I get how Molly must've felt when our parents were all about me becoming M's Consort while practically ignoring her. Not that having a future planned for her that she doesn't especially want is much better. Poor kid.

⁺₊

Since Kira drove her family's car to my house, we only manage a quick good-night kiss when she leaves, to both her frustration and mine.

By the time I pick her up for school the next morning, like I do every day now I have a car, I'm starving for another, longer taste of her lips. Fortunately, the moment she's in the car, she leans in for her good morning kiss. I savor it for all I'm worth, though eventually I have to summon enough willpower to pull away so I can drive.

"Mm," she murmurs, finally sitting back to buckle her seatbelt. "I wish we could just do this instead of going to school."

"You and me, both," I assure her, putting the car in gear. "Think you'll get home in time tonight for a nice long walk?"

Regretfully, she shakes her head. "I'll be lucky if I'm home before ten-thirty. Gilda's called for another double session today, then I have to go straight to my game way out in Oakmont."

I grimace. "And I can't come, because my parents want Molly and me to go with them to NuAgra for something or other. Tomorrow night I have a game, so I guess we can't get together then, either. Unless you can come?"

"I can't, sorry. Gilda wants me back for more Bodyguard training after basketball practice tomorrow and she's already warned us that'll go late, too. The way she's driving us, neither Tristan nor I will get a moment of down time until after Saturday's test."

Frustration tightens my grip on the wheel. "We haven't had *any* time alone except on the way to school since I got back from Kentucky. It's... driving me a little nuts."

"Same here." Her voice echoes my frustration. "But we'll make up for it after Saturday. Once I'm your official *Costanta*, I'll be *required* to spend as much time with you as possible."

"I like the sound of that. More time together will also mean more chances to work on our *graell* abilities, too. Not exactly something we can do on the way to school."

She puts a hand on my arm. *We can practice this, at least.* Removing her hand, she continues, *If we can increase our range, we'd be able to talk from classes we don't have together. Maybe even from home eventually.*

I smile over at her. *That would make being apart every night a lot easier. I swear the nights seem to be getting longer and longer.*

"Well, technically, they are," she teases, out loud. "At least for another couple of weeks."

"Showing off your Earth studies, are you?" I grin back. "But that's not exactly what I meant."

Sobering, she nods. "I know. I hate being apart, even when it's not long enough to make us sick."

"Me, too."

Missing Kira so much whenever we're not together has me thinking more and more about the future...our future. I haven't broached that subject with her yet, since we've only been dating for two months, but I really, really want to. Soon.

Funny that only half an hour after I think that, there's a reminder in the morning announcements that seniors are meeting with the guidance counselor this week, and today will be last names L through P. Which includes both me and Kira.

Halfway through third period Spanish I'm notified it's my turn to go see the counselor, so I grab my stuff and head to the office.

"Have you begun narrowing your college choices yet, Sean?" Ms. Campbell asks when I sit down. "I imagine by now you've received several basketball scholarship offers?"

"A few, yeah."

They started showing up before we went to State last spring, along with invitations to visit college campuses all over the country—all expenses paid. A lot more are flooding in now, but Mum and Dad are still chucking them all in the trash. That made sense last semester, when we all thought I'd eventually become M's Consort—on Mars.

Now? Not so much.

"I'm still trying to figure out whether I want to major in business or engineering before picking a school, since I can't count on playing basketball forever," I tell her, just like I rehearsed.

"With most college application deadlines looming, you'll need to make a decision soon, Sean," she admonishes me. "Talk to your parents. Then, if you need any advice from me, you can make another appointment."

"Thanks. I'll do that." I stand up to go.

She stands up too, smiling now. "I'd hate to see you limit your future options by making too hasty a choice, Sean. With your grades and athletic achievements, you can likely write your own ticket. Make it a good one."

Nodding, I thank her again and head back to class, thinking even harder about what I want most out of life...and the best way to get there.

In Weight Training sixth period, Rigel and I are taking turns spotting each other on the bench press when he whispers, "Guessing you need to work harder to tone it down in basketball this week?"

I lower the bar, the weights a fraction of what I can really lift. "Yeah, I could definitely tell a difference Monday night," I mutter back. "Getting a better feel for it in practice, though, so I should be fine for tomorrow night's game."

Liam and Alan, training on the next bench over, catch that last bit and join the conversation.

"We're all doing our best to, y'know, dumb it down," Liam assures us, also quietly enough no one else in the room can hear. Then he chuckles. "Or maybe I should say, 'Duchas it down?'"

Alan snickers, too, but I glare over at them.

"C'mon guys, not cool. You're talking about our teammates." I know it killed Rigel to let his team down—mostly for our benefit. I'll feel the same if the Council makes us do something similar.

"And some locals are smarter than you think," Rigel adds, "so don't underestimate them. Especially now."

He goes on to remind them about the growing suspicions in town, including here at school. "We all need to be on our toes, not do anything to attract more speculation. Right now it might be just a few crazies, but if their ideas start catching on, things could get ugly in a hurry."

Liam looks skeptical. "How? Pretty sure our people can handle anything they could throw at us."

I look at him like he's nuts. "Do you have any idea how many more of them there are than us? Not just in Jewel, but in this country? On this planet? Billions. Your Earth history should have taught you how violent they can be. Why do you think the Council came down on you so hard after our first game? If the truth gets out too soon, before our people can lay the proper groundwork, the Duchas could totally wipe us out—or at least lock us all up. Dunno about you, but I sure wouldn't want that on my conscience."

Both Liam and Alan turn a shade paler.

"I wasn't...I didn't mean... You're right," Liam mumbles. "Sorry."

Alan nods. "Yeah. When you put it that way—hefrin, maybe we should quit the team. You think?" He looks at Rigel, then me.

When I hesitate, Rigel says, "No, you can keep playing. I'd hate to think I lost that last playoff game for nothing! But you do need to be super careful. If these conspiracy nuts get the tiniest shred of proof they're actually right..." He lets the words trail off.

Because they both look positively scared now, I add, "Let's all just work a little harder to scale it back for the next few games, okay? It'll get easier if we can start a real *caidpel* team out at NuAgra. Then we'll have a *safe* way to play our hardest."

When I get home that afternoon after basketball practice, I notice several more envelopes from colleges in the stack of mail on the little table by the front door. I haven't opened one since the start of the school year, but now I pick one up and tear off the flap.

Reading the offer, my eyebrows go up. They're not just offering to cover my tuition, lodging and books, but throwing in a monthly stipend for "living expenses" that's more than twice what Kira's parents are paying in rent.

The school's in New Mexico, not a place I'd want to live, but I'll bet most of the other offers are just as good or better. The letter still in my hand, I go to the kitchen, where Mum's putting together my after-practice snack.

"Have you seen the kind of money these colleges are willing to throw at me?" I ask her, holding out the paper.

She turns to me with a puzzled expression. "Does it matter? It's not as though you're in a position to accept any of those offers anyway."

"Are you sure? Seems like a few years of college ball might net us enough to buy a bigger house, nicer cars, lots of stuff."

Now she frowns. "With everything going on right now, material things are hardly a main concern, Sean. I thought you knew that. I'd hate to think you're becoming infected by the *Duchas* love of money and possessions."

"I'm not," I'm quick to assure her. "It's just… What *am* I going to do after I graduate if I don't go to college? Hang around Jewel, hope you can find me some job at NuAgra answering phones or something?"

"Of course not," she snaps. "Don't be silly. With the necessary expansion of the *Echtran* government, there'll likely be several leadership roles you're suited for."

In other words, she has no idea. "Right out of high school? Why, just because I'm Royal?"

"Sean, you know as well as I do that we Royals have always been uniquely adapted for leadership. Someone in your station…"

"My station? What station?"

Mum prims her lips. "Despite current, ah, entanglements, according to tradition, you *are* still Emileia's presumptive Consort.

That will be true until you are both of age to formally refuse the pairing."

"Formally... Of age... What? Of course we both refuse! M's with Rigel and I'm with Kira. That's not going to change. I thought you'd finally accepted that."

She gives a little sniff, not quite meeting my eye. "Yes. Well. In any event, given your ancestry, I'll be surprised if you don't someday find yourself filling a very important role in our government."

"Someday," I echo. "But not right away. What am I supposed to do in the meantime? Twiddle my thumbs? I'd be better off going to a *Duchas* college and raking in the bucks. Maybe you and Dad don't much care about the money, but—"

She stops me with a look. "Of course you can't play basketball at some *Duchas* university. Jewel is remote enough and Jewel High small enough that you—and Rigel and the others—have drawn only limited attention. Even that has been worrisome enough that the Council considered forbidding sports completely."

"Then why are *Echtran* NBA players allowed? They're *way* more visible that I'd be on some college team?"

"There are only two. There were far fewer of us on Earth when they began their careers, so arousing *Duchas* suspicion was less likely. Now, with so many of us here, particularly in Jewel, the danger of discovery is much greater, with the potential for serious consequences."

I know she's right, so I just shrug and stuff a sandwich in my mouth, letting the subject drop. I don't stop thinking, though.

If basketball can't be in my future after high school, what will?

The next morning, I decide to at least hint to Kira about it during our drive to school.

"I, um, guess you met with the guidance counselor yesterday, too?" I say as soon as we pull away from her apartment complex. "She seemed a little put out that I hadn't made more of a decision yet. What did you tell her?"

She chuckles. "I was well prepped for that during Orientation in Dun Cloch. All the incoming seniors had to come up with fake future plans— colleges, studies we want to pursue, et cetera—to go with our cover stories. I told her I'm applying to Purdue, Cornell and Texas A&M, three of the top Agricultural schools in the country."

"Sounds plausible." Then, steeling myself, I ask, "So, um…what *do* you want to do after graduation? Have you thought about it at all?"

Kira's quiet for so long I glance over at her and see her frowning. Finally, she says, "When I first got to Jewel, all I wanted to do was to go back to Mars as soon as possible—if any of us are ever allowed. Now, though…" She trails off with a look at me that makes my heart speed up.

"Yeah. I was hoping to go back, too, if not during the next launch window, then someday. But now… I'd only want to go back if we were both going."

"Do you think that will ever be possible?" There's no mistaking the longing in her voice. "That we could go back and actually spend the rest of our lives in Nuath?" She doesn't *say* the word "together," but surely that's implied?

Focusing on her actual question instead of the part she didn't say, I have to shrug. "I honestly don't know. Maybe if they figure out a way to extend the power supply? Otherwise…"

She nods. "I know. I don't think Earth will ever seem quite like home, but it already feels a lot less, well, *alien* to me than it did a couple of months ago." Now there's no mistaking the meaning in her smile.

Smiling back, I put a hand over hers so she can feel the love I'm sending her way. "I'm glad to hear that. Because *where* I spend my future doesn't matter nearly as much as knowing you'll be there with me." There. I said it.

"I hope I can be." Though she's sending enough love back to warm my whole body, I sense a tinge of uncertainty.

Because she doubts it'll be possible? Or because she's not ready to commit to a whole future with me? I swallow, wondering if I dare pose that question.

When I hesitate, she asks, "What did you do at NuAgra last night?"

I snort. "I should've gone to your game after all. Mum just wanted to show us the office space Molly will eventually have there. It's huge, a whole suite of rooms, supposedly the same size M's will be. Mum thought Molly would be thrilled, but she called it ridiculous—which started them arguing. Totally wasted evening."

In fact, I'm sure the only reason they brought me along was so I wouldn't feel left out again.

"It bothers you, doesn't it?" Kira asks softly.

"What? No! Why would I want some palatial office?" The space *had* almost reminded me of M's quarters in the Royal Palace on Mars.

"I don't mean the office. I mean Molly suddenly being the important one in your family, when it used to be you."

I shoot a startled glance her way and find her watching me closely. Though I want to deny that, too, she just put into words the exact thing that's been gnawing at me even though I've done my best to ignore it.

"I...maybe a little. Which is dumb."

"No, I get it. Back home, I was practically a star, because of *caidpel*. The most exalted status I ever had, being an Ag. Then I came here, where I'm nobody."

I want to refute that, but she continues. "At least you're still Royal, which I'll never be. But you're the one who made me realize that being on the sidelines isn't necessarily a bad thing, that playing a supporting role can be important, too."

The truth in her words loosens something inside me I hadn't even realized was knotted up.

"You're right. Especially since no amount of status could ever matter to me a fraction as much as you do."

She catches her breath and smiles mistily at me. "Really?"

"Really." I almost ask if she also thinks being with me is worth giving up any chance of reclaiming the status she had in Nuath.

But I don't.

20

Genetic linkage

AT LUNCH THAT DAY, M again corrals our six person "Bond Squad" for a quick confab. "Any more progress?" she whispers to us.

Kira and I both shrug.

"We haven't had a chance to try our *main* thing since Sunday," I grumble, still irked by our lack of alone time. "Telepathy is definitely getting easier, though."

"Ours, too," Molly says. "We still have to be touching, but we can send complete sentences now."

"Most of the time," Tristan amends. "It still takes a lot of focus. Our other...things are trickier to practice. So far, I've mostly used mine to deflect people when they ask questions about NuAgra."

M nods approvingly. "That's probably the best possible way to use it right now, since the gossip seems to be getting worse. How about you, Molly? Did you ever try your push thing on Alan, to nudge him toward Trina?"

"Not yet. Think I should try now?" Molly asks, glancing over to where Alan's just leaving the lunch line with his tray.

"Go for it," Tristan urges. "Could be fun."

Molly gives a little snort, then shrugs and heads Alan's way, intercepting him on his way to his table.

"So, Alan," Molly begins, as our whole group listens in. "Trina's been talking a lot about you lately in cheerleading. Are you two becoming a thing?"

He stares at her, clearly startled. "A...thing? With Trina?" Then, so softly I have to strain my ears, "A *Duchas*? Are you crazy?"

Molly's smile tells me she's turning on the 'push' now. "It's not *so* crazy. I mean, she's awfully pretty. And we *are* supposed to be working harder to make friends with the *Duchas*, to deflect suspicion. I think you should ask her out." She holds his gaze as she says that last bit.

Alan blinks and frowns, but then his brows go up and he looks thoughtful.

"I guess just going for a soda or something couldn't hurt. Especially if it helps with...what you said. We...we all need to do our part, right? Thanks, Molly." Walking away, he looks slightly dazed.

So does Molly, when she comes back to our group. "Holy crap, I think it worked!"

We all chuckle.

"Sure looked that way," M agrees. "Clever, throwing in that bit about averting locals' suspicions."

"That tour should also help," I say. "Do you know when it'll happen?"

"Soon, I think," M replies. "I should find out at Saturday night's meeting. Which reminds me, Kira, I've been meaning to ask you if—" Her *Duchas* friends Bri and Deb are nearly to our table, along with a few guys from both the football and basketball teams, so she breaks off. "Later."

The next morning on the way to school, Kira tells me what M's last comment was about, since she didn't know yet when I asked her on the phone after her game.

"M called me after you and I talked last night," Kira tells me a few moments after our good-morning kiss. "She, ah, asked if I'm still in touch with any active Populists."

I glance at her in surprise. "Are you?"

"None on Earth, since the only people here I thought were Populists turned out not to be."

In other words, my Uncle Allister and ex-Governor Lennox, who played on her Populist sympathies to basically turn her into a bomb to use against M.

"But I told her I can probably contact at least one back in Nuath, if necessary," she continues.

"You can?" I ask in surprise. "Who?"

She doesn't talk much about the last year or so of her life in Nuath. I haven't pressed, figuring it's still a painful subject for her. Being forced to leave Mars when she was one of the top *caidpel* players in the whole colony—and right after getting her Ag team into the playoffs—had to be hard.

"I, ah...Brady. From my old *caidpel* team. M mentioned I'll probably get an omni once I'm officially your Bodyguard, so I could message him, find out how current sympathies are running."

"Whoa. Brady is a Populist?" We're stopped at Jewel's one stoplight, so I turn to look at her.

She nods, her gaze sliding away from mine. "He's...actually the one who recruited me to their cause. He took me to my first meeting and introduced me to Crevan Erc. Brady and I both carried messages for the Resistance while Faxon was in power, so they thought I could help the Populist movement, too. You know, subtly spread the word and drum up support, especially among younger people."

"So I, ah, guess you worked pretty closely with Brady even outside of *caidpel*, huh?" I know it's stupid for me to feel jealous, but...

"No, I never had the chance. My first and only meeting was the exact same night my mum and dad signed our family up to emigrate to Earth."

Do I detect a note of lingering bitterness in her voice? The light changes then, so I don't have time to decipher her expression.

Rather than let it gnaw at me, this time I just ask. "Is Brady one reason you wanted to move back to Mars?"

Kira reaches over and puts a hand on my arm to send a reassuring blast of love my way. "Maybe a little, when I first got here, but definitely not now. Sure, I briefly had a crush on him, but it never came to anything. I love you, Sean. Only you. I'd only want to go back to Nuath now if you were coming, too."

I let go of the wheel with one hand to clasp hers tightly. "Same here. I love you, too, Kira. I'm more than willing to spend the rest of my life on Earth if that means spending it with you."

.⁺₊

By Saturday afternoon, I feel like every cell in my body is starving for a good, long makeout session with Kira. A few kisses in my car before school every morning is all her crazy schedule has allowed since Thanksgiving, to our mutual frustration. We've both been looking forward to today's Bodyguard test as the light at the end of a too-long tunnel.

I give Molly a ride to NuAgra to watch Kira and Tristan get certified, since Mum and Dad claim they're too busy prepping for tonight's Council meeting. Molly's clearly as eager—and nervous—as I am.

"What if, after all this training, one of them doesn't pass?" she asks as I pull up to the imposing gated entrance. "I've hardly seen Tristan all week except at school and I'm starting to feel it. Not as bad as over Thanksgiving, but—"

The guard peers into the car and does a double take. Then, bowing deeply, he waves us through.

"Yeah, me, too," I reply, maneuvering the car to a spot near the main entrance to the central building. "If they're feeling as off as we are, I don't see how it won't affect their performance. Kira claimed she was fine when I texted her this morning, but maybe she just didn't want me to worry."

"Maybe we can give them kisses for luck before they start," Molly says hopefully as we approach the big glass doors. "That's sure to help some."

A woman in the enormous lobby area directs us to the room where they'll be testing. We enter a large arena-style space. The floor is covered with green foam mats except for a strip along one wall where a dozen chairs are lined up. Not quite like Rigel's back yard, where his Body-guard test happened last spring, just before we all left for Mars.

Kira's parents and sister are already seated. We're heading their way when M, Rigel and Tristan's mother come in, too. All eight of us exchange greetings as we sit down and I notice Molly and I aren't the only ones who look a little anxious.

"How are Tristan and Kira feeling?" M whispers, taking the chair next to Molly. "Have you talked to them?"

We both shake our heads.

"Only texts," Molly tells her. "They had to be here early this morning for more last-minute training."

"Kira warned me she wouldn't be at Taekwondo today," M says. "But Cormac tells me Gilda is an excellent *Costanta* trainer, so I'm sure they'll both do fine."

I hope she's right.

A door opens at the far end and the smallish woman who's been appointed Molly's Bodyguard comes into the arena, followed by Tristan and Kira. From here, they both look a little paler than usual.

Molly nudges me and I nod. Rather than ask—and risk being told no —we both hurry across the floor to them. Gilda's eyebrows go up but thankfully she doesn't try to stop us.

Kira looks surprised, too, but before she can say anything, I put my arms around her and cover her mouth with mine. She stiffens for an instant, but as strength and vitality flood into us both, the tension leaves her body

"Good luck," I murmur, raising my head after several deliciously healing seconds.

She smiles up at me. "Thanks. I...needed that."

"I figured, since I did, too. Bet you'll do great now."

She nods, the sparkle back in her eyes. "Bet you're right. See you...after."

Grinning, feeling a hundred times better than I did five minutes ago, I give her one last, quick kiss and head back to my seat.

"That was totally worth getting side-eye from Gilda," Molly remarks, catching up with me. "She's little, but I've noticed that up close she's kind of scary. She looks so...intense."

I can't disagree, but I'm in too good a mood now to care much, my earlier worry gone without a trace.

We've barely sat back down when Gilda motions to Kira, holding out a tiny silver energy weapon. Taking it, Kira strides out onto the mat, startling me with how confident she looks.

Gilda taps her tablet and three shadowy human-shaped holograms materialize by the far wall, then rush our way. Without the slightest hesitation, Kira brings the weapon up close to her body—the better to conceal it from any watching *Duchas*, I assume. She fires off three shots in rapid succession, all dead center, and the holograms vanish.

Nodding, Gilda makes a notation on her tablet, then calls out, "Next!"

Two huge guys I recognize from Rigel's Bodyguard test last spring burst through the far door, then separate to attack Kira from opposite directions. She goes into a slight crouch and when the first one reaches her, she seizes his arm, whirls and somehow pitches him into the other guy.

They both hit the ground, hard, but immediately scramble to their feet to go for her again. This time she doesn't wait but does a kind of flip into the nearest guy, catching him around the neck with her legs and crashing him back to the ground. Amazingly, Kira doesn't fall but bounces up and into the other guy, driving her shoulder into his stomach. Then, so quickly I can't quite see how she does it, she twists his arm behind him and puts it into some kind of joint-lock.

"Give," he grunts and Kira steps away.

"Well done," Gilda says approvingly. "Full marks."

I close my mouth, which I realize has fallen open. *Naofa flach!* I knew Kira was a phenom on the *caidpel* field, but that was sports. This is... deadly. Swallowing, I give her a shaky thumbs-up.

Tristan tests next with the same challenges, changed up only slightly. He does nearly as well but I barely notice, my attention still on Kira, now waiting off to one side. I'm still boggled by what I just saw her do. She must notice my stunned expression because she sends a questioning glance my way.

Forcing a grin, I try sending a thought to her, though we've never done it from this far away before.

That was amazing, I think to her as hard as I can. *You're amazing!*

Her eyes widen slightly, her gaze locking with mine, and I hear—barely—*That was...did you just...?*

I nod, my grin now a real one. This is a huge step forward for us—for our bond. *I guess practice does make perfect,* I send and she nods back, returning my smile.

Molly suddenly jumps to her feet and I realize Tristan's test is over. I didn't notice whether he also got full marks, but he clearly passed.

She rushes him, squealing, "You were so awesome!" before gluing her face to his.

I'm just two steps behind her and an instant later I'm at Kira's side, pulling her against me. "Guess I better never piss you off," I say, still grinning. "You'd flatten me."

She tilts her face up for a kiss. "No I wouldn't. I love you. And now I can protect you—officially."

"Which will give us a lot more chances to do this." I lower my lips to hers.

Two ecstatic seconds later, Gilda clears her throat. "Now that you're both certified *Costanta*, you are *expected* to follow a code of conduct that doesn't allow for what you're doing right now."

Kira and Tristan both take a step back from us, glancing guiltily at each other.

"Not in public, anyway," Gilda adds with a smile. "Do please try to observe the forms whenever possible, eh? I wouldn't want anyone to think I neglected that aspect of your training."

Molly grins impishly, threading her fingers through Tristan's as the rest of the spectators come forward to add their congratulations. "We'll do our best. Thanks so much, Gilda."

In response, the diminutive trainer bows, first to Molly, then to M, and finally, just as respectfully, to me. "It's been my honor, Excellencies."

Being included in the honorific startles me, but before I can process it, Kira tugs on my arm.

"I told my family you'd give me a ride home, so they'll be heading out in a minute. Do you want to tour the greenhouses before we leave, see what I do when I'm working here?" Despite what she says aloud, both her expression and her touch tell me she has something far better in mind.

"Absolutely," I reply, since I'm longing for the same thing. After confirming that Molly will ride back with Tristan, Kira and I leave the arena hand in hand.

.⁺₊

Kira leads me back to the main lobby area, then through the double doors at the rear of the NuAgra complex, where all the greenhouses are. It suddenly strikes me as odd that I've never even peeked into those before, considering how much time Kira spends in them.

As she steps up to it, the door of the nearest greenhouse hisses open and everything goes green and warm, like we've stepped into a jungle. All that's missing is exotic bird and monkey sounds.

Kira inhales deeply, then smiles up at me. "I just love the smells here. Like the very air is alive and growing."

Her enthusiasm is infectious. Sniffing, I nod. "You're right. It smells…rich. Vibrant. Like you."

"Rich?" She laughs. "Definitely not in the money sense. I can live with vibrant, though."

"Good. Because you are."

Nobody's around so I gather her into my arms. She melts into my kiss and it's like fireworks are going off in my brain, through my whole body. I haven't had a chance to kiss her like this in way, way too long. I've missed it even more than I realized.

"Mmmm," she murmurs after several blissful minutes. "You don't know how much I've needed this."

I grin down at her, reveling in how she feels pressed against me. "I can make a pretty good guess. It's like all these empty spaces I didn't even know I had inside me are filling up with... I dunno, something wonderful."

"Yeah. Like that."

We laugh together at how inadequate words are to describe what we're feeling, and then we're kissing again, making up for nearly two weeks of going mostly without. It's incredible.

Finally, with a contented sigh, I lift my head, though I keep my arms around Kira, unwilling to let her go just yet. "Since we seem to have this whole place to ourselves, maybe we should work on our new abilities some? It's been nearly a week since we've been able to."

She heaves a happy sigh of her own and nods. "You're right. Though I'd rather do this all afternoon."

"You and me both. But hey, I don't have to be anywhere for the rest of the day. Do you?"

"I guess not, especially if I call my mum and let her know I'll be late."

The thought of having Kira completely to myself for another whole hour or two is indescribably fabulous. "Don't worry, we'll get back to this—" I give her a quick kiss— "after we get some, uh, work done. Sound like a plan?"

"A great plan," she agrees, then looks around. "I haven't given you that tour yet."

"You mean that wasn't just an excuse to get me alone?" I tease.

"It mostly was, but as long as we're here—"

"Kidding," I assure her. "I do want to see what you do here." If nothing else, it'll help me visualize her better when we can't be together.

She slants a glance up at me from her amazing gold-flecked brown eyes. "Okay. This is greenhouse three, where I spend most of my work-study time, testing new plant strains. Took me a bit to get used to a whole new method of starting seedlings, but they seem to grow fine that way."

"What new method?" I ask curiously.

"New to us, I mean. Sticking seeds and plants into soil and watering them from above. You know, the way they've always farmed, here on Earth."

I never thought about it before, but of course no one does it that way in Nuath, where it never rains and water is so scarce. Everything there is grown aeroponically or, in some cases, hydroponically, I now recall from my required Ag classes back in Glenamuir.

"Wouldn't it make more sense to introduce the *Duchas* to our methods?" I ask. "They're a lot less resource-intensive, even if water's not so much an issue here."

Kira nods. "That's the long-term plan, but in the meantime we're working to develop superior crops that can be grown the regular Earth way, for both their benefit and ours."

She walks me through the greenhouse, showing me her various work stations with leafy greens in all stages of growth. With my Royal perspective, I'd assumed the Ag stuff here was just a cover for NuAgra's "real" function as our new government headquarters. But I realize now they *are* doing exactly what we've told the *Duchas*.

"This might be a good place to work on our telekinesis thing," she says when we reach the far end of the big glass building. "Plenty of stuff to practice with here."

"You're right." I look at the rows of open shelves full of empty plant pots, bags of soil and other gardening-type supplies. Reaching up, I take down one of the pots. It's lighter than I expect, composed of some kind of plastic or polymer fiber. "Want to start with this? I don't think it's breakable."

She nods, though she looks skeptical. Lightweight as it is, this pot is significantly bigger than anything we've ever attempted to move. Secretly sharing her skepticism, I set it on the floor in front of us, then take her hand again.

"Let's try to pick it up and set it back on the shelf," I suggest, even though the shelf is several feet away. Sensing her doubt, I shrug, grinning. *C'mon, it's worth a try,* I send silently.

You're right. Why not?

Together, we focus on the pot, willing it to rise. Almost at once, it does—which startles us both so much we immediately lose focus and drop it.

Wow, Kira thinks to me. *I didn't even remember to imagine a threat or anything.*

Neither did I. Maybe we don't have to anymore? That would make this ability way more useful. Let's try again.

We do. Still without pretending anything big is at stake, we're able to levitate the pot slowly to the level of the shelf, then maneuver it away from us until it hovers over its original spot. Lowering it, we let go a bit too abruptly and the pot falls over. Even so, I'm elated by our success.

"That. Was. Awesome," I breathe, not quite believing it. "Plus I'm nowhere near as drained as I was after moving that potato chip. Are you?"

Kira shakes her head. "Nope. Maybe because we got a lot longer to, ah, recharge first?"

"Or maybe being apart so much this week gave our bond another boost. Or both. I wonder what'll happen if we *do* imagine a threat? Want to try shifting one of those bags of dirt? They look a lot heavier than Rigel's math book."

"They weigh forty pounds apiece, so yeah. But hey, I'm game if you are. What's our pretend threat?'

I think for a second. "What if it's part of your Bodyguard test and if we can't lift it, you flunk?"

She chuckles. "Sure, okay. Not quite like getting blown to smithereens but still bad."

"All right. We'll pick up that blue bag on the bottom shelf, the one marked Premium Potting Mix."

Tightening my grip on Kira's hand, I imagine how devastated she'll be if she doesn't pass her test, how important it is that we lift the bag of dirt.

Amazingly, it works. In fact, it's only slightly harder to lift than the empty pot, though we're noticeably slower this time. As we focus, the heavy bag rises an inch, two inches. Three. Five. Unfortunately, we didn't discuss what to do next, since neither of us expected to get this far.

Let's flip it over, then set it back down, I silently suggest.

Kira gives a single nod, still focusing fiercely on the bag. I do the same, telling myself it's on me to make sure she passes her test. Slowly, one edge of the bag drifts higher than the other, then higher, until it's perpendicular to the one beneath it. We continue rotating it until it's turned completely over, then lower it again. This time, we maintain our concentration until it's fully at rest.

With a simultaneous gasp, we let go—of our focus, not our hands—and stare at each other.

"Okay, that was harder. But still," I say, slowly shaking my head. "I'm starting to think we may actually have something worthwhile here."

Kira's eyes are still wide, as awed as I am by what we just accomplished. "And if M is right, we'll keep getting better with practice."

I nod. "I'm sure we will. And hey, who cares about status or *fine* if we can become superheroes?"

She laughs. "Good point—though lifting forty pounds took a lot more out of me than the little pot did."

Grinning, I pull her against me. "I have an idea of how to fix that problem."

"You always have the best ideas," she says, grinning back as she tilts her face up for my kiss.

I immediately oblige. *I love you, Kira,* I tell her silently, since my mouth is otherwise occupied.

And I love you, Sean. So much, she thinks back. The accompanying emotion almost makes me dizzy.

Exultant, I deepen the kiss, my stupid petty piques and jealousies of the past few days evaporating in the knowledge that the most incredible girl in the whole universe is mine, and I'm hers. For always.

Tristan

21

Dominance

"HAVE I told you lately how incredibly amazing you are?" Molly asks when we pause our makeout session just long enough to catch our breath.

"Only about five times in the last hour." I grin at her from a few inches away, barely noticing my car windows are completely fogged on the inside. "You're pretty amazing yourself, you know."

She shakes her head. "Not like... I mean, you were unbelievable, the way you took those huge guys out. I'll never worry about my safety again, as long as you're nearby."

Her admiration only adds to the euphoria I'm already experiencing from her kisses. "I hope I never need to use any of that training in a real-world situation, but I'm glad I know how to protect you now, just in case."

"Me, too." Her adoring expression requires that I kiss her again.

"You can't believe how much I missed you this week," I tell her a few minutes later. "Missed this."

She snuggles against me as best she can. At least my car's center console is fairly low-profile. Makes parking together a little more comfortable.

"Of course I believe it," she replies, "because I missed you every bit as much. And this."

She leans in for another kiss and I immediately oblige. This is the first chance we've had to be completely private since before she left for

Thanksgiving. Nearly two weeks, though it feels more like two months. I revel in the strength and vitality permeating me as we take full advantage of some extended alone time.

All too soon, Molly looks at the clock on the dash and sighs. "I should get home—we always have dinner early on Council meeting nights. I wish you could attend, too…or that I didn't have to."

"Just part of being the Princess you are." I tweak her nose, then regretfully refasten my seatbelt. "You can tell me later about anything interesting."

"I will," she promises. "Tonight, if it's not too late."

I start the car. "I don't care how late it is. It's not like I'll be able to sleep before I hear from you anyway."

We head out of the deserted business park that's become our favorite place to make out and a few minutes later I pull up in front of Molly's house. "See you tomorrow?"

"Definitely. I'll text you after church." She gives me a quick goodbye kiss and gets out of the car. "Love you, Tristan."

"Love you, Molly. See you soon."

Driving home, I'm in the best mood I can ever remember. I passed my *Costanta* test with flying colors, got nearly as good a score as Kira, the famous athlete. Even better, I'm done with those grueling training sessions, which means I'll have tons more time to spend with Molly. Maybe the "Bond Squad" can get together again, too, see what kind of progress we're all making. At the moment I already feel like a superhero, after a whole hour alone with Molly.

I'm still grinning when I walk into the house…until I see my father sitting in the living room.

He stands up to face me as I enter. Mother stays seated, her expression strained.

"What are you doing here?" I demand. "Isn't Allister and Lennox's trial still going on? I thought you had to stay in Dun Cloch for that."

Predictably, he's wearing the same disapproving frown I've seen on his face a thousand times before. "The investigators released me two days ago. They had no grounds to keep me once I'd given testimony and answered their questions. I told your mother I'd be here today but I presume she didn't mention it?" He flicks a glance her way.

I hate the way she flinches—just like she used to before he left. I'd hoped a few weeks serving on the *Echtran* Council would have cemented the resolve she showed when she defied Father's demand that she and I leave Jewel with him.

"I, ah, didn't want to distract him from his certification test today," she explains.

I smile reassuringly in response to her mute apology to me. Because she's right—knowing Father was going to show up today would definitely have been a distraction.

"Ah, yes. I take it you've now been officially named the new Princess's *Costanta*? Quite a comedown from the position you might have had as Consort to Sovereign Emileia. Still, I appreciated receiving an invitation to attend the test. I used it to persuade the investigators to move up my release, that I might rejoin my family in time."

At my confused look, Mother tells me, "I invited him to come watch if he cared to. It seemed…the polite thing to do."

But of course Father couldn't be bothered to actually attend, any more than he ever took time to come to my football games or debate matches or any other activity I'd excelled at in my futile attempts to please him. To him, today's all-important test was just a convenient excuse to escape Dun Cloch sooner.

"So now what?" I ask, not feeling any particular inclination to be polite to him.

His frown snaps back. "I've come to take you and your mother back to Denver, of course. Despite the lack of support you showed by refusing to join me in Dun Cloch for what you had to know would be a trying time."

If he's trying to make us feel guilty it doesn't work. Not on me, anyway.

"Mother is on the *Echtran* Council now. Or hadn't you heard?"

"Of course I heard. But she can attend the meeting holographically from Denver, as I did myself for years."

He's not looking at her, so doesn't see the little negating motion she makes at his words. But I do.

"Mother likes it here. So do I. And I can't very well act as Mol— Princess Malena's Bodyguard if I'm in Denver."

Now he gets that pained expression I hate. "Bodyguard. Hardly a fitting occupation for someone of your lineage. Did no one bother to inform you that menial positions like *Costanta* are chosen from lesser *fines*, not ours? The Princess may have expressed a fondness for you while she still believed herself an Ag, but seeing you in such an inferior capacity will almost certainly give her a disgust of you soon. When the time comes for her pairing, she and her guardians will surely look higher than a mere Bodyguard."

"You don't—" I break off.

There's no point trying to explain to him the special relationship Molly and I have, something he could never understand. Just these few minutes of his nasty cynicism has already undercut my earlier euphoria. The sooner he's gone again, the better.

"Since Mother and I won't be going with you, do you need help packing the rest of your stuff?"

He glares at me for a long moment, then rounds on Mother—who flinches again. "Does our son dictate your actions now? If you're that spineless, you should resign from the Council and let me resume my place there. Maybe then I'd consider allowing the two of you to stay in Jewel for the remainder of Tristan's school year."

"Don't let him talk to you that way, Mother." I add a bit of charm to my words, the first time I've ever tried to use it on her. "You have more spine than he's ever had."

Rather to my surprise, she straightens her shoulders, then stands up to look him straight in the eye.

"Tristan is right. I let you treat me as an inferior for years, avoiding conflict in a mistaken belief that I was protecting our son from family disruption—from your temper. I realize now that by failing to confront you, I allowed you to set a dreadful example for him. Fortunately, he came to realize on his own that you typify none of the virtues we should rightly expect from members of the Royal *fine*...or from the *Echtran* Council."

I regard her with amazed approval. "Molly—Princess Malena—had a lot to do with me finally figuring that out," I admit. "Anyway, what makes you think the Council would take you back, after what you did? Especially since Mother's already proving herself a more valuable Council member than you ever were. Not surprising, since she's always been a better Royal than you. I'm lucky I had her as an example, too."

Father glares at the pair of us, now facing him side by side. "Everything I did was for the benefit of this family, to elevate our standing in the *Echtran* community."

"No," Mother snaps, startling me again. "All you cared about—all you've *ever* cared about—was your own status and whatever power and prestige might accrue from it. I gradually came to realize that was even true of our marriage. You charmed me into believing you loved me, with that ability you have, when in fact you merely saw me as a stepping stone to your ambitions. The only reason I can't regret pairing with you is Tristan."

The love and pride in her voice and expression gives me nearly as strong a boost as I get from Molly, though of a completely different type. My throat tightens with gratitude and an answering pride, in both myself and in her.

"How touching," Father rasps out sarcastically. "So the two of you have conspired to join forces against me. I knew it was a mistake to leave you here without my guidance for so long."

"We're doing just fine without your so-called 'guidance,'" I inform him. "Better than we ever have, in fact. If Mother wants to let you stay I can't stop her, but I'd rather you move back to Denver or Dun Cloch or wherever as soon as possible and leave us alone. It's not like you were ever really here for *us* anyway."

When Father flinches and pales a little, I realize I must have used some "push" without meaning to. For a long moment he looks back and forth between me and my mother, his face displaying a weakness I now realize has always been there, just better concealed. Finally, he gives himself a little shake. Ignoring me now, he speaks directly to Mother.

"Teara, you don't really want me to leave again, do you? I'd like to believe you missed me, at least a little. I certainly missed you."

I can tell he's putting all the charm he can behind his words but it doesn't exactly seem my place to intervene. They've been married for over twenty-five years, after all, and I have no idea what their relationship was like in the early days. Better, surely? I hold my breath, hoping Mother won't give in.

"I'm sorry, Connor," she says after only the briefest hesitation. "That talent of yours worked on me once upon a time, but no more. Nor do I believe you particularly missed us. If you had, I wouldn't have been the one to initiate every contact between us while you were in Dun Cloch. I had a misguided idea that we owed you that, that hearing from us might brighten your spirits, but if anything you always acted as though my calls were an inconvenience to you. Just as you've behaved toward us both for most of Tristan's life."

Father is clearly taken aback. "But…but Teara—"

"You can stay long enough to pack up the rest of your belongings and arrange for their transport to wherever you choose to live. But it won't be here." There's no compromise whatsoever in Mother's tone. I'm proud of her. "I need to finish putting dinner together now, which you're welcome to share if you wish. Then I have a Council meeting to attend."

Dinner is a mostly silent meal but still more pleasant than most I can recall with Father at the table. After what Mother said, I thought he'd just storm out—which would have been fine with me.

Instead, he grumblingly retreated to his office for half an hour, then came out and announced he'd stay till at least Monday. "Perhaps by then we'll be able to come to a somewhat better understanding."

Mother coolly responded, "Perhaps," and nothing else.

I keep shooting glances at her as I eat, alert for any sign she might be weakening toward Father. Thankfully, I see no evidence of that, but it makes me wish—a little—I could sense her emotions the way I do Molly's. None of this can be easy for her.

When she leaves for her meeting after dinner, I expect Father to either disappear into his office again or go upstairs and start packing. Instead, he invites me to join him in the living room.

"Son, I'd like to talk to you, unless you have plans this evening."

I don't, since Molly also attends the *Echtran* Council meetings these days. Warily, I take a chair across from where he's sitting at apparent ease on the couch.

"What's up?"

My tone borders on insolent but his smile only slips a fraction.

"I thought perhaps you could give me some insight into your mother's current frame of mind. Considering that she was the one who invited me here, I found her attitude this evening rather, ah, perplexing."

"Sounded to me like that invitation was for you to come watch my certification test, not for a social visit."

He lifts a shoulder nonchalantly. "I assumed that was merely a pretext to bring me back to Jewel, yet now she claims she doesn't want me to stay. Surely she doesn't expect me to abandon my family permanently? I thought she knew me better than that."

"I'm pretty sure she knows you better than you think she does.

Maybe better than you know yourself." I don't try to hide my contempt but he pretends not to notice.

Rather than respond to what I said, he leans forward to regard me intently. I can feel him using his charm-push even before he speaks.

"I fear that in my absence, some on the Council may have attempted to turn your mother against me. I'd very much like for you to intercede on my behalf, Son. For the sake of our family."

Knowing what I know about him, I don't feel even the slightest inclination to give in. Even before bonding with Molly, I suspected my charm talent was stronger than his. Now I'm sure of it.

Meeting his gaze straight on with one just as intense, I smile slightly. "What would benefit our family most, Father, is for you to admit how poorly you've treated Mother all these years. Not just to me, but to her."

He inhales audibly. "Treated—? What do you mean?"

"Blaming her for things that aren't her fault, snapping at her when you lose your temper for something she had nothing to do with. Telling her to shut up whenever she tries to offer an opinion, sometimes even threatening to hit her."

I continue to hold his gaze, keeping my expression pleasant while putting plenty of persuasive charm behind my words.

"I, ah... I suppose it's possible I haven't always kept as tight a rein on my temper as I should have," he finally concedes. "But I never intended — Never wanted her—either of you—to be afraid of me."

"Didn't you?"

A slight frown creases his brow. "Not... That is..."

"You had to realize, consciously or not, that intimidating us would make us easier to control. I'm sure you found that convenient, though it didn't make for a very healthy family atmosphere."

"No. I...I suppose not," he says uncertainly. "I never thought— Never meant—"

"Whether you meant to or not, your constant belittling nearly broke Mother's spirit. Not quite, though. Fortunately, she remembered in time who she really is—and that there are things way more important than appeasing you. Things like the good of our people. You used to claim that was what mattered most to you, too."

He stares at me, his uncertainty increasing to near-helplessness. "It did. Does. Of course I care about the good of our people."

"Unless it conflicts with your own self-interest. Even though you *knew* the Sovereign and Council suspected Devyn Kane of criminally conspiring with Allister and Lennox, you were willing to cover for him. Why? Because he promised you some position of power?"

"Yes, well, during the trial I realized I, ah, may have been misguided in shielding him—shielding all of them. It's…possible I allowed myself to be overly influenced by our long friendship to, er, turn a blind eye to how far their principles had strayed from what was right."

Surprised as I am by that admission, I don't relax my focus on him. "So you cooperated fully with the investigators? Told them everything you know about Devyn's plans?"

"I…believe so."

"Does Devyn know that? Are you still in contact with him?"

Now he looks startled. "How did—?"

"What exactly did you tell Devyn?" I try to ratchet up my persuasive powers another notch. "I need to know."

Father swallows. His head twitches like he's trying to look away but can't. "I…I told him he should abandon his plan. That the Council and investigators in Dun Cloch know he's up to something and that once they piece enough information together they'll figure out what. That it's too dangerous to move forward, no matter how much he wants to."

"And what did he say? Is he giving up on his plan?" I work to hide my elation at getting this much info out of him.

"No. He, ah, thanked me for the warning but said he's come too far to give up now. Even after I told him I'm no longer interested in being part of it."

"Part of what?" I press.

Father hesitates, his internal struggle obvious.

"What *is* his plan?" I persist, throwing absolutely everything I have at him, *willing* him to answer me.

Finally, haltingly, he does. "Devyn…I believe Devyn intends to either eliminate or subjugate the entire *Echtran* leadership. All at once. He…he means to create a power vacuum that…that he himself will fill."

"How?" I can't keep the urgency out of my voice. I almost ask if it will involve the stolen antimatter, but remember in time that Father doesn't—or shouldn't—know about that.

"I don't know, exactly," he replies slowly. "He may still be working out the details. Too technical to explain, he once told me when I asked. After my warning, he did say something about moving up his timeline. Before the Council can act on their suspicions. I'm afraid that's…that's all I know."

And all he's likely to, if he really has broken off with Devyn. I relax my focus, only now realizing I'm trembling slightly with the effort.

"Thank you, Father. That's very helpful. Or could be."

He regards me uncertainly. "I...I never wanted the Sovereign or Princess Malena harmed, Tristan. Please believe that. Even if Devyn implied at one point that might be part of his plan, I convinced myself he'd never actually go that far. Which I now realize was naive of me."

"Well, they're safe now, and I plan to make sure they stay that way. It's the main reason I wanted to become Molly's Bodyguard, degrading as you think that is."

"No," he surprises me by saying. "I...was wrong about that, too. Keeping our Sovereign line safe should be everyone's top priority. I regret now that it hasn't always been mine."

I smile—my first real smile at him in a long, long time. "I'm glad to hear that. But now I should probably do some homework before Mother gets back. I've let it slide this week, I've been training so much. Why don't you use that time to consider everything we just talked about." I add just a tiny bit of push to that last suggestion as I stand up.

"I'll do that. You've...given me a lot to think about this evening, Son. Thank you."

Startled again, I nod. "You're welcome."

Leaving him to ponder all the points I made, I hurry up to my room to jot down everything he told me about Devyn's plans before I forget. I'll pass the details along to Molly and the Sovereign first chance I get—tonight, if possible.

As I write, it occurs to me that I no longer have the least fear that I might somehow revert to the sort of person I used to be—that Father wanted me to be. I guess Molly's faith in me was justified. Huh.

When I hear Mother drive up an hour later, I go back downstairs to find Father still sitting in the living room, apparently lost in thought. For a moment I wonder if I went too far and scrambled his brain or something, but then he looks up at me and smiles—a genuine smile.

"Sounds like your mother's home," he says. "I, ah, hope she'll like what I have to say. Thank you again."

I'm still struggling to hide my amazement at such a dramatic change in his attitude when Mother walks in. She drops her keys in the metal bowl by the door, then looks up, sees us together—and freezes.

Father stands up, turning his smile her way. "I'm glad you're home, Teara. I trust the meeting went well? While you were gone, Tristan and I had a chance to talk about things, and—"

She takes two quick steps toward us, her expression both alarmed and angry. "You went behind my back to convince him to go along with your plan? To leave everything we've built here and move back to Denver? Tristan, I know he can be persuasive, but you can't let him—"

"No, Mother, that's not—" I begin.

"Please, Teara, just listen to me," Father says at the same time.

Though still clearly upset, she continues forward to join us in the living room. "I'm listening."

"Thank you." Father's voice holds no trace of his usual sarcasm. "As I said, Tristan and I had a talk after you left, and then I did quite a bit of thinking. He, ah, made me realize that my behavior toward you hasn't been exactly...kind in recent years. I seem to have allowed my ambition to blind me to what I was doing to my family along the way. I'm...sorry for that."

If anything, she looks even more suspicious. "Are you, Connor? Are you really?"

He nods. "Yes. Really. Tristan told me that you've both been—" He swallows— "happier this past month, with me gone. Much as I didn't want to believe him, I'm forced to admit he was probably right. I can see for myself that you're both more, well, confident than I remember. More like Royals."

That touch of his old arrogance makes me stiffen, but I'm watching Mother for her reaction.

Though her frown eases slightly, it doesn't disappear. "If you're truly ready to admit that's the case, what do you mean to do about it?"

Father presses his lips together for a second or two, then says, "It, ah, seems I have a bit of work to do—on myself—if I want to put our family back together. I'd like things to be...better than they were before. For that to happen, I think my best course is to return to Denver, alone. There I'll find someone who can help me manage my temper and other less-than-ideal personality issues. Perhaps a Mind Healer. I...I would very much like to stay in closer touch while working through this. If you're willing, Teara?"

Even I'm affected by his pleading look, a humility I've never seen in him before. Did I do this??

Mother only hesitates for a moment this time. "Very well, Connor. If you're actually willing to put in the work, I will support you in that, with all my heart. The impetus needs to come from you, though, not from me. I won't pressure you or even remind you to follow through on this, but I will be more than willing to take your calls whenever you wish to update us on your progress. I...very much hope you will be successful."

"So do I. Thank you, Teara. And you, Tristan, for making me face some hard truths." He stands up. "I'll go up now to pack a few of my things, then go to a nearby hotel where I'll make arrangements to leave in the morning. In time, I intend to demonstrate that your faith in me, thus far unearned, is not misplaced."

Mother and I watch him go upstairs, then exchange a disbelieving glance. I can tell she doesn't trust Father's sudden change of heart will be permanent. I'm not sure I do, either.

It seems too incredible to believe I could have wrought such a dramatic transformation in my father's outlook with just a half hour's conversation. Once away from my influence, will he revert to form? It seems likely. Unfortunately.

Meanwhile, I suppose there's no harm in hoping for the best.

M

22

Intelligent design

THE MEETING JUST ENDED, I tell Rigel telepathically on my way home from the O'Garas' house. *Early enough I can sleep in my own bed for a change.*

Good, he sends back. *That means we can talk longer. Any new developments?*

Nothing big, but you should have seen their faces when your dad told them you were the one who broke the code used in those messages. I grin at the memory.

I then tell him the *Duchas* tour of NuAgra has been set for a week from tomorrow, and that the Council approved my request for him, Tristan and Kira to have omni-phones similar to mine and Molly's. *I convinced them those should be standard issue for Bodyguards.*

Cool! Thanks, M. So no bad news at all tonight?

Not this time. But no good news, either. At least not on the antimatter front.

Fortunately, it's harder for Rigel to pick up any feelings I don't want to share with him from nearly five miles away. There's no need for him to lose sleep tonight over the impending sense of doom I can't seem to shake.

Let's focus on the positive, okay? he replies. *Consider it a reprieve from worrying. You need a break.*

In bed a little later, I try to take Rigel's advice. But instead of a reprieve, this lack of news seems more like the lull before a storm—a storm I can't prevent, because I have no idea when it will strike or what form it will take.

I fluff my pillow and stretch out, forcing myself to relax muscle by muscle. My breathing is just beginning to slow when the omni-phone on my nightstand pings softly. Rolling over, I pick it up and see a message from Molly.

Are you still up? Tristan just called and told me some stuff you'll want to know.

Wide awake again, I text her back. *Yes. Put your omni on secure and call me.*

A moment later her face appears on my screen, looking so worried my stomach clenches.

"Do you have your noise cancelation on?" I ask before she can speak, quickly enabling my own. She looks down, then nods. "Go ahead," I tell her.

"Believe it or not, Connor was at Tristan's house when he got home from his test today."

I stare at her. "Seriously? Teara Roark did say something to Kyna privately before the meeting started. That must have been it. I knew they'd have to release Connor since he wasn't charged, but I never thought he'd return to Jewel after all that happened. He just showed up without warning?"

"Not quite. Mrs. Roark invited him to the Bodyguard test but didn't tell Tristan in advance. She didn't want him to be disappointed if his father didn't come. Anyway, Connor and Tristan had a long talk while she was at the meeting tonight, and Tristan got some info about Devyn."

"Nothing good, I'm guessing."

She shakes her head. "No, definitely not good. Tristan couldn't give me any real details, since he doesn't have his super-secure omni-phone yet, but he sounded pretty worried. He said he'd tell me—and you—everything tomorrow, in person."

Though I'm frustrated she can't tell me more right now, I know it's not Molly's fault—or Tristan's. It was smart of him not to share anything classified or potentially panic-inducing over an unsecured line.

"Thanks, Molly. Tomorrow we'll figure a way to get all of us together. If it's something big, I'd rather know sooner than later."

"Same here. See you in church, M."

We click off then and I lie back down. Wondering what Tristan learned that has him so worried makes it even harder to fall asleep.

When I finally do drop off, my dreams are troubled, full of chase scenes, explosions and crowds of people screaming.

Remembering bits of those dreams on my way to church the next morning, I hope I'm just paranoid and not developing some weird new ability to see the future.

Molly's already in our church pew when I get there. The moment my aunt leaves for the choir room and Uncle Louie and Mr. O start talking, I lean toward her and murmur, "Anything else from Tristan?"

"Yes, we talked briefly this morning," she whispers, surprisingly cheerful considering what she told me last night. "Connor's leaving again—going back to Denver to get anger management therapy, if you can believe it! I'm hoping—"

She turns, craning her neck toward the back of the sanctuary. "Yes! They came!" Standing up, she motions to Tristan and his mother as they hesitate in the aisle.

They join us a moment later—the first time Teara Roark has ever been here—and I can tell they're both feeling pretty upbeat. Because it's church, Molly and Tristan clasp hands in greeting instead of kissing to get their boost from each other. The same boost I'm looking forward to when Rigel gets here.

"Did your father get off okay?" Molly asks.

Tristan nods. "He should be flying out of Indianapolis right about now. Whatever I said—or did—to shift his attitude, it still seemed to be in effect this morning. I'm taking that as a good sign."

His phrasing suggests he used his new, enhanced charm power to do a lot more than get info about Devyn out of him. Despite my impatience to know more, I feel my mood improving almost in spite of myself, the high spirits next to me are so infectious.

My mood improves even more when Rigel and his family arrive. We only have time for a quick touch and a whispered greeting before the service starts, but it's wonderful having him next to me in the pew. As soon as the music begins, I silently fill him in about what little Molly told me last night.

Then the lack of news last night wasn't such a great thing after all?

Maybe not. We'll know more when we can talk with Tristan ourselves. There is one bit of good news, though. I go on to tell him about Connor's change of heart.

That's great, Rigel thinks back. *Hope it sticks.*

Me, too. Partly because that would mean Tristan's powers are stronger than any of us realized.

As soon as the service ends, Molly, Tristan, Rigel and I hurry to join Sean and Kira at the back of the sanctuary, where they always sit with her family. Motioning them all a little apart from the crowd, I quietly ask everyone if they can get away for an hour or two this afternoon.

"Good idea," Tristan agrees, worry now marring his otherwise good mood. "I need to tell you all what I found out from my father."

"Arboretum?" Rigel suggests. "It'll probably be deserted, cold as it is. I'd say my place but my parents are having friends over tonight and will be home getting ready for that."

We agree to meet there at two o'clock, then disperse before anyone asks what we're talking about.

When Rigel and I arrive at the arboretum, Molly, Sean and Tristan are already there. A moment later, Kira jogs through the arched entrance.

"Sorry!" she pants. "Adina was showing off the new tricks she's taught her dog. Since I told my family I was just meeting Sean for a walk, I couldn't suddenly claim it was time-sensitive."

"It's fine," I tell her. "It's barely a minute past two."

Her obvious relief shows she still regards me as Sovereign first, friend second. I need to keep working on that.

Right now, though, I have bigger worries. I turn to Tristan. "Molly said you learned something important from him about Devyn?"

"Yeah. Maybe we should move away from the entrance before I tell you."

He's right. The arboretum is as deserted as we'd hoped, but as suspicious some of the locals are already, we can't be careless. Once we're all in a loose circle in a back corner of the big, walled garden, Tristan turns to the rest of us and takes a deep breath.

"Okay. So, I talked kind of a lot with my father yesterday. Some of it was great, like I told Molly. At first he tried to use his charm thing on me, but mine is definitely stronger than his now. When I 'pushed' back, he totally caved, admitted how awful he's treated Mother and me. Then, since he was already spilling his guts, I asked him about Devyn Kane and his plan."

"And he knew?" I ask excitedly. "More than he told the investigators?"

Tristan lifts a shoulder. "Not as much as I hoped. Not what the actual plan *is*. Just that the ultimate goal is to get rid of the Council and both of you—" He looks at Molly and me— "so Devyn can take over. Not sure if Father told the investigators that part."

"I don't think so," I say. "I've read all the reports from Allister and Lennox's trial, which included Connor's deposition. Under questioning, he admitted he arranged for Devyn to meet with them but claimed he didn't know what they discussed. Unfortunately, they couldn't confirm that with a memory extraction, since there wasn't enough evidence to charge Connor with anything. He did tell them Devyn is living out west somewhere, but insisted he'd never been told where."

"Father may not know exactly where Devyn is, but he knows how to get in touch with him," Tristan says. "He told me he warned Devyn the Council suspects him—that must have been after the investigators were done with him. When he tried to convince Devyn to abandon his plan, Devyn apparently said he's come too far to give up. Even implied he might speed things up, do whatever it is before anyone figures out what he's up to and how to defend against it."

I convulsively tighten my grip on Rigel's hand. "Speed things up? How much? Did Connor say?"

Regretfully, Tristan shakes his head. "I don't think Devyn told him. I doubt he'll tell him anything else, either, since Father supposedly told Devyn he's no longer interested in having any part in this 'new order' Devyn's hoping to create."

"So your father didn't know anything about *how* Devyn plans to get rid of us?" Molly sounds scared. I don't blame her. I'm pretty scared myself.

"No, but I'll bet it has to do with that stolen antimatter. He said he asked for more details one time and Devyn claimed they were too technical to explain. Which is probably true. Any ideas what we should do?"

Everyone looks at me but I don't have a good answer. "Keep digging, I guess, any way we can. Have you finished decoding all those messages yet?" I ask Rigel.

"Mostly, and they fit with what Tristan just said. There are definitely references to some kind of 'new order' and a power vacuum."

"Then whatever they're planning must have been in the works for a while," Sean says. "This is all pretty old info, right?"

Rigel nods. "The messages all stopped back in October, after Connor warned Devyn about them. Doesn't mean they're not still communicating. They probably just found another way that Dad hasn't discovered yet."

"Is Devyn mentioned by name anywhere?" I ask.

Rigel shakes his head. "Not that I've found. Just references to 'The Leader.'" He makes air quotes. "Maybe Devyn insisted his actual name never be used, even in messages as heavily encrypted as these."

"Yeah, he's always been super slick," I agree. "He'd want to make sure he has plausible deniability for whatever this group plans to do, so he can make a rational-sounding case for taking charge afterward." I hope I can convince the Council Royals of that.

"Those messages also mention the *Duchas* a few times, but they're a little vague on whether they plan to conquer them or join forces with them. Maybe both?"

I grimace. "Sounds like there's definitely some connection between Devyn's malcontents and the *Duchas*, then. The Royals didn't seem very concerned about that, even when I reminded them Mr. Farmer and that assassin, Carney, probably met at the local mental facility."

"Father was always the same way," Tristan says disgustedly. "He never considered *Duchas* worth taking into account. Hope that won't come back to bite us."

Sean frowns. "I know we can't take Farmer in for questioning or anything, but can't we have him followed, hack into his phone or computer or something? It would be good to find out what he's plotting or who he's been talking to."

"Cormac has him under surveillance," I assure him. "He'll tell me if he discovers anything dangerous."

"Maybe ask what he's found out so far anyway," Rigel suggests. "Could be helpful. I've been poking around in some online conspiracy forums, thinking Farmer might be in one, but there are thousands. Do you think Cormac can get me Farmer's IP address?"

"Um." I wrack my brains, trying to remember exactly what that means. Computer savvy, I'm not.

Rigel's clearly amused by my confusion. "Internet Protocol address," he explains. "It's a number that uniquely identifies his computer when he goes online. If I had that or, even better, his login info, I'd be able to narrow my search."

"Oh! Right. I'll ask him. Of course, it's possible Farmer doesn't use the internet at all," I warn him. "Some *Duchas* don't, like my aunt. Still, it's definitely worth looking into. Farmer may not be too bright, but plenty of idiots must spend time on the internet or all those conspiracy sites wouldn't exist."

That gets a tiny chuckle from the others, but their tension doesn't abate.

"How will we stop them, even if we do find out what they're planning to do?" Molly asks, worry creasing her brow. "Especially if it involves antimatter?"

"We'll figure that out once we know their plan." I try to sound more confident than I feel. "Did you all get a rundown on last night's Council meeting?"

Everyone nods.

Tristan glances at Molly, then me. "Mother said that NuAgra tour for the *Duchas* will happen a week from today?"

"Right," I confirm. "Then as soon as the tour's over and the *Duchas* are gone, there'll be a ceremony officially making NuAgra the *Echtran* center of government. All the local *Echtrans* will be invited to that. Kyna and Nara will fly in, too. For the *Duchas* tour, we're limiting it to the first hundred people who sign up online, and they'll have to provide matching ID to get in. That might help keep crazies out."

Rigel looks skeptical. "I'll bet Farmer and his buddies sign up the second they hear about it. You realize this could present a perfect target for Devyn's plan, whatever it is?"

"Yikes, you're right!" I exclaim. "I need to let Kyna know what Tristan learned. Maybe she'll postpone the whole tour and ceremony until we find out more."

"*If* we find out more." Sean pulls Kira tighter against his side. "For all we know, they could be massing for an attack right now." Then he looks at me. "Hey, what about that long-distance sensing thing you and Rigel can do? Can't you use that to detect any bad guys before they get here?"

"We have been," I tell him. "Every morning before school, and most days after, too. So far, we haven't found a threat within twenty miles or so of Jewel, but we'll keep checking."

I notice Tristan's also holding Molly closer than before. "Why not just do it all the time as a sort of early-warning system?" he asks.

"We have to be touching, for one thing," Rigel explains. "Plus it takes a lot out of M—more, the farther away she pushes. But now we know they could be speeding up their plans, we'll try to check more often. Right?" He looks at me.

"Definitely," I promise. "We'll do it before we go home."

Sean and Tristan both look relieved.

"Good," Sean says. "Of course, even if you do sense them coming, none of us except you and Rigel have enough power yet to stop them."

Which is unfortunately true. "Speaking of powers," I say, trying not to let my fear show, "what kind of progress are you all making with your abilities? Besides Tristan's charm thing, I mean."

"Our telepathy's getting easier," Molly tells me. "We used it a lot during church today."

"Ours, too," Sean admits. "Also, we experimented in one of the NuAgra greenhouses after Kira's test yesterday, and we managed to lift and move a forty-pound bag of dirt."

I blink, impressed. "Wow, that's a *lot* more than you could do a week ago."

"We weren't as drained afterward, either," Kira adds. "Though I can't claim it was *easy*."

"Easier, though," Sean says. "I wondered if having so few chances to be together this past week had a similar effect to an actual separation."

I turn to Molly and Tristan, who also look impressed.

"I haven't tested my 'push' thing since that bit I did to Alan a few days ago," Molly says. "But Tristan's ability is obviously way stronger than it was."

"It definitely had more of an effect on my father than I expected," Tristan agrees, "though I guess we won't know for a while how permanent my persuasion was. I'll honestly be kind of surprised if he actually follows through on getting help for his temper once he's in Denver."

Sensing how badly Tristan hopes he will, I smile encouragingly. "Hey, if he just takes the first step and finds someone to talk to, that'll be huge. So was getting that info about Devyn out of him. It makes me wonder what you could persuade someone to do with Molly boosting you."

They exchange a startled look. "I'm almost afraid to find out," Molly admits.

I don't say so, but I kind of am, too. "Have any of you tested things like your hearing since Thanksgiving? That should be getting better, too, especially when you're touching. You might be surprised what you can pick up from a distance if you try."

"Enough to maybe detect bad guys when you two can't be scanning?" Sean asks.

"It can't hurt to try." I shrug. "Any extra warning at all would be good."

"Why don't we all separate—couples together, I mean—and you each see how far you can push your hearing now?" Rigel suggests. "Meet back here in five?"

They all agree to that and the three couples move a bit apart from each other. The moment Rigel and I are screened by a spreading evergreen, we take advantage of our relative privacy for some serious kissing.

"Mmm," I murmur after several blissful minutes. "That was a great excuse you came up with to get me alone."

He chuckles. "Yeah, not quite up to Molly's standard, but it worked. Guess we should go see if anybody heard anything—though they might have put the time to the same use we did."

"I wouldn't blame them if they did." I grin. "Come on."

We indulge in another quick kiss, then we wander back to the corner we started from. A minute or two later, first Sean and Kira, then Molly and Tristan join us, from opposite directions. Judging by their smiles, both couples managed at least a bit of making out, too.

"So? Any luck?" I ask.

Sean and Kira exchange an intimate glance, then they both nod.

"When we focused, we could hear what people were saying down at Green's pub," Sean tells us. "Nothing worthwhile, of course, but it's cool we could do that."

"We didn't manage quite that far," Molly says, "but we were able to eavesdrop on a couple who were walking down Diamond, maybe a block away. Not that we can hold hands and listen all the time, either, especially at school. Unfortunately." She smiles up at Tristan.

I'm pretty encouraged, considering those were their very first tries. "Like everything else, it'll probably get better with practice, so keep working at it," I tell them. "You never know what'll come in useful."

Tristan grins. "Yeah, at this rate, we'll become a real Bond Squad yet! We should have a logo or something, like the Avengers or the Justice League."

The rest of us laugh.

"You don't think it might attract attention if we all start wearing matching t-shirts?" Molly teases him, getting another laugh.

"Okay, okay, fine," Tristan says. "But I'm starting to think we might actually be able to ramp up what we can do in time to make a difference. By the way, it's cool Kira and I are getting spiffy new omni-phones. Thanks for that," he tells Molly and me.

Kira nods, also smiling. "Those should make it easier for all of us to coordinate, if we need to."

Tristan glances at his current phone then. "Oh, hey, I should get home. Mother and I still need to talk about what happened with Father —we didn't have a chance earlier."

"We should probably all head home, if we plan to keep what we're doing secret," I suggest. "But let's plan to touch base before school every day, okay?"

Everyone nods and we all head toward the arboretum entrance.

.⁺₊

No one has anything new to report the next two mornings before school, beyond incremental improvements in telepathy and distance listening.

"Even that's great, though," I assure them.

"Any luck with those conspiracy forums?" Tristan asks Rigel Tuesday morning while we're still in the parking lot.

He shakes his head. "Not yet. Like I said before, there are a gazillion of them and lot are password protected, members-only. I can probably hack in, but just one at a time. I don't suppose Cormac had Farmer's IP address?"

"Oh! Yes." I get out my omni. "He sent it to me late last night—I meant to give it to you when you picked me up this morning. His team also captured a screen name Mr. Farmer has used online." I show Rigel the string of numbers and periods, followed by the name "Bullseye Buck."

He frowns at the screen for a second, then nods. "Got it. This should help a lot. Tonight I can start a more targeted search of those groups. You wouldn't believe some of the crap those people think is true—mind-control satellites, shape-shifting lizard people, you name it. Humans from a secret colony on Mars is so boring in comparison, it may not attract as many wackos as the wilder theories."

"Let's hope," Sean says. "But it'll be good if you can find out how close they are to the truth—and what they plan to do about it."

"Right, then we can work on how to stop them," Tristan agrees, then smiles self-consciously. "So, um, do you guys want to see my first idea for a Bond Squad logo?"

We all stare at him.

"I thought you were kidding," Molly exclaims.

He shrugs, clearly embarrassed now. "It's mostly just for fun. I tried to come up with something that wouldn't attract attention."

Pulling up his left sleeve, he shows us a design drawn on his forearm with blue ink—three grouped stars. "I tried six stars, but it was too busy. This way, each star is a couple and together the three couples make a little, um, constellation. I thought bringing in the space angle..."

"I like it," Molly declares, smiling up at him. "Subtle but distinctive."

Tristan regards her doubtfully. "You don't think it's stupid?"

"It's not stupid at all," I tell him. "Even if we can't show it to anyone else, having a visual symbol will make us feel more like a team. Definitely not a bad thing, since we may have to work together to deal with whatever's coming."

The warning bell rings then, so we all head to the school building. Before we separate, I suggest trying to get together again sometime before Sunday's tour.

"Kira's got a game tonight," Sean says. "I've got one tomorrow, then she has another one Friday. Right?"

She nods. "Plus practice on non-game weekdays. Maybe Saturday?"

"Let's talk more about it at lunch," I say, trying to stifle my impatience. "Meanwhile, everyone keep your eyes and ears open for *anything* that could give us a clue about what's coming. We may not have much more time to prepare."

23

Artificial selection

UNFORTUNATELY, there's no chance to talk privately at lunch because Bri and Deb drag us all into their discussion of the upcoming Winter Formal, a week from Friday—the last day before Christmas break.

"You guys obviously already have dates." Bri grins around at the three *Echtran* couples at the table. "So Deb and I were thinking maybe you could help *us* snag good ones. Kira, you know all the new guys. Think either of us might have a chance there?"

Kira blinks, clearly caught off guard. "Er…I don't think any of them have girlfriends, if that's what you mean."

Bri and Deb exchange a delighted glance.

"Can you put in a good word for me with Lucas?" Deb eagerly asks her. "He's in my sixth period Art class but he's so shy he hardly ever talks to anyone. He seems nice, though."

"Not to mention cute." Bri nudges Deb, who giggles. "I wouldn't mind getting to know his brother Liam better," Bri continues. "Every bit as cute, of course, and we're both into sports. It's the only thing I've gotten him to talk about so far, but I'd like to progress beyond that."

Though she's careful not to make any promises, Kira offers to drop a hint or two the next time she's in the NuAgra van with them. After that, they spend the rest of the lunch period and the walk to Government class trying to pry more details about the twins out of Kira and those of us who have classes with them.

. . .

Rigel's just about to drop me off at home that afternoon when my omni-phone pings to let me know the latest *Echtran Enquirer* is out.

"Want to read it now?" he asks, pulling up to the curb.

"Might as well." Leaning toward him, I bring it up on the screen so we can read it together.

I'm pleased to see that my latest article has top billing, since I worked hard on it last week. Hoping to shore up my support, I laid out several of my long-term goals for our people.

Among other things, I emphasized my plan to ensure broader repre-sentation of all *fines* in the new governments we're setting up on Earth and Mars. I also reiterated the importance of maintaining secrecy while we carefully work toward true integration with our *Duchas* neighbors, holding out hope that one day we'll no longer have to hide who we are.

A few Earth Scientists and political leaders are already aware of us, which proved useful during the Grentl crisis. A measured approach of gradually expanding awareness to those most likely to understand and accept will be key to avoiding unpleasant pushback, should the truth come out too quickly.

Reading to the bottom, Rigel turns to me with a smile. "Good job, M. Bet this'll undercut some of Devyn's recruiting efforts."

"I hope so. Now I guess we should check out Gwendolyn Gannett's latest bit of snark."

Scrolling past the updates on Allister and Lennox's trial, I click to the column headlined, *"Is the Echtran Council finally seeing sense?"*

I have now been able to confirm the rumor I hinted about to you last week, it begins. This coming Sunday, the *Echtran* Council plans to allow some of the *Duchas* residents of Jewel, Indiana to tour the new NuAgra agricultural and government facility. I'm told the purpose of this tour is to reassure the local populace that nothing sinister is going on there, as whispers along those lines have apparently begun circulating. My source assures me that all Martian technology will be carefully hidden from view.

Let's hope that this is just the first step toward letting the *Duchas* know enough about us that we can soon drop all the subterfuge and be ourselves around them. I've heard from many of you who are sick and tired of hiding your abilities, pretending to be less than you are. Perhaps the Council has finally realized that they're doing our people a disservice by insisting on this—particularly considering what those of you newest to Earth were promised by our Sovereign, back in Nuath. If this tour goes well, maybe it won't be long before we can all "come out of the closet," so to speak. Then we can start moving *Duchas* society in a better direction—one more like our own—for both their benefit and ours.

Why am I so optimistic? Because immediately following that tour the Council will hold a ceremony formally designating NuAgra as our new, centralized *Echtran* seat of government. The entire *Echtran* Council intends to be on hand for both this tour and the ceremony to follow. I, of course, plan to be one of the crowd so that I can report back to you with all the details.

Get a firsthand account of everything here next week!

"I was afraid of this," I mutter, frowning. "I wonder who her 'source' is?"

Rigel's clearly concerned, too. "Can't you talk Kyna into postponing the tour and stuff until we find out more about Devyn's plan?"

"I tried, but she's not convinced it's necessary, with no more to go on than what Connor told Tristan—especially since Connor has a history of lying. Nothing's come out at the trial so far to directly implicate Devyn in Allister and Lennox's plots, so some Royals are still making excuses for him."

"Like you said, he's slick. He must have known there was a chance they'd be caught and their memories probed, so he was careful never to say anything too incriminating in front of them."

I give a huff of frustration. "Meanwhile, Gwendolyn Gannett has let everyone know the whole Council will be at NuAgra in person on Sunday. If Devyn's looking for a chance to wipe us all out, we could hardly give him a better opportunity. I'm *sure* Devyn is at the bottom of all this. We need to prove it somehow, before it's too late."

"We will. Now that I have Farmer's IP and login, I should be able to do some serious digging."

"You really think you'll find anything?"

He raises a dark, perfect brow at my skeptical tone. "What, you don't think I can do it?"

"I know you can, if there's anything to find. It just seems like a long shot, even assuming Mr. Farmer knows how to use the internet."

"The very fact he has an IP address means he's *got* internet. Maybe he only uses it to stream pro wrestling or something, but it's worth checking out."

I can't disagree with that, considering how few leads we have—and how serious the problem might be. "Let me know what you discover."

"Promise," he says, leaning over for a lingering kiss. "Love you, M."

"Love you, too! See you tomorrow, if not sooner."

As I unlock the front door, I can't help thinking how wonderful it'll be once high school is over, with all these problems hopefully behind us. Whether we go off to the same college or whatever, Rigel and I will truly be together. Way more than now, anyway. I know it's dumb to look *too* far ahead, with so much uncertainty hanging over our heads, but I can't help imagining…

.⁺₊

Over dinner that evening, Uncle Louie is noticeably less talkative than usual. He also seems kind of fidgety, playing with his beef stroganoff instead of shoveling it into his mouth between funny stories from work. Judging by the curious glances Aunt Theresa keeps shooting his way, she's noticed, too.

I focus on him more closely and immediately pick up worry and traces of guilt. Uh-oh.

"Uncle Louie, is something wrong?"

He flinches, darting a look at me, then at Aunt Theresa. "Um, wrong?" he stammers, guilt and worry both ramping up. "What—? Why do you ask?"

"You've been on edge since you got home, Louie," Aunt Theresa snaps, frowning now. "What have you done?"

"Done? Me? Nothing, I swear! I remembered everything you told me, all the reasons we have to keep quiet about…you know." He nods at me. "So I was super careful not to let anything slip."

My alarm spikes higher. "Slip to who? Has someone been asking questions?"

For a long moment he hesitates, then nods. "Yeah. I wasn't going to mention it—didn't want to worry either of you." Or risk another scolding from Aunt Theresa, I suspect. "Anyway, I didn't tell them anything. At all."

"Who was asking you questions, Uncle Louie? About what? And when?" I try to keep my voice calm, though it's hard.

"Today, at the lot. Ted Farmer came by with a couple of his buddies. Seems he's, er, starting to remember at least some of what really happened that night he kidnapped you two. He wanted me to confirm it to his friends, but I wouldn't do it. No matter what he tried to get me to admit, I stuck to my story that it was all just an idea for a TV show, something I made up."

Aunt Theresa and I exchange a worried glance.

"Who did he have with him?" I ask. "Which buddies?"

"Joe Villiers and Arlo Smith. I've seen the three of them together at Green's but never knew they were talking about...this stuff. I promise, Marsha, I didn't tell them the truth about anything, even when they claimed they already know everything. They...they can't, can they?"

Could they? Surely Devyn wouldn't have—? "I doubt it," I say with more conviction than I feel. "What exactly did they claim to know?"

"That, um, you and Rigel are Martians, along with most of the new folks working out at NuAgra. That you're all part of an alien invasion force that's making Jewel its base of operations so they can take over the world. Stuff like that. I told them that was crazy. Then Farmer got mad, started yelling insults. His friends finally dragged him off when our security guy came over to see what the commotion was about."

I relax—a little. "Thanks for telling me, Uncle Louie—and for keeping your promise not to say anything. We already know Mr. Farmer can be dangerous, but it could be even worse if he manages to convince other people he's been right all along. Not that he is. At least not about the invasion part."

Uncle Louie looks at me doubtfully. "You're positive about that, right?"

"Yes," I assure him, adding a bit of 'push.' "I'm positive. They're only here because the colony on Mars is running out of power. Someday they —we—hope to help the people of Earth by sharing our technology. When they're ready. Meanwhile, I promise we don't mean any harm or have any plans to 'take over' anything."

I'm not about to mention Devyn and his possible plot. With luck, neither my aunt and uncle nor any other *Duchas* will ever need to know about that. Not if we can stop him, anyway.

And if we can't...

No. I'd rather not even imagine how badly that would set back *Echtran* hopes for eventual integration into Earth society and the brighter future I want for my people.

.+.

After dinner I go upstairs, supposedly to do homework but really so I can clue Rigel in on everything Uncle Louie said.

If he really didn't tell them anything, we shouldn't be any worse off than before, he reassures me. *We already knew Farmer was a nut job, that's nothing new. If he's still trying to convince others to go along with his conspiracy stuff, that probably means they're not all-in. Don't let it stress you out, M.*

Easier said than done. I ask if he's made any progress with those online conspiracy groups.

I'm just getting started on my searches. Pretty sure my dad won't approve of this kind of hacking, so I had to wait till I could do it on my laptop in my room. I'll keep you posted.

Okay. Love you, Rigel!

I've just finished the hour of Martian studies I try to do most nights after my homework is done when I get a secure call from Rigel on his brand-new omni-phone.

"M, I know it's too late for you to come over, but I wanted to let you know what I just found. Tomorrow I can actually show you."

From the excitement in his voice, I can tell it must be big. "Were you right about Mr. Farmer being involved with some conspiracy group?"

"Not just one, over a dozen. Looks like he's been into this stuff for years, since way before there were any Martians but you living in Jewel. But it's obviously the more recent stuff that we need to worry about."

My excitement nearly matches his, now—though it's mixed with a good bit of alarm. "Worry about? Have you figured out what Devyn's people are planning?"

"Not yet. And I still don't have anything the Council will consider proof that Devyn's actually involved. But I did just discover that at least one of these groups has recently started focusing on Jewel—on NuAgra, especially. And they're definitely getting info from somewhere that's *not* local."

"Which has to be Devyn—or someone working for him."

"Probably," he agrees. "I'm hoping a little deeper hacking might uncover some names. Anyway, I just wanted to tell you I wasn't wrong. In fact what I've found so far is probably just the tip of the iceberg—but I'll keep digging."

A glance at my nightstand clock shows it's already past eleven. "Okay, but try not to stay up all night doing it. We all need to be at our best for...whatever's coming. Tomorrow you can give me—and the others—more details."

"Will do. I'll, um, touch base again in a little while."

I know he means mentally, with our usual bedtime chat. "Can't wait."

.⁺.

On the way to school the next morning, Rigel gives me a few more details than he did mentally last night. We both prefer to spend our nightly falling-asleep "chats" just soothing and loving each other. Which has definitely been helping me to sleep better—and with great dreams.

"So, I found three separate groups that are talking about stuff in Jewel. Two are password-protected, but the other's just a private Facebook group. No wonder Farmer doesn't bother to keep his mouth shut around his friends."

"Or his kids, apparently, judging by what Molly's heard Ginny saying. Not that Mr. Farmer strikes me as all that bright...or at all balanced."

Rigel snorts. "Yeah, I don't think any of these people are, or they wouldn't believe half the stuff they do. Unfortunately, the bits I've seen posted about Jewel are at least partly true—though with a lot of fake scary bits thrown in, to rile people up."

"Yep. Scared people are both more dangerous and easier to control. Faxon figured that out early on. So did pretty much every dictator Earth has ever had."

"Oh. Right. Hadn't thought of it that way, but now it makes more sense. Still hard to imagine how people can believe some of the crap I've seen."

Remembering the rumors that were rife in Nuath last spring and summer, I'm not all that surprised. And that was with people who are supposed to be smarter than the average *Duchas*.

When we reach the school parking lot, the other two couples are already there so we join them to form a discreet huddle well away from the building.

Quickly, Rigel lets the others know he was able to find which conspiracy groups Mr. Farmer has been frequenting.

"Wow, good work," Sean exclaims. "M wasn't kidding, you're good at this stuff. What did you find out? Anything?"

"Not as much as I'd hoped," Rigel admits, "but I plan to keep digging."

Molly comments on yesterday's *Echtran Enquirer* then, complimenting me on my article but shaking her head over Gwendolyn Gannett's.

"She made it sound like we won't even have to bother with secrecy once this tour is over," she complains. "Does she think letting some locals see the inside of NuAgra will magically make all *Duchas* everywhere suddenly okay with the idea of aliens in their midst? It's a lot more likely going public would get us all thrown into internment camps."

At Tristan's emphatic agreement, I realize the two of them are probably extra-sensitized to that risk after researching the Korematsu case for their current Government project. Not that they're wrong.

"She's all about getting the eyeballs back next week, so she exaggerates all the time," Sean reminds them. "Everyone must realize that by now."

I nod. "Hopefully anyone who read her article also read mine, where I talked about a slow, measured approach, and how important it is to maintain secrecy for now. I'm more worried about how Devyn and his malcontents might take advantage of this tour, since Gwendolyn announced the whole Council will be there."

That worry ramps up even more the following morning, when Rigel shares more tidbits he's gleaned from those conspiracy groups. "On one sub-thread that mentioned Jewel, I found a reference to an upcoming 'opportunity.'"

Molly sucks in a breath. "The NuAgra tour, maybe?"

Rigel shrugs. "That was my first thought, but the person who posted it didn't include any details. If I can hack into their personal profile like I did Farmer's, there might be private messages with more info."

"How hard will that be?" I ask. "If this 'opportunity' they're talking about is this coming Sunday, that doesn't give us much time to prepare."

"It might be tedious, but definitely not impossible. Might go faster if you can come over again and help." He slants a smile at me that makes my heart speed up a little.

I immediately nod. "I'm in." Touching Rigel never gets old—even when it's for a reason like this.

"I'll see if I can get more info out of Ginny, too," Molly offers. "Maybe if Tristan and I approach her together—?" She glances up at him.

"Good plan," he agrees. "Let's sit with the cheerleaders at lunch and try it then."

Once I get to class, I discover the upcoming NuAgra tour is today's main topic of conversation. I didn't see it, but it was apparently mentioned on the local news last night, along with how to sign up online. Some people sound excited, while others think it'll just be boring. I mostly pick up worry from the other *Echtran* students, though obviously not for the same reason our little Squad is concerned.

When we get to the cafeteria later, I wait till Molly and Tristan set down their trays at the cheerleader table, then rest my arm against Rigel's.

You okay with listening in, so we'll know right away if they learn anything useful? I think to him. I know he's not a fan of eavesdropping on classmates this way.

For something this important? You bet.

The moment we focus our augmented super-hearing, we might as well be sitting right at the table with Molly and Tristan.

Molly makes a quick excuse for why they're there instead of here, pretending she has questions about the cheer schedule for the rest of basketball season. That's the first topic they discuss, then the conversation moves on to general gossip, including the NuAgra tour. That gives Molly her opening.

"Do you think your dad will do that tour, Ginny? I heard they're limiting it to the first hundred or so people who signed up."

"Are you kidding? Dad was probably the very first one to fill out the online form. He's been wanting to get inside that place ever since it opened. I warned him there's no way they'll let people see any of the secret stuff they're doing but he's still excited about it."

Molly shifts slightly, gripping Tristan's hand under the table. "What does he think he'll see there? The couple times I've been, it looked like they were just doing boring research on plants. Right, Tristan?"

He nods. "There's nothing very special about those greenhouses.

And when I've looked in the labs, it was just researchers in lab coats messing with trays and microscopes. They're probably developing new seed strains or something, but no one but a scientist would understand how. Definitely not my thing. Chemistry's hard enough." He gives an easy laugh.

"Yeah, well, Dad's heard a lot more is going on out there than they let on." Ginny smiles knowingly. "He says he'll have proof soon. I heard him telling Mr. Villiers so when I was out at his deer ranch yesterday."

"What kind of proof?" Molly asks, tightening her grip on Tristan's hand. "Tell us."

Even from here, I can hear the "push" behind Molly's words.

Ginny blinks at her, then blurts out, "Proof that there are aliens out there. Somebody's sending my dad a package he says will guarantee everybody will finally believe him."

24

Biodiversity

"A PACKAGE?" Molly presses "Of what?"

Ginny shrugs. "No idea. He noticed me listening and wouldn't say any more about it, at least not while I was there. I only help out in the store a couple hours a week, to satisfy visitation requirements. Even so, Mom doesn't like me doing it. She says Dad is a bad influence."

Clearly disappointed not to get more, Molly and Tristan release hands to finish eating their lunches.

Ginny blinks, frowning. "Um, I don't know why I told you that last bit. Don't...don't tell anyone else, okay? It's...kind of personal."

"Of course not," Molly assures her.

Ginny's expression instantly relaxes—one more example of how powerful Molly's 'push' is now. Stronger than mine. At least, I've never had that dramatic an effect on Aunt Theresa.

Don't be jealous. You have plenty of awesome abilities, Rigel thinks to me, making me start.

I didn't know you were listening in! Thanks, but I'm not jealous. Just... observing. I think it's great Molly's developing more powers.

Me, too. But don't let me hear you running down my favorite person in the world.

That gets a grin from me. *I'll do my best.*

· · ·

That afternoon, after a quick call home to check with his parents, Rigel drives me to his house.

"Dad has to help, um, 'Earthify' things out at NuAgra, but he'll wait to leave until Mom gets home from her shift in half an hour or so," he tells me as we get in the car.

Much as it sucks that they're sticking to their rule about the two of us never being there alone, I can't argue with their reasons. Still, "Someday..." I say wistfully.

Rigel instantly knows what I mean. "Yeah. Someday. Wish it didn't feel so far off."

"Me, too," I fervently agree, reaching over and taking his hand.

We drive mostly in silence, sharing our mutual frustration—and love. When we reach the house, his dad is just backing out of the garage. He stops to lower the window.

"Your mother got home a few minutes early, so I'm heading out. If you two decide to take a crack at Enid's files, I'll be interested to hear what you learn."

"Sure, Dad," Rigel promises, even though that's not what we have in mind.

"She used a whole different code than those messages," Rigel tells me as we get out of the car. "I'll mess with them at some point, but with that tour coming up in three days, I thought figuring out the *Duchas* connection was more time-sensitive."

That makes sense. "You still haven't told your parents you're poking around in those online groups?"

He gives me a crooked grin and shakes his head. "I didn't want to risk them stopping me. I get the impression they consider spying on *Duchas* a bit morally questionable—though I imagine that'll change if we find evidence they're an actual threat."

Dr. Stuart greets us just inside the door, still in her hospital scrubs.

"I haven't had time to put any kind of snack together for you, but I'm sure you can find something in the kitchen," she says apologetically.

"We'll be fine," I assure her. "Thanks, Dr. Stuart."

Smiling, she heads upstairs to change. Rigel gets milk and a box of graham crackers from the kitchen, then leads the way to his dad's office.

"I'd rather do this upstairs on my laptop, but Mom and Dad frown on you being in my room. Unfortunately." The suggestiveness in his look and tone makes my toes curl.

"We're alone right this moment," I point out, moving in for a kiss the instant he sets down our snack.

Trusting our enhanced hearing to give us ample warning of his mother coming back downstairs, we focus completely on each other for several blissful moments. At the sound of a door closing upstairs we reluctantly break apart.

"We need to figure a way to do this more often," Rigel murmurs, giving me a last quick kiss.

"Agreed. Though you *do* have a car now…" I wink at him.

"Mmm. We should definitely be taking more advantage of that. Let's build in some extra time for parking when I take you home."

That gets no argument from me. With a mutual sigh of anticipation, we move to sit down at Mr. Stuart's computer.

"Won't your dad figure out what you're doing if he checks the browser history?" I worry.

Chuckling, Rigel shakes his head. "C'mon, I'm better than that. I'll erase any evidence even Dad could find. And if Mom walks in, I'll just—"

He touches a key and one of the encrypted message files pops up to cover the screen, then he minimizes it again.

"Okay, here's that group where someone mentioned an opportunity. Let's see if he's posted anything since I last checked." He scrolls down. "Hm. Nope."

"You said Mr. Farmer's involved in a whole lot of groups?"

"I've found over thirty of them, yeah. Nearly half the sites he's a member of are conspiracy-related. You don't want to know about the rest."

I frown. "I don't? Why not?"

He grimaces. "Mostly porn. Trust me, you don't want to see it."

"Yikes, no. I don't," I agree, shuddering.

He's quiet for several minutes then, opening multiple tabs and typing stuff in at intervals, then reading, then switching tabs to type in more. Like last time, I don't contribute anything to his efforts except my touch. But, like last time, it seems to help.

Finally both boredom and curiosity get the better of me. "So what are you finding?"

"Oh, yeah, sorry. I had to keep rotating groups, since some sites will lock me out if I try too many wrong passwords in a row. I've hacked all of Farmer's profiles now—all the conspiracy ones, anyway. Along with the identical user name, looks like he mostly uses the same password everywhere, too. Dumb, dumb, dumb."

I just gaze at him admiringly—which wins me a quick kiss.

"Anyway," he continues, "I've found two others places besides the three I mentioned this morning where people have recently talked about Jewel. But I think this one bears the most watching." He clicks to a site called *ETs in America.*

I lean closer and see a long list of topics. "Latest government coverup... More strange lights seen in Nebraska... Two more abductions last week," I read aloud.

Rigel points at one a third of the way down: "Likely alien command centers."

"This one not only mentions Jewel, but NuAgra—along with about a dozen other places around the country that don't seem to have any connection to *Echtrans.* Guess it was too much to hope that the rumors about NuAgra would stay local." He clicks on the topic, then to the last page of comments in the discussion thread.

"That's Mr. Farmer, right?" I ask when he scrolls down to one by "Bullseye Buck" with the title *Indiana aliens.*

Rigel nods. "That's the name he uses everywhere, even the porn sites. Idiot."

I read through the diatribe on the screen about aliens that can take human form and what he thinks they might be putting in the water at NuAgra and in Jewel. The spelling and grammar are so bad, parts of it are hard to make out, but he finishes with a claim he'll be able to prove it all within a week or two. Then I notice the date on the comment is two days ago.

"Look. He wrote this before the NuAgra tour was even announced," I say, pointing.

"To the *Duchas,* anyway," Rigel says.

I stare at him. "You think Mr. Farmer has access to the *Echtran Enquirer*? How can he?"

"Probably not directly. But what if he's in contact with someone who does?"

"Like Devyn? Hm." I reread the last two lines of the rambling post. "He definitely implies he has inside information."

"Which is why I want to take a look at any private messages he's been sent," Rigel explains. "Just a sec."

He clicks a little icon in the upper right corner of the window and sure enough, it pops up a list of messages—the most recent ones from today. Rigel opens the last one, but it's from some other member of the forum demanding more information. So are the two previous ones. But then—

"Jackpot," Rigel murmurs.

I can send you something that will help you get the proof you want about NuAgra, it reads. *Expect to hear more from me in the next day or two, along with the tools you'll need. If you follow my instructions, you and your friends will be hailed as heroes for exposing the alien menace in time.*

"How much do you want to bet that's Devyn?" point at the screen name—SageOne.

"If it is, I'm guessing *his* account will be a whole lot harder to hack, maybe impossible. Didn't you say he's got some genius Informatics guy helping him?"

I grimace. "Yeah, an old friend of Enid's. Still, this proves they're planning *something.*"

"Something, but not what or when." Rigel scowls in frustration. "I'll keep checking back as often as possible between now and Sunday's tour, find out if that's the opportunity they're talking about. Can you come up with an excuse to not be there?"

"Just me? No. Once all the *Duchas* are gone, Molly and I are supposed to be part of that ceremony to formalize NuAgra becoming our new governmental center. All the Jewel *Echtrans* have already been invited. It's…a pretty big deal."

His worry floods into me. "I don't like it. You heard what Connor told Tristan—Devyn wants to get rid of you, Molly and the Council. I can't imagine a better setup for him to do that."

"I can let Kyna know what you just found, see if it's enough to convince her to postpone," I say dubiously, "though it would help if we had something more concrete than a single anonymous message."

"I'll do all I can to get more proof," Rigel promises. "I can't lose you, M. You know that."

"I know. And ditto. So you need to be careful, too."

He gives a mirthless snort of laughter. "I'm hardly in danger sitting in front of a computer screen. When Dad gets home I'll find out *exactly* what kind of security he's got out at NuAgra and see if it can be beefed up any more. Maybe even tell him what I've found so far, to get him on board."

"Good idea. So, do you think—?" I begin when Dr. Stuart comes in.

Instantly, Rigel taps the key that overlays the screen with an encrypted message—which he's already decrypted—and manages a fairly convincing smile. "What's up, Mom?"

"M's aunt just called, wanting to know if she'll be home in time for dinner."

A glance at the time in the corner of the computer screen shows it's already after five. "Oops, it's later than I thought. I should call her. Thanks, Dr. Stuart."

We wait till she's out of the room again, then look at each other. *What do you think?* I silently ask Rigel, in case his mom is still within earshot. *Should I stick around while you do more hacking?*

After a second's hesitation, he shakes his head. *I doubt I'll get much more this evening, though I'll keep looking. You already helped with the hardest part. Much as I love having you here, it may be more necessary later, if things start heating up.*

Okay. I was thinking we could work on our stasis field today, but maybe we can do that after school tomorrow.

I call Aunt Theresa to tell her I'll be home soon while Rigel wipes the computer's browser history.

"Even if I show Dad Farmer's messages, I'd rather he not know exactly how much hacking I've been doing," he explains when I look puzzled. "C'mon, I'll take you home. If we leave right now, we can stop along the way for ten or fifteen minutes without your aunt getting suspicious."

His expression tells me exactly what he wants to do with that ten minutes—and I'm in total agreement. "I like the way you think. Let's go."

.⁺₊

Friday morning before school, Rigel and I give the rest of the "Bond Squad" a quick recap of yesterday's breakthrough. They're as concerned by the implications of those private messages as we are.

"That definitely ties into what Ginny Farmer said yesterday." Tristan frowns. "Bummer she didn't know what'll be in that package, though. Think it could be an actual bomb?"

"The message said whatever it is would help Farmer and his fellow crazies get proof of aliens at NuAgra," Rigel reminds him. "So probably not a bomb? More likely some kind of listening or video device Farmer's supposed to hide there. But why? It's not like Devyn needs any proof—he already knows what's going on."

The warning bell rings, making us all jump. "Everyone keep coming up with theories," I suggest as we hurry from the parking lot. "We're for sure meeting tomorrow, right?"

Everyone nods, to my relief.

"Arboretum again?" Sean asks.

"We'll try there first," I reply. "Let's say two o'clock. There's a decent chance it'll be empty again this time of year. If not, we'll find somewhere else. This might be our last chance to figure out what they're doing and come up with a way to stop them."

Rigel nods grimly. "Hopefully by then I'll have something more definite."

No one else is there yet when Rigel and I reach the arboretum the next day, so we step just inside the entrance to wait.

"Want to try a wider scan of the area before the others get here?" he suggests.

"Good idea."

Taking one of my hands in his, he wraps his other arm around my shoulders. "Okay, go."

I grin at his phrasing, then focus my emotion-sensing to start a slow sweep of the area.

Oops, I think to Rigel almost immediately, when I pick up another couple inside the arboretum. Definitely *Duchas,* they're absorbed in each other and nothing else.

Stretching out farther with my senses, I gradually widen my search. I've pushed out more than a mile when the others arrive.

"Hey, guys," Tristan greets us, coming through the arch hand-in-hand with Molly. Sean and Kira are right behind them. "What's going on? Are you—?"

"Yeah, just checking for any baddies nearby," Rigel replies as I open my eyes. "Nobody to worry about at the moment."

We all continue into the arboretum then, startling the young *Duchas* couple already there.

"Uh-oh," Molly mutters. "Should we—?"

Before she can finish, the twenty-something man and woman smile nervously at us and scurry through the exit—presumably looking to be private somewhere else. I can't feel particularly guilty, considering the seriousness of what we might be facing tomorrow.

"So, um, strategy session," I say once I'm sure the couple is out of earshot. "Rigel hasn't found any more private messages yet, right?"

"No, unfortunately. I checked right before leaving. Though it occurred to me that if we've figured out Farmer isn't all that bright, Devyn has, too. Which means he probably won't let Farmer in on whatever his real plan is. More likely, he'll be fed some story that plays into what he already believes, so he'll willingly do whatever they need him to."

Kira coughs self-consciously. "Yeah, I can personally vouch for how effective that strategy can be. Allister and Lennox totally played on my existing prejudices. And even though they never told me what their real plot was, it came way, *way* too close to working."

"I wouldn't be surprised if that tactic was Devyn's idea, since he was apparently in contact with them the whole time. He's clearly a lot more clever than they are." I smile reassuringly at Kira to show I'm not holding a grudge. "So even if Rigel does intercept more messages to Mr. Farmer, they might not help us much."

"Could be," Rigel agrees. "Farmer himself has sent a couple more—he's obviously getting impatient. But Devyn or whoever hadn't replied yet, as of an hour ago."

Molly looks hopeful. "Then...they can't possibly be planning anything as soon as tomorrow, can they?"

"Or maybe they just decided not to involve any *Duchas* after all," Sean suggests. "Especially one as crazy as Farmer. Which puts us back at square one."

"Not quite," I say encouragingly. "The six of us are much better equipped to repel an attack than we were a few weeks ago. The longer they delay, the better prepared we'll be. Especially if Rigel finds any other ways they're communicating."

He nods. "I'm working on that. Since Dad's new network isn't operational outside of NuAgra yet, I've been pinging all over the internet looking for anomalies—anything using that same code, for example. Haven't found anything yet, but I'll keep looking."

"Meanwhile, since we have this place to ourselves now, let's work on those new powers you guys have." I speak briskly, trying to keep everyone's spirits up. "What Molly and Tristan did at lunch Thursday, with Ginny, was pretty impressive."

They exchange a grin, but then Tristan shrugs. "Not super useful, though. Too bad she didn't know more."

"I don't know," I say. "It helped confirm that bit about Mr. Farmer getting a package" I turn to Sean and Kira then. "I guess you two have been too busy with basketball to work any more on your telekinesis?"

"Mostly," Sean admits. "Though at Wednesday's game I sort of tried to use it on my own. Liam was getting a little overenthusiastic again, so I focused on him once when he was shooting. He did miss the shot, but I can't swear I had anything to do with it."

My brows go up. "Pretty cool if you can do that, even to a limited extent, when you're not touching Kira. Maybe she can, too."

"I'd have to experiment more before I can be sure," he cautions. "Guess we should both do that," he says to Kira.

"Um, I did try to move a dish on the kitchen counter after you told me what you did, but nothing happened."

Sean grins at her. "No biggie. You have your super Ag power—that's totally your own. Me, I don't even have regular Royal 'push.'"

"How do you know?" I ask, curious.

He snorts. "I tried plenty of times on Molly when we were growing up. I don't remember it ever working once."

"Nothing works on Molly, remember?" Tristan reminds him. "I found that out my first day at Jewel High."

Sean's brows go up. "Oh. Right. And I don't think I ever tried it on anyone else. Maybe I should—just to test."

"Yes, definitely test it sometime." I do another quick scan of the immediate area. "Meanwhile, why don't you and Kira show us what you can do together? Nobody's close, but let's go to the back corner anyway."

When we're all well out of sight of the archway, I motion for them to go ahead.

The two of them glance around, then exchange a long look—clearly communicating—before nodding. As the rest of us watch, they face one of the decorative boulders at the base of a nearby tree. Barely two seconds pass before the boulder quivers, then slowly rises several inches off the ground. They keep it suspended in midair for nearly a full minute before carefully setting it back in place.

"Whew!" Kira exclaims. "Okay, that was definitely the heaviest thing we've ever lifted."

"Yeah, that thing must weigh a couple hundred pounds," Tristan says, visibly impressed. "That was…wow."

Molly nods, her eyes wide with amazement. "Way more useful than anything we can do."

"Not necessarily," I tell her. "Being super persuasive—and then reassuring people, like you did Ginny—could have a lot of everyday applications. You know, like deflecting *Duchas* suspicions. If that starts to become a problem, I can't think of anybody better than the two of you to handle it."

They both look pleased by that idea.

"Wish we could practice the electrical thing again," Sean says. "But somebody might notice if we fried a tree or something."

I laugh. "Yeah, I think they would. Anyway, we had a different idea. Did you bring the multimeter?" I ask Rigel.

"Yup." He pulls it out of his backpack. "We can test lightning bolts, too, if you want, but M and I thought we should work on something that could be even more useful—and a lot more discreet. Remember that stasis field M and I created when my mom took that antimatter bomb out of Kira's neck?"

Sean nods slowly. "Oh, right. If we could all do that, we might be able to neutralize other antimatter bombs—if we figure out where they are. How does it work?"

"Sort of…the opposite of how we make bigger lightning bolts," I answer. "You know how imagining a threat increases the electrical charge we—each couple, I mean—can produce?"

Everyone nods.

"And how when you touched the multimeter together *without* a pretend threat, the charge was smaller than what you each produced individually?"

More nodding.

"Creating a stasis field goes even further in that direction," Rigel explains, "though it takes a lot of focus. You sort of tamp down everything negative or scary as much as you can. Together. I'm not explaining this very well…" He looks to me for help.

"It's like meditation," I offer. "You consciously empty your mind, your feelings, of everything stressful while inviting in peace and calm. Which was *super* hard to do when facing an actual bomb that might go off any second! We never could have managed it if we hadn't already practiced."

Sean's frowning now. "But...how can you tell if it's working? Other than a bomb not blowing up, I mean. How do we test it?"

"The only way we knew we'd done it the first time was when it froze the time on our phones," Rigel tells him. "When we experimented some more, we discovered we could sort of...suck the electrical charge out of things, like electronics. They mostly started working again as soon as we stopped, but we accidentally drained a couple of batteries. After that, we only used it on old stuff we didn't care about."

Tristan also looks dubious. "Doesn't sound like anything the rest of us can master by tomorrow, even if we're willing to destroy our phones and stuff."

"That's why I brought this along." Rigel holds up the multimeter. "I figured out how to recalibrate it to register negative charges. M and I practiced with it before I took her home yesterday afternoon."

"You probably won't get good at it right away," I caution them, "but Rigel and I thought you should at least try—see what it feels like to suppress a charge. If they do come at us with bombs, that might come in really handy."

Rigel sets the little machine on the metal bench and steps back. "Who wants to try first?"

With a shrug, Tristan steps forward, pulling Molly with him. "Calming thoughts. Right."

They look into each other's eyes for several seconds, a little smile playing around Molly's mouth, then reach for the multimeter. They have to actually touch it before it registers—a good sign. When they step back, Rigel picks it up to check the reading.

"Almost zero. Not negative, which is what's needed for a real stasis field, but definitely less than the first time you touched it together without a pretend threat."

"Can we try?" Sean asks eagerly, dragging Kira forward.

Just then, I hear voices approaching. "Better not not right now," I say quickly. "I think we're about to have company."

"Guess we'd better call it a day, then." Rigel stuffs the multimeter back into his backpack and we all head toward the archway.

As we reach it, a mother, father and three kids stroll into the arboretum, laughing and talking together. They barely glance at us as we pass them on our way out.

"If you get a chance, you guys can practice with your phones," Rigel whispers once we're outside. "Try to make the clocks stop. If we get more time to prepare than we expect, we can work more with the multi-meter later on. I'll tell M right away if I find out anything else online."

"And Molly and I will do our best tonight to convince the Council to postpone things," I promise. "But with just that one message to go on... well, don't hold your breath."

25

Molecular clock

AT SEVEN O'CLOCK THAT EVENING, the *Echtran* Council gathers at the O'Garas' house for one final time. Kyna and Nara are here in person tonight, since they plan to attend tomorrow's ceremony. After that, our weekly meetings will move to a special new conference room at NuAgra. Since Mr. O'Gara is sitting in, too, the little living room is even more crowded than usual.

After greeting us all and reading through the agenda, Kyna clears her throat. "As this will be our last meeting here, I'd like to thank the entire O'Gara family for graciously allowing us the use of their home these past few months. Your hospitality has been much appreciated."

Everyone claps.

Mrs. O blushes. "It's been our honor. But I'm sure we'll all feel safer at NuAgra, as the security there is apparently much more robust."

"It is." Mr. Stuart's smile is slightly apologetic. "The need for secrecy limited what we could do with private houses. Not so at NuAgra."

"In that case," Mr. O'Gara says, looking thoughtfully at Molly, "perhaps Princess Malena and the Sovereign should consider spending more time there and less at their homes once their sleeping quarters at NuAgra are furnished."

Molly and I exchange a startled look but Mrs. O immediately adds her support. "That's an excellent idea, Quinn. The safety of our two heirs to the Martian throne should be paramount, particularly with a possible threat looming." Noticing Molly's alarmed expression, she adds, "We can work out any details later."

Seizing that opening, I jump in. "Speaking of that threat...Kyna, have you told everyone what Tristan learned from Connor about Devyn?"

"I intended to do so tonight," she replies. Then, to the others, "A few days ago, Connor Roark informed his son that Devyn Kane intends to somehow eliminate the Sovereign and this Council and seize power himself...and that he may attempt to do so sooner rather than later. Though nothing was said about the stolen antimatter, was it?" she asks me.

"Well...no," I admit. "But Connor was already off the Council when the theft was discovered, so he wouldn't have known to ask. Whether Devyn's plan involves antimatter or not, don't you think it would be safest to hold off on tomorrow's activities at NuAgra? That ceremony would be a perfect opportunity for him to take us all out at once."

There's a lot of frowning at that.

"You've made your opinion of Devyn clear, Excellency, but Connor Roark is a proven liar," Malcolm points out, just like Kyna did earlier. "He could have fabricated whatever he told his son about Devyn, simply to deflect suspicion from himself."

"I agree," Breann says. "While it's true Devyn has always been ambitious, he has never shown any tendency to violence."

I barely suppress a snort. "Maybe not personally, but we know he was in contact with Allister and Lennox while they were plotting to kill me. Even if Devyn didn't orchestrate that attack, he did nothing to prevent it."

"Devyn may not have been aware of their plans," Malcolm protests. "Must I remind you that he was never directly implicated in the transcripts from the traitors' extracted memories?"

With an apologetic glance at me, Kyna nods. "I'm afraid that's true, Excellency. Circumstantial evidence aside, without more proof than Connor's word, we can't assume Devyn poses a physical threat, though he may well pose a political one."

I'm about to insist that we don't dare take that risk when I get an urgent mental message from Rigel.

M! Farmer just got a message from the guy we think is Devyn, telling him to expect a package and instructions tomorrow. You definitely need to get the Council to cancel everything out at NuAgra!

I glance wildly around at the others, but of course they didn't hear anything. Kyna looks ready to continue the meeting.

Can you text your dad? I think back to Rigel. *I can't blurt this out without explaining how I know.*

Oh. Right. Just a sec.

"Suppose someone does try to smuggle an antimatter bomb into NuAgra," I say before Kyna can introduce another topic. "Can the new security system detect one as tiny as what was implanted in Kira's neck?"

"It certainly should," Mr. Stuart assures me. "With the stolen antimatter in mind, I added a protocol to screen for negative energy signatures. Unfortunately, there's been no opportunity to test it beyond simulations, as we don't have access to—" He breaks off, glancing at his omni. "Just a moment."

I hold my breath while he reads Rigel's message.

He looks up, his expression now alarmed. "It appears we may have more than *Echtran* conspiracies to contend with. If you recall, Princess Malena's would-be assassin spent time in a *Duchas* mental facility frequented by the *Duchas* who sent that drone over NuAgra."

Most Council members nod.

"My son has apparently taken it upon himself to investigate a few online forums devoted to alien conspiracy theories. He now claims to have found recent communications between that same unstable *Duchas* and someone he believes is *Echtran*."

Kyna frowns. "That sounds…less than ethical, Van. I hope your son has not compromised our secrecy with his hacking or whatever?"

"I doubt it. Rigel is quite skilled enough to avoid *Duchas* detection— though I suspect he waited until now to tell me because he knew I'd be obligated to put a stop to his snooping. However, if these malcontents are recruiting *Duchas* to their cause, they're surely committing a far greater breach of our secrecy protocols than anything my son has done."

Malcolm snorts. "Even assuming young Stuart is correct, how could adding *Duchas* to their ranks possibly help those malcontents? Given how primitive their technology is, I can't imagine the *Duchas* will pose any additional threat."

"Are you kidding?" I stare at him. "The *Duchas* outnumber us by billions. Primitive or not, guns are as deadly as our energy weapons. Even if all they had were sticks and stones, they could overpower us by sheer numbers if they decide we're a threat."

"The Sovereign is right," Kyna says. "Every *Echtran* on Earth will be at risk if our secret is discovered before the proper groundwork has been laid. Tomorrow's tour of the NuAgra facility should be a solid first step in that direction."

"No!" I exclaim, looking to Mr. Stuart to back me up. "If whoever stole that antimatter is coordinating with the locals, they might use *Duchas* to smuggle in a bomb. We *have* to cancel that tour—or at least postpone it until we figure things out."

Kyna's not the only one shaking her head. "I'm afraid it's too late to do that now, Excellency. The tour and the ceremony to follow have been publicized to both the local *Duchas* community and our own people. Canceling it at the last minute would almost certainly make the citizens of Jewel more suspicious than before, the opposite of what we are trying to accomplish. It would likely draw criticism from much of Jewel's *Echtran* population, as well. Think how someone like Gwendolyn Gannett might spin such a decision."

"Does that matter, compared to preventing a possible catastrophe?" I ask incredulously. "If Devyn's looking to take over leadership of all the Martians on Earth, we'll be handing him a perfect chance to wipe out the monarchy and the whole *Echtran* Council in one fell swoop."

"Oh, come," Malcolm says scornfully. "You can't possibly believe Devyn Kane capable of such a thing?"

I totally do. "Can we take that risk?" I ask again, looking desperately around at them all. Surely at least Nara and Kyna will back me up?

"Every *Duchas* taking that tour had to register in advance," Breann reminds me. "No one else will be allowed in. They will each be scanned before entering and won't be permitted to carry cellphones or any other technology inside. That should minimize any risk."

To my dismay, even Nara agrees. "Don't forget, Excellency, that all *Echtrans* living in Jewel were also carefully screened before being allowed to settle here."

"What about the ones who just settled *near* Jewel? They weren't screened," Molly blurts out. "Didn't some of them turn out to be Anti-Royals?"

"It's true that there are *Echtrans* living in Indiana who did not make the, ah, cut for Jewel residence," Kyna admits. "Some for good reason. Still, if NuAgra is to become the Earth equivalent of the Thiaraway complex in Nuath, we cannot bar entry to our own people based on political leanings or vague suspicions. Van claims NuAgra's security system is now nearly on par with that of the Royal Palace on Mars. We simply have to trust that will be sufficient to ensure everyone's safety, both tomorrow and going forward."

They're not convinced of the risk, I think frantically to Rigel. *Nobody wants to cancel tomorrow's NuAgra events, they claim it'll look bad. What exactly are the bad guys planning? Do you know?*

No, not exactly, but it's definitely tomorrow, he replies. *I'll text my dad again. Maybe he can make them see reason.*

A second later, Mr. Stuart frowns at his omni again. I hold my breath, hoping…

"Rigel now tells me this *Duchas* and whoever he's communicating with are planning *something* for tomorrow, though he's not sure what. Is Ted Farmer on our list of attendees?"

With a barely-concealed sigh of impatience, Kyna turns to Breann. "Do you have that list?"

"Just a moment." Breann also looks irritated but pulls up a holographic screen. "Farmer…Farmer… Ah. Yes, Ted Farmer was among the earliest to sign up for the tour."

"We can't let him in," I insist. "Not only did he send that drone, he threatened to kill my aunt and me back in September. The guy is seriously nuts."

Breann raises a brow. "In that case, won't he cause a scene if he's barred from the tour?"

"I wouldn't be surprised, judging by his behavior when he collected his drone," Mr. Stuart confesses. "But allowing him inside could pose a greater danger to others."

"We'll have him closely watched," Kyna assures us. "If he causes the least disturbance or tries to access any area not on the tour, we can remove him for cause, which is less likely to arouse suspicion than denying him entrance for no apparent reason. We can hardly explain that Rigel Stuart hacked into a private *Duchas* forum."

I'm close to panicking now. "But if Rigel is right, letting Mr. Farmer inside could put everyone in danger, *Echtran* and *Duchas*. Is avoiding bad press worth that risk?"

Malcolm clears his throat. "Perhaps, Excellency, if you could tell us what, exactly, the risk is? Surely you don't believe this *Duchas*, Farmer, can stroll into NuAgra with an antimatter bomb in his pocket?"

I glare at him in frustration. "You make it sound absurd, but we can't know he won't."

Now everyone in the room looks skeptical.

"I'm confident Van's security system will prevent that, Excellency," Kyna says dryly. "Our security team will also be told to keep a close eye on Farmer. With so little in the way of specifics, I simply can't justify doing more than that. Now, shall we go over the program for tomorrow's dedication ceremony? The plan is to clear the NuAgra facility of *Duchas* by four-thirty. Local *Echtrans* may arrive as early as five o'clock, as events are to commence at five-thirty."

They still refuse to cancel, I tell Rigel. *Your dad's assured them NuAgra's security system will detect any bomb someone tries to bring in. I wish we had more details about what they're planning!*

I'll keep checking Farmer's messages, but they could wait until just before the tour to send those instructions or just include them in the package. You're the Sovereign. Can't you just...order them to cancel it?

I bite my lip, carefully probing the feelings of everyone present as they discuss who'll speak in what order tomorrow. Molly's the only person who shares my anxiety, though not to the same extent. Tamping down my fear, I force myself to think rationally.

If I do force them to cancel, what's to keep Devyn from trying again later? I send to Rigel after a moment. *At least now we have fair warning. Canceling might tip him off that we know something. He could do something even sneakier next time and catch us completely off guard.*

Wow, I hadn't thought of that, Rigel admits. *You're right. Once NuAgra's our main government center, he'll probably have lots more opportunities to wipe out you and most of the Council. We'd better use what little advantage we have now to try and stop him.*

After that I try to act interested in the various other items on the agenda—retrofits of the transport ships in Nuath between launch windows, the approaching elections there, and plans for our own elections in the spring.

Unfortunately, I can't shake a looming dread that by this time tomorrow, everyone in this room could be dead.

.⁺₊

"If you believe the bad guys plan to blow up NuAgra this afternoon, why didn't you go all Sovereign last night and overrule the Council?" Molly whispers to me before church the next morning. "I totally expected you to."

We couldn't talk privately after the meeting, because Mrs. O insisted on choosing Molly's outfit for the ceremony before bedtime.

"Rigel wanted me to," I admit, "until I pointed out we might not get any warning at all if they back off and regroup—especially if they figure out why we canceled. We figured this little bit of advantage is better than none at all."

She looks doubtful, but then nods. "I guess that makes sense, though I wish we had more time to prepare."

"Other than your abilities getting stronger, what more could we do? Oh, here comes Rigel."

Anything new? I think to him as he and his parents come up the center aisle.

Not yet. His frustration comes through as clearly as his thought. *I'll check again the second I get home.*

The moment he slides in next to me, his presence and touch ease my fears so much, I'm half convinced we'll handle whatever happens... somehow. On my other side, I notice Molly and Tristan discreetly holding hands, too. A moment later, when Tristan glances over and gives me a tiny nod of understanding, I know Molly silently relayed everything I just told her.

She still looks worried, though, so I reach over to pat her arm, trying to share some of my confidence that we'll all get through this together. She gives me a half-smile. Then, weirdly, I hear a faint echo of what sounds like Tristan's voice.

Seriously, they have a point. Could be worse later.

Startled, I look at Rigel. *Did you hear that?* I silently ask him.

I thought...was that Tristan? How—?

I don't know, it's never happened before.

"M?" Molly whispers then. "Did you just...? What...?" She looks just as amazed as I am.

"I...I thought I heard Tristan's thought just now," I mutter back. "Did you—?"

She nods, wide-eyed. "I heard you, then Rigel. That's...new. And kinda freaky."

"No kidding! It could be useful, though. If we can all do this, it would make it a lot easier to coordinate as a group." We're both using that almost sub-vocal whisper no non-*Echtran* can hear—no *Echtrans*, either, unless they're nearby.

For a long moment, she and I stare at each other, not quite daring to believe. Then, tightening my grip on her arm and Rigel's hand, I think to both of them, *Let's test this! Rigel, what did you have for breakfast?*

I... French toast, he thinks back, looking past me to Molly and Tristan, who's staring at us in disbelief.

Taking my hand off of Molly's arm, I whisper, "Did you get that?"

Tristan nods first. "French toast," he whispers back. "Right?"

I sense excitement welling up in the others, matching my own. "Yes! I wonder—"

Letting go of Rigel's hand, I motion for Tristan and Molly to do the same. Then I put my hand on Molly's arm again and think to her, *Can you hear this? Does this work with just the two of us?*

She watches my face, clearly concentrating, but doesn't reply. After several seconds, she whispers, "If you said anything, I didn't hear it, sorry."

"Ah, well. It was worth a try," I reply, shrugging. "Maybe eventually?"

The singing starts then, but the four of us continue discreetly experimenting with this new-found ability off and on during the sermon that follows. By the time the service ends, we've verified we can each communicate with all three others, but only when all four of us are connected by touch.

That'll make doing this in public a little awkward, I think to the others during the benediction. *Even so, it's great to know we can do this!*

Definitely, Tristan sends.

As we all stand for the closing hymn, Molly sends, *Let's check if it works with Sean and Kira.*

I nod. The moment we're dismissed, the four of us hurry through the crowd toward the back of the sanctuary, where Sean and Kira sit with Kira's family.

They must know from our expressions that we want to talk. Kira whispers something to her parents, then she and Sean join us as we make our way outside, where we can be a little more private.

"What?" Sean whispers when we're well away from the nearest group. "Did Farmer get another message with the actual plan?"

Rigel shakes his head. "Not by the time I left for church, but we discovered something else. Maybe not as time-sensitive, but definitely cool. M, you want to show them?"

"Yeah. C'mere, you two." I lead everyone down the little brick path that winds around the side of the church, farther from the crowd. "Sean, Kira, keep holding hands. Now..."

My own hand firmly in Rigel's, I reach over and hold lightly to Kira's wrist. *Can you guys hear me?* I think as hard as I can.

Both Sean's and Kira's eyes go wide.

"Holy crap," Sean breathes. "How—?"

"We just found out during the service we could do this with Molly and Tristan. Molly, you two try with them now."

She and I trade places and she reaches over to touch Kira. A few seconds later, all four of them are nodding.

"Yep," Tristan tells Rigel and me. "It definitely works both ways. Let's see if we can do it with all six of us."

I glance back toward the door of the church but don't see the O'Garas, the Stuarts or my aunt and uncle yet. "Okay, but quickly. We may not have long."

Keeping a wary eye on the gradually dispersing crowd near the door, I take Tristan's hand, since the other four are still linked. Then Rigel thinks, *Can everybody hear me? Nod if you can.*

They all do.

"How cool is this?" Tristan exclaims. "And if we ever get to where we can do this without touching, we'll be able to—"

He breaks off as the O'Garas emerge from the church, my Aunt Theresa and Uncle Louie right behind them. Tristan's mother and the Stuarts are also visible just inside the doorway.

"We'll work on it more later," I promise them all.

"And I'll let you all know the second I find out more about what Farmer's up to," Rigel adds. "Speaking of which, I'd better get home and check his messages again."

He gives me a quick kiss and hurries to join his parents.

"Do you think we'll get enough warning to stop them?" Molly asks worriedly.

"We will." I inject a lot more certainty into my voice than I feel now that I'm not touching Rigel. "Somehow."

.•.

By two o'clock that afternoon, I'm increasingly nervous. The NuAgra tour is supposed to start in an hour and we still have no idea what the bad guys are planning to do. Maybe nothing?

As Rigel reminded me the last time I reached out mentally for an update, we don't actually *know* it was Devyn who contacted Mr. Farmer. It could be another crazy conspiracy kook pretending to have inside info —one who just happens to sound more literate than most.

Anything? I send yet again, barely ten minutes after the last time I asked.

I'll check, he thinks back. *Dad's on his computer, so I need to go upstairs and log in with my laptop.*

I can tell from his mental tone he's losing hope we'll get an answer in time, just like I am. So I'm surprised when he reaches out to me excitedly a few minutes later.

Finally! Message for Farmer popped up about two minutes ago from the same guy, telling where the package is and what to do with it.

Where? I think back, hope and fear rising up in equal measure. *Can we get to it first?*

Out at the deer ranch, so I doubt it. But Farmer hasn't replied, so maybe he hasn't seen the message yet?

We have to try! I send back. *Can you pick me up? I'll be ready by the time you get here.*

I hurry to the kitchen where my aunt is mixing up yet another batch of cookies. "Aunt Theresa, I need to leave early for the NuAgra tour. The Council wants me to go over a few things for the ceremony afterward I told you about. Rigel will come by for me in a few minutes. Are you and Uncle Louie still planning to go?"

She glances at the clock on the stove. "Goodness, it's nearly two-thirty already. I'd best make sure he isn't asleep in front of the television again. Louie's been very curious to see the inside of that complex." From her expression, she doesn't share his curiosity.

"Great. I'll, um, see you there, then."

I run up to my room, throw on the outfit Molly picked out for me to wear today and give my hair a last brushing. Rushing back downstairs, I open the front door just as Rigel pulls up. Calling a hurried goodbye to my aunt and uncle, I race down the porch steps to his car.

"Has Mr. Farmer seen that message yet? Did he respond to it?"

"Not by the time I left, but that was less than a minute after we talked." He leans over and gives me a quick, hard kiss. "For luck. For both of us."

I kiss him back. "We'll need it! Did the message say what's inside the package?"

"Supposedly three tiny listening devices." He turns down Opal toward Diamond Street. "Farmer and his friends are supposed to hide them inside NuAgra, spacing them as far apart as they can. I doubt that's what they really are, though."

I suck in a breath. "You think they're bombs? Spreading those out would make sense, too, to cause as much damage and kill as many people as possible."

"My thought exactly," he replies grimly, turning on to Diamond Street.

The moment we're out of downtown Jewel, Rigel picks up speed. The clock on the dash shows it's already past two-thirty. We'll be cutting this awfully close.

Sensing my worried thought, Rigel reaches over and puts a hand over mine. "It'll be okay," he assures me, though he can't possibly know that.

"It will," I agree, not fully believing it. "As long as we're together."

Once we're on the two-lane road leading to the turnoff for the deer hunting ranch, Rigel suggests we watch for Mr. Farmer's truck, in case it passes us going the other way—which would mean we're too late to beat him to the drop point.

"Do you remember what it looks like?" he asks me.

"Vaguely." I think back to the one time I saw it, when Aunt Theresa drove me to his store without us knowing he planned to keep me prisoner. "Black, pretty beat up. I never thought to check the license plate or anything, though."

Almost as soon as I say that, I see a black pickup approaching. Craning my neck, I try to get a look at the driver. It's an elderly man— and the truck looks almost new.

"Not him," I tell Rigel. "I'll keep watching. You just…drive."

Two more black pickups pass us before we reach the smaller county road heading north to the deer ranch, but neither is Mr. Farmer's. I don't think. "Could we have missed him?" I ask worriedly.

"Yeah, there are at least two ways to get to NuAgra from here. The other one's shorter than how we just came. We'll go that way after we check the drop point."

No more trucks pass us before Rigel turns at the weather-beaten wooden sign reading "Bulls-Eye Whitetail Ranch & Specialty Meats." We wind along the dirt and gravel road until we reach the store where

Mr. Farmer held Aunt Theresa and me hostage in September. There's no truck there, either.

"Either Farmer hasn't seen the message about the package yet, or he's long gone," Rigel comments, driving around behind the building to check the dirt lot there. Also empty. "Let's see if it's still where the message said it would be."

We get out of the car and Rigel runs to an overflowing dumpster off to the side of the back lot, me right behind him. The stench from the dumpster is overpowering as Rigel checks the hollow in a rotted section of tree trunk lying behind it.

"Gone." He indulges in a second or two of cursing, something he almost never does, then grabs my hand, a newly determined look on his face. "We need to get to NuAgra—fast. The tour's supposed to start in ten minutes."

"Maybe they can stop Mr. Farmer before he gets inside," I say hopefully as we scramble back into the car. "I'll call Kyna."

She doesn't pick up, so I'm forced to leave a message. "Kyna, Rigel intercepted another message to Mr. Farmer a little while ago and he's definitely planning to bring something—tiny recording devices or maybe bombs—into NuAgra today. He needs to be detained and searched the moment he shows up. I'm on my way."

Clicking off my omni, I turn to Rigel. "No idea if she'll check her messages in time. She's probably too busy dealing with any *Duchas* who are already there. Hurry!"

26

Character displacement

UNFORTUNATELY, though Mr. Farmer's hunting ranch and NuAgra are both well outside of Jewel, they're on opposite sides of it. There's no possible way we can be there in ten minutes.

While Rigel drives, I try calling Molly. She doesn't answer, either, so I send her a text explaining everything and telling her to alert the others. I've just hit "send" when my phone rings.

"Molly?"

"Sorry I missed your call, I was in the bathroom. Is there news?"

I quickly repeat everything I just put in my text to her. "I take it you're not at NuAgra yet?"

"No! Since we hadn't heard anything more about the bad guys, we were just going to come with our parents later on. I'll grab Sean and call Tristan and we'll all get out there as fast as we can."

"Good. If you get there before the tour starts, make sure they don't let Mr. Farmer inside. We'll be there as soon as we can. Be careful!"

Fifteen minutes later, Rigel finally pulls up to the guard house at the NuAgra gate. I see dozens of cars in the big lot by the main building but no people milling around.

"Crap. The tour must have started right at three." Leaning forward, I catch the guard's eye. As I hope, he immediately straightens up, bows, and waves us through. Rigel guns it up the short drive and swings into the first parking spot we reach.

"C'mon," he says, jumping out of the car.

We both run flat-out toward the entrance, where a few stragglers are still waiting to be allowed in. Mr. Farmer isn't one of them.

"Do you...think he's already inside?" I gasp between breaths as we run.

"Probably. Is that his truck?" Rigel points and my heart sinks.

Then I see something that worries me even more—Sean, Molly, Tristan and Kira getting out of Sean's car just ahead. Changing our trajectory slightly, Rigel and I race over to them.

"We came as quick as we could," Molly says, "but apparently not quick enough." She looks toward the building. "At least nobody's blown it up yet."

"No, they'll want to wait till you and I are both inside, along with the Council," I point out. "We need to find Farmer and those bombs before they all arrive for that ceremony."

Sean looks past Molly. "Do we know for sure they're bombs?"

Rigel shrugs. "Not for absolute sure. They *could* be recording devices, like the message said, maybe even sent by some other *Duchas* conspiracy nut. But can we take that chance?"

We reach the entrance as the last two local *Duchas* are let in after being checked off on the tablet a security guy is holding. Like the guard at the gate, he immediately snaps to attention when he sees me, but when he starts to bow I shake my head.

"Not here!" I hiss, nodding toward the crowd visible through the big glass doors.

"Of...of course. My apologies." Rattled and embarrassed, he ushers us all inside.

Once in the main lobby area I start looking around wildly before common sense intrudes. Taking a deep breath, I motion the others off to the side.

"Okay," I whisper, "we know Farmer's here somewhere, probably with whatever was in that package, since I never heard back from Kyna."

Just then, I spot her near the hallway leading to the government offices, motioning curious *Duchas* on past, though with a smile.

"I'm afraid there's nothing of interest down here. Just empty offices."

Telling the others to keep looking for Mr. Farmer, I hurry over to her. "Did you get my message?" I whisper the moment the *Duchas* are out of earshot.

Her fist comes halfway to her chest before she self-consciously drops it to her side. "Message? No, Ex— er, I'm afraid not. People began arriving a full half hour before the tour, so I've been otherwise occupied. Has there been a development?"

"Yes. Rigel intercepted another message less than an hour ago from the person we think is *Echtran*. Mr. Farmer's truck is out front, so I assume he's here somewhere?"

Alarmed now, Kyna nods. "Yes, his name was checked off the list of attendees. I believe he was one of the earlier arrivals. Since we agreed we had no specific reason to detain him—"

"Now we do. That *Echtran* he's been talking to sent him something to plant here—supposedly miniature recording devices, but it could be antimatter bombs. We need to find him."

She frowns. "Wouldn't Van's security system—?"

"I don't know. Apparently not? If Mr. Farmer's inside, whatever he brought must be, too. We need to find him—now," I repeat, urgently.

"Agreed." Scanning the lobby, Kyna motions another woman over. "Thea, can you please divert the, ah, tourists away from this corridor while I help the Sovereign with something?"

The younger, darker-haired woman takes up Kyna's post and we head across the wide reception area.

"I haven't seen Mr. Farmer since he checked in." She finally sounds worried. "Do you recall what he looks like?"

"Definitely. But I don't— Oh, there's my uncle. Maybe he knows where he is. Just a sec."

I move to intercept Uncle Louie and Aunt Theresa, who've just emerged from one of the labs on the opposite side of the main area.

"—way they combine genes like that is so cool," my uncle is saying. "If they really can extend the growing season and double yields, that could mean— Oh, hi, Marsha. Did you just get here? This place is amazing! Why didn't you tell us they—?"

"We can talk about it later, Uncle Louie," I interrupt. "Right now, I need to know if you've seen Mr. Farmer."

He blinks. "Um, yeah, when we got here he was out front talking with Joe Villiers and Arlo Smith, but they all went in ahead of us. I saw Joe over there before we went into the genetics lab." He points toward the rear of the huge central concourse.

I look, but unfortunately, I don't know either of those men well enough that I'd definitely recognize them. "Is he there now?"

My uncle shakes his head. "There's Arlo, though, by the information desk. The one with the red ball cap," he clarifies before I can ask, since there are several people there.

"Thanks, Uncle Louie. I'll catch up with you both later, okay?"

Nodding, he gives me a wink. "Oh, right. I guess you have, like official stuff you have to do, huh? Since you're the—"

"Sshh! Louie!" my aunt shushes him.

"Um, yes," I whisper. "Back in a bit." I hope.

Motioning to Rigel and the others, who are still waiting just inside the front doors, I stride across the big room toward Arlo Smith. Catching my eye, Kyna moves that way, too.

"Hello, ah, Mr. Smith?" I say when I reach him.

Clearly startled, he turns. "Uh, yeah?" He regards me warily, radiating nervousness. I can make a good guess why.

"You're friends with Mr. Farmer, aren't you?" I ask as Rigel moves to my side, flanked by the other two couples.

Arlo's nervousness ramps up several notches and he swallows convulsively. "I, ah, yeah, I guess. Why?"

I put some 'push' into my voice. "Tell me, did Mr. Farmer give you anything before you came into NuAgra?"

His frightened gaze darts from me to Rigel to Kyna, who's standing off to one side, frowning. "Er…I don't remember."

Molly steps forward, clasping Tristan's hand just behind her. "Are you sure you don't remember, Mr. Smith? It's important for us to know."

The man blinks several times, his eyes going slightly unfocused. "Oh. Right. Um, yeah. Ted got these three teensy recorder things from somebody who said if we stick them all around here—" He waves a vague hand— "they'll prove we were right that there are aliens in Jewel, disguised as regular humans. He gave me and Joe one each to, um, deploy."

"I'm sure getting that proof is important to you, Mr. Smith. Have you already hidden yours?" Molly asks persuasively. He nods. "Can you please tell me where you put it?"

The 'push' behind that question is so strong, even I can feel it. Arlo Smith doesn't stand a chance.

"Sure," he says without hesitation. "Over there near the door, in that plant pot." He nods toward a flourishing palm in an ornate planter.

"Thanks, Mr. Smith," Molly says with a brilliant smile that makes him blink again. "Enjoy the rest of your tour. No need to mention our little talk to anyone else, okay?"

His head bobs jerkily in agreement. "Right. Right. Won't say nothing to nobody. I never quite believed— That is— Ted's always been a little nuts, you know."

With an understanding nod, Molly steps back, releasing him from her thrall. He blinks dazedly for a moment, then scurries for the front door. A moment later, he's gone.

"Great work, Molly," I mutter. "Now we know where one is. Two to go." I turn to Sean and Rigel. "Do either of you know what Nate Villiers' dad looks like?"

Sean nods. "He comes to all the games. Looks a little like Nate. I don't—" He gazes around the huge atrium. "Wait, there he is—and isn't that Farmer with him?"

I whirl to see two men—one definitely Mr. Farmer—coming through the double doors at the back that lead to the greenhouses.

"Yep. C'mon." I head their way, everyone else behind me. Kyna brings up the rear, reading something off her omni-phone. My message? This would have been way easier if she'd checked sooner.

The men see us coming—and Mr. Farmer obviously recognizes me.

"Should'a known you'd try to stop me, alien queen," he snarls, drawing curious glances from some of the other *Duchas* milling around. "You're too late, though."

Fighting down sudden panic, I force my voice to stay calm. "Oh? Too late for what?"

"You'll never find 'em. In a few days we'll have all the proof we need to call the cops or maybe the feds. Your whole plot will be exposed. They'll round y'all up and ship you off to one of them FEMA camps where they keep the alien bodies. Hell, they'll probably put up a monument to us for saving the world from your alien scourge!"

"What is it we supposedly won't find?" Tristan asks, using his own 'push' this time.

Though Mr. Farmer sneers, he does answer. "Recorders, practically microscopic. If they haven't already picked up enough evidence to take to the feds, they will soon."

At that, Kyna steps forward. Slightly taller than Mr. Farmer, she looks down her nose at both men, exuding an impressive air of authority.

"You gentlemen should know that corporate espionage is a crime, per the Economic Espionage Act of 1996, which makes theft of trade secrets a federal offense. If it's true that you've planted recording devices anywhere in this facility, it will be a simple matter to have you both arrested and brought up on charges."

Mr. Villiers blanches visibly. "We're not...we didn't... Corporate espionage? We're not after any trade secrets, just proof of aliens! Ted here said..." He trails off with a panicked look at Mr. Farmer. "Tell them we're not doing economic whatever, won't you?"

Using some 'push' of my own, I hold Mr. Villier's gaze. "I'm sure if you cooperate by telling us where the devices are hidden, we can arrange to have you released with only a warning. Otherwise, a big, important corporation like NuAgra will almost certainly do whatever it takes to protect their proprietary information."

"Right. Right. I'll cooperate," he replies, nodding spasmodically. "I put one just behind that door there." He hooks a thumb over his shoulder toward the one they just came through. "Right down near the floor. And Ted here—"

"Shut up, you idiot!" Mr. Farmer turns on him fiercely. "She's using some alien mind trick on you. Don't tell them anything else!"

Mr. Villiers shakes his head. "Forget it, Ted. I ain't going to prison! None of your other crazy theories panned out, dunno why I thought this one might."

"Don't call me crazy!" Mr. Farmer yells, getting red in the face and lunging for his friend.

Rigel steps up to block him and Kyna motions to two burly security guards standing near the central desk. They immediately head our way, their holstered *Duchas* weapons clearly visible.

As an interested crowd starts to gather, I tug Mr. Villiers away from Mr. Farmer. "Where's the other recorder?" I ask urgently, doubling down with my persuasion. "If you tell us, I'm sure they'll let *you* go."

"He...he stuck it under the counter of that desk there." Mr. Villiers nods to the one the security guys just left. "Over on the right side. The things have some kind of stickum on them. Arlo Smith had one, too, but I dunno where..." He looks wildly around.

"That's all right, we've already spoken with Mr. Smith and he was equally helpful," I assure him. Then, to Kyna, "What do you think? Will that do?"

She nods. "I believe so. Mr. Villiers, you are free to go. I recommend you do so immediately."

Like Mr. Smith, he doesn't have to be told twice. With one last, fearful look at Mr. Farmer, now screaming curses at the guards restraining him, he scrambles for the exit.

Mr. Farmer's yelling has drawn an even bigger crowd of interested *Duchas* onlookers now. I'm trying to figure out the best way to keep things from escalating out of control when Kyna does it for me again.

Totally ignoring their captive's wild ranting about the "alien menace," she speaks to the guards holding him, raising her voice enough to be heard by everyone nearby. "Suppose you escort Mr. Farmer to a quiet area where he can calm himself while we call for assistance from the local authorities. I understand they have experience dealing with his, ah, irrational outbursts."

A chuckle ripples through the crowd of onlookers as the guards march the still-resisting Mr. Farmer away.

"We'll be concluding our tour in twenty-five minutes," Kyna announces as the *Duchas* start to disperse. "If there are tour areas you would still like to see, please do so now."

The crowd disperses then, hurrying off in different directions.

"I apologize for superseding your authority just now, Excellency," Kyna says quietly, "but under the circumstances—"

I shake my head. "No, you were right to take charge, Kyna, thank you. To those people, I'm just a nobody high school junior. It would have looked weird if I'd acted like I was somehow in charge."

"My thought exactly. Shall we go somewhere more private to discuss how we should proceed?"

"Good idea." Still clinging to Rigel's hand, I invite the other two couples to follow.

When we reach a door near the hallway Kyna was guarding earlier, she glances curiously at the others.

"It's okay," I tell her. "I'd like them to be part of this discussion."

Though her brows go up, she doesn't question me. "Very well."

She opens the door and we file into a room lined with video monitors and various complicated-looking panels—the security control center, I assume.

Rigel's dad turns in surprise. "Is there a problem? The guards seem to have Mr. Farmer well in hand." He gestures toward one of the screens.

Kyna shuts the door behind us. "I'm afraid Mr. Farmer may be the least of our problems. Excellency?"

"Yes, it turns out Rigel was right last night," I tell Mr. Stuart. "Somehow, Mr. Farmer and two of his buddies managed to sneak something past your scanners. We don't know for *sure* it involves antimatter, but—" I break off at his sudden frown.

Swinging back to the screens behind him, Mr. Stuart leans in to examine one of the smaller panels. "A tiny aberration did pop up during a handful of individual scans as people entered, but as it wasn't limited to Mr. Farmer, I assumed it was a calibration error—or perhaps *Duchas* heart pacemakers."

"Let me guess," Rigel says. "Were the other ones Mr. Villiers and Arlo Smith?"

His father pulls up a second window on the same screen he was just looking at and runs a finger down the list displayed there. "I'm afraid so. Not a mere calibration error after all, I take it?"

"No. They *claim* what they brought in are just tiny recording devices. Would your scanners have registered those?"

"Definitely," he replies. "In fact, we confiscated two small digital recorders from other guests. These anomalies were rather different, though not what I would expect from antimatter bombs. Where are those devices now?"

"Still where Farmer and his friends hid them," Rigel answers. "We need to collect them and get rid of them somehow."

I nod. "Though we should wait till all the *Duchas* are gone. If they *are* bombs, they're probably timed to go off when the whole Council is supposed to be here."

"I believe everyone on the Council except Van and myself are in our new conference room by now," Kyna tells me. "The plan was to meet there briefly before the dedication." She glances at her omni. "The local *Echtrans* will expect the doors to open again at five, so the building will be largely empty for half an hour. I'm unclear, however, on how we are to, ah, 'get rid' of possible antimatter bombs?"

Rigel and I look at each other, then at his dad.

Mr. Stuart clears his throat. "Rigel and the Sovereign were able to neutralize the one implanted in Miss Morain, here, by essentially reversing their electrical ability to produce a dampening field. That allowed my wife to extract the bomb so it could be safely detonated."

Kyna blinks. "Ah. Yes, I remember that. You mean to attempt something similar now?"

"It should be a whole lot easier to get bombs out of a building than a person," I point out with a half-smile at Kira.

"Very well." Kyna becomes brisk. "I'll oversee clearing out the rest of the *Duchas* so you can proceed."

We follow her back to the atrium, where a few small groups of guests are still reading the placards explaining NuAgra's purpose. Kyna speaks quietly to the woman at the central desk, who nods and picks up a microphone.

"This concludes today's tour of NuAgra," her amplified voice announces throughout the building. "Please make your way to the exit. If you have further questions, feel free to call or email us. Thank you for coming."

Though a few look disappointed, everyone willingly heads for the main entrance. A security guard stationed by the door checks off names as people exit. My aunt and uncle are among the last to leave, pausing next to me on their way out.

"Really glad we came, Marsha," Uncle Louie enthuses. "Everyone seems impressed by all the cool stuff they're doing here, even if they don't know—" He breaks off at my expression. "Um, everything."

"Come along, Louie," Aunt Theresa admonishes with a quick, apologetic smile for me. "We'll see you at home later, Marsha."

The one visitor most resistant to leaving is Gwendolyn Gannett. "I don't see why I can't remain inside, as I plan to cover the dedication ceremony as well," she hisses when Kyna motions her toward the door. "It's not like I'm one of *those*." She nods toward the last few *Duchas*, now exiting.

"Sorry, ma'am," a guard says. "We need to clear the facility so it can be prepped for the next group. You'll be allowed back in when we reopen the doors at five."

Still grumbling, she follows the last visitors outside. Kyna then asks all the *Echtrans* who helped with the tour to go out front, to oversee the visitors' departures. "Please make sure no *Duchas* linger on the grounds," she tells Mr. O'Gara. "I'd like them well away before our own people begin arriving."

He nods and marshals the small group toward the doors. Kyna waits until they're all outside, then rejoins us. "That should be everyone. We rechecked the list as the *Duchas* left to ensure none remain lurking in odd corners. Overall, I'd say our tour went quite well—apart from possible bombs, of course."

Her caveat gets a nervous laugh from all of us.

"I recommend we all work quickly," Kyna says then. "Van, why don't you seal the front doors? I'll fetch the rest of the Council and send them out back, just...just in case."

Mr. Stuart leans over the main desk and pushes a button. "The doors are sealed. What now?"

"Our first step is to find the things," I reply. "If they're where we were told, one should be under this counter, somewhere along here."

I crouch down and look up at the underside of the big, semi-circular desk. So does everyone else.

A second later, Tristan exclaims, "Found it!" He points at a metal ball half the size of a BB stuck to the underside of the counter.

"Should I just...pry it off?" I ask Mr. Stuart.

Pulling a small scanner from his pocket, he passes it over the tiny sphere, looks at the screen and frowns.

"Hm. No antimatter reading, but it is emitting a barely-detectable signal. Definitely one of the anomalies I picked up earlier."

"Whatever it is, it shouldn't be here." Reassured that it's unlikely to explode on contact, I'm reaching down to detach the little device when I hear a babble of voices.

Straightening, I turn to see the whole *Echtran* Council heading toward us.

"I thought you were taking them out back?" I say to Kyna.

She huffs out an irritated breath. "I tried, but they insist on knowing what's going on. I told them explanations could wait, but—"

"Yes, what is this, Excellency?" Malcolm demands. "Kyna says a few *Duchas* managed to smuggle in possible bombs? We were assured that couldn't happen." He looks accusingly at Mr. Stuart.

"I don't believe they are bombs," Mr. Stuart says, "but—"

"Whatever they are, we don't have time to discuss this in committee right now," I interrupt, stepping forward. "I'd like you all to follow Kyna outside, past the greenhouses, to wait for the all-clear. With luck, you won't have to wait long."

Mrs. O'Gara frowns. "Excellency, if there's a risk, surely you and Princess Malena should come with us? Sean as well. These others—" She motions toward Mr. Stuart, Rigel, Tristan and Kira— "can handle whatever needs to be done."

"No," I tell her. "Rigel and I need to be here in case—"

I'm interrupted by a tiny *pop* and all the lights go out.

"What on Earth?" Mr. Stuart exclaims.

A babble of frightened voices breaks out from the others. I'm groping for Rigel's hand in the dark when the lights come back on as suddenly as they went out.

"Oh. Just a power flicker, apparently," Breann comments as everyone's brief panic subsides.

Mr. Stuart is frowning, though. "Even an outage that brief shouldn't have been possible. Along with the new security system, we installed enough redundancy to prevent so much as a millisecond of power loss. Nothing short of an EMP could have—"

Before he can finish, thick gray fog starts billowing out from under the counter. Everyone scrambles backward, but Rigel and I, the closest, aren't quite quick enough. A second later, we're both coughing and gagging.

"Tear gas!" Rigel croaks. "Everyone outside!"

There are no more arguments. I glance over my shoulder as we all hustle toward the back of the building and see another cloud of smoke coming from the planter by the front door. From what Mr. Villiers told us, there'll probably be more up ahead.

"Everyone hold your breath!" I shout as loudly as my constricted throat will allow as Mr. Stuart pushes open the back doors. "Now!"

Sure enough, another cloud of tear gas greets us on the other side. Frantically, I motion for everyone to keep moving. A few seconds later, we're through the fog and into the clear space between the main building and the greenhouses. I gratefully suck a deep breath of cold, clean outdoor air into my starved lungs.

We all stagger on past the greenhouses before finally stopping. Eyes still streaming, I turn to count heads. To my relief, all seven Council members plus our Bond Squad of six are safely outside and well away from the gas.

"Is everyone okay?" I ask, my voice still gravelly.

Though clearly shaken and confused, they all nod.

"Good. That's the important thing." Then, before they can start asking more questions, I continue, "We should wait out here a few minutes, let the air clear. Then we need to figure out—"

I break off, interrupted by a high-pitched whirring hum that strikes me as unpleasantly familiar. My heart suddenly in my throat, I pivot toward the sound and see a large, silvery orb about twice the size of a basketball hurtling toward us across the empty fields.

An Ossian Sphere.

27

Convergence

ALL THIRTEEN OF us stare at the approaching Sphere in horror. Though deathly pale, Kyna finds her voice first.

"That's impossible! Those were all supposed to have been destroyed."

"Impossible or not, how much do you want to bet that's where the missing antimatter is?" Rigel asks.

His father whips out his scanner again and points it toward the rapidly-advancing orb. "No question about it. I'm detecting more than a billion times as much as the last bomb contained."

Rigel turns to me, his fear matching mine. *Can we create a stasis field that big?*

We have to try, I think back, grabbing his hand as the thing slows, then stops, to hover ten feet above the ground. Desperately, we work to suppress our mutual fear so we can focus.

We're just about to raise our free hands to point at the sphere when Devyn Kane himself steps from behind the nearest greenhouse.

"You!" I exclaim. "How did you—?"

He holds up both hands, palms out, in a gesture of apparent surrender. "Please don't be alarmed, Excellency. I'm here to help," he says in that soothing, measured tone I remember all too well. "When I learned what the local *Duchas* intended today, I came as quickly as I could to offer you my assistance. I must say, I am sincerely delighted to find you all still alive and well."

Weirdly, my alarm starts to recede, but Rigel takes a half step forward, still gripping my hand.

"No thanks to you!" he says angrily to Devyn. "We know you've been egging them on."

"On the contrary," Devyn responds, smiling benevolently. "When I discovered a radical *Echtran* element meant to provide the Terrans with Martian technology while enflaming their prejudice, I hurried here to intervene on your behalf."

"How?" I ask suspiciously.

Devyn's smile broadens. "With this, of course." He gestures toward the Ossian Sphere now hovering just behind him.

Rigel and I both stiffen. *We need to get rid of that thing,* I think to him, lifting my other hand again. *He's somehow using it to—*

"Please, Excellency," Devyn interrupts my thought, "I implore you not to do anything foolish. I truly have no desire to harm any of you."

"Then why did you turn that thing into an antimatter bomb?" I demand, pointing at the Sphere.

He looks genuinely startled. "A bomb! That wasn't my intent at all. I simply used the antimatter to enhance the power of this remarkable device, for the good of us all. However, if you destroy this Sphere as you did the previous one, everyone within a mile of us likely *will* be vaporized. None of us wants that, I'm sure. Right now, I merely wish to talk."

I exchange a baffled glance with Rigel. "Talk?" I repeat suspiciously. "About what?"

"The best possible future for our people, of course. I want that for them as much as you do. I always have." His voice is totally calm and rational. "I'd like to offer my help to you and the *Echtran* Council as we all press forward toward that mutual, worthy goal."

"You...you..." I struggle to remember what I know about this man. "You've been trying to undermine us these past few months."

Devyn chuckles understandingly. "It may have seemed that way, Excellency, but in truth I've been facilitating cooperation among certain segments of our people who are less than resigned to your leadership. You are aware of these groups, I believe?"

I nod and see most of the Council doing the same. No one speaks.

"Though these groups originally had widely varying intentions, I have undertaken the difficult task of uniting them. Over time, I'm confident I can shore up their waning confidence in you and the Council, to our mutual benefit. In the meantime, however, a growing number believe that my taking a leadership role will move our people forward more quickly."

"What…what kind of leadership role?" For some reason, I have difficulty getting out the words. Devyn seems to be making a lot of sense.

"Appoint me your *Echtran* Regent here on Earth," is his reasonable reply. "With that authority, I can begin taking the necessary steps to more quickly integrate our people into *Duchas* society without any loss of our own autonomy. I now have both the knowledge and the technology to ensure that both Martians and *Duchas* will more readily accept coexistence on this planet. I'm sure you can agree that will reap unprecedented rewards for both peoples, as we all move into that brighter future together."

I find myself nodding again at the sense he is making. Off to the side, I hear pleased murmuring from the Council.

"He makes some very good points, Excellency," Kyna says.

"Indeed," Malcolm and Breann agree together.

Glancing at Rigel again, I see he's also nodding.

Have I been wrong all this time, as prejudiced as Malcolm has claimed? Apparently so.

"Shall we put it to a vote?" Kyna says then. "With your permission, Excellency, I move that we appoint Devyn Kane Regent on Earth. I am also more than willing to step aside to allow him to take leadership of this Council."

I'm about to agree to all of that when Molly grabs my free hand, the one not already clasped in Rigel's. Instinctively, I try to pull away, but then her thought penetrates my consciousness.

M! Don't listen to him! He's using some kind of amplified 'push' to make you believe anything he says. This is Devyn! The guy who helped wipe Rigel's memory and lied to you. The one who's been stirring up opposition to you. You need to push back!

Emerging from a thick mental fog, I shake my head and look at Molly. Her other hand is holding Tristan's. He nods urgently to me, boosting the resistance Molly is sharing with us both. Looking the other way, I see Rigel blinking as though just waking up, too. On his other side, Kira and Sean are still smiling bemusedly at Devyn.

Grab Kira's hand, I think to Rigel and he immediately reaches over and does so. Luckily, she's already holding Sean's.

Now I feel the combined power of our group surging through me and sense Rigel's feeling the same. All six of us stand up a little straighter, our minds now clear.

"All in favor?" comes Kyna's voice from behind me.

Wow, that's some powerful mind control! I hear Sean's voice in my head. *He had me completely convinced.*

Me, too. Molly seems to be the only one who can resist it, I silently reply. *Good thing she can share it with the rest of us.*

One after the other, I hear Nara, Malcolm and Breann say, "Aye."

We need to take him out! Tristan thinks urgently. *Quick, before he realizes we're not buying it any more.*

Wait! I mentally shout before he and Sean, at opposite ends of our chain, can let go and lose our connection—and Molly's protection.

They pause while I focus on Devyn—and realize he isn't giving off any emotion or even *brath*.

He's just a holo! I tell the others. *If you'd tried to tackle him, you'd have gone right through him—and he'd know we're no longer under his control.*

What should we do, then? Tristan's frustration comes through with his thought.

Create a stasis field, I reply. *Now! We need to neutralize that Ossian Sphere before he realizes we've broken free, or he might blow it up after all. That's probably his fallback plan, in case the mind control doesn't work. As a holo, he's not in any danger himself.*

I let my reasoning sink in, then think, *Ready?*

They are.

Together, we all focus on the Ossian Sphere hovering behind Devyn's image while Rigel and I put our minds to creating the biggest, strongest stasis field we've ever managed. Augmented as we are by the others, it's not nearly as hard as I expect.

I think it's working! Kira silently exclaims from Rigel's other side.

"Excellency?" Devyn's voice intrudes. "I believe Council Leader Kyna is waiting for your agreement."

Keep him talking! Distract him until we can get rid of it, Sean thinks to me.

Right, I send back.

"What about Regent Shim, back in Nuath?" I speak slowly, as though still under Devyn's spell, while simultaneously fighting to maintain my concentration on the stasis field.

"I will coordinate my efforts with him, of course," Devyn gently assures me, clearly believing us still in his thrall. "As well as with you and the Council. I've no doubt we can all agree on the best possible measures to take toward our ultimate goal."

As he's talking, I send a silent message to Sean and Kira. *If it blows up this close, it'll kill us all and probably destroy NuAgra. See if you two can—*

Got it, Sean thinks back.

Almost immediately, the Sphere starts moving backward. Through our linked hands and minds, I can feel the effort he and Kira are exerting, even while I focus on maintaining the stasis field with Rigel.

Where to? I can hear the strain in Sean's mental words.

From my other side, I feel Molly and Tristan sending more power their way. Maintaining the stasis field suddenly gets easier, too.

"What—? What are you doing?" Devyn suddenly sounds alarmed. "How—?"

Up! I respond to Sean, not daring to look away to see what the Council is doing. *And backward.* Other than a few scattered farmhouses, there's nothing in that direction before the next town, several miles from here. *As high and as far as you can.*

At once, the Ossian Sphere begins to rise, gathering speed the higher and farther away it goes.

"Stop!" Devyn shouts, his voice no longer soothing. "You can't—"

He cuts off mid-sentence, his image vanishing as the Sphere moves beyond hologram range. Faster and faster it flies, up and away. Soon it's no more than a tiny speck of silver reflecting the setting sun.

Rigel and I maintain our stasis field until it's at least ten miles up, well above even the highest airplanes' flight paths, before letting go.

Zap it! comes Tristan's thought from Molly's other side.

He and Sean, at opposite ends, reach up to point at the orb and on a mental count of three, all six of us together unleash a blinding, blue-white bolt of lightning that sizzles up, up, up toward the barely-visible metallic glint.

There's a spectacular flash in the sky and we all start cheering.

"We did it! We really—" Tristan is cut off by an ear-splitting *boom* and a shock wave that knocks us all to the ground.

Shaking my head, I look first to Rigel, who seems fine, then scramble up to check on everyone else.

"Is anyone hurt?" I ask as they all start getting dazedly to their feet. A quick probe of emotions reveals more confusion than fear among the Council. Everyone in our group of six seems okay, too. Relieved, I turn toward NuAgra, which also appears completely intact.

"What…what happened?" Kyna looks around. "How did—?"

Immediately, the rest of the Council members also start demanding explanations.

"We'll explain later," I tell them. "First we should make sure no one out front was injured by that shock wave."

"Yes, of course," a still-dazed Kyna agrees, pulling out her omni.

We should see if Devyn's anywhere nearby, I think to Rigel as Kyna makes a call.

He could have sent that holo from anywhere, he points out. *Though he might have wanted to be close enough to take charge if his plan worked.*

Rigel clasps both of my hands in his and I stretch out with my emotion-sensing, sure I'll recognize Devyn's distinctive vibe if it's out there. I'm pushing my senses past the NuAgra grounds when it suddenly gets way easier—because Molly's hand is now on my arm, the other three touching her.

With that boost, I'm able to scan a five mile radius within moments. No Devyn. I do detect two or three *Echtrans* nearby who feel icky, but without names, descriptions, or any other specifics, I'm not sure what to do about them.

Just stay vigilant, I guess, Tristan thinks to the group.

We all release hands just as Kyna turns to face us. "I've been assured that no one was injured," she tells me. "However, they'll be expecting the doors to open momentarily, so we should all get back inside."

All thirteen of us head back the way we came, several Council members wondering aloud what just occurred. Most of them still seem pretty confused, though I imagine their full memories will return shortly.

Passing the greenhouses, I'm glad to see no damage worse than a few cracked glass panes. At the double back doors to the main building, we hesitate.

"Will the tear gas be gone yet?" Molly asks.

Mr. Stuart blinks, then nods. "It should be. NuAgra's air filters are quite powerful." He cautiously opens a door. "Yes. Yes, it's fine."

Sure enough, everything inside looks completely normal. When I get to the central desk, I peek underneath. A tiny charred spot is all that remains of the device that was there. I straighten up and turn to the Council members, wondering how best to explain what happened out back.

"So, you all probably—" I begin when Kyna interrupts me.

"I'm sorry, Excellency, but explanations will have to wait. It's already two minutes past five. We need to let everyone in for the dedication ceremony."

⁺⁺

Needless to say, the question on every *Echtran's* lips as they file into the big reception hall is, "What just happened?"

"We've got this." Molly gives me a wink and she and Tristan step forward to greet the shaken crowd of *Echtrans*.

"Sorry, sorry!" she exclaims the moment they're all inside. "We didn't mean to scare anyone. There was supposed to be a surprise fire-works display just before we opened the doors, but as you could prob-ably tell, it didn't exactly go off as planned."

The majority of heads nod in understanding. Probing the mood of the crowd, I sense pleased relief—not surprising, since the 'push' behind Molly's words almost made *me* believe her.

Gwendolyn Gannett hurries forward then, demanding more details, which Molly cheerfully makes up on the spot.

At a quarter past five, Kyna takes charge with her usual authority, seemingly back to normal. She herds the rest of the Council, as well as Molly and me, onto a small platform at the rear of the atrium and has us take our places for the ceremony.

NuAgra's official dedication goes off without a hitch, following the program we discussed at last night's meeting. At its conclusion, the holographic symbol designed for the new *Echtran* government appears over the main desk: red for Mars, blue for Earth. Everyone applauds.

Kyna informs the crowd that the Council will be available for ques-tions in a moment, then turns to those of us on the stage. "Once our visi-tors leave, I'd like to have a brief meeting," she quietly tells us. "We need to discuss what happened earlier...and have a few things explained."

When the Council members step off the dais a moment later to circu-late among the crowd, Molly and I hurry over to the rest of our "Squad."

"Kyna wants us to hang around after everyone's gone," I quietly inform them. "I'm sure we'll have to answer some questions."

"Let's find a place to talk privately before people start mobbing M and me," Molly suggests.

We all head down the nearest corridor, past all the government offices, then duck into an empty conference room.

Closing the door, I turn to the others. "Kyna made it pretty clear the Council's going to want an explanation, so we need to decide how much we're willing to tell them."

"They saw us all working together to get rid of that Ossian Sphere," Rigel points out. "They'll probably want to know how we did that."

"True—assuming they remember it," I add. "They still seem a little out of it. If they do, should we admit you guys also have *graell* bonds?"

Sean and Kira exchange a nervous look. So do Molly and Tristan.

"What if—?" Molly starts to say when the door to the conference room bursts open.

Three large men fill the doorway, all broadcasting the same "bad guy" *Echtran* vibes I picked up when searching for Devyn.

"You were right," the one in front says with an unpleasant grin. "The Sovereign, her sister and a couple more precious Royals, all back here on their own, no security. This'll be easier than I thought."

I suck in a panicky breath. It's true no one knows we're back here— and we're out of sight and earshot from the lobby. Before I can pull out my omni to signal for help, all three men rush us.

What happens next is almost too quick to see. Kira, Tristan and Rigel dart forward, each intercepting a different attacker. Kira ducks low, catching hers mid-thigh, and uses his momentum to send him crashing into the table. Tristan executes a quick jab to the next guy's windpipe, then grabs his arm to pin it behind him in a joint lock. Rigel keeps it simple, letting his guy run straight into his fist, which knocks him flat on his back.

"You were saying?" Tristan asks pleasantly, giving the leader's arm an extra twist that makes him gasp.

"How—? What—?" the man sputters. The others struggle fruitlessly, securely pinned by Kira and Rigel.

I make my call then and a moment later half a dozen security guards come running. Quickly sizing up the situation, they haul the three bad guys to their feet and hustle them away, motioning us to follow. Kyna meets us all in a nearby room, where we recount what just happened while the guards fasten the miscreants' hands behind their backs.

"Well done!" Kyna congratulates the three Bodyguards. "I see my faith in allowing the two of you to train as *Costanta* was not misplaced. I know Gilda will be proud," she adds to Kira and Tristan, who both look gratified.

At Kyna's direction, our attackers are frog-marched off to a holding area to be dealt with later. She then suggests Molly and I return to the reception hall before hurrying back there herself.

Molly, Sean and I add our own private thanks to our personal Bodyguards the moment we're alone again...with kisses.

After that, we all reluctantly return to the crowded reception hall, where Molly and I are immediately surrounded by local *Echtrans*. Several of them ask about our plans for the future but Molly, I notice, is deliberately vague with her answers. So am I. It's not something we've discussed much...yet.

There's no other chance to speak privately with the rest of our "Squad" before Kyna again summons Molly and me to the stage for her parting words to the crowd.

"Thank you all for coming," she tells everyone. "Again, our apologies for the inadvertent scare earlier. Going forward, please feel free to visit this facility whenever you like, though I recommend making an appointment if you wish to speak with someone specific. Enjoy the rest of your evening."

As the visitors file out, I ask Kyna whether she wants Rigel, Tristan, Sean and Kira to stay, along with Molly and me. She seems startled by the question.

"Is there some reason you think they should?" she asks, brows raised.

"Um, no, I guess not. I just thought— But no, that's fine." I step off the dais to let the others know they can leave if they want to.

"Let's wait in the parking lot," Rigel suggests to Sean, Kira and Tristan.

"Good idea," Sean agrees. "We'll want to hear right away how much you tell them."

Molly and I give our boyfriends quick kisses, then follow Kyna and the Council to the room where we'll hold our future meetings. A dozen or so comfy-looking chairs are spaced around a large central table. On the walls are pictures of Nuath, Bailerealta, Dun Cloch and Jewel.

"I hope someone here can fill me in on exactly what happened earlier," Kyna says when we're all seated. "After we all left the building to escape the gas from the devices those *Duchas* smuggled in, I seem to recall what looked like an Ossian Sphere approaching. However, I'm having difficulty remembering anything between that and finding myself on the ground after some sort of large explosion."

Glancing around the big table, I see the others look similarly confused.

"Don't any of you remember what happened after the Ossian Sphere showed up?" I ask.

Everyone but Molly shakes their head.

"Was it really an Ossian Sphere, then?" Nara asks. "I...I don't see how that can be. Didn't we have the other ones Boyne Morven brought to Earth destroyed a year ago? The Council received a complete report on it at the time."

A sudden suspicion occurs to me. "Who was in charge of having them destroyed? Did the report say?"

"Devyn Kane," Breann replies.

"That's what I figured. He obviously kept at least one Sphere for himself and modified it using the stolen antimatter," I tell them. "That's how he managed his mind-control trick that almost worked."

Teara Roark furrows her brow. "Now that you mention it, I do have a vague memory of Devyn talking to us outside. Something about an Earth Regent?"

I nod eagerly. "Yes! The Sphere projected his hologram, so it looked like he was really here. He nearly convinced us all that he should be Regent and lead the Council, too, before....um, before the Ossian Sphere blew up."

"But...how was the Ossian Sphere dispatched?" Kyna asks. "Did your security system do that, Van?"

"Er, no." Mr. Stuart darts a glance at Molly and me. "I'm afraid not. It should have kept the Sphere from entering the grounds, but I realize now that brief power failure must have been caused by a localized electromagnetic pulse, the only thing capable of disabling that system, even temporarily. Produced by the same devices that emitted the tear gas, I presume. I tried to review the security video logs after the dedication but, ah, apparently the exterior sensors were also affected by that EMP."

He sends another questioning look our way, making me wonder what he *did* see on that video.

Kyna huffs in frustration. "Then we have no way of confirming what transpired unless we remember? Or... Excellency, do *you* have a clear memory of what happened?"

I freeze. How much should I say? The other two couples never got a chance to tell me whether they were okay letting everyone know about their *graell* bonds.

Molly, ever resourceful, comes to my rescue.

"M and I are apparently immune to Royal 'push,' so Devyn's mind-control didn't work on us," she explains. "By combining our own 'push,' we turned the tables and controlled *his* mind. We convinced him to move the Ossian Sphere to a safe distance, then M and Rigel blew it up with their lightning thing."

I stare at Molly in astonished admiration—then quickly nod before the Council can suspect I'm hearing this story for the first time.

"Well! It appears we once again have you to thank for saving us all, Excellency," Kyna exclaims. "Along with Princess Malena and Rigel, of course."

"I, ah…" I stammer.

To my relief, Molly again steps smoothly into the breach. "We just did the best we could. I wish we could have defused the situation without creating that massive explosion, but…we *did* get rid of the stolen antimatter."

Surprising myself as much as anyone, I burst out laughing—then the rest of the Council joins in. The tension in the room dissolves as we all finally relax for the first time in hours.

Kyna is the first to regain control. "As no one was hurt, I believe we can forgive you for that," she says, still smiling. "Thank you, Excellencies."

Everyone else also expresses their thanks—thanks we'll be sure to pass along to the rest of the "Squad," since we couldn't have done it without them.

"We'll discuss this more thoroughly at our next meeting," Kyna says then. "The men who were just apprehended will of course be questioned, and efforts to locate Devyn Kane will be stepped up. Perhaps the rest of us will recover our own memories of events by then, as well. Meanwhile, I suggest we all go home and try to unwind. It's been rather a trying day."

.⁺.⁺

Outside, in the NuAgra parking lot, Molly and I quickly fill the others in on what transpired at the meeting.

"Molly was amazing," I tell them. "She came up with a totally plausible explanation without mentioning your *graell* bonds at all."

"Yeah, hopefully that won't get us in trouble down the line if they end up remembering everything," Molly says. "I felt bad about fudging, but I wasn't sure Sean and Kira were okay yet with everyone knowing about their bond—especially Mum."

They both nod gratefully, clearly relieved to hear they weren't 'outed.'

"Unfortunately, that means you guys aren't getting the credit you deserve," I tell them. "You all played at least as big a part as Molly, Rigel and me."

"No biggie," Tristan assures me. "Secret identities are part of being superheroes, right?"

Everyone laughs at that.

The moment I get home, my aunt and uncle ask about the big explosion.

"It rattled the windows," Aunt Theresa tells me. "And Mrs. Crabtree across the street saw a big flash in the sky."

Rather than scare them, I use Molly's explanation. "Yeah, there was supposed to be a big fireworks display after the tour, but something set them all off at once. They exploded way up high, luckily, so no one on the ground was hurt."

"I'll bet Ted Farmer and his buddies had something to do with it," Uncle Louie theorizes. "I could tell they were up to something out there."

"Oh, uh, maybe," I say noncommittally.

Uncle Louie's not the only one to jump to that conclusion, I discover he next day at school. Apparently, everyone in town heard about Mr. Farmer getting hauled off by the cops after his meltdown at NuAgra. At lunch, so many people demand details from Ginny Farmer, she runs from the cafeteria in tears.

"I'd feel sorrier for her if she weren't nearly as mean as Trina," Molly mutters, watching her go. "Maybe now she'll stop hassling Jana and Adina about NuAgra."

Somehow, word gets around that the six of us were also out there, so we get questions, too. We all stick to Molly's fireworks story—and carefully don't confirm *or* deny that a group of crazy conspiracy theorists might have been involved.

Gwendolyn Gannett's *Echtran Enquirer* column that week is particularly amusing.

When I get to Molly's house Tuesday evening—our boyfriends are meeting us for another walk to Dream Cream—I pull the article up again so we can reread it together.

Titled, *"A conspiracy—and coverup—unmasked at NuAgra,"* she claims to have cleverly uncovered an *Echtran* Council attempt to hide the truth.

> During the course of the evening, I was able to catch Princess Malena in an unguarded moment. She confided to me that the cache of fireworks had been inadvertently left accessible during the *Duchas* tour, clearly a huge oversight by someone in authority. A small group of *Duchas* conspiracy lunatics apparently took advantage of that opportunity to somehow set off the entire display prematurely, causing the explosion we all witnessed Sunday evening. Their goal, no doubt, was to create panic and possible damage to the NuAgra facility. Had they succeeded in that goal, it could easily have set back *Echtran-Duchas* relations for years, perhaps decades. In this reporter's opinion, our people should demand an inquest into how this could have happened.

"Unguarded moment?" I repeat to Molly, chuckling.

She grins. "I figured if I let her believe she was getting something out of me I didn't mean to let slip, she'd run with it. If she thinks she's stumbled onto a scandal, she's less likely to go hunting for the truth."

"Brilliant." I shake my head admiringly. "That's an amazingly useful skill you have. Even after being bonded with Rigel for a year, I can't do anything like this—" I point at the article. "Or making up a story like the one you told the Council Sunday, right on the spot."

"Yeah, well, I may be good at inventing excuses on the fly," Molly admits, "but you're way better than me at this."

She reaches over and clicks to my own piece in this issue of the *Enquirer.* "You always tell people what they need to hear, even if they'd rather not hear it. And you do it so diplomatically, it never sounds like you're criticizing them for being wrong."

"It's a whole a lot easier when I can outline in advance, then edit a few times before anyone sees it," I reply with a laugh. "No need to be a quick thinker for that."

Molly shakes her head. "I've seen your press conferences, M. You're better than you think. And judging by this week's poll numbers, these articles you've been writing lately are working."

"About time," I say. Then, on sudden inspiration, "Speaking of poll numbers, what would you think of us doing some on-air interviews together when the new *Echtran* News Network starts broadcasting after the holidays? I could write up the ideas we want to get across, then you could use your super-convincing improv thing to work them into our answers."

She looks startled, then thoughtful. "Interesting idea. Have you run it past Mr. Stuart yet?"

"No, I just now thought of it. Let's kick the idea around a little first. If we decide we want to do it, he can tell us who to talk to. With Devyn's antimatter-enhanced Ossian Sphere out of the way, we should start reaching out to his followers before he comes up with another plan. Maybe counteract his brainwashing with with our own 'programming.'" I make air quotes.

Rigel and Tristan arrive then, and on the way to Dream Cream we share my idea with them.

After asking a lot of questions, they both agree it's a good plan. The four of us then spend the next hour or so cheerfully hammering out possible broadcast formats over ice cream sundaes.

.⁺₊

Friday is the last day of school before winter break, and that night is Jewel High's annual Winter Formal. Last year's was more frustrating than fun, since I was supposedly there as Sean's date. But this year I can dance every dance with Rigel, instead of the *one* we managed last time— while a glowering Sean looked on.

Like before, the school gym is festooned with recycled paper snowflakes for the occasion. Rigel and I join Sean and Kira just inside the door and a moment later Molly and Tristan come in from the parking lot.

After we all exchange greetings, Molly pulls something from her coat pocket with a slightly sheepish smile.

"I thought these might be fun to have tonight, unless you guys think they're stupid..." She opens a bag from Glitterby's, a jewelry shop in downtown Jewel, and hands around six little packages.

"Remember Tristan's idea for a Bond Squad logo?" she asks. We all nod. "Well, I wasn't too keen on getting an actual tattoo, so I had these made up instead."

Curious now, I unwrap a tiny brooch—a silver replica of the little constellation of three stars Tristan drew on his arm with pen last week.

"These are awesome!" Tristan exclaims, affixing his to the lapel of his navy suit. "Thanks, Molly. And I can wear it on a pocket or collar at school."

Charmed, I give Molly a hug. "I love these. They're beautiful! Subtle but distinctive, like you said." I pin mine to my dress. So do Molly and Kira, while Sean and Rigel follow Tristan's example, using theirs as lapel pins.

Touching my brooch, I smile around at the others. "I feel like these make us an official team—not that we should need to play superhero again any time soon."

"Hey, you never know. Devyn Kane's still at large and might try something else," Tristan says with a wink. "If he does, the Bond Squad will be ready."

That gets a chuckle from all of us.

Still, when I'm in Rigel's arms for a slow dance a short while later, I mutter, "I hope Tristan's wrong and our troubles—the big ones, anyway —are finally behind us for good."

So what if they're not? He thinks to me. *You've proved time and again you can handle anything.*

WE can handle anything, I correct him. *Together. Trying to do it on my own last spring and summer totally sucked.*

He smiles tenderly down at me. *I plan to make sure you never have to handle anything alone again, M. Bond Squad or not, you'll always have me. Always.*

Lowering his lips to mine, he turns that promise into a vow—one I fervently return. *Always. I love you, Rigel.*

The whole evening is magical, worlds better than last year's awkward Winter Formal. Halfway through the dance, Molly points up the contrast, too. Our group of six is briefly together at the punch table when she nudges Sean, then me.

"Aren't you two going to dance together tonight, for old time's sake?" she asks with a mischievous grin.

Startled, I look at Rigel. *Go ahead if you want,* he thinks to me, smiling. *I won't mind a bit...now.*

The glance Sean and Kira exchange suggests a similar exchange going on between them.

Sean and I look at each other. "Nah, we're good," he and I say simultaneously, getting a laugh from the others.

Looking around at them all, my heart feels suddenly full to overflowing. "You know, guys, cool as our *graell* bonds are, the ones we have as friends make me every bit as happy. I feel incredibly lucky to have you all in my corner, super powers or not."

Just then, "We Are the Champions" starts to play. We all laugh and head back to the dance floor. Singing along with the others, I feel sure that no matter what the future throws at us, we'll come out on top—as long as we face it together.

＊
＊＊

About the Author

Brenda writes novels of sparkling romantic adventure spanning Regency England, Americana, contemporary teen science fiction and more. Which ever you pick up, you'll find excitement, romance and, always, an uplifting happy ending. In addition to writing, Brenda is passionate about embracing life to the fullest, to include scuba diving (she has over 60 dives to her credit), Taekwondo (where she's currently working toward her 4th degree black belt), hiking, traveling…and reading, of course!

✦

For a free Starstruck short story and the earliest news about Brenda Hiatt's books, subscribe to her newsletter at: brendahiatt.com/subscribe

Connect with Brenda at:
brendahiatt.com

CPSIA information can be obtained
at www.ICGtesting.com
Printed in the USA
LVHW041011131120
671368LV00002B/93